IMPERIUM
DEFIANT

BOOK SIX
OF THE DUCHY OF TERRA

IMPERIUM
DEFIANT

BOOK SIX
OF THE DUCHY OF TERRA

GLYNN STEWART

FAOLAN'S PEN
PUBLISHING

faolanspen.com

This edition published in 2019 by:

Faolan's Pen Publishing Inc.

22 King St. S, Suite 300

Waterloo, Ontario

N2J 1N8 Canada

ISBN-13: 978-1-988035-92-5 (print)

A record of this book is available from Library and Archives Canada.

Printed in the United States of America

1 2 3 4 5 6 7 8 9 10

First edition

First printing: September 2019

Illustration © 2019 Tom Edwards

TomEdwardsDesign.com

Faolan's Pen Publishing logo is a trademark of Faolan's Pen Publishing Inc.

Read more books from Glynn Stewart at faolanspen.com

CHAPTER ONE

"THIS IS *JEAN VILLENEUVE*, REQUESTING CLEARANCE THROUGH the shield."

It would probably have been more appropriate to have her communications officer handle the request, but Commander Morgan Casimir was well aware that *Jean Villeneuve* was playing for an audience today.

The brand-new superbattleship had been built *inside* Jupiter, in a bubble of vacuum opened up by powerful shields. Now the ship was leaving that bubble for the last time, to enter the service of the A!Tol Imperium.

Morgan was *Jean Villeneuve*'s First Sword—her executive officer —newly transferred to the navy of the A!Tol Imperium from the Duchy of Terra Militia.

"*Jean Villeneuve*, this is DragonWorks Control," a calm Spanish-accented voice replied, and the blonde Commander's lips quirked. Commodore Ariel Ortiz had no more business answering basic communications for her security region than Commander Morgan Casimir had sending the coms in the first place.

"Shield segment thirty-one-B-thirteen has been reduced in

strength to allow for passage. It's been a pleasure hosting you, *Jean Villeneuve*. Fly straight."

Morgan's smile expanded. *Villeneuve* had been built and done most of her initial testing there. DragonWorks had done more than host the A!Tol Imperium's newest and most advanced superbattleship.

"It's been a pleasure working with you, DragonWorks. We have thirty-one-B-thirteen on our displays and are making our way out."

She dropped the channel and glanced over at *Villeneuve*'s navigator. Speaker Cosa was a Pibo neuter, a small gray-skinned alien that looked a *lot* like some old Earth myths.

"Destination is laid in," Cosa told her. They were speaking their own language, but every member of the Imperial Navy had translator earbuds as part of their working uniform. They weren't universal translators, but they held about thirty languages.

There were eleven species represented aboard *Jean Villeneuve*. Mixed-race ships were a rarity in the Imperial Navy, but everyone had agreed that Jean himself would have had it no other way.

He'd been Morgan's "Uncle Jean" until she was eighteen and entered the Militia Academy, and she still missed him fiercely.

The arrival of the superbattleship's Captain shut down that familiar train of grief, and Morgan rose from the command seat and saluted.

Tan!Stalla—the *!* was a glottal stop for humans, a beak-snap for the A!Tol themselves—was a recruiting-poster perfect example of the A!Tol warrior female. Her bullet-shaped torso with its sharp beak and large black eyes was suspended in a seeming forest of tentacles.

There were only sixteen of those tentacles, but that was enough to human eyes. Twelve manipulator tentacles allowed the squid-like aliens to control a technology far beyond humanity's when they'd met, and four locomotive tentacles moved her around.

At her full height, Tan!Stalla was over two and a half meters tall. She was large for an A!Tol female, though Morgan had known bigger. A!Tol females kept growing until something killed them, after all.

"We are cleared to commence the final tests?" Tan!Stalla asked, returning Morgan's salute with several manipulator tentacles smacking against the central point of her uniform harness.

"The Militia has laid out targets for us along the designated course," Morgan replied. "Course is laid in and we are on our way out of the DragonWorks shield."

"And our audience?" the A!Tol Captain asked, glancing at the main holographic display at the center of the circular bridge.

Morgan had been intentionally keeping her focus very narrow, on *Jean Villeneuve*'s own targets and missions. The number of icons in that display and the *nature* of many of those icons sent a chill down her spine.

"The Empress's representatives are aboard the Militia superbattleship *Emperor of China*," Morgan noted. Another phrasing of that would be *my stepmother and my new boss are aboard the temporary flagship of my old service*, but that one would be unprofessional.

"The Eleventh Pincer of the Republic is watching from his flagship," she continued, her gaze drifting across the holographic sphere to a set of icons she'd never expected to see as actual allies. Ten wardreadnoughts of the Laian Republic, the closest of the more technologically advanced Core Powers, now orbited Sol. Today, they were in a high orbit of Jupiter to watch the tests of *Jean Villeneuve*'s new systems.

"And the Mesharom?" Tan!Stalla asked.

Morgan nodded slowly and considered the rest of the "allied" icons. She was familiar with the Mesharom, the oldest of the Core Powers—the oldest known species in existence—and had served as the Duchy of Terra Militia's "Mesharom expert."

Even to her, however, the Mesharom war spheres were basically a myth. Now forty of the twelve-kilometer-wide spherical warships were watching her tests, with sixty of the battlecruisers she was used to seeing with them.

"Grand Commander Tilsan is aboard their flagship, watching," she reported. *Watching* summed up a lot of what Tilsan did. They weren't an Interpreter, one of the rare Mesharom trained to deal with aliens. They were...simply in command of the largest Expeditionary Fleet the Mesharom had deployed in the five hundred years the A!Tol Imperium had been aware of the eldest Core Power's existence.

"Hopefully, they're impressed," Tan!Stalla murmured, a flush of dark green covering her skin. The A!Tol showed their emotions on their skin, and *that*, Morgan knew, was fear and determination.

Which meant that she and her Captain were on roughly the same page.

"Emergence from the DragonWorks shield...now," Cosa reported. "Entering Jovian atmosphere. We will bring the drive to full power and commence the tests on your order."

"Tactical?" Tan!Stalla asked.

Lesser Commander Nidei, a tall and gaunt red-skinned Ivida, muttered to themself in a language the translator didn't understand. Morgan had almost no familiarity with Ivida languages—not least because, as an Imperial Race, neither did most Ivida!

"All systems are green," Nidei reported. "I've asked Lesser Commander Tanyut to take a closer look at some specific sections of the plasma lance, but there's no major problem."

"All right." Tan!Stalla's black eyes focused on Morgan. "First Sword. Any concerns?"

"I'm concerned that we get to do this in front of *two* Core Powers," Morgan replied. "Other than that, I believe *Jean Villeneuve* is ready to show her talents to the world."

"As do I. Nidei, Cosa...commence the demonstration."

JEAN VILLENEUVE WAS unlike any ship built before her in the A!Tol Imperium. Ships across the nation were being refitted with the same basic technologies, but she and her three sisters were the first superbattleships built from the ground up with everything the

Imperium had begged, borrowed and stolen over the last twenty-five years.

She was a twenty-one-million-ton beast, with a twenty-five-hundred-meter-long core hull in the shape of a double-ended spindle. Four arched "wings" covered the rear half of the ship, stretching out to her full twelve-hundred-meter height and width, and shallower extended arches spread defensive systems away from her core all along her hull.

Cosa brought her out of Jupiter's atmosphere at a delicate ten kilometers a second, then brought the ship's engines to full power.

The interface drive—the gravitational-hyperspatial interface momentum engine—only played fair with Newton when measured across *both* real space and hyperspace—and needed four more spatial dimensions in both to do it. *Jean Villeneuve* went from ten kilometers a second to fifty-five percent of lightspeed in slightly over seven seconds.

"First targets live," Nidei reported. "Firing Echo batteries. Second targets in the line in twenty seconds."

Forty proton beams flashed in the void. Once the main close-range ship-killer of the Imperial Navy, the energy weapons had survived into the *Galileo*-class superbattleships only because half of her *other* weapons didn't work in hyperspace.

Obsolete the beams might be, but the shielded and armored targets laid out for them vanished in the single salvo as the capital ship blazed away from the planet.

"Second targets in the line; firing Foxtrot batteries."

One of the technologies the Imperium had stolen from the Laians had been the spinal plasma lance. *Jean Villeneuve* and her sisters were the first to use the technology without basically building the ship around it. Now, specially designed conduits flashed plasma out into the superbattleship's wings. Instead of firing a single lance from the nose of the ship, *Villeneuve* fired a lance from the tip of each of her four wings.

Those four targets didn't last as long as the first set, but Cosa was already flipping the ship around, keeping them within a light-minute of Jupiter as they hammered toward the third set of targets.

"Alpha and Bravo batteries firing on third targets, loading the fourth targets...firing Charlie and Delta batteries," Nidei continued their chant.

Missiles screamed toward the third set of targets, a hundred and twenty interface drive weapons moving at eighty percent of the speed of light. The fourth targets were farther away but actually died *first*, as Charlie and Delta batteries were the first of *Villeneuve's* FTL weapons: the hyperfold energy cannons vaporized the fourth set of targets before the missiles arrived at the third.

The targets, Morgan noted absently, *were* moving. They carried interface drives of their own and were evading at forty percent of the speed of light. It just hadn't been enough to save them yet.

"We are receiving hyperfold telemetry from the fifth set of targets," Morgan announced as the data came on the displays of her own seat. She had less data there than she would in her actual combat station in the combat information center, but for this she'd wanted to be on the bridge.

The fifth set of targets was a *lot* farther away, several light-minutes from Jupiter: near the maximum range of *Jean Villeneuve's* primary weapons and outside the range of their instantaneous tachyon scanners.

A recon drone near the targets, preplaced along with them, was now feeding their location to *Villeneuve* by a hyperfold communicator. Like the weapons, it was instantaneous at this range. Unlike the weapons, it was transmitting at a low-enough intensity to have a range of nearly a light-year.

"Firing."

Nidei's last report hung in the bridge. There were twenty-four targets this time, a test for the superbattleship's main armament: the hyperspace missiles that could reach this range.

A blip on Morgan's displays told her that the portals inside *Jean Villeneuve* had opened and closed, launching the weapons into hyperspace. A few seconds later, new icons appeared on the drone's feed.

Moments after that, all twenty-four targets vanished.

"Full sweep, Lesser Commander Nidei," Morgan declared. "Every target down with one salvo from each battery."

"Well done, Lesser Commander," Tan!Stalla agreed. "Speaker Cosa, set our course to rendezvous with *Emperor of China*. The Fleet Lord awaits us."

Jean Villeneuve would be under Fleet Lord Harriet Tanaka's command, but the need to refit so many ships meant Tanaka's command was somewhat...theoretical at the moment. Today, Tanaka had joined the Duchess of Terra aboard the current flagship of Earth's Ducal Militia.

Duchess Annette Bond. The woman who'd turned humanity's conquest by the A!Tol Imperium into the greatest opportunity they'd ever had. Who'd negotiated with the Mesharom for much of the technology that underpinned *Jean Villeneuve*. Who'd negotiated the unexpected alliance with the Kanzi, the Imperium's age-old enemies, that had saved Terra once again a mere three months before.

And also Morgan Casimir's stepmother.

No pressure living up to *that* example.

CHAPTER TWO

Fleet Lord Harriet Tanaka watched *Jean Villeneuve* streak across the star system and wished the lump in her throat was a mere cold or something similarly easily healed. She'd risen to command a sublight battleship under the old Frenchman's command before she'd become an Imperial officer, after all.

She'd worked with him since, too, as the Imperial Navy and the Duchy of Terra Militia had secured the stars around Sol against pirates, Kanzi and now the Taljzi genocides.

And she'd commanded one of the fleet detachments in the last Battle of Terra where Jean Villeneuve had died. Harriet missed the stubborn old Frenchman.

Watching his namesake tear through the targets brought a smile to her lips as well, though. The *Galileo*-class ships were the ultimate combination of years of secret R&D at the DragonWorks base. She'd have three more in a few weeks, but *Jean Villeneuve* was the first.

"Jean would have been impressed with her," the tiny Japanese woman said to her companion. Age and a second pregnancy hadn't been kind to Harriet, but she was still petite and short. She might be graying and worn now, but no one was going to mistake that for weakness.

Pregnancy and time had both been *much* gentler to Annette Bond, who still looked far too much like the Idaho cheerleader she'd once been. The Duchess of Terra's golden hair was beginning to fade to silver now, and stress lines marked her face, but there was no question of her iron will—or of her accomplishments.

"We lost too many good people getting here," Bond finally said, her gaze on the warship's icon. "Jean and Li are at the top of the list, but they're not the only ones."

Jean Villeneuve had been the Councilor for the Duchy of Terra Militia, once Bond had finally talked him into partial retirement. Li Chin Zhao had been the Duchy's Treasurer. Neither had survived the Battle of Terra, one dying in battle and one in a medical crisis that had gone unnoticed too long because of the battle.

Thousands upon thousands of human spacers, A!Tol Imperial spacers, Kanzi spacers and even *Mesharom* spacers had died as well. Victory had come at too thin a margin and too high a cost...but now they could repay that debt toward the Taljzi.

"How long until your fleet is ready to deploy?" Bond asked.

"Not as soon as I'd like," Harriet admitted. "I'm waiting on refits everywhere. The first of my squadrons will be coming out of the Raging Waters of Friendship Yards here in a few weeks, but until then, I'm running with a single squadron of *Bellerophons*."

The *Bellerophon*-class battleship had been the predecessor to the *Galileo*. *Bellerophon* herself had died covering the retreat of the scouting fleet that had found the Taljzi home systems, gaining the knowledge they'd soon be ready to use.

The Taljzi had burned entire worlds clean of life. Harriet had no intention of returning that favor...but she had even *less* intention of letting them repeat the act.

"It's looking like three months," she finally estimated. "The Taljzi brought thousands of ships. Even with our new Core Power friends, the Empress has made it clear: we don't move against the Taljzi without at least forty squadrons of capital ships."

Harriet was used to the Imperium's sixteen-ship squadrons now. She'd been tasked to command a fleet anchored around over *six hundred* battleships and superbattleships. With every ship refitted with the new weapons, it would be a more powerful force than the one the Imperium had committed to defend Sol three months earlier.

It was also a force they could *not* afford to lose. Tanaka could do the math. Even with new construction, losses at the Battle of Terra had reduced the Imperium to around ninety squadrons of capital ships. If she lost the fleet the Empress was entrusting her with, the Imperium would be crippled.

The good news was that their most likely enemy was the Kanzi Theocracy, and *they* were committing a similar fraction of their own forces. If they lost this fight, they would at least have also exhausted the resources of anyone likely to pick a *new* fight with them.

THE TEST COMPLETE, Harriet and Bond joined Admiral Kurz-man-Wellesley in his office next to the flag deck. The broad-shoul-dered Englishman produced beer bottles and glasses for the three of them, which Harriet regarded with scant favor.

"Could you be a little *less* stereotypical, Patrick?" she asked. "I'm sure you have green tea somewhere on this ship."

"Probably," he agreed. "But I like beer, and my people find me some good ones. At least give it a try."

Harriet leveled her best glare on him and he gave her an unabashedly cheerful grin. Admiral Patrick Kurzman-Wellesley and his husband General James Wellesley-Kurzman ran the Ducal Militia for Annette Bond now.

Before either of them could say anything more, the door slid open to reveal a second man, a tall man with graying black hair, who stepped in holding a tray with two steaming cups on it.

"James! I didn't know you were aboard," Harriet said as she smelled the tea on the tray Wellesley-Kurzman was carrying.

Despite his advancing age and the inherent desk-flying nature of his job, the General of the Ducal Guard was still well muscled and fast. He had the tray on the desk before Harriet had finished speaking and carefully selected one of the two teacups for himself.

"I prefer to keep a careful eye on Her Grace," he noted in a precise British accent, a stark contrast to his husband's lower-class British tones. "And it gives me an excuse to see Patrick."

He gave his husband a kiss and gestured to the teacup he'd left on the tray.

"That one is green," he noted. "Mine is...British."

"Black tea, overbrewed to death?" Harriet said sweetly as she scooped up the cup.

"Exactly. The only way to properly caffeinate."

"I'll stick to beer," Kurzman-Wellesley told his husband as he reclaimed the beer he'd pulled out—but hadn't *opened*, Harriet noted —for her.

"James came up with me to see the demonstration," Bond told Harriet. "We both wanted to get a feel for how *Villeneuve* and her sisters will stack up against the Kanzi and the Taljzi fleets."

The Taljzi were a rogue Kanzi offshoot. They'd apparently acquired a Precursor cloning facility that allowed them to produce soldiers and factory workers in vast numbers, but their ships were built on very similar lines to the Kanzi.

They just had Precursor-derived tech woven through them that the Kanzi couldn't match. That was why the Mesharom were here, after all. The galaxy's oldest race had been slaves of the Precursors before their empire fell, and they kept a careful eye on their previous masters' technology.

"And your conclusion?" Harriet asked.

"If we're upgrading the rest of the fleet to similar standards, I'm confident in Sol's security," Bond replied. "I won't pretend I wouldn't rather be rebuilding my Militia, but I understand why the Empress ordered every yard to build for the Navy."

"And the licensing fees for all of that DragonWorks-researched tech does *not* hurt our patience," Kurzman-Wellesley noted. "The Navy is getting a bargain rate, but when you're refitting fifteen hundred capital ships and planning on building at least half that in new ships, well...it pays for *my* new fleet, that's for sure."

"That's for different minds than mine," Harriet told them. "My job is just to make sure that the fleet they're building does its job. No more dead worlds."

The humor in the room faded. The Taljzi had destroyed more colonies belonging to their estranged siblings, the Kanzi, but multiple human worlds had suffered under the orbital bombardment of the Taljzi Returns.

An alert pinged Harriet's communicator and she eyed it cautiously. In this level of meeting, there was a priority lock on it... which meant the message had already gone through her operations officer and been flagged as important enough to reach her.

She pulled the device out and swallowed hard as she read the message.

"Fleet Lord Tanaka?" Kurzman-Wellesley asked carefully.

"Grand Commander Tilsan's flagship, *Blade,* has left their formation and is heading directly for *Emperor of China,*" she told them, as calmly as possible. "The Grand Commander has not yet sent any communications, but..."

There was no reason for the Mesharom war sphere to be coming *there* unless the Grand Commander wanted to speak to someone in person—and while Harriet Tanaka was the highest-ranking Imperial *officer* in the system, Duchess Annette Bond had been designated the Empress's personal representative.

If Tilsan wanted to talk to someone, it would be them.

BY THE TIME they made it back to the flag bridge, Tilsan's intentions were clearer, if still vague. The Mesharom, as a race, didn't like dealing with other individuals very much. That disinclination was even stronger when dealing with aliens, which was why only a handful of Mesharom, designated Interpreters, did so.

Tilsan was *not* an Interpreter, so their orders were sent via a computer that coded them into a text message.

Fleet Lord Harriet Tanaka and Imperial Representative Annette Bond are to report aboard my ship immediately upon our arrival.

That was it.

"You know, the Mesharom are usually terse, but this is bad even for them," James Wellesley-Kurzman said softly. "No orders against guards, though they rarely *say* that."

"No guards," Bond said sharply before Harriet could.

"Neither of us is actually allowed to go anywhere unescorted," the Fleet Lord pointed out. She agreed with Bond, but one of them had to say it.

Bond pointed to the screen.

"That ship is twelve kilometers across," she said sharply. "I doubt we can assume we know its full arsenal, but we *know* it carries molecular disruptors, point eight *c* interface missiles and hyperspace missiles. Alone, it could probably defeat what's left of the Ducal Militia and level Earth.

"Hell." She shook her head. "Adamase once threatened to level Hope, and all they had was *battlecruisers*. Not these monstrosities."

Unspoken was that Adamase, now the Interpreter-Shepherd of this region of space and the senior Mesharom bureaucrat for light-years in any direction, had a long track record of being the Imperium's friend.

Tilsan did not.

"We don't have a choice," Harriet conceded. "Even if we called in the standby fleets, they're days away and..."

"Still wouldn't be enough in the face of *forty war spheres*," Bond replied. "We have to go meet them, Tanaka. On their terms."

The Duchess shook her head.

"Whether we like it or not."

Tanaka nodded and sighed.

"My shuttle should already be fueled up and ready to go," she noted. "Shall we?"

CHAPTER THREE

Harriet had never been aboard a Mesharom ship before, and the stark white space they found their shuttle in was strange to her for several reasons—not least that it didn't have any doors. Even the big hatch that their shuttle had entered the ship through was gone.

There were no features at all on the smooth white walls of the space the shuttle was tucked into, and the Fleet Lord shivered as she fell into step behind Bond.

"Shouldn't there be a door or something?" she asked.

"There will be one," Bond replied. "Look."

The Duchess pointed and Harriet followed her hand to see a part of the wall rippling away. Two serpentine robots, each the height of a large adult man, slithered through the opening and approached them.

"Fleet Lord Harriet Tanaka and Imperial Representative Annette Bond," one of the robots greeted them. "We are your escorts to meet the Grand Commander. Come with us."

Harriet joined Bond in stepping in between the robots, but she wanted to shake her head at the machines. Not even a "please"—and while Harriet might be a mere military commander slated for a fleet of over a thousand warships, Annette Bond was the designated ruler of an entire planet and the direct personal representative of the Empress A!Shall.

And A!Shall was the ruler of a *lot* of planets and twenty-eight species spread across them.

Harriet had been raised in a relatively formal Japanese household for the late twenty-second century. Now, six years into the twenty-third century, she'd learned to relax much of that etiquette in most company. The Imperial Navy was, in many ways, even less formal than the United Earth Space Force she'd been trained in.

Both had been informal, to her at least, for the same reason: when combining dozens of cultures, it was impossible to create a set of etiquette rules that were going to work for everyone.

The complete *lack* of anything she'd regard as etiquette or even common politeness from the Mesharom, though...that was just irritating.

The robot behind her made a strange *plink* noise and both machines stopped in the corridor. Harriet paused, looking around and sharing a look with Bond.

The robotic servitors made up the vast majority of the "crew" of the war sphere. If they were likely to just...stop, that would be a spectacularly bad idea for the Mesharom.

"This is a recorded message for Duchess Annette Bond," the robot behind them said, in a different voice...one that both of the women recognized.

Harriet had rarely dealt directly with Interpreter-Shepherd Adamase, but they'd commanded the Mesharom fleet that had fought at the Battle of Terra. She and they had spoken extensively then and she recognized the particular tones of their chosen translated voice.

"I warned you that there would be consequences for your choices, my old friend, and I have done all I could to mitigate them," Adamase told them. "Tilsan is a Battle Fleet commander. The flexibilities required to operate out here without destroying our soft power are...offensive to them.

"I have no authority to overrule Tilsan and he has now seen *Jean Villeneuve*'s tests...a flagrant demonstration that even I would have been forced to act over.

"Be prepared, Duchess Bond, to lose *everything*." There was a sadness to the translated voice, but that was easily faked, Harriet supposed. "You should never have kept the scans of the Precursor ship. That alone is the stone Tilsan will drown you for."

The recording ending, the robot *plink*ed again, and both machines started forward like they'd never paused. The humans were quickly shuffled along, unable to do more than share a nervous look unbefitting two women of their power and stature.

———

TILSAN LOOKED like a giant fuzzy caterpillar. Lifted to their full height, Tilsan had a good meter and a half of body on the floor and two and a half meters raised up, towering over the humans as the robots escorted them into the room.

Dozens of long feelers, clearly usable for both movement and tool manipulation, covered the Mehsarom's underside, and dark blue-and-purple fur covered Tilsan's body.

If they hadn't been clearly trying to be intimidating, Harriet might have almost found the Mesharom pretty. The colors and the fur twisted through fascinating patterns, and it wasn't like the Mesharom went in for clothes a human would recognize.

There were no chairs waiting for them. The room wasn't colored in relaxing tones as Harriet had heard others describe meeting with Mesharom. There was no attempt to make them relax, and Tilsan was alone in the room with them and the two robots.

The machines slid back to where the door had been, taking up flanking positions behind Harriet and Bond—and Harriet was grimly certain the robots were armed. If Tilsan wanted to commit a war crime, he could easily have them both killed.

"Fleet Lord Tanaka. Representative Bond." There was no tone to

Tilsan's translated words. They were using their own systems to make sure they controlled the tone and other secondary communication of their English...and they weren't conveying *any*.

"I arrived in this system three days ago and began the necessary investigations to make up for the shortfalls of the local Mesharom forces," Tilsan told them. "As I was completing these investigations, your demonstration began."

A hologram appeared in the room without Tilsan seeming to do anything, showing *Jean Villeneuve* flying the test circuit.

"She is an impressive ship, isn't she?" Harriet ventured. "I'm looking forward to having her under my command."

"That won't happen," Tilsan told them. "*Jean Villeneuve* and her sister ships are to be surrendered to me immediately. All ships with similar systems will be interned until Mesharom inspectors can confirm those systems have been removed.

"Your Imperium's theft, lies, and betrayal end now. You will not be permitted to benefit from your deceptions."

Harriet caught herself staring at the Mesharom in shock. She wasn't even sure what to *say* to that.

Bond, thankfully, had clearly taken Adamase's warning to heart and expected this.

"Are you mad?" she asked bluntly. "You have no such authority, even if you had proof of some kind of theft...which you can't have, since none of *Jean Villeneuve*'s systems were stolen."

Whatever Tilsan's initial response to that reply was, it was untranslatable. A hissing series of clicks emerged from the alien, and none of the translators in the room turned it into English as the Mesharom crossed to the hologram.

It zoomed in, highlighting chunks of *Jean Villeneuve* as Tilsan gestured.

"None of the systems were stolen?" they demanded. "Mass-conversion power cores here."

Half a dozen sections of the ships highlighted on the hologram, all along the spinal power trunk.

"Stolen from the Reshmiri," Tilsan noted flatly. "The local Shepherd had records proving that theft. It was not our responsibility to solve the Reshmiri's problem, though I wonder now if we should have taken that as a warning of what was to come."

The Mesharom gave a whole-body shiver and then highlighted the wingtip plasma lances.

"Plasma lances, stolen from the Laians," they continued. "Potentially purchased from the Exiles, obsolete in any case compared to the hyperfold cannon we so foolishly gave you ourselves."

Harriet was expecting to hear Bond jump and glanced over at the Duchess. Bond gave her a *shush and listen* gesture. Clearly, she was going to let Tilsan run the list of "charges" out.

"Hyperspace missiles, stolen from us," Tilsan continued. "Tachyon scanners, stolen from us. All of this built on a hull with a mixed microbot-and-nanobot underlying matrix...based on the Precursor tech you should never have had access to."

The hologram snapped out of existence, and Tilsan turned back to them.

"This ship is built on lies and theft," he concluded. "To protect the Precursor tech and to reclaim our own technology, it *must* be turned over. All of the duplication of its technology must also be stopped and all examples turned over."

"That isn't happening," Bond said calmly. "None of that is happening, because everything you've said is wrong. Our original experimental matter converters were based on a reverse-engineered Reshmiri design, yes. That was fifteen years ago. There's only the most tenuous of connections between our current generation of matter-converter power plants and the stolen Reshmiri technology.

"As for the rest? We stole *nothing* from you. We saw the hyperspace missiles, the tachyon sensors, your own active microbot hulls and interior starship spaces, in action. Hell, Grand Commander, we saw them all in action in *Alpha Centauri*, a system we have wired with more sensors than you have aboard this ship.

"My husband is an engineer, and he says that knowing something is possible is half the battle. We knew the system we'd seen you use worked, so we set out to duplicate them. We succeeded."

Bond's words were fierce, and Harriet suddenly had an entirely new level of appreciation for the amount of work and brainpower that had gone into creating the technology behind her fleet.

"We duplicated your hyperspace missiles exactly, but with our tech, they were immense things. So, we found a different way," Bond continued. "Our HSMs don't work on the same logic as yours. Our hull matrices don't work on the same logic as yours. We had data-compatibility problems trying to interface our tachyon sensor networks with Interpreter-Shepherd Adamase's force's tachyon sensors in the Battle of Terra, because our system doesn't work the same way as yours.

"So, we have stolen *nothing* and all you have proven today is that you are so lost to your ego that you cannot conceive of the possibility that the best minds of *twenty-eight species* could combine to dupli-cate what we saw."

The room was silent.

"I am not Interpreter-Shepherd Adamase," Tilsan said into that silence. "I will not be turned by your brilliance or fooled by your lies. The proof is in front of my eyes, in the sensor data of your own ship. My dictate is unchanged."

"Then your dictate is refused," Bond said calmly. "Are you prepared to wage war on the A!Tol Imperium for your ego, Grand Commander?"

"It would be a very short war. I suggest you consider your choices carefully."

Harriet was frozen. She could do the math about the fate of every warship in the Sol System if Tilsan decided to launch that war. Even if the Laians decided to help them against the Core Powers' first among equals—unlikely at best—it would only add to the death toll.

"I think you overestimate how much territory you can hold with forty war spheres," Bond replied. "And how much damage you would do to your cause in the long run. You have no authority to demand what you are asking for. There are no treaties that give you that claim, no reason for us to accede but naked force.

"Do you understand what you will sacrifice if you use that force? That you will destroy ten thousand years of carefully built reputation? That you will throw aside the work not merely of Interpreter-Shepherd Adamase but of *every* Shepherd to ever hold the title?

"Your people's power out this far is based on respect and honor, not coercion. You don't have the ships to compel even the Arm Powers to bow to your will by force—and there are enough Arm Powers with cozy relationships with the Core to require more.

"Are you prepared to set your people against all the galaxy because we managed to build technology you have determined is your own?"

The room was silent again and Harriet coughed to clear her own frozen fear.

"And you may overestimate the firepower of your fleet," she said quietly. "Your weapons are not *that* much more powerful to allow you take forty ships against a thousand.

"You and I are military officers, Grand Commander. If I lost even *half* my fleet on a side project, unrelated to my actual *mission*, I would be court-martialed. Your superiors sent you to deal with the Taljzi, not start a new war."

"And if you turn on us, Grand Commander, you have my word that you will fight that war against the Taljzi alone," Bond said quietly.

"So, I repeat myself: your dictate is refused. We will not accede to your *request*. This meeting is over, and we will return to our shuttle now."

Bond turned and walked toward the wall where the door had been with perfect confidence. Still more than a little in awe, Harriet Tanaka followed.

Fortunately for *their* egos, the wall slid open to allow them passage.

CHAPTER FOUR

By the time Harriet and Bond made it back to *Emperor of China*, the rumor mill was in full overdrive. The Fleet Lord could tell from the way the deck crew were looking at them as they came out of the shuttle, and she wondered just what news *had* reached the fleet.

Patrick Kurzman-Wellesley entered the shuttle bay before they reached the exit, the Admiral moving with the solid pace of an angry glacier. His bulk, still more muscle than fat even with his desk job, did as good a job of scattering people out of the way as his stars.

Normally, Harriet knew Kurzman to be more careful about abusing those factors than this, and a chill ran down her spine.

"Admiral," she greeted the Militia's commander, half a second ahead of Annette Bond. "Something happened. What?"

"I was hoping you could tell me," the Admiral admitted. "We got cut out of the Mesharom hyperfold communications network when you were halfway back. Not just the multi-system net but the coms with the local fleet as well."

The chill was turning into a sheet of ice across her lower back. Hyperfold communicators relays only had a ten-light-year range and suffered from a two-hour delay at that distance, but they were vastly cheaper and easier to build than the instantaneous starcom stations.

As part of their recent alliance with the Mesharom, they'd been given access to the Mesharom's interstellar communications. That wasn't needed for their own territory, but it had let them negotiate the deal that saw Laian war-dreadnoughts ready to go to war against the Taljzi.

Its loss wasn't a big deal in itself, but it was a disturbingly good sign of just where Grand Commander Tilsan's mind and mood were.

"We appear to have lost the alliance with the Mesharom," Annette Bond said calmly.

Kurzman was stunned to silence, barely managing not to stare at his Duchess. Harriet had been there and known what happened, but the frank phrasing still sent a shiver down her spine.

"Grand Commander Tilsan demanded the surrender of all Gold Dragon technology and ships built with it," Bond continued. The Gold Dragon systems had been the most classified array of technology to come out of DragonWorks, most notable the single-portal hyperspace missiles.

"Starting with *Jean Villeneuve*. That wasn't fucking happening."

"No, no it wouldn't be," Kurzman confirmed after several more seconds of silence. "What do we *do*, Your Grace?"

"Ki!Tana is aboard, yes?" Bond asked.

Ki!Tana was an odd creature, a member of an ancient and special breed of A!Tol that had served as Bond's friend and advisor since Bond had fled the A!Tol conquest of Earth. From privateer to Duchess to chosen representative of the Empress A!Shall, Bond had risen with Ki!Tana at her side.

"She is," Kurzman-Wellesley confirmed. "We hid her quarters down behind the Guard to make sure no one bothered her."

"Get me a guide, Patrick. Ki!Tana knows these people better than anyone else in the star system. She can tell me how deep a hole Tilsan may have invited us into."

"I'll show you myself," Kurzman replied. "I get the feeling this might be important."

Bond sighed. "True. Harriet, you're with me as well."

Harriet nodded silently and followed the Terran Admiral. The ice at the base of her spine wasn't going anywhere. Ki!Tana was part of the reason they'd had any support from the Mesharom, but *she'd* known Interpreter-Shepherd Adamase and their predecessors.

Grand Commander Tilsan seemed like a very different caterpillar.

HARRIET TANAKA HAD SPENT twenty years in the service of the A!Tol Imperium, since the day she'd discovered that Imperial medicine could cure her then-ten-year-old son's aggressive cancer—and that while that medicine was *coming* to Earth, it would be made immediately available for volunteers for the Imperium's military and their families.

She'd been the first of the United Earth Space Force's officers to make the leap. She remained the most senior human in Imperial service, having risen to the highest rank the Imperial Navy *had*.

Along the way, she'd grown familiar with the A!Tol and their oddities. The worst of these, from the perspective of a human woman who'd now had three children, was that A!Tol females didn't have wombs.

Their birth cycle was parasitical—and fatal. They'd developed egg extraction and artificial gestation before they'd developed *computers*. A!Tol females were bigger and stronger than their males and grew until they died.

But their biology assumed they'd die breeding...and their hormones conspired against them to make sure they did. Every A!Tol female eventually reached the point where the demands of their body grew too much, at which point they usually quietly suicided.

A small but significant portion of the population had at least some of their eggs fertilized and reimplanted, dying in "childbirth" as their ancestors did.

Some tried to make it through the birthing madness and come out the other side. Most who tried failed, but a tiny number made it through. On the far side of insanity, they found a new balance of lost memories, self-control...and near-immortality.

The Ki!Tol were the trickster demons and wise advisors of A!Tol mythology, a reputation that Ki!Tana had never disabused anyone around her of. Bond's advisor was one of only two Ki!Tol Harriet Tanaka had ever met, and she was the older of them as well.

When the three humans entered the sitting area of Ki!Tana's quarters, the A!Tol was waiting for them. Even by the standards of A!Tol females, she was immense, a three-meter-tall squid capable of cracking unpowered armor with her bare tentacles.

Today, however, that height and strength were undermined by the color of her skin. Flickers of red pleasure at seeing them were visible but mostly lost in the deep purple sadness that covered her entire ever-shifting flesh.

"Ki!Tana," Bond greeted the old alien, giving the Ki!Tol an awkward hug. "You look like you already know some of what I need to ask you about."

"In two hundred long-cycles of working intermittently with the Mesharom, I have had a dozen different levels of communication with them," Ki!Tana replied. Two hundred long-cycles was roughly a hundred and five years. All of the humans in the room were distinctly familiar with A!Tol time units by now.

"But in all that time, I have *never* been entirely cut off from communicating with them," the Ki!Tol concluded. "I am guessing that the Imperial Fleet and Militia were cut off as well?"

"They were," Kurzman-Wellesley confirmed. "Less than five minutes after the Fleet Lord and the Duchess left their meeting with Tilsan."

"I take it that meeting didn't go well," Ki!Tana said dryly.

"Tilsan demanded the surrender of all Gold Dragon technology," Bond said flatly. "So, basically, to hand over every active warship currently in the Sol System and then let his people gut every ship the Imperial Navy has spent the last three months refitting."

The purple on Ki!Tana's skin grew darker and shades of fear-black were starting to be clearly visible.

"They presumed the technology was stolen," Ki!Tana guessed aloud. "They would be wrong, and the evidence would have been easily accessed by someone with their cyberwarfare systems."

Harriet twitched at how casually Ki!Tana assumed the Mesharom could access the most secured computers in the star system.

"Tilsan couldn't accept that," Bond replied. "They doubled down. I called their bluff and pointed out that forcing us over false pretenses would destroy any moral authority the Mesharom claimed to have."

"I do not know Tilsan, but Adamase knew them by reputation," Ki!Tana admitted. "The Mesharom Conclave does not pick Expeditionary Fleet Grand Commanders at random, Annette. They will have chosen a Mesharom of extraordinary will and stubbornness.

"They would not have expected Tilsan to ignore their primary mission in favor of this kind of distraction, I imagine, but the control of Precursor technology has been their primary objective for a hundred thousand long-cycles."

There was something more to that...something Harriet didn't know but was clearly bothering Annette.

"So, they got sent out to deal with a problem and got distracted by their usual objectives," Harriet concluded. "That doesn't help us much."

"No," Ki!Tana confirmed. "Though it does give us one piece of reassurance: Tilsan won't start a war without checking in with the Conclave. That'll take a day, at least, and...well, the Conclave is mostly likely going to tell them to get back on mission."

"Which raises another unpleasant question," Kurzman said. "If their main mission is to deal with the Taljzi, why would they demand that their own allies gut the forces we're going to support them with?"

"Oh, that's easy," the A!Tol said with a sad chuckle. "Tilsan doesn't think they need you."

CHAPTER FIVE

EVEN FROM HER FLAGSHIP, THE *BELLEROPHON*-B-CLASS battleship *Ajax*, Harriet Tanaka didn't feel any better about the situation. It didn't help that the *Bellerophon*-class battleships had been the testbed for what had become the *Galileo*-class superbattleships...and the B type was every bit as "guilty" of having been built with Gold Dragon technology as their larger siblings.

"Any status change?" she asked her operations officer as she stepped onto the flag deck. Koanest was a Yin, a tall blue-skinned alien who might have passed for a human woman in body paint if not for the fact that her head more closely resembled a featherless blue raven.

Koanest had been recommended by her previous right-hand officer, Sier. *Squadron Lord* Sier now commanded the sixteen *Bellerophon*-Bs that were most of Tenth Fleet's current firepower.

Forty squadrons of capital ships might be the plan, but right now, she had one. There were a dozen squadrons in various locations near Sol, guarding the approaches and ready to be called back if Sol was attacked, but they were only loosely assigned to Fleet Lord Harriet Tanaka's fleet.

None of them had been refitted. Once Harriet had her squadrons of Gold Dragon–refitted capital ships, those vessels would return to the yards for their own overhauls.

Koanest was responsible for tracking all of that, keeping an eye on the status reports of the ships destined for Tenth Fleet and making sure Harriet's flagship had a stockpile of real Japan-grown green tea for the Fleet Lord.

The last thirty-six hours, though, she'd been watching the Mesharom.

"They're just...sitting there, Fleet Lord," the Yin told Harriet. "They pulled all the battlecruisers in from around the system two hours after Tilsan met with you. No activity since. They're out of the allied tactical network; they're not responding to hyperfold or radio coms."

"They're *ignoring* us, Fleet Lord."

"Tilsan's an asshole," Harriet replied conversationally. "Any update on the *Galileos*?"

"*Jean Villeneuve* has completed her trials. There's some paperwork for you to go over and then we'll need to arrange a formal ceremony to buy her into Imperial service," Koanest told her. "The other three are about four weeks from their own trials. Barring unexpected problems, we'll have a full division of *Galileo*s by the time Tenth Fleet is ready."

"We'll attach them to Sier's squadron," Harriet decided. "They're going to be our most powerful single ships by a significant margin. I want them close to hand."

"Will you be taking command from one?" Koanest asked.

"No, we'll stay aboard *Ajax,* I think," she replied. "Better to get everyone used to where to find the Fleet Lord, after all."

Plus, the *Bellerophon*-Bs punched above their weight and were extremely well defended while still not being superbattleships. The superbattleships were going to attract a *lot* of fire once the battle closed, and the *Galileo*s were almost four megatons bigger than the

Vindication-class ships that were now the Imperium's *second*-biggest superbattleships.

Ajax would attract a lot less attention than the bigger warships and could survive what attention did get thrown her way. Hopefully.

Harriet hummed softly to herself as she reached the main holographic display and surveyed it.

"What are our Laian friends up to?" she asked.

"They moved the war-dreadnoughts away from the Mesharom shortly after coms got cut," Koanest reported. "They're keeping well to themselves otherwise, but they're at least linked into our hyperfold coms and *talking* to us."

Ten war-dreadnoughts and a hundred escort cruisers. Once, that fleet would have terrified her—it was two and a half billion tons of Core Power warships, after all.

Now she'd seen a fleet of a thousand capital ships swarm Sol. Seen a threat from beyond any known territory field over *twenty* billion tons of warships against her home. The new Gold Dragon technologies had changed the balance between the A!Tol Imperium and the Laian Republic.

That change was part of why Eleventh Pincer of the Republic Kanmorad was there. The Republic had agreed to a pact of mutual nonaggression with the Imperium as they engaged in a conflict with the Wendira, their neighbor amongst the Core Powers.

That agreement had been made with an inferior they'd pissed off. Now, though, that inferior was closing the gap far faster than they'd expected, and the Republic was still exhausted from the latest round of war with the Wendira Hive. Helping the Imperium now came with the unspoken proviso that the Republic would call for the Imperium to return the favor.

Ton for ton, *Ajax* was actually more powerful than the war-dreadnoughts now. They just outmassed the battleship twenty to one, and the Republic could build a war-dreadnought in the time it took the Imperium to build two *super*battleships.

"All right." Two Core Power fleets hanging out in her star system, and one of them wasn't talking to her—and she didn't have the power to fight either of them. Not right now. Maybe once she had everything she'd been promised, she'd feel comfortable taking on *one* of them.

For now, all she could do was hope that Tilsan was *merely* an asshole and not utterly mad.

"WE HAVE movement in the Mesharom formation!"

The barked report had the attention of everyone on *Ajax*'s flag deck. Its equivalent probably had everyone's attention across the combined fleets gathered in the Sol System.

It wasn't just movement. The Mesharom Conclave's Expeditionary Fleet had gone from motionless to sixty percent of lightspeed in under three seconds. That was five percent of lightspeed faster than the new cruise speed the A!Tol Imperium was standardizing, reached in slightly less than half the time.

Harriet breathed a sigh of relief as she saw the Mesharom fleet was heading *away* from Earth. Despite all of the assurances she and Annette Bond had given everyone, the fear that Tilsan would turn his weapons on the Imperium had never quite faded.

"They're leaving the system," Koanest reported. "They'll reach hyper portal distance...now."

Space tore in front of the Mesharom war spheres, massive portals sized for ships of a scale no one else could build. There was a flicker on the hologram as the ships entered the portal, and then emptiness.

"All the Mesharom units moved together," Koanest reported. "There's nobody left. Not even a scout ship."

"We know damn well they have stealthed sensor platforms hidden in the Kuiper Belt," Harriet pointed out. "They've been watching us for a while. Still, to leave like this..."

Ki!Tana had said that Tilsan didn't think he needed the A!Tol and their subject races. Harriet, on the other hand, had seen the

Taljzi invade Sol with three thousand warships. She suspected Tilsan might be underestimating their enemy.

"Fleet Lord, we have an incoming communication request from the Eleventh Pincer of the Republic," her Frole reported. The ambulatory fungus was more dependent on machine translators than most of the crew, since they didn't naturally communicate by sound.

Like the rest of the Imperium's subjects, they'd adapted.

"Put him through," Harriet ordered.

Pincer of the Republic was technically a junior rank compared to her...except that Kanmorad was the eleventh most senior Pincer, which made him the thirty-first most senior officer in the Laian Republic military.

Plus, he had ten war-dreadnoughts. That bought a certain degree of respect his rank might not earn on its own.

"Pincer Kanmorad," she greeted the Laian.

"Fleet Lord Tanaka," he replied. Kanmorad was a massive scarab beetle–like creature, his shell and underside glittering with opalescent purples and greens. Laians were often gorgeous to human eyes—Harriet was familiar with the colony of Laian Exiles on Earth—but Kanmorad was spectacular.

"You saw our esteemed Mesharom allies leave," he continued. "I am guessing that Grand Commander Tilsan did not share their plans with you?"

"They did not. They appear to be rather upset with us," Harriet said calmly.

Kanmorad laughed, a chittering sound with a clicking of mandibles.

"Your Imperium has a habit of developing technology from scan data at a speed that really *should* require reverse-engineering," he pointed out. "Considering the rings you ran around Kandak, I can't imagine you weren't able to prove your systems were fairly developed."

"We had the proof," Harriet confirmed carefully. She wasn't sure what relationship Kanmorad had to the junior Pincer of the Republic who'd once threatened Sol with a war-dreadnought, but he certainly didn't seem *bothered* by the facts of that confrontation. "Grand Commander Tilsan was...unimpressed."

"Grand Commander Tilsan is a dung bug without the brains to see what's shitting on him," Kanmorad said cheerfully.

Harriet had enough practice at controlling her face to make sure her amusement didn't leak, but she didn't argue with the Laian, either. She was going to have to remember that description.

"Did the Grand Commander communicate with you?" she asked.

"That is why I reached out," Kanmorad replied. "He wanted us to accompany him, apparently believing that our fifty capital ships combined would be more than sufficient to deal with the Taljzi."

"And you didn't?" Harriet asked.

"The Grand Parliament made no promises to the Mesharom Conclave," Kanmorad pointed out. "We made promises and commitments to the A!Tol Imperium and to Empress A!Shall. My assigned task is to protect the Sol System until the Imperium has completed refitting the first wave of their ships and then to accompany Tenth Fleet against the Taljzi.

"I am *not* tasked with destroying the Taljzi alone or with going anywhere without a few hundred Imperial capital ships alongside me," he concluded. "More importantly, Fleet Lord Tanaka, I do *not* believe that forty war spheres and ten war-dreadnoughts would suffice to stand against the fleets the Taljzi have so far deployed.

"We must assume that they will gather as great of a force to defend their shipyards and worlds as they gathered to attack you. Grand Commander Tilsan's vessels are more powerful than any other in the galaxy, but even they can not stand against a hundred times their numbers."

The Laian laughed again.

"So I remain here, with you, until your fleet is ready to deploy. I suspect we will see our Mesharom friend return with a dented shell, asking for our forgiveness and help. It never hurts to remind those who think themselves all-powerful that they, too, have limits."

Harriet would have described the Imperium's interaction with the Laians as being that kind of reminder...and from the way Kanmorad said it, so might he.

"I appreciate you passing on what Tilsan told you," she said. "You think they're going to move against the Taljzi alone?"

"I do not believe the Grand Commander's ego would allow anything else," Kanmorad noted. "More importantly, I know that returning without dealing with the Taljzi would be a violation of their orders.

"If they have left Sol, Fleet Lord, they intend to attack the Taljzi. He will fail. We must hope that they do enough damage to clear the path for us."

Harriet grimaced.

"You are not wrong, Pincer of the Republic. Your aid and presence are appreciated, as is your...wisdom."

CHAPTER SIX

THERE WERE A LOT OF DOWNSIDES TO BEING THE STEPDAUGHTER of a planetary ruler. Most of the time, it was, in Morgan's opinion, a pain in the ass. You got all of the assumptions of nepotism and shadows to live in, without any chance at actually *inheriting* said planet.

In her more self-reflective moments, she'd admit that trying to pick out where she'd benefited from being Duchess Annette Bond's stepdaughter was like asking a goldfish to point out water.

One thing she *had* learned was that even fully booked-up restaurants tended to find an extra table somewhere when the Duchess's daughter called for an emergency reservation. With both her and Victoria Antonova being active-duty military, arranging dates in advance was hard.

"You know, you don't *need* to find the fanciest restaurant on half the planet to feed me at," Victoria teased after they'd been seated. The current venue was a small two-person table next to the balcony railing of a rooftop restaurant...on the rooftop of Hong Kong's largest mixed residential-commercial building.

The building was so tall that Morgan had picked up smaller

versions of a warship's shield generators as she approached. Those shields were there to protect the guests from the wind and chill of the eight hundred and seventy-six meter height of the restaurant.

Morgan had been there before with her parents and had to stop and think about what Victoria had said before laughing.

"You're probably right, but I keep going to the restaurants I *remember*," she admitted. Her father was the man who'd built the first interface-drive ships for humanity. After the Annexation, he'd ended up building ships for the Ducal Militia and then for the Imperial Navy.

"And your parents only go to the fanciest places?" Victoria asked, glancing hesitantly over the balcony at Hong Kong. "That doesn't strike me as right."

"My parents only go to the most securable places," Morgan said quietly. Even if the waiter hadn't chosen that moment to arrive, that might have killed the conversation. Morgan was aware that while the shield wasn't primarily intended to stop military weapons, it would stand up to everything short of someone firing missiles from orbit.

They ordered their drinks, Victoria wincing at the prices, then Morgan reached across the table for her girlfriend's hand.

"I'm sorry," she said softly. "Goldfish in a fish bowl. I don't always recognize when water's wet."

"It's okay," the blonde Russian woman replied, squeezing her hand. Victoria had stayed in the Ducal Militia when Morgan had transferred to the Imperial Navy. Once Tenth Fleet moved out, Victoria would remain behind.

Morgan wasn't going to let any chance to get together pass.

"I do tend to forget that money isn't really...a thing to you, though," Victoria continued. "I think I just ordered a drink that cost more than my first phone."

The fish bowl in *this* case was the trust fund that took care of Morgan's expenses whenever she wasn't aboard a starship. Morgan didn't actually *know* how much money her father had put in the semi-blind trust that managed her funds and her Hong Kong apartment.

"I'll...try to remember better," Morgan admitted. "My treat?" she offered plaintively.

"There's no other way I can afford to eat here!" Victoria replied, but she was laughing as she did.

"I'm guessing they have oysters?" she asked with a wink as she opened her menu.

ONE OF THE other advantages of going to places Morgan's parents had frequented was that Ducal Consort Elon Casimir—the once-CEO and still-primary-shareholder of Nova Industries, Sol's biggest shipbuilder—had a nearly allergic reaction to the type of places that put their focus on presentation over quality *or* quantity.

The two women were quite happily full by the time they made it back to Morgan's apartment. The unit was on the lower floors of the building her stepmother lived in. The official Ducal Residence, however, filled the top five or six floors—Morgan wasn't even sure—of the building with a full-floor penthouse and multiple floors of security.

Being in the same building meant that the Residence's staff and security could watch Morgan's place when she was gone. There'd only ever been one attack directed at Morgan—as opposed to what-ever warship she was aboard—in her life, but that was enough for "Uncle James," AKA General of the Ducal Guard James Arthur Valerian Wellesley-Kurzman, to insist her apartment was regularly checked.

A green light after she flagged her ID card told her a team had been through since she'd come through around lunchtime, and she shook her head.

"What is it, love?" Victoria asked.

"Having the head of security for the planet as your honorary uncle means his professional paranoia gets applied to you," Morgan told her. "There was a security team in here today to make sure there were no..."

She stepped into her kitchen and discovered what the "security" team had *actually* been doing. Her normally empty kitchen had suddenly acquired several neatly arranged flowerpots, their smell wafting delicately through the space.

The one-bedroom apartment wasn't very large, and the plants were enough to change the tone of the entire space. A glance into her bedroom showed that she'd also received professional-grade turn-down service.

"So, is this normal with the security sweep?" Victoria murmured, resting her head on Morgan's shoulder. That took some bending, since Victoria was definitely the taller one of the pair.

"No, this is probably someone working out I had a date." Morgan shook her head and then found a note on the table. "Apparently, my little sisters."

Hope this helps smooth the night. Meet us at the Residence tomorrow.

Leah and Carol.

PS: There's breakfast in the fridge. For two.

Morgan chuckled.

"Apparently, they want me to come by the Residence in the morning. But not *too* early, since they put breakfast in the fridge for both of us."

Victoria giggled and gently bit Morgan's ear.

"How much time do you have?" she asked, her voice serious.

"Tonight, all night," Morgan replied. "In general?" She shook her head, knowing what Victoria was asking. "Two months or so. We're starting to get confirmations of ships finishing their refits and heading our way."

"Then it sounds like we need to take *full* advantage of tonight."

CHAPTER SEVEN

THE TWINS WERE WAITING FOR MORGAN WHEN SHE GOT TO THE Residence in the morning. They were at least waiting while doing their schoolwork, but Morgan had no illusions as to why the heir and the spare of the Duchy of Terra were doing their homework in the front sitting room of the Ducal Residence.

The pair of sixteen-year-old girls attended Hong Kong's premier academy, a school that had leveraged having the twins *hard* to get funding and patronage to turn themselves into *Earth's* premier educational institute.

At sixteen, they were probably studying what Morgan had learned in her first years at the Militia Academy.

"Morgan," Leah greeted her big sister. There was a moment where the three young women attempted to be all formal, then Carol laughed and jumped up to embrace Morgan.

Morgan gleefully returned the embrace. Like her and the younger sisters' mother, the twins were blonde. Unlike Morgan's golden blond, Leah and Carol had hair so platinum blond as to be nearly white.

No one was quite sure *where* that had come from, since Elon

Casimir was dark-haired and Annette Bond had been even more golden than Morgan at the twins' age.

"It's good to see you two," Morgan told them. "When did you get back?"

All four of her younger sisters had been evacuated when the Taljzi fleet had been looming down on Sol. They hadn't known for sure that they'd be able to hold, and a lot of people *had* died when the Taljzi had besieged the system.

Once the Return had been beaten back, though, the twins had managed to talk their way off of the ship they were on and onto a ship heading back to Earth.

"A couple of weeks ago," Leah said. "Still getting angry messages every time Megan's ship drops out of hyperspace and she can send a hyperfold transmission to the nearest starcom."

Morgan snorted. Megan was the second-youngest of her half-sisters, which meant she was old enough to fully understand *why* she and Alexis, the youngest, still had to go to A!To. And old enough to be angry that the twins had decided to turn themselves around.

"Has Mom forgiven you yet?" Morgan asked.

"I'm not sure Mom actually managed to get *angry* over it," Carol said. "It's a little too much...something she would have done."

"That's fair." Morgan took a seat and noted there was already an extra coffee on the table. Plain black, strong...the way both Morgan and their father took it. "This mine or Dad's?"

"Yours. Dad *is* currently somewhat angry at us," Leah pointed out. "But...also well aware that this was inevitable given who he married. He's at DragonWorks, though, they wanted his brain to help with something."

"And you asked me to meet you here," Morgan said as she took a swallow of the coffee. "Much as I appreciated the reminder you two were home and I *could* see you, I'm guessing you had a reason."

Both twins shifted body language ever so slightly. Their shoulders straightened, their eyes leveled and their smiles faded a bit. Suddenly, Morgan was no longer talking to her half-sisters.

She was talking to the heir of the Duchy of Terra and the heir's right-hand woman.

Morgan had seen the transition before. She'd seen them *practice* it in front of a mirror and had, at one point, sat with the twins and helped grade their particular level of "stern stateswoman."

That robbed the transition of much of its impact on her, but she also knew that it had value for them.

"We wanted an update on Tenth Fleet's status," Leah told her. "We get the official reports, but since you're right in the middle of it..."

"I'm also bound by a whole bunch of rules and chain of command," Morgan pointed out. "I can tell you some stuff but not everything."

"We know," Carol replied. "We get the lecture from Mom and Admiral Kurzman-Wellesley at least every two weeks. But Leah, especially, *needs* to know. Tenth Fleet's mission is critical to the safety of the Duchy."

Morgan took another sip of coffee and studied the two younger women. Her sisters were identical twins, attractive platinum blondes in matching haircuts and matching slacks and blouses. The only difference anyone other than close family would pick out would have been the golden brooch of a Hong Kong–centered globe on Leah's collar, marking her as heir to the Duchy of Terra.

"I can give you the high level," she said, echoing her earlier comment. "Tenth Fleet is a little over two months from deployment. We attempted to accelerate that after Grand Commander Tilsan took the Mesharom Expeditionary Fleet out on their own, but the timeline was set for a reason.

"What we managed to gain in accelerated refit timelines, we then lost on the insistence that we deploy a stronger force to make up for the lack of the Mesharom fleet," she continued. All of this should have been in the reports the twins had seen, but if they wanted to hear it from her, they'd hear it from her.

"What about morale in the fleet?" Leah asked. "It's only been a month since our most powerful ally pulled one of the more epic flounces I've ever heard of."

"That didn't help," Morgan admitted, considering some of what she'd heard and dealt with. "We all had a moment of terror when the war spheres came out of hyperspace, but knowing they were on our side was reassuring. Those ships are terrifying, but…"

She shrugged.

"Only a handful of the fleet's officers dealt with the Mesharom at all. A lot of people only interacted with them via translated text messages. Those are abrupt at their best and rude at their worst. It didn't help the fleet's opinion of our allies…and then they heard about Tilsan's demands.

"The general reaction to their exit has been 'good riddance.'"

"But don't we *need* the Mesharom?" Carol said. The twins were passing the questions back and forth with practiced skill. Their rhythm wasn't perfect…and Morgan realized they were practicing their technique on her.

She was about as safe an "interrogation subject" as they were going to find.

"We're not sure," she admitted. "Between Tenth Fleet and what the Kanzi have promised to put up, we're looking at fifteen hundred capital ships. And that's before the Laian war-dreadnoughts get counted.

"We're deploying half the star fleets of two major Arm Powers, plus significant numbers of a Core Power's main-battle-line units. If we *can't* carry the day, we could be in serious trouble."

Morgan shook her head.

"It's intentionally set up that we and the Kanzi are each committing the same percentage of our line of battle," she noted. "Even if we fail, we will probably smash the Taljzi badly enough that we'll achieve a peace of mutual exhaustion for a few years—and the Kanzi will be in equally bad shape."

Leah sighed.

"That's a *shi* calculation to make," she replied, the Cantonese curse slipping in without thinking. Morgan's younger sisters were very much children of Hong Kong in many ways.

"That's on Mom," Morgan said, taking another sip of her coffee. "I've probably already told you more than I should have, but most of that should have been in the reports you get as members of the Ducal Council. Have fun practicing your interrogation?"

She'd timed the question perfectly. Carol was halfway through a sip of her tea and spat it halfway across the room in surprise.

Leah, on the other hand, simply raised her own tea in salute as she relaxed out of Heir Mode.

"You owe me twenty marks," she told her younger sister. "I *told* you Morgan knew us well enough to guess." She turned back to Morgan with a smile as Carol started cleaning up the mess.

"We did need the update and the in-the-fleet point of view," she noted. "But yes, we were using you as practice for some of what Minister Camber is teaching us."

Amanda Camber had taken over the intelligence functions of the Duchy of Terra after Li Chin Zhao had passed away. That man had been enough of a titan that it had taken *three* extremely competent people to replace him.

Camber herself had once been a corporate spy in the...*fascinating* milieu of pre-Annexation Earth. After getting herself pulled into helping stop a terrorist movement's attempt to kill the newborn Duchy in its cradle, she'd ended up as one of Zhao's right-hand women.

Now she was apparently teaching the twins interrogation tactics.

"There are worse teachers, I see," Morgan replied. "You're going to do fine, though you'll excuse me if I wish for you to have a long and boring adult life before you need them."

"Another ten years of education while serving as a generic 'voice of the people' on the Council for us both," Carol put in. "After that, I'm sure Mom will have work for us both. But yeah, we get your point."

"And we agree completely," Leah finished for her sister. "I've already spent enough time training for the job to know I need, oh, five or six *decades* more experience before I'm ready to take it over from Mom."

With Imperial medical technology, that was actually likely…but from Morgan's conversations with their mother, Leah was underestimating just how long it would take for her to be ready.

From what Annette Bond said, being Duchess of a world simply wasn't something you *could* be ready for.

CHAPTER EIGHT

THE GRAND BRIEFING CHAMBER THAT HARRIET TANAKA currently stood in front of didn't exist. It was an image that her communications software was showing on the walls of the tiny briefing room next to her office.

Every illusory figure in the briefing chamber was connected to an actual living person, though. Not all of them would be able to respond to the briefing in real time, though most of her assigned Division, Echelon and Squadron Lords were within real-time hyperfold-com range of a starcom.

Hyperfold coms didn't have a noticeable delay until the distance was over a light-day. Most Imperial systems had starcoms, which had no delay at any distance but were far more expensive and difficult to build. Some of the ships were in systems without them and would get the briefing after the hyperfold delay. Others were in hyperspace, where capital ships could at least receive starcom transmissions but nothing could send hyperfold coms. They'd get the briefing, but they couldn't ask questions.

"Greetings, everyone," Harriet told them. "I'm sure this probably could have been sent out as a recording, but tradition says I waste at least a few thousandth-cycles of everyone's time."

After twenty years, she could translate between A!Tol cycles and Terran measurement with ease. A thousandth-cycle was roughly a minute and a half—and she'd probably need more than eighty-four seconds of everyone's time to get through her talk today.

"With the reactivation of the superbattleship squadrons undergoing refitting here in Sol, High Command has seen fit to formally declare Tenth Fleet an active force," she told them all. Everyone in the briefing, which included members of all of the A!Tol Imperium's twenty-eight species, was designated to join Tenth Fleet.

Less than a tenth of them were in Sol so far. That still left Fleet Lord Harriet Tanaka in charge of five squadrons of Imperial capital ships—and no sane sentient was going to argue that eighty battleships and superbattleships didn't count as a fleet.

There was a smattering of applause and equivalents from the gathered officers, and Harriet smiled grimly.

"Unfortunately, it's also my responsibility to inform you all that it has now been two full twenty-cycles since the Mesharom Expeditionary Fleet left the Sol System. We have had no contact with the Expeditionary Fleet since then.

"Our forward scouting forces did see the Mesharom pass them heading towards Taljzi space, but that is the last record we have of Grand Commander Tilsan's force. At this point, the Imperium has no choice but to assume that the Mesharom Expeditionary Fleet has been destroyed."

Those forty war spheres would have made Tilsan's fleet the largest component by mass of the Allied Fleet they'd been planning to gather. Now the Imperium and the Kanzi Theocracy had to judge whether they needed to somehow come up with *more* ships—which wasn't happening—or deploying with what they had.

Harriet had been promised five more squadrons, though no one was entirely clear on where they'd come from. The Kanzi had increased their commitment from seventy ten-ship squadrons to eighty, but both of those commitments were going to strain the nations providing them.

No star nation could deploy *eight hundred* capital ships without giving something up. The Kanzi had to worry about rebellions and internal difficulties more than the Imperium did...but both of them were still carefully watching each other across the border, too. And while the Imperium had agreements with the Laians, the Wendira were within striking distance of Imperial territory too.

The briefing had exploded into chaos when Harriet had made her announcement about the Mesharom, and she waited for it to die down.

"Both our commitment and the Kanzi's commitment to this mission have been expanded," she told them, knowing that her own thoughts would be echoed in all of their briefings. "With the support of the Eleventh Pincer of the Republic and his ships, I feel that the Allied Fleet should suffice even without the Mesharom.

"Bluntly, even if the Mesharom were utterly destroyed, they would not have gone down without a fight," Harriet noted. "Grand Commander Tilsan may have failed, but even in failure, they would have almost certainly opened a pathway for us to achieve our shared goals.

"We have moved some target dates around, and I'll go over those quickly. While I'm doing that, I want you to hold any questions you need to ask."

She smiled.

"I'm sure another thousandth-cycle or two isn't going to reduce the number of *those* you have!"

THE END of the briefing found Harriet back in her office, staring at the pot of green tea her steward had made for her...and the bottle of expensive French brandy sitting next to it. The brandy had been Jean

Villeneuve's favorite brand, and he'd corrupted her into enjoying it at some point.

She'd lost track of when. The old man had been an influence in her life, one way or another, for a very long time.

His namesake and her sisters were going to *keep* being an influence for a while yet, too. She'd stack the four *Galileo*-class ships up against a Laian war-dreadnought without blinking, even if the war-dreadnought outmassed them five to two.

A chime told her that her next scheduled call was up and she sighed and put the brandy away before hitting Accept.

A familiar A!Tol appeared on the screen. Smaller than any adult female, male A!Tol were still in the process of fighting for a level of gender equality humans would regard as acceptable. They were *winning*, but it had been a surprisingly long fight, from what Harriet knew.

There was no question about *this* A!Tol, though. Especially not in Sol. Tan!Shallegh—the *Tan!* marked him as a close relative of Empress A!Shall—had commanded the fleet that had conquered the system.

Twice since, he'd commanded fleets that had saved it. Earth and Tan!Shallegh went way back.

"Fleet Lord Tanaka," he greeted her. "I skimmed the recording of your briefing to the fleet and the question session. Any concerns?"

"About fifteen hundred of them on one hand, and forty on the other," she replied. That was how many ships she was going to command when the dust settled and how many war spheres were missing.

"I understand. You have the command because you're ready," Tan!Shallegh told her. "Because *I* think you're ready." Flashes of red amusement and green determination crossed his skin.

"And also because A!Shall recalled me to become First Fleet Lord," he admitted. "If she hadn't decided she needed me within manipulator reach, I wouldn't have given the command up to anyone.

"But since I had to give it up, it had to be you. No one has commanded a fleet of this scale in three hundred long-cycles...and the Duchy of Terra, for whatever reason, has been the center of this whirlpool so far."

"We're talking about going out and fighting an enemy that appears to have just disappeared forty war spheres," Harriet pointed out. She'd say a *lot* more to Tan!Shallegh than she could to any of her subordinates. She didn't have to hide her concerns from her boss.

Just her subordinates. Downsides of the job, she supposed.

"Everything you said about Tilsan going down without a fight is true, Tanaka," Tan!Shallegh told her. "I don't care what surprise they pulled out of the waters, they didn't take forty war spheres without paying for it."

"I'd feel better if I knew I was getting those extra squadrons I'd been promised," she pointed out. "Everyone has been promising that they'll find them, but I'm not sure where they're coming from."

"The Indiri Great Houses," Tan!Shallegh said flatly.

She outright gaped at her boss. The Indiri's Duchy was the manifestation of the old American joke of *one nation under copyright.* The Great Houses were the family-owned central corporations that ran their Duchy—and the megacorporations that had worked with Nova Industries and others to help leverage the Duchy of Terra into the top half of the duchies by wealth in less than two years.

Of course, that process had moved the Duchy of Indir from the third-wealthiest Duchy to the wealthiest. They weren't the richest system in the Imperium, though. The richest systems in the Imperium weren't Duchies—they belonged directly to the A!Tol or the Imperial Races.

But among the Duchies, the homeworlds of the species who *hadn't* seen their cultures accidentally destroyed in their annexation, the Indiri Great Houses now represented the single largest concentration of wealth and industry...and the largest Ducal Militia.

"We already gutted the Terran Ducal Militia," Harriet said quietly. "They, at least, fought in the defense of their own star system. Does the Indiri Militia even have Gold Dragon–tier ships?"

She figured she knew the answer. If they didn't, Tan!Shallegh wouldn't even be suggesting it.

"The Indiri and Nova Industries have been in each other's back pockets for most of the last forty long-cycles," Tan!Shallegh replied with the red flash of an A!Tol chuckle. "What would you say to five squadrons of *Bellerophon*-Bs?"

Most of the ships she'd been promised were refits. Shipyards across the Imperium were ripping out proton beams and antimatter power cores to install matter converters and hyperspace missiles. Only about half of the refits would have hyperfold cannons, but all of them would be carrying single-portal hyperspace missiles.

Bellerophon-Bs, however, were built from the ground up with Gold Dragon tech. They had the active-microbot hull supports to shore up the near-impenetrable compressed-matter hulls all of the warships used. They had plasma lances and hyperfold guns and...

Well, her own flagship was a *Bellerophon*-B for a reason.

"I'd do cartwheels on my flag deck," she said. "They've got them?"

"The Indiri Ducal Militia has eight squadrons of capital ships as a rule," Tan!Shallegh told her. "Their plan was to retire the older five in favor of these ships and then replace the remaining three with *Galileo*s. Once the news about Tilsan's fleet made it to Duke Natar Forel, he offered to sell the ships into Imperial service."

Tan!Shallegh's tentacles fluttered nervously.

"You don't want to know what premium we paid for them," he concluded, "but crews are taking possession of them for final trials now. They'll be a five-cycle later than your original planned launch date, but I will make waiting for them an order if necessary, Fleet Lord."

"For another eighty *Bellerophon*s, sir? That won't be necessary at all."

CHAPTER NINE

While the hyperfold communicator had made short-range and mobile faster-than-light communication possible, a real-time conference across any distance still needed a starcom on both ends.

Fortunately, both Sol and Arjzi, the Kanzi capital system, had the massive installations. That allowed Fleet Master Shairon Cawl, the commander of the Kanzi's Third Armada, to participate in at least some of the meetings putting together the offensive against the Taljzi.

Cawl was old for a Kanzi. Like all of his people, he looked basically like a human...a human that was roughly a hundred and twenty centimeters tall and covered in blue fur, at least.

He had darker fur than many Kanzi, but streaks of paler fur were visible on his face. Some of it was almost gray, the effect of age, but there was also the white splash of a scar crossing his face and his right eye. The eye had been regrown, but the scar remained.

The hologram of the Fleet Master sitting in Harriet's conference room was complete enough to show the powered brace around his right leg as well. Most of the video she'd seen of the old Kanzi moving showed him using a cane as well.

She didn't know quite what had happened to Cawl's leg or face, but the Kanzi had spent a long time in the service of the Kanzi Theocracy—culminating in leading an entire fleet to the relief of Sol in the Battle of Terra that had caused so much destruction.

"We've finalized our numbers," Cawl announced after the initial pleasantries were over. "The Third Armada is going to be lighter on superbattleships than I hoped, only twenty-five squadrons, but once Her Holiness got involved, the people trying to saddle me with *light* battleships finally shut up."

Harriet had dealt with a similar problem. Both the Kanzi and the A!Tol had an inventory of light capital ships, ranging from four to seven million tons, designed to be more strategically mobile than heavier units.

Those ships didn't really *count* as capital ships in her mind. Like the old British battlecruisers, they had *enough* of the traits of capital ships for people to try and use them as such—and lacked enough of the traits to burn like kindling in the main line.

She'd forwarded the people who'd wanted to give her A!Tol fast battleships to Tan!Shallegh. She hadn't heard the idea raised again.

"So, fifty-five squadrons of battleships?" she asked, glancing over at the other members of the room. Kanmorad was also present by hologram, but Bond was actually present aboard *Ajax*. Five hundred and fifty battleships was a mind-boggling number to her still.

It was just also the kind of number needed to take the fight to the Taljzi.

"They're currently scattered across half the Theocracy, but I now know which squadrons and ships," Cawl confirmed. "There's still argument going on over weight and type of escorts, but I've been promised at least a hundred squadrons."

"We're looking at similar numbers on our side," Harriet agreed. That would give them around two thousand escorts and fifteen hundred capital ships. She had to shake her head at the numbers.

"If everyone manages to honor those commitments, we'll have enough ships to match the Second Return," she continued. "We have to assume they'll muster a force of at *least* a similar size to defend their home territories, and they'll have the advantage of fixed defenses and interior position this time."

"But you will have actual war-dreadnoughts to reinforce you this time," Kanmorad interjected, the big beetle leaning back in his oddly constructed chair to study them. "No illusions or games."

Harriet concealed a wince behind an only semi-forced smile. Kanmorad, at least, seemed to regard the actions of his people's exiles as *hilarious*. Ten attack cruisers belonging to the Laian Exiles had shown up at the end of the Battle of Terra, using powerful ECM to pretend to be modern war-dreadnoughts.

It had been the final straw to send the survivors of the Second Return fleeing, but it had also been a giant bluff. Now, as Kanmorad pointed out, they had real war-dreadnoughts. The ten Laian capital ships could easily mass as much as the thousand escorts either of the main star nations were bringing to the Allied Fleet.

"Which leaves us, I'll note, with an interesting question that no one seems to have addressed," Kanmorad continued. "The dates in these reports everyone has so kindly shared with me suggest that we are all rendezvousing in six weeks. One of the most powerful fleets assembled by any of the powers in a very long time.

"And nothing has been decided about who will be in command."

Laians didn't smile, but Harriet did *not* like the tone of Kanmorad's mandible clicks as he dropped that bomb. The Laian reminded her of Ki!Tana some days...and *not* in a good way.

"I presume you don't intend to put yourself forward for the role?" Annette Bond interjected, her sweet tone a warning to anyone who knew her.

The mandible clicks accelerated into outright laughter.

"Much as it is beyond my usual tunnels to conceive it, my war-dreadnoughts will be the smallest of the three components of the fleet by any measure," he noted brightly. "While I will require some independence both as an ally and the representative of a Core Power, I will concede that overall command authority must be held by either Fleet Lord Tanaka or Fleet Master Cawl."

Harriet met the eyes of the hologram of her Kanzi counterpart. Cawl was probably senior to her by any rational measure, but there was no way in *hell* the Imperium was putting forty-five squadrons of hyperspace-missile-equipped capital ships under the command of a Kanzi.

"The Taljzi are our mistake," Cawl said quietly and calmly. "They are our kin, however far removed and lost to God they may have become. It was our worlds that burned first and our people who suffered—and we are bringing the largest number of capital ships.

"My ego is not lost to the mountains and winds like others I've known, but I think it is entirely reasonable for my High Priestess to insist that I command the joint fleet."

"Shairon," Bond said sharply. "We're bringing three hundred and twenty superbattleships to your two hundred and fifty. Most of our capital ships are larger, too—especially after the refits both of our fleets have gone through.

"You're bringing more hulls but we're bringing more *tonnage*. Not to mention that your fleet lacks hyperspace missiles entirely."

"That's a low blow, Duchess Bond," Cawl replied—but the smurf was smiling as he said it. "You yourself denied us any ability to develop that technology."

As part of the price of the alliance, the Kanzi fleet had been provided schematics for a number of systems the Imperium had struggled to keep out of their hands. Cawl's fleets would have hyper-fold coms and hyperfold cannon.

They wouldn't all have compressed-matter armor like the Imperial ships—the Kanzi had developed that tech on their own, but it was far more difficult to re-armor the entire hull of a battleship than it was to remove and replace relatively modular weaponry.

Harriet's understanding was that the Kanzi had demanded hyperspace missiles as part of the treaty. In Bond's place, she'd probably have walked away at that point. There was no way the Imperium was *ever* giving up the single-portal hyperspace missile technology. In some ways, the S-HSMs were superior to the Mesharom version of the weapon!

"I can't speak to what your fleet does or does not have," Harriet told Cawl. "What I can note is that my orders leave me unable to place hyperspace missile–equipped ships under the command of anyone except an Imperial officer. To my mind, that would mean I could not place Tenth Fleet under your command, Fleet Master Cawl."

Something flashed across the old Kanzi's face.

"And again we see the arrogance of the A!Tol," he murmured. "Some days, I think your masters do not understand just how self-righteous they are."

A chill ran through the room, only to shatter as Cawl shook his head.

"I suggest a joint command," he conceded. "Myself and Fleet Lord Tanaka sharing command decisions on a day to day basis...and to rotate battle command. There can be no confusion in the fire of the battlespace."

"The details of that sound complicated," Kanmorad interjected. "But the fundamentals are reasonable. What do you say, Duchess Bond?"

From the way the Duchess's eyes flashed, she was only slightly more tolerant of Kanmorad's poking than Harriet was.

"Those details will be very important, I think," she replied. "But I think that is for a conversation between Cawl and Tanaka. Presuming that you will accept third-in-command, Eleventh Pincer of the Republic?"

"I have a *mere* two billion tons of warships to bring to the field," Kanmorad replied. "I am more than an observer, yes, but this remains your war, Duchess Bond."

CHAPTER TEN

"COMMANDER CASIMIR. ANYTHING TO REPORT?"

Tan!Stalla waved the bridge crew back to their seats with a fluttering tentacle gesture as she stepped up next to the main command chair. She was early, Morgan noted.

"Six more squadrons arrived over the night watch," Morgan told her boss. "One of refitted *Vindication* superbattleships, two of cruisers and three of destroyers."

"That's got us up to what, sixty percent of target?" the A!Tol asked. Morgan was technically in her seat, but Tan!Stalla hadn't officially taken over the watch yet either.

"Just over," Morgan confirmed. "That's our twenty-fifth capital ship squadron but we're up to forty-five escort squadrons. Everything's on their way at this point."

Tan!Stalla clicked her beak thoughtfully.

"And our sister ships?" she asked.

"*Pasteur* is finishing her trials in two days," Morgan told her. "*Newton* and *Einstein* will be another three days after that. Nothing significant has fallen out of the tests yet, so all three should commission on schedule."

The sheer number of icons swarming across the main display was crazy. The Grand Fleet had mustered more ships in Sol for the Battle of Terra, but the Grand Fleet was primarily a *defensive* formation.

Tenth Fleet was going to rival the largest Grand Fleets ever mustered in the Imperium's history. Morgan wasn't certain why Tenth wasn't being called a Grand Fleet, for that matter. She was still a very new officer in Imperial service.

"A twenty-cycle," Tan!Stalla noted. "And then we deploy."

It wasn't a question and Morgan didn't reply initially. She was checking her own repeater screens to check in on the fleet as she mulled her thoughts. The smaller screen didn't even have icons for *squadrons*, let alone individual ships.

"Captain, may I ask a question?" she finally said as her screens settled into a listing of warships by class.

"Always, First Sword," Tan!Stalla replied. "Part of my job, after all, is to make sure you're ready for your own command in a few long-cycles."

Morgan swallowed a snort of disbelief at that. She was one of the youngest humans to rise to the rank of Commander in the A!Tol Imperial Navy—partially because she had been the second-youngest officer to make Commander in the Ducal Militia.

She liked to think she'd earned the rank in the hellstorms that had been the First and Second Taljzi Returns, but she knew she was inexperienced.

"A few long-cycles" was *maybe* two years...and Morgan knew she needed more seasoning than that before she took on command of her own ship!

"Your question, Commander?" Tan!Stalla said politely after a moment.

"Apologies, sir. I don't think of myself as getting ready for command," she admitted. "I meant to ask...why is Tenth Fleet not the Grand Fleet? It seems like we certainly have enough ships!"

The A!Tol chuckled, a series of disturbing beak-snaps.

"We do. And the answer is politics, as you might have expected," she explained. "The Grand Fleet is the premier formation of the A!Tol Imperium, the ultimate expression of our power and might.

"The Grand Fleet, therefore, could not and cannot be a portion of a larger force," Tan!Stalla concluded. "That would be contrary to the nature of the Grand Fleet. Since Tenth Fleet was intended to be one part of four of the Allied Fleet—one part of three, now—it cannot be the Grand Fleet.

"Even though, as you say, by any reasonable standard, Tenth Fleet is the current Grand Fleet."

Morgan shook her head and glanced at the time. Her shift was just about up, and more crewmembers were starting to filter in to replace the night watch.

"Politics," she echoed. "I grew up with them, I understand them, but I'm not sure I like them."

Tan!Stalla laughed again.

"I am Tan!," she pointed out. The prefix meant she was a member of the Imperial family line. Morgan wasn't sure of Tan!Stalla's relation to A!Shall or even to Tan!Shallegh, but they were all part of the same family.

"So, you get it," Morgan guessed.

"We share similar hatching stories, my First Sword," Tan!Stalla agreed. "But the shift has changed and I have the watch. I relieve you, Commander Casimir."

Morgan rose from the command chair and gestured Tan!Stalla to it.

"I stand relieved. I know I have a stack of files waiting in my office," she noted. "*Pasteur*'s XO wanted me to go over some of the test results and see how they stacked up to ours."

"Duty never rests, Commander Casimir," Tan!Stalla replied. "Carry on."

JEAN VILLENEUVE HAD GONE through a lot more testing before the demonstration than DragonWorks admitted to in public. No one had wanted the lead ship of the new class of superbattleships to fall on her face in front of the Imperium's allies.

That hadn't necessarily ended well, but Morgan had ended up with a lot more information on just how a *Galileo*-class superbattleship worked and broke than anyone else in the galaxy.

That was why she had the current test results of her three sister ships spread around the wallscreens of her office, comparing them against each other and against *Villeneuve*'s own test results.

Most of it was fine or going to be fine. The four ships had been built in tandem, after all, with *Villeneuve* slightly ahead of the others to let them catch unexpected problems.

Most was not *all*. *Louis Pasteur*'s crew had flagged hundreds of items for minor repairs and efficiencies to be implemented before the ship entered final service. Only the most critical of those were going to require—or going to get, with Tenth Fleet moving out in less than three weeks—shipyard time, but the rest would be corrected over time by the ship's own crew.

All of those were the obvious and not-so-obvious items that the crew could pick out on their own. Morgan's job was to find the subtle problems, the ones that looked fine on the initial scans and tests.

The flashing orange item on the compared reports was just that. Matter-conversion plants had an operating frequency. Morgan herself was only so sure what that *meant*, but it was one of the critical metrics for tracking the health of the power cores.

Pasteur had six conversion cores. All six were within the tolerances that had been written by the manufacturer, nothing that would flag a concern on its own.

Except that Morgan was looking at the records for twenty-four of the matter-conversion power cores used in the *Galileo*s, a slightly larger and more advanced version of the one used in *Bellerophon*.

Outside of a handful of test cores built by Nova Industries, those twenty-four cores were the only ones in existence. They were certainly going to be the only ones in active use for a while yet. Twenty-three of them were within a far tighter range than the estimated tolerances.

Louis Pasteur's Core Five was not. It was still inside the estimated tolerances, but it was drastically out from the other twenty-three operating cores.

Morgan shook her head. It could be nothing. It was inside tolerances, after all.

But it was enough different that either twenty-three *other* cores were a problem...or *Pasteur*'s Core Five was.

She tapped a communicator.

"Commander Elstar?" She waited while *Villeneuve*'s Rekiki chief engineer got onto the channel. "I need to borrow you for a few minutes. Can you come up to my office?"

LESSER COMMANDER ELSTAR was a Rekiki Noble, the politically powerful and physically larger breed of the centauroid reptilian race. He towered over Morgan, rivaling Tan!Stalla's two-and-a-half-meter height with a long-mouthed head that resembled a hungry crocodile.

The Rekiki were one of the several races whose needs meant that Imperial warships were far more spacious than any spaceship built purely for humans would ever be. Elstar took up as much space in Morgan's office as her desk.

He studied the indicated set of reports in silence for several minutes, then gestured toward the controls on the wallscreen.

"May I access your office systems, Commander Casimir?" he asked politely.

"Go ahead," she instructed.

The text and numbers from the reports vanished on the wallscreen Elstar was using, replaced with a schematic of the matter-conversion core. Schematics of both *Pasteur* and *Villeneuve* appeared on the screens on either side of the power core as the engineer studied the schematic.

"You're right, Commander," he noted. "If all the cores but one are within one range, then that one is a concern." He gestured at the schematic.

"This is our Core Five," he noted. "It's inside the same range as the rest of the normal cores."

Elstar fell silent for several more moments, then tapped a specific part of the diagram and pulled out his own communicator.

"Speaker Indel," he addressed one of his subordinates. "I need live footage from your core. I'm sending you the exact location now."

A few seconds later, the schematic was replaced with a video feed from one of the maintenance drones operating in Core Five.

Even to Morgan's eyes, the array of cabling and conduits was neatly organized and labeled. She didn't necessarily understand it, but she could see the organization and color-coding.

The Rekiki studied the feed.

"Indel, have the drone move conduit K-Eight-Eight-Six-Five-B," he ordered. "I know it doesn't have much flex, but let's move it towards conduit D-Six-Six-F as close as we can. I have a live status feed."

There was a pause. Morgan couldn't hear the other half of the conversation.

"Of *course* you stop moving it if you see a problem," Elstar replied to the unheard question. "Don't wait for my order if you see a danger, Speaker."

On the video feed, a mechanical arm reached out and latched on to one of the conduits. Slowly and gently, it pushed the pipe toward a set of cables. For a second, it didn't do anything.

And then the status feed shifted.

"Operational frequency is rising by zero point zero four percent for each centimeter that conduit moves," Elstar noted calmly. "Thank you, Speaker; please have the drone put the conduit back. Add reviewing the K-series conduits' electromagnetic insulation to our to-do list. Thank you."

He cut the channel and turned back to Morgan.

"That might not be the only potential problem," he noted. "But that was the place where one of the ionic conduits was closest to an electrical line. There's only so much shielding and insulation we can manage with this kind of power load, so we use separation *as* insulation.

"I'll touch base with Lesser Commander Rogo if you wish," the engineer officer added. Lesser Commander Rogo was the chief engineer aboard *Louis Pasteur*. "It may be easier for me to explain this than you."

"Much easier, Lesser Commander Elstar. Thank you," Morgan told him.

"Thank *you*, Commander Casimir. With everything going on, we were all focused on making sure all of the plants were within tolerance. Our winds would have swung to comparing them against each other eventually, but if we have to relocate the K-series conduits..."

The Rekiki shivered.

"I'd rather do it with a shipyard to hand," he concluded.

CHAPTER ELEVEN

Tokyo didn't really celebrate Christmas as Americans did. Hundreds of years of cultural cross-contamination meant that Christmas Eve was still a spectacular affair in the city, but it was arguably not a Christmas celebration.

Harriet Tanaka didn't really care what the reason was. She was home and there were lights on the buildings and snow in the air as she walked the streets with her husband. Kenji Tanaka was smaller than she was and had seen more of the celebrations than she had, but he kept up gamely as she crossed through the park in the snow.

"Hiro should be home in an hour or so," he told her. Their son was an officer in the Ducal Militia, serving on the defensive fortifications at DragonWorks. "Fuyoko is home with my parents. Waiting for us."

Their sixteen-year-old younger child was causing a small hurricane's worth of havoc, as usual. That was the job of a teenager, so far as Harriet Tanaka knew. It had been a long time since she'd been one, after all.

"I'm glad I managed to be home for this," she told Kenji. She wasn't often home...at all, let alone home for any kind of celebration.

Kenji wasn't quite a single parent, but he carried the lion's share of the burden.

"We're glad to have you, always," he told her. They walked a perfectly appropriate half-step away from each other, even as younger couples danced through the park, holding hands. Both of them had been raised to a far more formal standard, one long regarded as obsolete even here.

She shook her head.

"I once thought I could never come home," she murmured.

"And my parents have never quite forgiven you for divorcing me," Kenji said with a chuckle. "They're hurt you thought they wouldn't understand."

Harriet chuckled.

"I was trying to protect everyone," she noted. She'd been ashamed of herself for putting on an Imperial uniform, so she'd divorced Kenji and cut herself off from her family after making sure that Hiro got his medical treatment.

She'd been *wrong* and she'd misjudged both her family and Kenji's, but she still understood what she'd been thinking. *Her* mother, after all, had taken far longer to accept what she'd done than anyone else had.

Even saving the planet from the Kanzi hadn't been enough for Hikaru Ueno, not initially anyway.

"You learned better," Kenji said in a self-satisfied tone. "Didn't even argue with marrying me again, either. I always said you were the smartest girl I ever met."

Harriet laughed.

"I seem to recall something about that, yes," she admitted. They'd met in high school, though they hadn't dated until she'd come home on leave as a junior United Earth Space Force officer.

"And making that judgment call always told *me* that you were reasonably intelligent," she continued. "Any idea what your mother is making for supper?"

"It's Christmas Eve. She is once again attempting to make turkey Japanese."

Harriet laughed and leaned against her husband for a precious moment.

"That is always fascinating. I guess we should pick up the pace?"

Kenji leaned back against her and chuckled.

"Probably, but I won't rush you!"

HARRIET AND KENJI entered the apartment to Fuyoko explaining the use of the singular *they* in English to their grandmother.

"But *they are* makes no sense in the singular," Ume Tanaka was saying as the door closed and her parents were shedding their shoes. "If it's just one person, shouldn't it be *they is?*"

"If English was a sensible language, probably," Fuyoko agreed. "But English is *dumb* for a language we all have to learn."

Ume Tanaka responded with a spiel of Japanese that was... roughly as coherent as *they is*. Probably the slang from the Tanaka matriarch's own misspent youth.

"Hi, Fleet Lord Mom!" Fuyoko said as they spotted Harriet. "Saved us all from the tentacle horrors yet?"

Harriet bowed to her mother-in-law and youngest child. The formal gesture ran contrary to the tone of Fuyoko's commentary, but everyone in the family was used to that. The youngest Tanaka had absorbed the etiquette rules her grandparents taught...and then completely rejected them.

The family dealt. That was what you did with your children, after all.

"I work for the tentacle horrors, I believe," she pointed out. "Ritually scarred smurfs are the current problem."

Fuyoko laughed and made a throwaway gesture.

"I'm helping *obaa-san* with the turkey," they said cheerfully. "With her help, we'll even survive my cooking!"

Kenji's father came in and exchanged bows with Harriet.

"It's good to see you," he told her. "Your youngest is insisting on English tonight."

"I noticed," Harriet said. "I spend my life with a translator bud in my ear, but it doesn't speak Japanese. I'll be fine."

"It should speak Japanese," Ume Tanaka said sharply. "We've sent enough of our young people to the Imperium and Duchy alike, after all."

Harriet was spared having to admit that the Imperium's translation program *did* have Japanese programmed into it—she just didn't use it because she was so used to speaking English in a work environment—by the arrival of her son.

Lieutenant Commander Hiro Tanaka slipped through the door as quietly as he could, but there was no sneaking into this house. Fuyoko had their arms wrapped around their brother before he'd even shed his shoes.

"Uniform?" they demanded. "For Christmas Eve dinner?"

"I was in a Militia vehicle thirty seconds ago, Fuyoko-*kun*," he pointed out. "And I'm back on duty in twenty-four hours. The car will be returning for me soon enough."

"They can't spare you for this?" Ume demanded. "And your mother the Fleet Lord!"

Hiro looked uncomfortable.

"Neither of us is inclined to use my rank to smooth Hiro's way," Harriet told her mother-in-law. "And his work is important."

The young officer chuckled.

"Well, what we *guard* is important," he corrected, then sniffed the air. "I smell turkey...but what *have* we done to it this year?"

"Come, come!" Ume replied. "Let me show you."

The party, as all parties do, ended up in the kitchen.

LATER THAT NIGHT, after the family was asleep, Harriet snuck into the office Kenji kept for her to catch up on Tenth Fleet's affairs. Most of her human crews had been given leave for the next several days, but that was less than five percent of her personnel—that was *why* she could let the humans take Christmas, since they were at Earth.

But an organization of Tenth Fleet's size didn't sleep just because the commander was spending Christmas with her family. Another squadron of battleships had arrived during dinner, and the Tosumi commander was apparently complaining about her orbital assignment.

The Squadron Lord in question was far too junior to be raising *any* kind of fuss that made it to the senior Fleet Lord's desk in a force of this scale. On the other hand, the junior Fleet Lord she was reporting to had clearly dismissed her concerns, so she'd escalated.

Harriet took a look at the complaint and shook her head.

Orbital assignment was part of the problem, but the *actual* complaint was that the squadron had lifted off with some kind of pest in several of the ships' food storage facilities. Six of the sixteen ships had been forced to dump their entire supply of Universal Protein, the artificial tofu-like substance that every species could eat.

Spreading the food supplies out meant that the squadron was low on food supplies and their position meant that restocking was taking far longer than it should have. The Squadron Lord was clear that they *would* be fully resupplied before they left, but that the delays were impacting the morale of her ships' crew.

"Fleet Lord Uridos," Harriet recorded. "I received both Squadron Lord Otal Fen's concerns and your own dismissal of said concerns. I *suggest* that you reread Lord Fen's message and consider the potential impact of low morale in a full quarter of your force—let alone the impact on morale of all of your squadrons when you disregard requests like that.

"What I'm *not* suggesting is that you move Lord Fen's squadron. I am *ordering* that you and Fen sort out a means to get her squadron fully resupplied on food inside one cycle." She smiled grimly. There were multiple ways to pull that off...but the easiest would be to move the squadron to the "place of honor" in the task force's formation, which would put Fen's ships within easy reach of the supply depots.

"So long as those battleships are stocked on food by then, I will regard the situation as resolved. Carry on."

She cut the recording and sent the message. A moment later, the door to the office opened and Kenji stepped in.

"I see you are no more able to get away from work than you ever were," he said quietly. "Crises and crises?"

"Always," she said apologetically. Harriet rose and embraced her husband. "You've always been more patient with me than I deserved."

"Perhaps. But I knew what I was getting when I married you—both times!"

Kenji chuckled and kissed her cheek. "But it is late and we are celebrating in the morning. You should get *some* sleep."

Harriet chuckled and leaned her head against him.

"I checked the critical messages," she promised. "But I thought we'd made sure the bedroom was well soundproofed? If we're both awake, after all, why would I waste that by *sleeping*?"

CHAPTER TWELVE

CHRISTMAS IN THE RESIDENCE HAD ALWAYS BEEN A HUSHED affair. Morgan and the rest of the Duchess's family had always been far too aware of the sacrifices others made to assure their safety for their Christmases to be spectacularly extravagant affairs.

The first thing she did every Christmas morning she was home, in fact, was bring coffee and hot breakfast—made the morning before by the Residence's conspicuously-absent-on-holidays kitchen staff—down to the security three floors down.

She left Victoria sleeping as she and her half-sisters converged in the kitchen to pull out the trays of par-baked croissants and ready-to-toast sandwiches.

"Oven at two thirty for the sandwiches," Carol reminded her as Morgan turned on the big stove. "Just a few minutes for each tray."

"This one's for the croissants," Morgan replied with a grin. "Leah, toss those trays in once it's heated."

The Heir shook her head at both of her siblings but obeyed promptly when the oven beeped. Leaving her half-sisters to the ovens, Morgan found the rolling table in the same place the kitchen staff left it every year.

She didn't even *remember* the first time she'd done this. Morgan, for reasons her therapists preferred her not to poke at too closely, had pretty scattered memories of her life before about age six.

Given that she'd spent six months as a hostage in there, she was willing to let most of those memories go. There'd been good years in there, but she'd had enough of those. Despite running a planet, her parents had done a *good* job raising her, in her extraordinarily biased opinion.

But every Christmas since her parents had married, she'd helped Annette Bond deliver food to the guards who drew the short straw for Christmas duty. On one memorable occasion when she'd been nineteen, one of the guards she'd been making eyes at had received more than a sandwich, too.

That wasn't a story she was telling her sixteen-year-old half-sisters. It had nearly cost the young man his job—and *had* cost him the prestigious posting to the Family's security detail.

Morgan had got a *long* lecture from Uncle James after that. She figured her half-sisters were smarter than she was—and even if they weren't, she'd bet marks to carrots that the Ducal Guardsmen assigned to the detail were better warned now.

She was trying to transfer coffee from the big industrial coffeemaker into the equally monstrous dispensers that would go downstairs with them when Victoria drifted in. Her lover was wearing fluffy blue pajamas, a determinedly unsexy garment that still left Morgan wanting to drag the other woman back to their shared room.

"What's going on?" the tall blonde Russian asked.

"Tradition," the twins chorused in perfect unison.

"We bring food and coffee to the guards who get stuck with the Christmas shift," Carol continued after the pair giggled. "Mom started it when she first moved in. A lot of people would say a planetary ruler shouldn't do something like that, but Mom is Mom."

"And tradition is tradition," Morgan continued.

Victoria looked around the only partially organized chaos.

"I'm guessing you're used to more hands?" she asked.

"Alexis is still too young to really help, but Megan has helped the last few years," Leah admitted.

"May I help?" Victoria asked.

"Of course!" Carol exclaimed. "You're family now!"

From the warm flush on Victoria's face, Morgan realized the answer to a question she'd been wondering: the kitchen staff had always set the trays up for the right number of people before. She'd thought they'd been expecting Annette Bond to help out herself...but now she suspected that her mother had given quite specific instructions to the kitchen.

And those instructions had been intended to make Victoria feel part of the family.

THE DUCHESS HAD DONE her best to secure Christmases and Sundays away from work for the entire time period of having kids. To Morgan's memory, what they'd *actually* succeeded at was having either Annette or Elon home for every Sunday and every major holiday.

Having both of them home for Sundays and most holidays had been rare. They'd *tried* for Christmas, at least, but they ran a star system. They got lucky only so often.

It was phenomenally strange to Morgan, however, to be gathering for Christmas breakfast with both of her parents...and *missing* her two youngest sisters.

Having Victoria there helped. The other woman was mostly lost to stunned silence, though, and Morgan wasn't quite sure what to do about that. The meal itself had passed without her finding a solution, but as the twins cleared the plates, Elon looked down the table at Victoria and cleared his throat.

Morgan's father was a chubby man of average height. The only intimidating thing about him was his eyes and the piercingly insightful gaze of an unquestioned genius.

"Victoria, it seems I have to remind you that none of us bite," he told Morgan's girlfriend gently. "You're with Morgan, so you belong here. If you're worried about living up to ridiculous extravagant gifts, Morgan should have already told you that we don't really *do* gifts."

The Ducal family simply had too much money. In the main, if one of the girls had wanted it, it had simply materialized shortly afterward. Some things had been withheld as rewards for success at school or until they proved capable of handling the responsibility, but they'd been *denied* nothing.

Megan had been the first of them to pass Annette's requirements to actually own her own horse. The rest had been taught to ride—Annette had grown up riding, so it had been expected—but they didn't own horses. Megan did, and had apparently been heartbroken to leave Dancing Diamonds behind.

Morgan suspected the only thing the horse was in danger of was getting fat from being spoiled by the stable taking care of her.

"She did tell me that I didn't need to worry about gifts or anything," Victoria said quietly, squeezing Morgan's hand. "But... well..." She gestured helplessly.

"If it helps, when I was Morgan's age, I was just beginning the investigation that got me cashiered from the UESF," Annette said drily. "She's done as much—if not more!—by age twenty-six than I ever did."

Morgan snorted.

"You were, what, the third-youngest person to ever make UESF Commander?" she asked. "I think you did okay."

"Third-youngest *woman*," Annette corrected carefully. "Eighth-youngest *person*."

"And *that* is a minefield the only man in the room is *not* stepping into," Elon said brightly. "I believe you and Morgan are spending the whole day with us?"

"We are," Victoria said, her hand still gripping Morgan's under the table. "I haven't had a...well, a family Christmas in years. Morgan promised me quiet..."

"God, I hope this was quiet," Annette replied. "This was just breakfast. What comes next will probably be quieter without Alexis, but without the youngest, Elon's competitive streak is going to come out."

Morgan grinned as Victoria squeezed her hand harder.

"What comes next?" she asked carefully.

"Tradition," Morgan repeated. "It's family time, so that means Monopoly."

CHAPTER THIRTEEN

"WELL, THAT'S THE LAST DANCE, ISN'T IT?"

Morgan and Victoria stood on the transfer station observation deck, watching shuttles swarm away from the space station in droves. Even to the naked eye, it was clear that *something* was going on farther out. Even the immense Laian war-dreadnoughts were too far to be more than tiny dots, but there were just *so many* ships in Sol.

Entirely new starfields glittered across the dark that Morgan could see as she looked out into space, each star a shuttle under power, a capital ship, or even a collection of escorts. Tenth Fleet was fully assembled, and that meant that Morgan Casimir had run out of time.

Which was exactly what Victoria was talking about. Morgan sighed and reached out for her girlfriend's hand. To her gratitude, Victoria still took it.

"Not the *very* last dance, I hope," Morgan told the taller woman. "I'm planning on coming back, after all...and I'd hope that I'll learn to actually *dance* before my very last dance."

Victoria snorted and squeezed her hand.

"And how long is Tenth Fleet going to be gone?" she asked.

"Without the Mesharom to play hyperspace games, it's sixteen days to the shipyard system we found," Morgan said. That system was *nuts*. The Taljzi shipyards were built into and on an old Precursor ring station that encircled a significant gas giant. That station alone represented more living space than multiple habitable planets.

If the Taljzi weren't driven by the dual whips of wanting revenge against the Theocracy that had tried to wipe them out and a "divine order" to exterminate the "false faces of God," that station alone would have occupied their expansion for centuries.

But all non-Kanzi bipedal sentients were false faces of God. Imperfect mirrors of the near-perfect replica represented by the Kanzi. The Theocracy had its own issues with interacting with those "mirrors," resulting in their being one of the largest slaveholding nations the A!Tol knew of.

The Taljzi had decided that all of the false faces were to be destroyed. Since the main Kanzi nation and people had tried to wipe the Taljzi out for that belief, the Kanzi Theocracy was also on the chopping block.

"So, even if *nothing* else happened, you'd be gone over a month," Victoria said. "And that's not happening. You're going to be gone, what, six months? A year?"

Morgan sighed.

"We're stocked for an eighteen-month voyage," she said quietly. "We'd need to refuel repeatedly to pull that off, but we have food— Universal Protein and its additives—and the rest of our consumables for that long. Even with the fleet train, though, we only have the munitions for *maybe* three serious fights."

"Eighteen months," Victoria repeated, and then she squeezed Morgan's hand *hard*. "I'm going to wait," she promised. "Shit may happen, I won't pretend otherwise, but I expect to be pretty damn busy."

"Busy enough not to fall for pretty boys in the Guard barracks?" Morgan asked.

Victoria laughed.

"*I* don't have that problem," she pointed out. "Should I be worried about the Marines?"

"Nah—most of *Villeneuve's* Marines are Tosumi, and birds are *not* my type."

"Mmm, fair." Victoria pulled her closer and kissed her. "I'll admit, I've seen a Yin or two that might break that rule for me...but I'll wait for you. Eighteen months."

"I'll be back," Morgan promised.

"I know. Just...don't die."

MORGAN HAD CUT her return to *Jean Villeneuve* far closer than she should have. She had *just* enough time to drop her duffel off in her quarters before she needed to be on the bridge, relieving Lesser Commander Nidei, the ship's tactical officer, of the watch.

"Any news?" she asked the Ivida as the hairless red-skinned biped rose from the command chair.

"Our departure time was just delayed by two hundredth-cycles," Nidei told her. Their face was unmoving, a hard shell that Morgan was only just getting used to after working with the Ivida for six months.

She had grown used to the fact that Ivida's long arms and legs were double-jointed more quickly, but it was still odd when Nidei easily reached behind themself to produce a datapad that they passed over.

"One of the *Majesties* refitted by the Pibo has a frequency twitch in her core drive unit," Nidei told her. "Your father's people got her opened up in record time, and she *will* leave with the fleet. Her squadron will just be the last out."

Half an hour wasn't a bad delay for a major capital ship being out of commission, Morgan noted. The *Majesty* class had been the most powerful unit in the Imperial Navy when the A!Tol had conquered humanity. It was outdated now, behind *Vindication*s and *Galileo*s, but it was still a superbattleship.

"I'll run through the movement order," she promised. With the delay, it would be three hours—the original scheduled tenth-cycle plus the thirty minute delay— before they were scheduled to depart.

"The *Galileo*s are assigned to escort *Ajax*," Nidei told her. "I think that's new since you went on your last leave."

Morgan's leave had been *two days*. *Villeneuve* and her sisters had been assigned to Squadron Lord Sier's Sixty-Seventh Squadron already, but directly escorting the flagship was a whole new order of trouble.

"Thanks, Nidei," Morgan replied. "Are we in position for that?"

"As of a tenth-cycle ago," they confirmed. "We're ready, Commander. *Villeneuve* won't let anyone down."

"Our namesake would never have let us," she said with a smile. "Go rest, Nidei. My turn."

The Ivida followed their watch shift out of the bridge, and Morgan settled into the big chair. A few commands to the repeater screens confirmed everything Nidei had told her.

Jean Villeneuve was ten thousand kilometers in front of *Ajax*, the lead point of a slanted cube formation of capital ships around the flagship. Four of those positions were *Galileo*s and the other four were other *Bellerophon*-Bs.

Sixty-Seventh Squadron had twenty capital ships with the *Galileo*s added in. It wasn't the most powerful formation in the fleet— even disregarding the Laians, *that* status went to the six full squadrons of *Vindication*-C superbattleships—but nineteen of those twenty super-modern warships shared one purpose:

Protect the flagship.

CHAPTER FOURTEEN

THE FLAG DECK HOLODISPLAY WAS SUFFERING A NOTICEABLE problem to Harriet's mind. If they zoomed out far enough to see the entirety of Tenth Fleet, they could no longer make out individual ships.

She probably should have had someone else fiddle with the controls, but she was honestly enjoying herself. Finally, she managed to find a compromise of flagging individual eight-ship echelons.

"Keep it on this setting for now," she told Koanest. "It seems like the best compromise to try and keep track of the fleet."

"Yes, Fleet Lord," she confirmed. Yin shook their heads in disbelief in much the same way as humans did. "That's a *lot* of warships."

"Hopefully, it's enough," Harriet said quietly, stepping back to review her fleet.

Twenty-five squadrons of superbattleships. Five of those squadrons were the fully updated *Vindication*-Cs, the biggest ships in the fleet after the *Galileos*. The other twenty were a mix of refitted *Majesties* and other classes, all fully armed with hyperspace missiles and hyperfold cannon.

Twenty squadrons of battleships, half *Bellerophon*-Bs built from the keel out with the new technology. All of the *Bellerophon*s had been built either by the Indiri or there in Sol. It was only in the last year that any other yards had had full access to the DragonWorks technology, after all, and capital ships took several years to build.

To escort those forty-five squadrons of capital ships, she had forty-six squadrons of cruisers of assorted sizes and sixty squadrons of destroyers.

All told, she commanded over *twelve billion* tons of warships— and the Laian formation hanging off to the side of her fleet was another two and a half billion.

The Kanzi had promised roughly equal tonnage. They were going to be bringing almost thirty *billion* tons of the most advanced warships two Arm Powers had to the fight.

"Have we confirmed the rendezvous with Fleet Master Cawl's staff?" she asked Koanest. She'd talked high-level dates and concepts with Cawl herself, but it always fell to the staffs of fleet commanders —whatever the actual *titles* of said commanders—to sort out actual details.

"We have," Koanest confirmed. "The Gloried Armada will meet us in the Kanda System in six cycles."

The Gloried Armada. The Kanzi Theocracy had numbered formations, Harriet was quite certain of that, but when it came to fleets of dozens of squadrons of capital ships, they refused to hang anything as prosaic as, say, "Tenth Fleet" on them.

So, Cawl's fleet was the Gloried Armada. He'd already left, if he was going to be in Kanda in six days, too. The Kanzi system was actually far closer to Earth than to most of the Theocracy.

One of the treaties and galactic standards that the Mesharom enforced was the Kovius Treaty. That particular document declared that all stars within forty light-years of the homeworld of a sentient race belonged to that race.

That was often honored as "belonged to that race's overlord." The A!Tol actually gave their subject species property rights to those systems. The Duchy of Terra didn't *rule* Alpha Centauri, for example, but was the primary shareholder in the Centauri Development Corporation and owned the planets and resources of the Imperially administered star system.

When the dust had settled around humanity's emergence onto the galactic scene, the Kovius zone around Sol had cut a chunk out of space the Kanzi had traditionally regarded as theirs. Fortunately, none of that space had actually been colonized—but several systems on the Rimward side of that zone *had* been.

The largest was Kanda. The planet had been home to over half a million people, two-thirds of them slaves and a third of them Kanzi.

Then the Taljzi had come.

It was a graveyard now, but it was the closest system in Kanzi or Imperial space to the one known Taljzi system with any refueling infrastructure. Both Tenth Fleet and the Gloried Armada were accompanied by hundreds of freighters and tankers, but Harriet wasn't going to turn down an opportunity to fill those tankers.

"Any problems other than *Seacrest's* that are going to delay us?" Harriet finally asked Koanest. Reorganizing the departure schedule so that *Seacrest's* squadron left last had been surprisingly easy. It was going to take almost twelve hours for her to safely extract her fleet from its position scattered through Sol's infrastructure.

It would be a full day, still, before everyone was in hyperspace and organized to travel. At least stopping at Kanda would be easier. Once they'd assembled the entire fleet, they'd only need one hyper portal to exit hyperspace.

"Twenty-five hundred warships and eight-hundred-odd logistics ships produce an effectively infinite number of problems," the blue-skinned Yin operations officer pointed out. "None are going to delay our departure or impact combat effectiveness."

"Then I see no reason to change the plan," Harriet replied. "Departure in one tenth-cycle?"

"That's the schedule," he confirmed. "Everyone knows their schedule and vector."

"Then all I need to do is watch for problems," the Fleet Lord said with a chuckle. "Hopefully, I get to be unneeded today!"

"That seems...unlikely."

AT THE LEADING edge of Tenth Fleet, dozens of ships linked their exotic-matter projectors to open larger hyper portals. A single super-battleship *needed* a portal three kilometers across and had the projectors to open a portal nearly twenty kilometers across.

The synchronized projectors of an entire squadron of superbattleships opened a portal two hundred kilometers across. The lead elements of Harriet Tanaka's fleet opened eight of those, and a sequenced handoff kept the portals open as ships flashed through them.

"Did the entire squadron *really* need to be set up as ablative armor around *Ajax*, Squadron Lord Sier?" she asked the commander of Sixty-Seventh Squadron.

Sier had once held Koanest's job, rising from the First Sword tapped to keep the first human Captain from screwing up too badly to operations officer for the first human Squadron Lord and then Fleet Lord.

The promotions that had come along with that had eventually pulled him out of her staff and into an echelon and now squadron command of his own. Harriet's flagship wasn't in his squadron by accident, though Sier flew his own flag from *Aris*.

Harriet felt some sympathy for the Yin that ship was named for. Like her, Fleet Lord Aris had been the first of his species to join the Imperial Navy. The Duchy of Terra had been in more need of Imperial protection than the Duchy of Yin had been, though, and his people had taken longer to reconcile with his service.

Sier had probably picked his flagship with intent, she knew. She held his gaze levelly, raising a questioning eyebrow at the beaked alien.

"Seven hundred and twenty-four capital ships," Sier pointed out. "Forty-five squadrons and some stragglers. We can afford to have a squadron mostly focused on protecting the senior Fleet Lord much more easily than we can afford to *lose* that Fleet Lord."

He shrugged, a gesture he'd learned from her.

"Besides, the *Bellerophon*s and *Galileo*s still carry more S-HSM launchers on a ton-for-ton basis than anything else in the fleet. If we're pushing this squadron into the heat of the fray, we are either doing it wrong or we're already in the hunter's nest."

And being fed to its children. Or, at least, that was how Harriet interpreted that idiom.

"And you thought I might not notice you arranging nineteen warships around *Ajax*?" she asked.

"You are keeping track of over two thousand warships," her old friend pointed out. "It was reasonable to hope you might miss how I arrayed my twenty. If you order me to choose a different formation..."

Harriet laughed.

"I am not *that* stubborn, Sier," she replied. "Keep the squadron as you wish." She shook her head reprovingly at him. "How long until we transit?"

"A hundredth-cycle, no more. Our journey is upon us."

Harriet nodded silently, leaving the channel open as she turned her attention back to the main display. Hundreds of her ships had made transit. Hundreds more were still ahead of *Ajax* and a thousand or so would follow her.

A combat transition would be faster, but she had the time to take it slow and do it right. There would be plenty of time for necessary risks when they reached Taljzi space.

CHAPTER FIFTEEN

It was one thing to be told that the Taljzi had burned Kanda to ash. It was quite another to *see* it.

Kanda wasn't the first dead system Morgan had seen. If she was very lucky, it would be the last...but they were heading into Taljzi space, and the Taljzi had secured the area around their worlds by exterminating anyone nearby, regardless of their actual threat level.

She could see why the Kanzi had planned to anchor their new colonization sector on the Kanda system. Four gas giants had dragged most of the debris that would normally haunt the inner part of a star system into their own trail, providing an easily accessed supply of raw materials close to near-infinite supplies of fuel.

The stations that had once gathered that fuel and refined it were still there. They were abandoned, though most of their crews had managed to last until a Kanzi scout flotilla could evacuate them.

Morgan tried to keep her focus on those stations and the flight of tankers that *Jean Villeneuve* was playing high guard for, but every so often, her gaze slipped to the data codes for the inner system.

Kanda III hadn't been a perfect world—there weren't very many of those—but it had been readily habitable across most latitudes, with vast oceans and plains of rippling red grass.

All of that was now hidden beneath vast black clouds. Theoretically, those clouds would eventually precipitate out and refill the empty oceans. Eventually.

Morgan hadn't seen any estimates for how long it would take. Kanda III had been written off by the powers responsible for the world. The Theocracy had evacuated a few thousand survivors from the space stations and scanned the world for life.

The system might be of value later, but before Tenth Fleet's arrival, it had been utterly dead—and once Tenth Fleet departed, it would be utterly dead again.

"Are we early?" Commander Nidei wondered aloud. "It can be difficult to tell with how many ships *we* brought, but the Kanzi don't appear to be here yet."

"If you've found a way to accurately gauge the length of a hyper-space trip, Her Imperial Majesty would love to speak to you," Morgan told the Ivida with a chuckle. "Our average speed over the fifty light-years from here to Sol was almost double your usual speed if you're going from Sol to Alpha Centauri. The Kanzi are going over a hundred light-years and allocated twice the time, but..."

She shrugged.

"If hyperspace was predictable, life would be easy," she concluded. "We know the Gloried Armada left on time. Their expected arrival window should have had them arriving six hours before our earliest arrival, but we beat that by four hours."

"Which means they're still late," Nidei replied. "Am I allowed to hold that against them?"

"They're our allies today, Lesser Commander," Morgan told the junior officer pointedly. "So long as they're our allies, we play nice."

Her smile thinned.

"The moment they're *no longer* our allies, then you can bring out a list of grievances and we'll talk about what shitty allies they were. Until then, we play nice."

"As you and the Empress will."

Nidei clicked their tongue in imitation of an A!Tol beak-snap laugh, and Morgan shivered.

The Ivida were an Imperial Race. It sounded like a special status and it *was*, but the reason for it was terrifying. The A!Tol had now annexed and absorbed twenty-seven species, with humanity as the most recent.

They had uplifting and integrating a space-age civilization and culture down to a science...but that kind of science required learning what *not* to do. The first three races that they'd absorbed were the Imperial Races: the Tosumi, the Pibo and Nidei's people, the Ivida.

The Imperial Races had been the A!Tol's mistakes. Vast pieces of their culture and knowledge base had been lost. In many ways, Nidei had been raised in a culture that was more A!Tol than Ivida.

Including, apparently, *laughing* like an A!Tol.

"Just do your job, Nidei," she told them. "And let me know when the Kanzi finally show up."

NO ONE NEEDED to let Morgan know when the Kanzi arrived. Anyone within sight of a hologram, tactical display or even a *window* knew the moment the Gloried Armada arrived.

The couple of times Morgan had seen fleets of similar size emerge from hyperspace, they'd been light-minutes and light-minutes away. This time, the Gloried Armada arrived less than two million kilometers away from the Imperial and Laian fleets, and the brilliant light of the hyperspace portals' opening lit up the fleet like a new sun.

An *open* hyper portal wasn't as bright to the naked eye, though the odd radiation of hyperspace meant that they still glittered to her sensors, but the moment that half a dozen thousand-kilometer portals opened was awe-inspiring.

Moments later, the first ships came through. Serried ranks of Kanzi attack cruisers led the way, hundreds of the three-megaton warships scouting the way. Destroyers flared out around them as the first of the battleships emerged, followed by superbattleships and freighters in a seemingly unending chain of flying metal.

A flashing note popped up on her screen and Morgan grimaced.

"Nidei, link our systems into the flagship's," she ordered. "Captain Koanest is trying to coordinate traffic control for a couple of thousand starships, and the command staff is getting overwhelmed.

"For our sins of being right by *Ajax*, we got tapped to help out. So, get us linked in to the tactical network and get ready to play traffic controller."

Their main hologram zoomed in on a smaller portion of the screen as Koanest sent instructions to a dozen ships' tactical teams at once. They were responsible for a specific arc and zone of the orbit of Kanda V.

Existing assigned orbits were on the board in green. Instructions flowed onto Morgan's screen, and she made sure they were on the screens of the tactical department as well. They needed to home three superbattleship squadrons and seven cruiser squadrons, a hundred ships.

Minimum-thousand-kilometer clearance between ships, minimum-ten-thousand-kilometer clearance between squadrons...and minimum-hundred-thousand-kilometer separation between Imperial and Kanzi units.

"Everyone got the instructions?" she asked. "All right. They're holding for now, but we need people in place in twenty minutes."

The Kanzi had been supposed to do this for *them*, but she still couldn't help feeling that they should have had a plan.

It wasn't a good omen for how this mission was going to go.

CHAPTER SIXTEEN

GIVEN THE COMMUNICATION TECHNOLOGY AVAILABLE TO THEM all, there was no reason for the commanders of the three fleet components to meet in person. Even assuming there was a reason for that to be required, it could have been done on any of the flagships or any designated vessel in the immense armada surrounding Kanda V.

There was no logical or technological reason for the three commanders to meet in orbit of Kanda III... and yet none of the other two had objected when Cawl had suggested it. There was no *reason* for them to stand on a glass-floored observation deck and look out at the wrecked planet.

And there was no way they could have held this meeting anywhere else.

"How many people were here?" Kanmorad asked, the big Laian's voice soft even through the translator.

Cawl grunted and leaned on his cane as he studied the planet.

"Six hundred and fifty thousand people from four species," he told them. "They were laying the groundwork for several new waves of colonists that were *supposed* to arrive years ago, but there were some political problems."

Harriet muffled a chuckle. Those *political problems* had been the Kanzi losing control of several of the intended staging systems to the Imperium, thanks to Sol's Kovius Zone.

"I thought that had all been sorted out," she asked.

"They had. The corporation running the effort had been recruiting for a new wave of about ten million." Cawl shook his head. "The infrastructure was all in place, but they were trying to keep a specific ratio of slaves to Kanzi. The bastards."

It was just the three of them in the observation deck. That was apparently enough for the Fleet Master to be a bit clearer about his opinions of the Theocracy's practice of slavery.

"I always found the practice of slavery on this scale...odd," Kanmorad noted. "Surely, you don't need that much physical labor with your technology."

Cawl snorted.

"Who do you think is running most Kanzi technology, Pincer?" he asked. "At its best, our slavery resembles a permanent workers' caste. Even at its worst, it's not purely manual labor. My people are very good at convincing people that they should follow orders and running audits to make sure that even our IT slaves weren't causing trouble."

"And then there's the sex slaves," Harriet pointed out. "The attempt to get humans to sell as exotic meat did *not* endear your people to us."

The old Kanzi winced, putting both hands on his cane as he kept his focus on the dead planet beneath them.

"Why would you have reacted any differently?" he asked. "Any system has its abusers, Fleet Lord Tanaka...but I will not pretend that ours does not enable them. I have not quietly enabled the Reformers for nothing."

"So quietly that you freely tell us," Kanmorad pointed out.

"You have no interest in Theocracy politics," the Kanzi replied. "And Tanaka's people *want* the Reformers to succeed. My High

Priestess wants to move things slowly. She's *wrong*, but at least her error is a question of speed, not of direction."

"And the Taljzi?" the Laian asked.

"They take the same logic that my people use to justify slaves and twist it just a bit further," Cawl said flatly. "If we are the one true image of God, then anything that looks like us but isn't us is a twisted mirror of the divine.

"Lesser images, my people call them. The High Priestess believes we are charged to protect and guide them." He shook his head. "The Taljzi believe they more truly know the mind of God, hence their name. They believe all the 'lesser images' are blasphemies and should be destroyed."

Taljzi meant *minds of God*, much as Kanzi meant *faces of God*.

"And this?" Harriet asked, gesturing to the planet. "Hundreds of thousands of Kanzi died here."

"Everyone should understand this," Cawl told them. "This was pure revenge."

CAWL HAD BROUGHT eighty more squadrons of capital ships and a hundred of escorts. With another two hundred and fifty super-battleships, they were up to over six hundred of those immense warships *alone*.

Rows upon rows of holographic warships surrounded the three fleet commanders as they went through their strength, class by class and squadron by squadron. With Harriet and Cawl sharing command of the Allied Fleet, they all needed to be completely cognizant of the sword at their fingertips.

Over fifteen hundred capital ships and almost twenty-eight hundred escorts. A total of over twenty-six billion tons of warships and *another* ten billion tons of freighters and tankers. The logistics train alone of the Allied Fleet outmassed almost any other force Harriet had ever seen.

As they finished, she leaned back in her chair and shook her head.

"I started my career on a million-ton battleship with fusion engines, you know," she said conversationally. "The last twenty years have been a hell of a ride."

"In the last twenty years, the problem of the Ascendancy's survivors has been politically resolved and the Grand Parliament has come to realize that the Arm Powers are both potentially stronger allies and potentially greater threats than we ever realized," Kanmorad replied. "In any other age, Kandak's actions and failures at Sol should have ended his career.

"Instead, because he ended up laying the channels for the unofficial pacts that put me here today, well, his career survived." The Laian chittered his mandibles softly. "The galaxy changes around us, and only the blind think they can choose not to change with it."

"It's not you humans, if that's what you're thinking," Cawl told Tanaka with a purring laugh. "The conflict between the Imperium and the Theocracy was driving much of this before the Taljzi showed up—and both that and the Taljzi have been brewing for...eternity, it seems."

"Someone would have dug up that ship at Centauri," Kanmorad agreed. "You dragged our Exiles, those Ascendancy survivors, back into the light and got the Parliament to officially recognize that we couldn't proscribe the Ascendancy's descendants.

"Some of us had been pushing that for a while, but it took your Imperium first giving them a home and then defying Pincer Kandak to actually get it *written*."

The room was silent for a few moments, all of them studying the wrecked world again.

"You and Kandak," Harriet finally said. "You're related?"

"Born of the same line-creche," Kanmorad confirmed. "Might have even had some of the same parents, who knows? We don't track those things. Kandak is... Everyone has that one creche-mate who hates everything not purple, right?"

Harriet considered the metaphor for several seconds, then smirked.

"My American acquaintances refer to that as 'the racist uncle problem,'" she told them. "I think I understand."

Outside of a small portion of their population, mostly confusedly accepted by the majority now, Laians didn't pair-bond for child-rearing. They engaged in the kind of group marriage that occasionally showed up under the "line marriage" label among humans, continually adding males and females to a group that raised children together.

She didn't know what kind of color and racial prejudices the Laians had amongst themselves, but labeling Kandak as a bigot made sense of large chunks of the Alpha Centauri incident.

Especially if you assumed he was a *smart* bigot, the kind who could get past it when they really needed to.

"He didn't do *too* badly," Kanmorad allowed generously, "but I can't help but feel there were at least a hundred or so better officers to send." His mandibles chittered in amusement. "Including myself, of course."

"It's a strange time we live in," Cawl said quietly. "And now we have gone through the administration, there remains one final question the three of us have to sort out."

Harriet ran over her mental agenda. They'd addressed everything immediate on her list, primarily making sure all three of them were as aware of the capabilities of each other's fleets as possible.

"Which is?" Kanmorad asked. There was a tone to his translated voice that suggested he was no more certain of what Cawl meant than Harriet was.

"What we do in response to this," Cawl replied, gesturing at the ruined world. "The Taljzi burned over half a dozen worlds. Millions dead. According to the High Church, they are still formally proscribed as heretics."

"That calls for rather...specific treatment, doesn't it?" Harriet asked.

"They must either recant their heresy and accept sterilization or die," he said flatly. "I haven't received official *orders* to that effect, but the fact that several Grand Priestesses made the point about the proscription still standing means I know what they want."

"And the *High* Priestess?" Harriet asked. She hadn't met Reesi Karal, the High Priestess of the Kanzi Theocracy, but Annette Bond *had*...and from Bond's description, Harriet didn't get the impression that Karal was going to sign off on mass murder.

"She has given no specific instructions," Cawl noted. "According to my formal orders, what to do with the Taljzi is up to my discretion."

"I don't see the concern," Kanmorad noted calmly. "We pay evil unto evil. They destroyed worlds, so we turn the same fire on theirs. These Taljzi have clearly demonstrated that they cannot be permitted to survive, as anything less than extermination will leave them as an active threat."

Harriet was stunned to silence. It was easy to forget that as easy to get along with as Kanmorad was proving, he was still an alien from a race with very different value on sentient life than humans. Or the A!Tol, for that matter.

"I place somewhat higher value on the life of even the lost than that," Cawl said quietly. "We know nothing about what the Taljzi have become. Are we looking at the actions of a government without the support of the populace? Are the clones we have seen a separate part of their society?

"We do not know the answer to these questions, and I hesitate to slaughter billions without certainty of their guilt."

"Regardless of their guilt, my own orders and authority are clear," Harriet told them. "We destroyed *one* star system once. We have no intention of doing so again—and my orders do not permit saturation planetary bombardment."

Some of the details of the one time the A!Tol had deployed a starkiller weapon were starting to leak out now. Harriet now knew they'd blown up the Taljzi capital during a vicious three-way war between the then-young A!Tol Imperium and the two factions of the civil war in the older Kanzi Theocracy.

She also knew, though her understanding was that the information was very closely held still, that they'd done so at the request of the Mesharom, as the Taljzi had been digging into Precursor technology.

It was inaccurate to say her orders forbade mass bombardment of a planet. That was actually the A!Tol Imperial Tablets of Military Legality—the legal rules that bound the Imperial Navy. The destruction of a world and its inhabitants was a war crime, and the Imperium would punish it as such.

Starkillers could be deployed only on the order of the Empress, but every starship commander had the ability to ruin a world. The Tablets made clear that it was forbidden.

Of course, in practice, the Empress had the authority to issue orders that overrode the Tablets, and Fleet Lords had the *ability* to issue those orders. A Fleet Lord who issued those orders would face a court-martial, regardless of their reasons. Depending on context, though, they had a good chance of simply being forced to retire early.

"Your people are very young still, I suppose," Kanmorad finally said. "You two are the joint commanders of this fleet. I certainly won't open fire on any planets without your approval, but I warn you that you may be making a mistake."

"We need to know more," Harriet told him. "More about their society. More about where these clones are coming from. It's entirely possible that simply destroying the cloning presses will end their threat—if they have to actually send their own children to war instead of running their soldiers out of a factory, their attitudes may change."

"We will learn more," Cawl promised. "I will not destroy innocents unless I must."

Harriet shivered but nodded. She didn't think she would ever see a circumstance that required her to murder innocents by the billions...but then, there'd been a point in her life where she'd never expected to meet aliens, too.

CHAPTER SEVENTEEN

"HAVE A SEAT, EVERYONE," TAN!STALLA ORDERED AS *JEAN Villeneuve*'s senior officers drifted into the meeting.

Morgan was the last to follow that order, making sure that each of the officers—all seven of them a different species—had seats that worked for their physiologies before taking her own seat to the Captain's right.

"I've been going over the latest round of exercises," Tan!Stalla told them all. "They are starting to edge into acceptable territory, though Speaker Cosa's navigation team is still ahead of everyone else."

The Pibo Speaker was the most junior officer in the room, though everyone knew their current posting was basically ticking the box to promote them to Lesser Commander. Cosa had no combat experience yet, and for a Navy that had found itself in the middle of an apparently genocidal war, that was essential for higher rank.

Morgan literally had Cosa's promotion paperwork in her computers, authorized by Navy HR for as soon as *Jean Villeneuve* had seen action.

"*Acceptable*, the captain says," Nidei said slowly. "Deep waters she lures us into."

Tan!Stalla's skin flashed red with amused pleasure as Morgan joined the general round of amusement and gestured for the eighth officer in the room, a human Lesser Speaker—junior lieutenant, basically—to put the results of the exercise on the holodisplay.

"The first set of numbers you can see are our target times," she told the others. "The second set are *our* numbers from the most recent exercise."

The numbers were color-coded, fading from green to a dark orange.

"Green means we beat the target by ten percent," she told them. "It fades towards orange from there as we reach the target. If anybody had actually *failed* to make the target time for the exercise, you'd see red on the board."

She smiled.

"I don't see any red on the board, do you?"

"Acceptable, as I said," Tan!Stalla noted. "This is the first *Galileo*-class ship, and we are named for Duchy of Terra's greatest Fleet Lord. Jean Villeneuve meant a great deal to the Terrans, to the Imperium, and, personally, to our First Sword."

The A!Tol gestured to Morgan, who bowed her head in acknowledgement. She still missed the old Frenchman. A superbattleship wasn't a great replacement for an old family friend.

"The targets are already accelerated from the Fleet standard to account for the *Galileo*'s improved automation and other systems," Lesser Commander Elstar pointed out, the Rekiki chief engineer slumped lazily in the couch-like seat his people used. "The difference between one hundred and ten seconds and ninety-nine seconds on ejecting a failing fusion core may save the ship.

"The difference between thirty-six seconds and thirty-three seconds on deploying a conduit-cleaning drone..." The centauroid alien had two sets of shoulders, both of them immense, which made for truly impressive shrugs.

"Wasn't it a conduit-cleaning drone you used to test the frequency error on matter-conversion Core Five?" Morgan asked.

The Rekiki paused thoughtfully for a second, then laughed.

"So it was. I suppose if we have debris on the conduits, the cleaning drones might be critical," he admitted. He gestured at the display. "We deployed in thirty-two seconds. There's only so much accelerating you can *do* on some of the drone launches without rewriting parts of their code."

"Have we tried rewriting that code?" Tan!Stalla asked. "That strikes me as the kind of efficiency that could be shared with the other *Galileo*s, at least."

"We haven't yet," Elstar admitted. "The conduit-cleaning drones aren't where I'd start with going over the drones' code, either. They might be critical in a niche situation, but the general maintenance bots are far more likely to save the ship. We've cracked their code open already, but I haven't made a project of it."

"Make one of it," Tan!Stalla instructed. "We're going into the fire, officers. It appears that Fleet Lord Tanaka intends to take full advantage of the detached nature of the two divisions of *Galileo*s. Our division is being temporarily transferred to Fleet Lord Mira Castil's task force."

Morgan had been briefed on this and brought up details of the task force—TF10.5—under the Indiri Fleet Lord.

Five superbattleship squadrons and ten cruiser squadrons. TF10.5 was a heavy force, even with all of its superbattleships being the *Majesty*-D type.

"Pincer Kanmorad is also putting two of his war-dreadnoughts and a squadron of his escort cruisers in the task force, and we're picking up ten Kanzi battleship squadrons and their escorts," Morgan noted. "It's being designated Joint Task Force Twenty-One."

"And it's going be the tip of the spear in PG-Three," Tan!Stalla told them.

PG-Three was Precursor Gold Three, one of the systems noted in gold in the ancient Precursor map Morgan's previous ship

Bellerophon had found. They knew that the gold icons indicated Precursor installations, and PG-Three had held one hell of an installation.

The ring station they'd found there surrounded an entire gas giant, and the Taljzi had been using it as the anchor for an immense shipyard. From what the allies had learned, the Taljzi had refitted three thousand warships—half of them capital ships—with new systems in response to Imperial weapon systems there…in under six months.

"JTF Twenty-One is going to be first through the portal and scanning the system," the A!Tol Captain continued. "If something goes wrong, it will be our job to make certain the rest of the fleet knows in time to either not enter the system or to turn around before they come under fire."

Tan!Stalla's skin flashed green in determination.

"Which also means that it will fall to us to cover the hyperspace portals through that withdrawal. We will be the first in, and, if something goes wrong, we will be the last out. Adjustments to our place in the formation will be forwarded to Cosa's department by the time we wrap this up. I'll check in with you later, Speaker, to make sure there's no problems."

"I'll touch base with *Pasteur*'s First Sword," Morgan promised. "We'll make sure everyone is linked in."

There *should* have been two Division Lords among the four *Galileo*-class ships. Morgan suspected their absence was due to the sheer scale of Tenth Fleet and of the construction and rearmament programs.

The Imperium was starting to come up short on officers at every level, and her impression was that a lot of junior flag officers were being bumped to higher ranks or at least higher responsibility.

The immediate impact for them was that Tan!Stalla commanded the two-ship division made up of *Jean Villeneuve* and *Louis Pasteur*.

"Thank you, First Sword," Tan!Stalla told her. "We'll want to set up some exercises with the rest of the Joint Task Force. We have at least four days before we reach PG-Three. Our assignment to Castil's command is temporary, but let's make sure we leave a positive impression on the Fleet Lord!"

LOUIS PASTEUR HAD A MORE normal crewing arrangement than *Jean Villeneuve*. *Villeneuve*'s multi-species crew certainly had advantages in terms of bringing different perspectives and abilities to any given problem, but maintaining an atmosphere and humidity level acceptable to multiple species always meant creating one that wasn't comfortable for *any* of them.

And then there was every other additional requirement stacked on top of that. Food for multiple species—you *never* ate anything except Universal Protein with additives on a multi-racial ship, where a single-species ship could have real food aboard. Extra protection and moisture for *just* the quarters of the amphibious species. That kind of thing.

Louis Pasteur had an entirely human crew. Since they'd launched from Sol, Morgan was enviously certain that they had real food in their freezers and pantries.

Like *Jean Villeneuve*'s First Sword, though, Commander Loni Tequila was a recent transfer from the Duchy of Terra Militia. The petite Asian-American officer greeted Morgan with a grin as the connection between the superbattleships came online.

"So, you heard we're getting stuck on the tip of the spear, huh?" she asked.

"Sounds like the place for the most modern warships in the Imperial Navy," Morgan agreed. "We're moving up to join the Joint Task Force in about an hour. What's your timeline looking like?"

It was almost a relief to be able to give times in regular Terran measurements. The translator could handle the conversion from cycles to days and so forth, but it made it a lot easier to *align* time frames when everyone was thinking in the same scales.

"Pretty similar," Tequila confirmed. "Captain Vilhjálmsson asked *me* to ask *you* to ask Tan!Stalla about organizing joint exercises. If we're taking squadrons from three separate fleets into battle, some kind of virtual maneuvers in advance might be handy."

"Captain Tan!Stalla already has me organizing it," Morgan replied. "I'll want to bend your ear about ideas before we're done."

Tequila chuckled delicately.

"How about the scenario of 'a fleet twice the size of the last Return is waiting for us and we have to run like hell'?" she asked. "That's my personal nightmare."

"Mine, too," Morgan admitted. "We don't know enough about what these assholes are playing with. I don't *think* they can replace a thousand-plus capital ships in six months, but we don't know the size of their overall fleet or industrial base."

"Or how fast their cloning machine is spitting out people," Tequila replied. She shook her head. "That still blows my mind. They just...print soldiers?"

"So far as we can tell," Morgan agreed. Tequila had been tactical officer on a *Duchess of Terra*–class battleship in the Battle of Terra, but she hadn't been there for the early clashes out beyond the Imperial border *or* the scouting mission that had found Taljzi space.

That meant she hadn't seen the rows of identical corpses as the Ducal Guards took their samples. Video of it wasn't quite the same as watching a live feed.

"Soldiers, spacers, engineers, miners," Morgan reeled off, then shook her head. "I don't know what their society looks like, but it's got to be weird as hell. We're guessing they're producing adults with existing skillsets at the very least, which is *utterly* beyond anyone's tech these days."

"I didn't think that was even possible," Tequila replied dryly. "But then, I suppose my parents thought hyper travel was impossible at one point."

"We deal with the world we've got," Morgan confirmed. "Do you need anything from us to be ready for the transfer?"

"It's pretty straightforward at this point," the other woman said. "We'll be in formation with *Sunwing* by the same time as you. We'll sort out the exercises then."

"All right. We'll be in touch."

WITH THE INITIAL calls and conferences out of the way, Morgan started pulling together the data she'd need for the big virtual battle she and Tan!Stalla were hoping to convince Fleet Lord Castil to authorize.

The first part was the information they had on the Taljzi forces. Fast ships with compressed-matter armor, multiple varieties of sublight missiles, and a molecular disruptor for close-range combat.

Everyone in the battles to come would be using a functionally standard interface-drive missile capable of traveling at point eight cee. The Taljzi also had an extended-range version with a range of over four light-minutes.

They were surprisingly short on mid-range energy weapons. Their ships carried a handful of proton beams, but they were also equipped with an antiproton curtain that negated that particular system. Their real close-range shipkiller disrupted molecular bonds, turning hulls and systems into atomic bombs at ranges of up to a light-second.

That was mutual suicide range in space combat, but as defenses grew more powerful, Morgan could see the value. The Mesharom used the same system, after all.

They didn't have any Mesharom on their side, which actually meant that all three components of the Allied Fleet were equipped with a very similar array of weapons.

Laian, Kanzi and A!Tol all used a point eight cee missile with no real tricks. Laian missiles were a bit smarter, with more powerful ECM and slightly longer range, but nothing material. All three powers were carrying hyperfold cannons as their main mid-range energy weapon.

The Laian system was noticeably longer-ranged and more powerful than the A!Tol weapon—but the Kanzi were *using* the A!Tol weapon. That had been their price for the alliance.

The A!Tol ships were also equipped with plasma lances, heavy weapons the Laians had phased out after bringing the hyperfold cannons into commission.

All three fleets used proton beams. The Kanzi actually had the most powerful beams there, with a marginally greater range and significantly greater hitting power. What the A!Tol Fleet was keeping quiet was that they'd actually duplicated the Taljzi antiproton curtain.

It had actually been installed on every ship in Tenth Fleet...and it was the *Kanzi* they were worried about in that case. The Taljzi didn't use the weapon, after all.

The real game-changer and the one distinct advantage that the Allied Fleet had over the Taljzi was the single-portal hyperspace missiles loaded onto the Imperial ships. With the mass refit that had started after the first contact with the Taljzi, every capital ship and cruiser in the fleet had at least one six-launcher battery.

They were the longest-ranged weapons in play, but they were vulnerable in their terminal mode after exiting hyperspace. The Taljzi had gone from zero active defenses when they'd first encountered Imperial forces to an antimissile suite capable of shooting down hyperspace missiles in their final real-space approach.

Morgan shook her head as the data all flowed onto her screen, and she began to put together a hypothetical Taljzi defense force. The Kanzi offshoots had surprised them before, which meant that she had a lot of options for what their enemy might pull out of their hat.

The very first scenario she put together gave them hyperspace missiles.

CHAPTER EIGHTEEN

"THAT WAS SUPPOSED TO BE AN *ACCURATE* SIMULATION?" NIDEI demanded in the debrief. *Jean Villeneuve* hadn't been destroyed until the very end of the battle—but she'd been critically damaged in the opening salvos when Morgan's Taljzi defenders had concentrated her hypothetical hyperspace missiles on the heaviest units in the lead allied formation.

"Accurate in what way?" Morgan replied. "Do I believe that the Taljzi are in possession of hyperspace missiles equivalent to our own and the tachyon scanner–equipped hyperfold drones required for precision targeting?" She paused, letting her mixed audience from all three fleets consider that thought.

"Probably not," she conceded. "I put the chance of them having duplicated Imperial or Mesharom hyperspace missiles at about thirty percent. But I guarantee they're working on it—in the single long-cycle between first contact and the attack on Sol, the Taljzi deployed new offensive and defensive systems to counteract our hyperspace missiles.

"That included superior active defenses, the long-range bombardment missiles, and a tachyon-scanner jammer. They cut the effectiveness of our long-range fire twice over and matched much of its range.

"It is a *given* that we will face some kind of surprise when we arrive at PG-Three," she concluded.

"I presume, Commander, that there are other surprises in the scenarios you drew up?" Fleet Lord Castil asked. The holographic image of the Indiri officer was mostly an observer in this conversation. His staff had observed the ten-ship exercise *Jean Villeneuve* had just run to see if he wanted to run the test for the rest of the joint task force.

"Of course," she confirmed.

"Are they that unfair?" Nidei asked.

"The challenge was not unfair," Four Hundred and Twenty-Third Sword of the Republic Instildan replied. The Sword was the first female Laian Morgan had encountered from the Republic side—one of her honorary "aunts" was a Laian Exile—and commanded one of Kanmorad's war-dreadnoughts.

Instildan was one of the two war-dreadnought captains assigned to the Joint Task Force—*both* of which had agreed to take part in Morgan's test exercise.

"That we all failed to meet it as completely as we did is on us, not on Commander Casimir," Instildan continued. "It is also a sign that these exercises are *very* required."

That was more generous than Morgan had expected, given that she'd used the massed launchers of a thousand Taljzi capital ships to turn both war-dreadnoughts into scrap metal in the first few minutes of the fight. Even with all of the information on the ships, they'd *still* taken more killing than she'd really expected.

Given that only ten ships on one side had even had bridge crews "active" and the rest of the ships in the exercise had been AI-run, they'd done well to even successfully cover the retreat of the rest of the fleet.

But since JTF 21 had been completely wiped out, it hadn't been a *great* showing.

"I must agree with the Sword of the Republic," Fleet Lord Castil said calmly. "Fleet Master Do Kan?"

Aral Do Kan was the commander of the Kanzi component of the fleet, and her hologram was in the meeting for the same reason as Castil's: to decide whether to put the entire Joint Task Force through Morgan's scenarios. Scenarios that were apparently even more hell than she'd intended.

Do Kan had the kind of body a lot of human women would pay for, with curves in all of the right places and frankly outlined in the skintight black leather uniform of the Kanzi fleet. Of course, Do Kan was covered in blue fur and short even for a Kanzi, at one hundred and ten centimeters tall.

Morgan had watched at least one human male have a serious mental train wreck on first encounter with female Kanzi and, in the privacy of her own head, would admit to having done much the same herself. Kanzi were shorter than humans and blue, but otherwise, the proportions were identical.

"My own ships have been engaging in internal exercises, but I did not think that joint exercises would be beneficial," she admitted calmly, studying the hologram showing the hypothetical shattered wreckage of their combined forces.

"If nothing else, it appears that Commander Casimir has as much sympathy for weakness as her mother. Are the rest of these scenarios as deadly?"

"That will depend on who is running the op force," Morgan replied. "But yes, each of the eight scenarios I drew up gives the Taljzi a surprise."

Some of those surprises were less atrocious than others. They wanted the JTF to win at least some of the scenarios, after all.

"I think that preserving those surprises would be invaluable," Do Kan noted. "Fleet Lord Castil, I suggest that we recruit officers from outside the Joint Task Force to work with Commander Casimir to run the op force for task force–level exercises. The evidence suggests that we should run through all of Commander Casimir's scenarios at least once."

The Kanzi grinned.

"And while we do that, I suggest that you and I, Fleet Lord, think of some *more* surprises for some additional scenarios. The last thing we want is for our fleet to cross into PG-Three without being ready for *anything*."

THREE *GRUELING* DAYS FOLLOWED. Morgan found herself tapped to act as the coordinator for the opposing force even when she wasn't, somehow, acting as the commander of the op force in a scenario against multiple *flag officers*.

The simplest surprise she had for JTF 21's officers, though, was an enemy fleet four times the size of the one that had attacked Sol. That one hadn't possessed any upgraded weapons above the Taljzi at the Battle of Terra, though, and the Joint Task Force had actually pulled out of the fight with no losses.

That was the only scenario where they hadn't been hammered. Hyperspace missiles, super-long-ranged energy weapons, upgraded stealth fields...if Morgan, Do Kan, or Castil could think of it, it had played a role in the scenarios. JTF 21 had *won* every single scenario, in the sense of covering the main Allied Fleet's emergence and, where necessary, retreat., at least.

After twenty-three scenarios, Morgan was hoping for a break when the latest scenario came to its close. It was a rerun of the initial scenario with hyperspace missiles, and the allies had just handily demonstrated that their current antimissile weaponry was entirely capable of duplicating the Taljzi's stunt of shooting down incoming HSMs.

"I wasn't expecting that," she admitted aloud as a hypothetical Allied Fleet came through behind JTF 21. With the path cleared for the thousands of capital ships of the main fleet and her own criteria suggesting that the Taljzi would have run out of HSMs, the end result of the scenario was pretty obvious at that point.

She was coordinating the op force—basically acting as Squadron Lord Sun's operations officer while the human ran the Taljzi fleet—from the superbattleship's secondary control center. The rest of *Jean Villeneuve*'s bridge crew was fighting the virtual version of their ship from the bridge. She had an open channel to her tactical officer now that the battle was wrapping up.

"Everything that lets the Taljzi shoot down *our* missiles is applicable in return," Nidei pointed out, the Ivida's smug tone coming through the translator nicely. "And unlike them, *we* have instantaneous sensors and weapons across the terminal attack range."

"And they were used well," Morgan agreed. "Well done, Nidei. If we can duplicate that efficiency in the actual action, we'll be doing just fine."

There were scenarios where using tachyon-scanner-aimed hyperfold cannon for close-range defense wouldn't change anything, but Morgan was reasonably confident that Taljzi hyperspace missiles were a middlingly likely "surprise."

Of course, the problem with expecting surprises was that you were never going to guess the *right* surprise.

Screens flipped from training mode over to active mode on both the bridge and secondary control as Tan!Stalla cut into the channel.

"It appears we have all done well," the A!Tol told them. "Orders are coming down from Fleet Lord Castil: all ships are to go to minimum cruise status for the next cycle. Everyone involved in the exercises is to take as much rest as possible."

The Captain paused.

"You two, especially, are to take at least four-fifths of the next cycle completely off. That's an order," she said calmly. "We enter the enemy system at the end of that cycle, and I want you as fresh as possible.

"I'd also suggest that you both record messages for your loved ones. JTF 21 will be acting as mail-carrier for the entire Fleet, linking into the hyperfold relays the first scout mission left behind once we're in real space."

Those relays were light-years away from PG-3, but unless the entire task force was destroyed in the first few seconds, their messages would still get home. One last chance to tell loved ones what they meant.

After all, no matter how well they did, they were looking at one hell of a battle in PG-Three. At least some of their ships and crews wouldn't be coming home.

BACK IN HER QUARTERS, Morgan took the time to shower the day off before putting an undress uniform on. Aboard ship, she didn't have much in terms of clothing that *wasn't* a uniform—and the uniforms doubled as safety gear with their built-in gloves, boots, emergency helmets and oxygen supplies.

She wanted to hope that they were going to face a relatively small defending force, maybe even only the survivors of the Battle of Terra...but she'd done the calculation for how much industrial capacity would have been required to refit the Second Return with the LRMs and active missile defenses.

Barring some kind of ship-production methodology unknown to the Imperium—not *impossible*, given that the Core Powers built ships far faster than the Imperium could—that industry wouldn't let them produce capital ships in six months.

The back-of-the-envelope calculation she'd done, though, suggested that they could have built as many as *ten thousand* cruisers. When the enemy had forty billion tons of warships, she wasn't sure how much it would matter that their ships would be bigger on average.

Quantity had a quality all its own.

Sighing, she settled down into her chair and brought up a recording program. *Jean Villeneuve* would be mailman for the entire fleet—every ship crossing into normal space would do so with a full copy of the fleet's messages and would send it just in case—but Morgan had her own messages to record.

"Hey, love," she started the first message. "As I'm recording this, we're about to make our first real-space entry in Taljzi space. I can't say more than that. I honestly have no idea how briefed the Militia or even the general population is on this mission."

She figured the civilians knew the mission was taking place but not much more than that. The details would be relevant only when they succeeded—or failed.

"I don't think I realized how much I liked having you on the bridge with me, even before you asked me to join you for 'lessons,'" she continued with a grin. "I think you may have got your hooks into me long before you got my clothes off.

"Transmission delays being what they are, by the time you get this, the battle will probably be over. I'll do everything in my power to survive and come home to you, but we both knew the deal when we started this game."

She kissed her fingers and pressed them briefly to the camera.

"Know that I'm thinking about you and I miss you," she concluded. "I love you and I'll see you when I get home. Be patient with me, Victoria. We both know I suck at this, but I'm *trying*."

In more ways than one, she heard the other woman say in her head, and laughed as she ended the recording.

With a swallow, Morgan saved the recording and attached routing. Once that one was ready, she straightened her back and set another recording to begin.

"Hi, Mom and Dad."

CHAPTER NINETEEN

"Hyper portal in thirty seconds."

Morgan nodded silently in response to the report that echoed across the secondary control center. Right now, her job was to be ready to step in as *Villeneuve*'s commander if something happened to Captain Tan!Stalla.

Well, that and coordinating with *Louis Pasteur* and making certain a thousand tiny details of the formation were in order and that Tan!Stalla was aware of everything *she* was seeing.

Right now, everything looked as perfect as it could. The hundred and eighty-four capital ships of the somewhat misnamed Joint Task Force—not merely a fleet but a *large* fleet by normal standards—were assembled into the formation the exercise had helped them put together.

It served a number of purposes, but one of them was setting their positions so that the largest ships—the ones most likely to be targeted by long-range fire—were within the defensive envelopes of the largest number of other ships.

Villeneuve and *Pasteur* and the two war-dreadnoughts made up the "heavy hammer" of the task force, but they would also draw the most fire as the four clearly largest targets on the map. So, now each of the big ships had entire squadrons of other capital ships wrapped around them to protect their flanks.

Everyone was where they should be. *Villeneuve* was at battle stations and all of her crew was ready. There was nothing left to do but wait out the last few seconds until...

"Hyper portal opening."

The holographic display in the center of secondary control was a mirror for the one on the main bridge or the flag deck. The massive portal torn open by sixteen superbattleships sliced across the entire hologram like the axe of an angry god—and then another wave of sixteen superbattleships smashed through that tear and began relaying their data back.

"Getting our first visuals on PG-Three now," Lesser Speaker Jessica Haig reported. The Scotland-born young officer had been raised on Alpha Centauri, one of the first recruits to officially come from the colony at Hope.

"Anything out of place?" Morgan asked.

"The planets are all still there," the junior officer told her. "Still resolving details beyond that." She paused. "We're getting drone feeds now, too. I'm not picking up any Taljzi engine signatures."

That was odd...but on the other hand, they hadn't picked up much when they'd first visited the system, either. All of the ships that had chased *Bellerophon* and her fellows back to Sol had been docked at the ring around the gas giant.

"Do we have eyes on the ring station yet?" Morgan asked, blinking against the momentary nausea as *Jean Villeneuve* passed through the portal. "If there's a response, it's going to come from there."

Her own screens reported that JTF 21 was now in the system. The plan called for the rest of the fleet to wait just over ten minutes, long enough for the Joint Task Force to swing by the gas giant with its artificial ring world.

"Casimir."

It was Tan!Stalla on their private channel.

"Are you seeing anything?" the Captain asked. "Because this place is looking pretty dead to me."

"It looked relatively dead last time, too," Morgan warned. "Right up until the ring started spitting hundreds of warships at us."

"True." The Captain paused. "These waters feel murky, Casimir. If you see something you think I might have missed…"

"It's my *job* to tell you if that happens," Morgan pointed out with a chuckle. "I'm watching, but…"

It finally hit her as she looked at the gas giant again.

"What's important is what I'm *not* seeing, sir," she told Tan!Stalla. "And that's the ring world's energy signature. We didn't know what we were looking for the first time, but I do now…and it's not there."

MORGAN HAD a small advantage over many of the officers in JTF 21 from having been to PG-Three before, but she wasn't the only one. She was the first to realize the ring world was missing, but by the time it bounced by the chain of command, the report was coming from a dozen officers.

"We're sending more drones in toward the gas giant," the tactical officer of the lead superbattleship reported. "We should have a clear image about…now."

The primary tactical network for the task force had thousands of sentients on it. Captains, executive officers, tactical officers, flag officers…all of these and more had access to the network. There were a thousand sub-channels, but the main channel almost always had *someone*'s voice overlaying the data.

As the data report from the lead drones hit the network however, that channel was silent in stunned shock.

The ring world had been the largest construct any of them, including the Laians, had ever seen. A space station built as a ring two kilometers thick and a hundred kilometers high with a radius of forty thousand kilometers, it represented literally a *trillion* cubic kilometers of living and working space. They hadn't been certain of how many people lived on the station, but just the shipyard capacity alone would have required tens of millions of workers with hundreds of millions of support workers.

Given the size of the station, Morgan figured it was probably home to at least a few billion people.

And someone had blown it to hell. Entire sections had been vaporized—the scale of the damage suggested massive use of antimatter warheads. Other chunks had clearly fallen *into* the gas giant.

At least half of the immense station was gone. The defenses had clearly been bombarded with antimatter weapons until the facility had stopped firing back, but that didn't explain the damage.

"It had to be the Mesharom," Morgan half-whispered on her private channel with Tan!Stalla. "I didn't think they were this...ruthless."

"They threatened to level Hope once," the A!Tol replied. "There were, what, a couple million humans there at the time?"

"That was millions. This was *billions.*"

"Once you're prepared to regard any number of sentients as acceptable damage, the difference between a million dead and a billion is just zeroes," Tan!Stalla said flatly. "The Mesharom have always been *very* certain of their cause."

Morgan heard the unspoken word. *Fanatic.* The people they were fighting were fanatics...and it was easy to sometimes forget that the Mesharom, the grand old race of the galaxy, were also fanatics.

"Must be something in the Precursors' water," she muttered. "What do we do, sir?"

"Mission profile calls for us to scout the ring world area to assess opposition while we wait for the fleet," Tan!Stalla reminded Morgan. "We're to get as close as safe."

There was a bitter tone to the forced beak-snap laughter.

"It looks like that's going to be *very* close."

"WAIT, WHAT WAS THAT?" Morgan demanded. "Someone get me control of drone DS-13," she snapped.

The drones were flying an automated pattern, and it only took a handful of seconds for her to take control of the particular robotic spacecraft she'd seen *something* move through.

"There's nothing out there, Casimir," the tactical officer of the superbattleship *Darkstar* told her. The Lesser Commander was human, but Morgan only barely registered that as she turned the probe around.

"Can I have my drone back?" *Darkstar*'s officer asked after a second. "We're trying to catalog the debris he—"

Morgan muted him without even thinking about it. *Something* had moved near the chunk of debris that *Darkstar*'s drones were surveying. What was there?"

She reran the scan. There wasn't anything there, just the debris cloud that had been an automated industrial node of some kind.

Just a debris cloud.

"*Darkstar*, are you running post-processing for stealth ships?" she demanded as she reopened the channel. The standard first-pass analysis of the scan data wouldn't pick up ships under a stealth screen. If you committed enough processing power to it, a secondary run could at least tell you the ships were present.

"Of course," the man replied grumpily. "Results started filtering in a minute or two ago."

With the Imperium's best computers and software, they'd cut what had once been a forty-five-minute data analysis down to ten. That was part of the reason for the ten-minute delay on the arrival of the rest of the fleet.

"Get me the post-processing for the area DS-13 is in," Morgan ordered.

"There's nothing there; I already checked the data," the officer replied.

"Check it against the debris cloud," Morgan told him. "Taljzi stealth screens are more vulnerable to particulate interference than the Core Power ones we're used to."

There was a few seconds' silence.

"Forwarding you it now," the Lesser Commander replied. "I'm still not certain...but it looks like there might be *something* there."

Morgan pulled up the data and swallowed a curse. Her junior officer aboard *Darkstar* was right. There was nothing solid—ten minutes before, the drones had been a long way out. They *should* have picked up any stealthed ships...but there were a lot of factors in play in that assessment.

It looked a lot like something—potentially a battleship—had been in that debris cloud and had moved at just the right time to be spotted by the drone. There was no certainty, though, and the entire Joint Task Force had taken the destruction of the ring station as a sign that the region was safe.

"Captain Tan!Stalla," Morgan pinged her boss. "I think we may have at least one stealthed unit in play. Permission to poke a possible hive with a missile?"

The fleet was still well outside any of their energy weapons, almost a light-minute away from the planet, but even their sublight missiles could manage that.

"Permission granted. Use an HSM," Tan!Stalla ordered. "My tentacles *itch,* and it's not just because someone murdered a lot of civilians here." She paused. "In fact, if you think you can avoid damaging what's left of the structure, use *six* HSMs."

"Yes, sir." That was a full salvo from one of their batteries, the standardized number of launchers per shipboard portal.

Morgan plugged the numbers in. The safety radius of an HSM's antimatter warhead. The likely survivability of the remains of the station. Where she figured the ship was...

"Firing," she reported.

Six icons flickered on her display and then reappeared in the ring world debris field. Four detonated harmlessly, vaporizing some hopefully minor wreckage and ice fragments.

Two didn't detonate. Two had been shot down the moment they flashed out of hyperspace in a hail of laserfire that broke the stealth fields.

"Captain, I have at least six Taljzi battleships on the screens," Morgan reported calmly. "Orders from the flag?"

———

THE JOINT TASK FORCE had advanced in battle formation, just in case. Morgan's determination to convince everyone in the combined force to expect surprises had paid its dividends there. No one had even dropped from full battle stations as they swept the wreckage.

"Targeting orders from the flag. We have Bogey Three," the communication officer on the bridge reported.

Morgan was once again an observer whose job it was to make sure she was aware of what was going on, and she pulled the entire fleet targeting plan to her console. Moments after she did so, she felt the almost-imperceptible vibration of *Jean Villeneuve* opening the portals for her hyperspace missile batteries.

Five of the six battleships she'd located were the target of the firepower of a full squadron of HSM-equipped superbattleships apiece, with the cruisers targeting the sixth. Morgan doubted they'd found all of the Taljzi ships, but that hammer of antimatter fire would probably be enough to convince the rest they'd been spotted.

Over seven hundred missiles erupted from hyperspace around each Taljzi battleship. New stars flared in the orbit of the gas giant, and five of the Taljzi ships vanished.

The sixth reeled away, spewing atmosphere from a dozen critical wounds. After a moment, she stabilized her course and ran—and she didn't run alone.

Defensive fire from other ships had joined in as the hyperspace salvo arrived. It had been too late and not enough to save the targeted ships, but it *had* revealed just what the Joint Task Force was dealing with.

"I make it one hundred and twenty-four battleships with four hundred destroyers," Morgan reported. "They brought their tachyon jammers up when they dropped the stealth fields. They must have already had their stealth fields up before we even arrived, though. Paranoid as hell for searching a graveyard."

"They were watching for the people who *made* this a graveyard," Tan!Stalla replied. "They're outnumbered and outgunned. This should be straightforward enough."

"And if they have a surprise, sir?" Morgan asked.

The A!Tol laughed harshly.

"I'm expecting one," she confirmed. "But they're already running, so I think they agree with me." Tan!Stalla paused. "Orders from the flag," she told Morgan after a moment. "Pursue and engage with HSMs. They have the speed advantage, so we'll let them *try* to escape."

The Task Force smoothly moved from "investigate the wreckage" mode to "pursuit" mode. The Taljzi ran at sixty percent of lightspeed, and JTF 21 followed at fifty-five percent of lightspeed. The Imperial ships *could* match the Taljzi's speed for limited periods of time, as could the Laians.

The Kanzi fleet didn't have the same sprint capabilities as the Imperials though, and Castil was clearly not giving up their defenses against the inevitable long-range Taljzi fire.

They might outnumber their prey, but a hundred-plus battleships could fling a lot of the Taljzi's big long-range missiles back at the allies—and they proceeded to do just that as Morgan thought about it. HSMs were detonating in an antimatter stormfront across the rear edge of the Taljzi fleet, and massive point eight cee missiles dropped back toward the JTF at effectively lightspeed.

Point eight cee missiles heading toward a fleet moving at point five five cee. The interface drive did not play particularly fair with

Einstein, but the relative velocity still managed to stay below the speed of light.

Somehow.

Morgan didn't pretend to understand how that whole mess worked. She had to account for the fact that their lightspeed sensors could only give fractions of a second of warning of the incoming fire. Their defenses had been designed to try to compensate for that once —but now they had tachyon scanners.

She watched the first salvo come in and nodded approvingly as over ninety percent of the missiles were shot down. Real-time target tracking and engagement across a ten-light-second window made up for a *lot* of shortcomings.

Shields handled the missiles they didn't stop, and the task force continued to barrel after the enemy. Another half-dozen battleships died under the hyperspace missile fire, and Morgan studied the screens and wondered what they'd missed.

The Taljzi had been invisible under their stealth screens. They had to know that invisibility only lasted so long, and they had to have seen that they were badly outnumbered by even the vanguard of the Allied Fleet. Why had they *still* been in among the wreckage? They could have been five light-minutes away by the time the JTF realized they were there.

Unless...

Morgan started tapping commands. *Jean Villeneuve* was only firing hyperspace missiles currently, so it was easy for her to commandeer half of the interface-drive missile tubes and launch another spread of drones at maximum velocity.

"Casimir?" Tan!Stalla said calmly. "Would you care to *ask* before firing sixty-plus drones into space?"

"There's no time," she snapped. "Captain, remember DLK-5539? They lured us into a *minefield*."

DLK-5539 was a black hole the First Return had used as the anchor for a logistics base. When *Bellerophon*—with Morgan aboard as tactical officer—had investigated one of the depots, they'd run into a massive minefield of antimatter charges backed by automated missile platforms.

"We'd see those mines," Tan!Stalla replied. "Without the accretion disk to hide them, the antimatter signatures would stick out like a rock in calm waters."

"They have stealth fields, sir," Morgan pointed out.

Most of her attention was on the drones flashing out ahead of the fleet when her sensors were momentarily blinded by the massive hyper portals opening behind them. The rest of the fleet was arriving.

That momentary blinding was enough to confuse her drones for several critical moments...and, apparently, confuse the mines. The drones shouldn't have set off any of the warheads, but the flash of radiation from the portals' opening clearly overwhelmed the sensors enough to leave them erring on the side of caution.

A dozen of Morgan's drones vanished as antimatter mines detonated. The backflash from the mines allowed her to flag the *rest* of the minefield.

"Transmitting minefield location to the JTF," she snapped, swallowing her fear at the sheer scale of the trap that had been laid for them. She couldn't distinguish between antimatter mines, beam-weapon platforms and missile launchers. Not with dozens of stealth-field generators covering tens of thousands of mines. An entire region of space three light-seconds across and a light-second thick had been turned into a death zone.

A death zone directly on the path of the advancing JTF 21.

"All ships, this is Fleet Lord Castil," the Indiri flag officer's voice cut into the main tactical network. "The Taljzi apparently like their minefields. We're estimating over fifty thousand platforms ahead of us. At least some are missile launchers or disruptors...We take no chances. Target the field with your interface-drive missiles.

"Clear a path."

Targeting orders were already spreading through the data channels. As soon as Castil had finished speaking, *Jean Villeneuve*'s sublight weapons spoke. Her HSM launchers continued to pound the fleeing Taljzi force, but the main focus was now the minefield in their path.

They could evade it but only if they let the Taljzi escape. Instead, over two hundred capital ships opened fire on the mines with their primary weapons.

Against any single mine, a point eight cee missile was overkill. But with the stealth fields still in place, the odds of any given missile hitting a mine were only about fifty percent.

Thousands of missiles crashed into the minefield and thousands of mines died...but the JTF was still charging into the teeth of tens of thousands of platforms. They could survive the antimatter mines and missiles...but if Castil was correct about there being molecular disruptor platforms, the Joint Task Force had no defense against the Taljzi's thankfully short-ranged hell guns.

Morgan brought up their energy weapons, tasking them with automatic fire. Their hyperfold cannon and proton beams wouldn't make much difference...

"Break off," Castil ordered. "All ships, break off and go around the minefield. Maintain a million-kilometer safe radius." He paused. "We can't burn through fast enough to get through safely, and I won't risk ships when I don't have to."

He paused, but there was grim satisfaction when he spoke again.

"I suppose we can settle for only blowing up a hundred battle-ships, after all."

CHAPTER TWENTY

AJAX WAS IN THE SECOND WAVE OF SHIPS TO ENTER PG-THREE. By the time Harriet's flagship approached the hyper portal, she had heard about the fate of the Precursor-built ring station and that Joint Task Force Twenty-One had located a major Taljzi force in the system.

The reports on the minefield came in just as Harriet was finally in the system and getting live updates. Radio transmissions could be sent through the portal, but hyperfold coms were normal space to normal space only.

"We're not going to get them all," Koanest concluded as their main display finally updated. "We could redirect some of the ships still in hyperspace to intercept them."

"We could," Harriet agreed, studying the vector for the alien fleet. "But remember that we know *nothing* about what's out here. Get me a link to Pincer Kanmorad. We need to follow them—but we need them to not *know* they're being followed."

Kanmorad had brought four of his war-dreadnoughts through in the second wave. None of the fleet commanders had been in the first wave...and none of them were waiting for the third, either.

"Fleet Lord Tanaka," the Laian greeted her cheerfully. "This is an impressive mess. You would agree with me that it was the Mesharom, yes?"

"Almost certainly," Harriet agreed. She was still trying to compute the horror of just what the Mesharom had done there. All of the estimates agreed that her sometime-allies had murdered at *least* several billion people.

"I need a favor, Pincer of the Republic."

"My fleets are at your disposal, though I don't think my war-dreadnoughts are much better equipped to catch our slippery friends than anyone else. If they were, I'd order the vessels in the Joint Task Force forward."

"We could cut them off as they enter their hyper portal," Harriet reminded him calmly. "Our vessels are more defanged in hyperspace than theirs are, though."

And they were running out of time. It would only be a handful of minutes at best before the Taljzi would flee into the strange grayness of hyper travel.

"We need to follow them. We don't know enough about what's out here, and while we know *their* stealth fields don't work in hyperspace...I believe yours do?"

Kanmorad paused to consider, his mandibles chittering slowly in thought.

"Battered as their fleet is, they would still be a threat to any force of escort cruisers I sent," he noted. "But you are correct. I will contact my subordinates and have two squadrons in position. Twenty escorts with stealth screens should suffice for this end—"

"Fleet Lord!" Koanest interrupted. "The Task Force!"

Whichever Taljzi had put together the *second* layer of the trap had to have been feeling very clever. There was the central minefield, already a massive investment of industrial might and resources. There was an entire *fleet*, allowing itself to be hammered into near-uselessness to lure the Joint Task Force forward.

And then, "above" and "below" the minefield in relation to the ecliptic, they'd positioned missile platforms. Each of them was stealth-screened in its own right, and Harriet doubted they were protected beyond the most basic shields, but the platforms were half the size of a battleship.

Each of them started spewing missiles at JTF 21 from a range of barely four light-seconds. At point eight cee, they crossed the gap in five seconds.

Five seconds for the preprogrammed responses aboard JTF 21's ships to kick into action. They might not have been expecting this, but Harriet had been following the exercises the JTF's commanders' twisty brains had produced.

They'd been expecting *something,* and an automated protocol built to protect them against hyperspace missiles proved more than sufficient to get their defenses targeting incoming sublight missiles.

There were just so *many* missiles. Thousands of them crashed down on JTF 21—where they collided with solid lines of Imperial and Kanzi capital ships backed by the two Laian war-dreadnoughts.

The first two salvos arrived unanswered, every weapon in the Allied Fleet turned to protecting themselves and their fellows. Hyperfold cannons spoke by the thousands, with lasers, ECM and shields backing them up.

Whoever had coded the missiles had targeted the Laian war-dreadnoughts primarily. Despite everything that the massed fleet could do, at least a thousand missiles flung themselves on each of the immense warships.

Their mighty shields shrugged aside the salvos, and Harriet felt a chill of memory—of another war-dreadnought facing another fleet, and how the massed missiles of a combined Imperial–Ducal Militia task force had failed to do much more than distract the war-dreadnought they faced.

Missiles made it through the shields on the second salvo, but the war-dreadnoughts carried vast amounts of heavy compressed-matter armor. The ships were hit, but they were still clearly in the fight.

And then, finally, the Joint Task Force returned fire. Hyperfold cannon were dedicated to defense still, but all of the three fleets had proton beams—and many of the Imperial ships had plasma lances.

It was the lances that took the most devastating toll. The two *Galileo*-class ships alone obliterated eight platforms in the first salvo, each of their plasma beams aimed at a different target.

Even Harriet was shocked at the success of the strike. Over half of the platforms died in a single blast of flame—and most of the other half died over the ensuing seconds as the weaker proton beams claimed their own toll.

Perhaps a third of the platforms were left when the plasma lances spoke again and finished off the trap. *Ajax*'s flag bridge was silent enough that Harriet had half-forgotten she still had Kanmorad on an open channel.

"I see that my people need to reconsider our decision to remove plasma lances from our more modern ships," he noted calmly. "The enhanced design your new warships carry is...most impressive."

"I think your ships might be the only reason we survived long enough to use them," Harriet replied. She was checking loss numbers. Despite the focus of the Taljzi fire, the Imperial component of JTF 21 *had* lost ships.

There'd been enough missiles in play that escorts could be over-whelmed by *accident*. The losses were light, though, with only three cruisers destroyed outright and another dozen wounded.

The war-dreadnoughts had taken the brunt of it, and she didn't have damage reports for them. Kanmorad did, but from what she could read of his body language...it hadn't been as bad as it looked.

"The purpose of a war-dreadnought, more than anything else Fleet Lord, is to *survive*," Kanmorad told her. "We're still counting losses, but it looks like a few hundred or so injured. Some may not survive, but our medicine is among the best in the galaxy."

He turned his gaze back to his own display.

"They hurt us," he noted calmly. "Not many have done that. I came on this mission prepared to lose war-dreadnoughts, I thought... but they have bloodied the Republic."

Harriet found herself wondering if the *Imperium* had "bloodied the Republic" in their one battle—or if the intervention of the Laians' old Wendira enemies meant the Wendira took the blame for any dead the Imperials had inflicted.

Kanmorad certainly looked angrier than she'd seen him yet.

"Those escorts are already in motion," he continued. "This system is certainly not the beating heart of our enemies. We need to find that heart, Fleet Lord Tanaka.

"And when we do, the Republic will help tear it to pieces."

CHAPTER TWENTY-ONE

HARRIET HAD NEVER SEEN THE PRECURSOR RING INTACT WITH her own eyes. Footage and sensor data of it had been awe-inspiring, enough to make her reconsider some of her own assumptions about just what the Precursors had been capable of.

Looking at its ruins inspired an entirely different feeling. Awe at what it had been, yes, and awe at the level of firepower used to destroy it...and a sinking feeling of utter terror that anyone would that cavalierly destroy an artifact and population of that scale.

There was something about the Precursors that terrified the Mesharom. She'd suspected that just from Grand Commander Tilsan's reaction to thinking the Imperium had any systems based on Precursor tech, but looking at the old ring station, she was certain.

The station had been designed to be self-stable. Its orbit was high enough and fast enough that even without sentient intervention, it would have effectively circled its gas giant anchor forever. Harriet didn't know how long it had done so before the Taljzi had descended on it, but the *minimum* time frame possible was basically fifty thousand years.

It would have lasted forever. Instead, the Mesharom had

destroyed it and she couldn't help but feel that they had done so as much to destroy a Precursor artifact they couldn't haul home as to defeat the Taljzi.

Either way, she was grimly certain that the billions of workers and inhabitants aboard the station hadn't registered in Tilsan's calculations one way or another.

"We're still completing our cataloging of the surviving fragments," Koanest said over her shoulder, joining her in her examination of the ring. "The Mesharom did a very thorough job, but with something of this scale, you're still looking at fragments a hundred kilometers long."

"They're still doomed," Harriet pointed out. "Nothing out there has a vector that will escape the gas giant's gravity well. We're looking at what, ten years until it's all gone?"

"Less," her operations officer admitted. "Five to seven. Half that for the larger pieces. It looks like the Mesharom hit every potential defensive installation with antimatter warheads, then came in closer and blew out every single power core and life support facility they could detect."

Koanest snapped his beak shut hard and paused.

"Captain?" she asked calmly.

"Anyone who survived the initial radiation pulses from the antimatter warheads suffocated within a few weeks," he concluded, his voice shaky even through the translator. "Emergency bunkers or similar supplies might have bought them that long, but the Mesharom left no one here to evacuate them—and evacuating billions isn't an easy endeavor to begin with."

The inhabitants of the station hadn't just died. They'd died slowly and unpleasantly...and it was the doing of a species, of a *specific sentient*, Harriet had thought of as an ally.

"I think I might actually be glad we weren't with them," she said softly. "I don't think I could have stood by while this was done."

"If we were here, we would have had the troops to at least

consider trying to take control of the station," Koanest responded. "That was the *plan*, after all."

Harriet didn't have an invasion force to hand, but the Marine and Marine-equivalent detachments of three thousand–plus warships would have sufficed to secure power cores and life support facilities until one could be brought up.

The Imperium was certainly prepared for her to *need* an invasion force, but officially, the troops in question were engaging in exercises in Alpha Centauri. It was a lot easier to carry out field maneuvers simulating a full-scale planetary invasion when you had an entire planet to work with. Hope was in the sweet spot of populated enough to provide logistics and unpopulated enough to give them vast spaces to land troops.

Harriet wasn't actually sure how many troops were involved in those exercises, but she had been assured that if she needed an invasion force, she'd have it.

Unfortunately, it looked like the Mesharom might not have left her anything to invade.

EVEN THE BEST holographic conferencing software cried for mercy when it was instructed to set up a conference with over four thousand starship captains, their executive officers, and the division-, echelon-, squadron- and task force–level commanders of that fleet.

Only a handful of the ten thousand sentients on the conference were expected to say anything. One of that handful was Harriet Tanaka. She stood in the center of a real briefing room aboard *Ajax* and looked out at a sea of faces.

If she focused on any of them, the software would make them more visible. With only six sentients actually present in the *Ajax* briefing room, that was surprisingly handleable.

"All right, everyone," she greeted them. "Fleet Master Cawl and I are currently dealing with the headaches of joint command, and orders will get issued shortly, directing you where to go on at least a task-force level."

There were days she was convinced that the Imperium, at least, should have given up and carved Tenth Fleet into three distinct formations at the fleet level. Instead, she had eight task forces, each consisting of five squadrons of capital ships and a proportionate amount of her escort squadrons. Each of the Fleet Lords commanding a task force reported directly to her.

It was unwieldy, but it seemed to be working at least as well as whatever the Kanzi were doing instead.

"Before the fleet command gets down into the details, I wanted to make certain that *all* of us are on the same page as to where we are and what we have to achieve," she continued. "I'll leave some of the details we do have to Captain Koanest, but there's one key confirmation you all need:

"It was *definitely* the Mesharom that blew up the PG-Three ring world. We've analyzed a lot of the data we have, and there's no question. They were here ninety-two cycles ago." She shook her head. "At least that confirms that there isn't *another* mysterious alien hostile out here. As for where we go next, I'll pass that over to Captain Koanest."

The Yin seemed completely unbothered at being asked to brief ten thousand sentients. That definitely put her ahead of Harriet! Harriet could handle commanding a fleet in action, but looking out at that many faces staring back at her was...uncomfortable.

"Our core strategic problem at this point, officers, is that we don't have a map of Taljzi space," Koanest told them. "We have an extraordinarily powerful fleet but no enemy to fly out against.

"Our immediate objective, then, appears to be *locating* other Taljzi systems."

The holographic display behind the Yin lit up with the image of the fleeing remnants of the Taljzi fleet that had been poking around PG-Three.

"The most likely lead we are following is the route of the fleet that was present here when we arrived," she noted. "Two squadrons of Laian escort cruisers are pursuing that fleet in full stealth. We have not had any updates from them and likely won't until their quarry reaches their destination.

"Unfortunately for the likelihood of them leading us to mission-critical locations, we have established that there would have been no one left here for them to be evacuating," Koanest said. "They were searching for usable hardware and tech, not survivors."

That had been a relief to Harriet's conscience. In the heat of the moment and faced with armed combatants, no one had considered that the battleships might have been carrying civilian survivors. They *couldn't* consider that, not once the Taljzi started shooting, but the possibility had nagged at her afterward.

The holographic image shifted from the retreating Taljzi fleet to an image of a three-dimensional star map consisting of various spheres marked in different metals.

"Our second set of leads is the same one that led then-Admiral Sun of the Duchy of Terra Militia to PG-Three in the first place," Koanest told them. Octavius Sun was now Squadron Lord Sun of Harriet's Tenth Fleet. She'd intentionally poached most of the scout force that had been out there before.

"This map was discovered at the bottom of an archeological dig at an abandoned interim Taljzi colony. The Precursors appear to have used this as some kind of ceremonial place marker or local map."

The Yin shrugged.

"We don't know why the Precursors have this, to be honest," she admitted. "It was near the control center of a Precursor-built starcom, so it may have been a communications directory. At some point, it may even have had localized data tags included in the structure.

"All we can use from it, though, is the star map itself. Squadron Lord Sun's scouting flotilla scouted one copper-flagged system and one gold-flagged system. PC-One was a graveyard, the home of a sentient species with a limited space capability when the Taljzi arrived."

Koanest paused, presumably to let his audience remember that the Taljzi were still some of the worst mass murderers known to anyone in the room.

"We are in PG-Three: Precursor Gold Three. Ten stars in the map are marked with copper, and we are presuming all held sentient species at the time of the Precursor's presence in this area."

Given what the Imperium and humanity knew of the Precursors —that they had consisted of a single master race and several second-tier, not-quite-slave races like the Mesharom...well, those ten systems had probably been lucky they hadn't been advanced enough to be of use to the Precursors.

"Based off what we found here, we have reason to believe the other four gold-flagged systems represent the location of similar Precursor facilities or colonies. Logically, one of these systems should contain the cloning facility the Taljzi are using."

"So, we're scouting those systems?" someone asked. The conferencing software told Harriet it was one of her Echelon Lords.

"I believe that's part of the plan, yes," Koanest replied. "Our greatest chance of certainty, however, is here."

The hologram shifted to the gas giant they were all orbiting and the shattered ring stations.

"We have cataloged two hundred and eleven fragments exceeding one cubic kilometer in size so far," the Yin told them all. "Without knowing anything about how the Taljzi were using the station, we have no real way of prioritizing any particular fragment.

"However, we *do* know that this station was a key component of their military infrastructure and was used as a staging point for their assault on our space. There had to have been thousands—*millions*—of maps of their territory on that station.

"Searching the station appears to be the only option that has a chance of getting us a full view of our enemy," Koanest concluded.

Harriet stood again as several dozen people tried to raise questions and arguments, gesturing the Yin to a seat and sharing an amused smile with Fleet Master Cawl.

"Captain Koanest has laid out our options quite handily," she said firmly. "We have three. We also have over four thousand warships and hundreds upon hundreds of transports and tankers.

"We're going to do all three," she stated. "A force will be assembled to follow in the direction that the fleet here retreated. They won't be perfectly positioned once our scouts find the enemy destination, but they will be closer than if they stayed here.

"Other forces will scout the periphery of the other gold systems in the Precursor map. The majority of the fleet will remain in PG-Three and engage in a detailed sweep of the ring world's wreckage.

"Hopefully, all of these operations will bear fruit," Harriet said. "Multiple sources of information to compare to each other will tell us more than a single source of data in isolation. It may be true that there is only one core world for the Taljzi and we just need to find it... but I don't expect our lives to be made that easy!

"As we noted at the beginning, Fleet Master Cawl and I will need to sit down and sort out some details before anyone gets distinct orders. That is our basic plan, though: we're going to chase *every* lead and see where we meet up in the end."

And if Harriet Tanaka and her people were *very* lucky, they'd all meet up in the same place and find the cloning presses.

IT WAS A VASTLY SMALLER gathering that Harriet met with an hour later. This time, she and Koanest were in her office, facing holographic images of their counterparts in the Kanzi and Laian fleets.

She had a pot of green tea steaming on her desk, and both she and the Yin held cups. Harriet had apparently been a good influence on the much younger, blue-feathered alien.

"Three different tasks," Cawl stated once they were all linked together. "It's quite the plan."

"We already discussed this," Harriet pointed out. "And my response is still what it was then: forty-three hundred warships."

The old Kanzi made a throwaway gesture.

"And I agree now, as I did then. It's still ambitious and putting a lot of weight on our junior flag officers."

Harriet snorted.

"I don't know about you, Shairon, but I have officers who are qualified to command entire fleets and are doing basically that, only we're calling the fleets 'task forces.'"

Cawl gave a purring chuckle in response to that.

"I am in much the same state, I suppose," he conceded. "My concerns are less around competence and more around..." He shrugged.

"Trustworthiness." The word hung in the air after Guard Keeper Anson Karal spoke. Cawl's aide was roughly equivalent to a Terran Commodore or Imperial Division Lord. He was also a not-particularly-distant relation of the Kanzi High Priestess—a second cousin or something similar, Harriet believed.

"The internal politics of our fleet are mostly irrelevant," Karal continued after a few moments of silence. "But they do impede our ability to trust a significant portion of our flag officers in independent commands."

Cawl winced, leaning back in his chair and clenching his cane fiercely.

"I wouldn't have phrased it *quite* so bluntly," he said delicately. "But the Guard Keeper's familial connections have some value in shielding him from politics."

"Fleet Master, you are a *Companion of the Divine Chosen*," Karal pointed out. "You are as much under Her Holiness's protection as I am."

"In either case, he's right," Cawl admitted. "I am only *certain* of the trustworthiness of a disturbingly small portion of my Fleet Keepers and Fleet Masters."

His Squadron and Fleet Lords, in Imperial parlance.

"We don't need that many independent commands," Kanmorad interjected. "Keep your enemies close, Fleet Master. The Republic has learned *that* lesson."

He chuckled.

"Otherwise, we end up with the children of our former enemies in the fleets of our new allies."

Harriet mostly ignored that. There was a grand total of *seven* Laians in her fleet, volunteers out of the enclave of Laian Exiles living on Earth. Their existence was now formally accepted by the Republic, not least because they were now subjects of the A!Tol Imperium and didn't claim to be the heirs of the Ascendancy.

"I see us needing four detachments," Harriet told the other fleet commanders. "One to follow Kanmorad's escort cruisers, three to investigate the gold and silver systems from the Precursor map. Each scout force is to search two systems. The astrography works well for that. Koanest?"

Her ops officer brought up a holographic star map. Their own location at PG-Three was a blinking green icon, but gold and silver icons marked the other locations from the Precursor map.

"We can send a task force here that will investigate PG-One, then PG-Five," Koanest explained, drawing a green line on the map. "Another one here can hit PG-Two then PS-One, then the last will hit PS-Two and PG-Four."

Three green lines now marked the map.

"This," an orange line appeared, "is the course that the Taljzi fleet from here retreated along. As you can see, it doesn't directly cross any of the gold or silver systems."

All six of them studied the orange line in silence for a moment.

"It comes close to that system," Kanmorad pointed out, a long finger indicating one of the copper icons. "That's...PC-Three?"

"We haven't investigated that system yet, but it is a potential destination," Harriet agreed. "My suggestion is that we detach another heavy Joint Task Force, this one under Kanzi command, to PC-Three.

"We'll relay any reports we receive from the escort cruisers to the starcom at Sol," she continued. "That way, they can redirect to a different destination if needed. Their updates will be thirty-plus hours out of date, but that's not that bad, all things considered."

"You're volunteering to put ships under Kanzi command?" Cawl asked with that purring chuckle. "I was going to insist and expected to have an argument."

"We agreed to rotate command," Harriet replied. "It makes sense to put the subordinate forces through a similar logic. Do you have an officer you'd suggest?"

"Fleet Master Odel Rist," Cawl replied instantly. "If nothing else, the man is courting my eldest daughter. If I can't trust a flag officer brave enough to take to the savannah in chase of one of the more famously Reformist senior priestesses...well, I have other reasons to trust him as well."

"I'll put up Fleet Lord Nobo," Harriet told them. "They're my most junior task force commander, with five squadrons of battleships, two of them *Bellerophons*."

"A Pibo, I presume?" Cawl asked. "Rist has worked with several Pibo in the past. He'll be fine. What about the scout task forces?"

"I was thinking smaller forces, two of my squadrons or three of yours," Harriet said. "Their purpose isn't to get into a fight, after all, but since we *have* battle squadrons to send..."

"We have no reason to hold them back. I suggest one squadron of each of ours," Cawl replied. "That would give us twenty-six ships, more than sufficient to deal with any incidental Taljzi forces but small enough to easily escape any major forces."

"And if pursued, they must lead them here," Kanmorad said firmly.

"I agree, with one addition," Harriet said slowly. "I want to attach one of my *Galileo*s and, if Pincer Kanmorad agrees, one of his war-dreadnoughts to each of the scouting fleets. Those ships punch well outside their weight and draw a lot of attention."

"The purpose of a war-dreadnought is to *do*, not wait," the Pincer of the Republic replied placidly. "My ships will accompany these task forces."

CHAPTER TWENTY-TWO

"CAPTAIN TAN!STALLA. COMMANDER CASIMIR, REPORTING AS ordered."

Morgan was stepping inside the Captain's office as she spoke, the door sliding automatically shut behind her. Tan!Stalla gestured her to a seat and slid a tray of coffee and fixings over to her.

Taking the carafe from the tray, Morgan poured herself a black coffee and ignored the other contents of the tray in their little refrigerated box.

"I did. I just got our new orders for *Jean Villeneuve*'s place in the grand plan," the A!Tol told her. "We'll go over it all with the rest of the staff later this morning, but I wanted to fill you in immediately."

"Of course. What are we doing?"

"The Fleet Lord appears to have decided that the *Galileo*s make the perfect stiffening for lighter forces," Tan!Stalla told her. "JTF Twenty-One has been dissolved—it was only ever intended to be a temporary formation—and it looks like we're putting together four new Joint Task Forces.

"Joint Task Force Twenty-Two will be going after the fleet we kicked the crap out of. Similar strength to Twenty-One but with a heavier focus on Kanzi and Laians. The other three are lighter forces, which is going to leave you with a sense of old waters."

That metaphor went right over Morgan's head and she blinked.

"Sir? I don't follow."

"We're being assigned to Joint Task Force Twenty-Five, under Squadron Lord Octavius Sun," Tan!Stalla told her. "So, you are once again, Commander Casimir, aboard a capital ship looking for the Taljzi under Lord Sun's command."

Déjà vu. That was apparently what *old waters* meant.

"I see your point, sir," Morgan agreed. "I can't say it ended all that well last time, though we definitely *found* them."

And led them home. And triggered the largest space battle in the history of the A!Tol Imperium, a battle the Imperium had won only by the skin of their teeth and several unexpected and expected allies.

"From the copy I received of Squadron Lord Sun's orders, that whole sequence of events was very much in Fleet Lord Tanaka's mind when she wrote them," Tan!Stalla noted. "If we encounter major Taljzi forces, we are to fire hyperspace missiles at them from long range and lure them back to PG-Three."

"Poke them with a stick and see if they'll follow us into a trap of our own," Morgan translated.

"Yes. Our objective is to find their bases and potentially their home systems. We know *they* were following the same Precursor map we were when they came out here, so the hope is that their core world or worlds are among the gold-flagged stars."

"Do we know our particular destinations yet?" she asked.

"There'll be an all-hands briefing for the Captains and XOs in six hours," Tan!Stalla told her. "Somewhat smaller than the one for the entire Allied Fleet, thankfully. Squadron Lord Sun will command the task force, and we're bringing his squadron of *Bellerophon*-Bs, but we're also bringing Fleet Keeper Reesi Tone and her squadron of Kanzi superbattleships, and Six Hundred and Fifth Sword of the

Republic Mordak's war-dreadnought. Plus escorts from all three fleets."

A small task force by the standards of Tenth Fleet and their allies, but still twenty-eight capital ships. Morgan brought up the numbers on the hologram between them with a tapped command and nodded.

They were getting a squadron of escort cruisers from the Laians and then two squadrons of Imperial cruisers, plus two squadrons of Kanzi cruisers and a squadron of Kanzi destroyers.

Seventy-two escorts—and all of the Imperial cruisers were *Thunderstorm*-Ds with full modern arsenals. Refitted ships would only really lack the plasma lances, but there was an efficiency to ships built for a weapons loadout that no refit could ever match.

"Not shabby for a scout force," she noted. "We had a *lot* fewer ships when we poked the hornet's nest the first time."

"Agreed. As for our destinations, we're hitting Silver Two then Gold Four. We're not sure what the silver systems hold, and we'll hit Silver Two before JTF Twenty-Four hits Silver One."

"We get to find out what horrors the Precursors left behind this time," Morgan agreed. "Lucky us."

"Most of what I've seen of theirs I'd call wonders, not horrors," Tan!Stalla pointed out. "Even here, the horror was more what the Taljzi did with the place."

The younger First Sword snorted.

"Wonder and horror are two sides of the same coin, sir, and with Precursor artifacts...well, you flip the coin every time you find one. There's one thing I *am* certain of, and it makes the nature of the Taljzi cloning press truly terrifying for me."

"And what is that, Commander Casimir?" her Captain asked.

"I've spoken to and worked with a lot more Mesharom than anyone else in the Imperium," Morgan reminded Tan!Stalla, "and they made one thing very clear: Precursor technology doesn't work anymore. They were never clear why, but they were very sure of it. Nothing the Precursors built works the way it was designed to.

"So, anything that still functions is doing something *very* different than the Precursors meant for it to do."

"Ah." Tan!Stalla studied the hologram for a few seconds as a layer of concern drifted into her skin. "I think I begin to see what you mean by *horror*, Commander."

EVEN THE RELATIVELY "SMALL" Joint Task Force Twenty-Five still had over two hundred sentients in the Captains and XOs conference. Morgan and Tan!Stalla were detached from most of the groupings, too, as *Jean Villeneuve* was assigned directly to Squadron Lord Sun instead of being part of one of the squadrons.

"All right. That's the basic plan," Sun concluded, having just laid out the plan that Tan!Stalla and Morgan had discussed earlier that day. "You all knew that eight hours ago. You've had time to mull it over and think about it.

"Now is your chance to ask questions."

Sun, Morgan noted, hadn't made the transition from using Terran time units to using Imperial ones. The translator could handle it, though, and with half of the JTF being non-Imperials, they couldn't avoid the usual slight confusion of hearing "three point four tenth-cycles" as they could have in an Imperial force.

Everyone was getting a weird set of numbers for the time units. Using tenth-cycles or twentieth-cycles might have made it easier for the Imperials to understand—that was why the Imperial Navy insisted on its officers learning to *think* in Imperial time—but it wouldn't help the Kanzi or the Laians.

"Why are we going to the Silver system first?" one of the Kanzi escort squadron commanders—a Guard Master—asked. "Surely, the Gold system is more likely to be our actual target."

"Two reasons," Sun replied, holding up fingers as he spoke. "One, PS-Two is functionally on the way to PG-Four. Going via PS-Two only adds an average of thirty-six hours to our flight time to PG-Four, ignoring whatever time we spend in PS-Two.

"Two, we really don't *know* which system is more likely to have a major Taljzi presence," Sun reminded them. "We know PG-Three was a major Precursor installation and we're assuming that's what the gold icons mean, but we are *assuming*."

And assuming makes an ass out of you and Ming…and Ming the Merciless does not like to be made an ass of.

Elon Casimir's joke had only made so much sense to Morgan, even after she'd looked up who the fictional alien overlord was. It still covered the dangers of assumptions, though.

"Regardless of what the gold icons stand for, however, we also don't have any idea what the silver icons mean," Sun continued. "Our best guess is that they are for systems like the one we found the map in, secondary installations at least equipped with a starcom, but we don't *know* anything.

"So, we're hitting all of our bases and we're tagging PS-Two on our way. Does that answer your question, Guard Master?"

The Kanzi officer nodded his understanding.

"Do we know what kind of forces we're expecting to collide with?" one of the *Bellerophon*-B commanders, Captain Loto Ondi, asked once the silence made it clear that question was resolved. He was a big Tosumi officer with deep purple plumage wrapped around his four arms, leaning forward as he studied the map.

"Our understanding is that the Taljzi mostly use Kanzi-style deployments but are operating with a far higher industrial density than the Theocracy," Sun replied. "We expect to see anything of value guarded by at least a ten-ship squadron of capital ships and two or three times that in escorts.

"If we encounter a force of that scale, we are to engage and destroy. Any force comparable or superior to our own, we are expected to lure back to PG-Three to be engaged by the main fleet."

"So, we're shark bait?" Ondi asked.

Morgan snorted. The exact term Ondi used was A!Tol, referring to a long-extinct major sea predator that had harassed their early settlements. Like the other Imperial Races, though, the metaphors and culture of the Tosumi were mostly long lost.

"If we're shark bait, we're shark bait with *very* big guns," Sun replied with a cold smile. "It will be a big shark to threaten us, but if we do run into a shark that big...well, we have a bigger boat waiting back home."

CHAPTER TWENTY-THREE

HARRIET WATCHED FROM HER FLAG DECK AS THE TASK FORCES set out. Her hands were behind her back and she was softly humming to herself as she did the math.

Four task forces of twenty-eight capital ships apiece and one heavy task force of twenty Kanzi squadrons and ten Imperial, another two hundred and sixty ships.

She'd detached four *fleets* she was calling task forces, but the force still under her and Cawl's joint command still numbered over a thousand capital ships and three thousand warships overall.

She stayed there in quiet contemplation as the task forces opened their portals and vanished into hyperspace. It would be days now before Tenth Fleet and the Gloried Armada heard from any of the forces they'd sent out.

Her focus now should be the wreckage of the ring world around the gas giant, but she stayed there, watching where the hyper portals had been for several long minutes before Koanest, as usual, appeared from nowhere at her left elbow.

"The landing forces are going in," Koanest told her. "Superbattleships for cover." She shook her head. "Half ours, half Kanzi. Do we trust them to tell us everything?"

"I trust Cawl to tell us everything he learns," Harriet replied. She turned her attention to the gas giant and its once-immense ring. Seventy green groups, each consisting of a single superbattleship and a squadron of cruisers—each carrying three-quarters of the Marines from four other ships—descending toward the debris field.

Another seventy groups were marked in blue. Each of those was two battleships and a ten-ship Kanzi squadron of cruisers. Like hers, those ships carried troops pulled from other ships to assemble real landing forces.

"Do you expect Cawl's people to lie to him?" Koanest finally asked. It was the question her comment invited, and Harriet considered the answer carefully.

"Yes," she admitted. "Not all of them. Not even most of them, by any stretch. But the loyalties of the Gloried Armada are far more divided than the loyalties of Tenth Fleet. I don't necessarily trust *our* people not to take the opportunity to bag themselves an 'accidental' dead smurf or six—that's why each of us has our own list of targets—but I trust them to have the same orders and objectives as I do.

"With Kanzi politics as they are..." Harriet shivered. "From what Bond told me, Cawl has *tried* to remain as above the fray as he could while still being the kind of political animal that gets major fleet commands.

"He's associated with, not *part* of, the major reformist faction. Right now, the High Priestess and her loyalists have a tentative truce, if not necessarily an alliance, with the reformers. Which, of course, means that their own traditionalists are in a quiet uproar and the anti-A!Tol militarists are furious."

The Fleet Lord shook her head.

"Any of those groups, *including* the reformers, will have agents and adherents among his officers whose loyalties are to those groups above their orders or their chain of command. I'm not going to pretend we *don't* have that," Harriet admitted. If nothing else, the

Duchy of Terra had spread its economic and political tentacles widely through the Imperium. Humanity might have knelt to the A!Tol, but they were damned well going to have their say in which way the Imperium jumped.

They were more successful at it than some, but all of the Imperium's twenty-eight races were doing much the same. The Imperium was a constant multi-way tug-of-war with the Empress as the referee.

"I trust our factions not to undermine the chain of command in the field," Koanest pointed out.

"The very *nature* of the Taljzi themselves, plus the alliance with us, drags a lot of those factions right into Cawl's orders and mission," Harriet replied. On the hologram, the first of the landing groups was launching shuttles.

It was petty, but she was still pleased to see it was one of hers.

"He's aware of the problem; we know that. But *we* need to be aware of it as well."

She shook her head, her thoughts only half on the display showing the better part of a million soldiers launching a hundred and forty assault landings.

"Because the first people a bunch of those factions are going to stab in the back are us."

NONE of the landings moved particularly quickly. The wreckage they were boarding had no atmosphere, no artificial gravity, nothing.

The Mesharom had destroyed anything that looked like a weapon or a power source, which left the Allied Fleet guessing where the best place was to land. The solution, as most of the solutions had been for this operation, had been the use of massive numbers to deal with them in parallel.

"Anything particularly interesting come up yet?" Harriet asked Koanest two hours later. "I'm going to head back to my office and start digging through the paperwork involved in being in charge of a fleet of three million people."

"Nothing mission-critical, not in two hours," the Yin replied. "Some fascinating stuff. A good third of the chunks we boarded never had artificial gravity by any means we can detect."

"Did the place used to spin?" Harriet asked, a momentary vision of a centrifuge with a forty-thousand-kilometer radius.

"Not so far as we can tell, but it looks like the Taljzi installed their own artificial gravity plating," Koanest told her. "In fact, it looks like there's a lot of...well, new installations. I'm not sure the Taljzi found anything truly functional here."

"That would fit with the state of the Precursor ship on Hope," Harriet pointed out. "Nothing in the ship was really functional. Rolfson found a barely functioning power source, and the doors were working. That was it, though it wasn't like we had a lot of time with the ship before we gave it to the Mesharom."

"Sold it to the Mesharom," Koanest corrected her. "Best kind of deal, too, from what I can tell. Everyone thought they got the better end."

Harriet chuckled.

"Rolfson said it was like a bunch of the stuff should never have worked," she echoed the Militia officer. Harold Rolfson had been in the heart of the Alpha Centauri Incident and the initial contact with the Taljzi. She'd *tried* to poach him, but he'd been given the Duchy's squadron of *Vindication*-class battleships in the wake of Vice Admiral Tidikat's death.

Plus, his wife was in Sol. She hadn't tried that hard in the end, especially once she'd heard that Ramona Wolastoq was pregnant.

"That's some of what we're seeing reported," Koanest confirmed. "It looks like most of what was functioning was the Taljzi's installation. They had a lot of space to work with, but they might have only been using the place for just that: space."

"Let's not assume that just yet," Harriet instructed. "The Taljzi appear to have access to Precursor tech to one degree or another—or do you want to think it's coincidence that the only *other* people with molecular disruptors are the Mesharom? Who *also* have access to Precursor artifacts?"

"I doubt it," she agreed. "I'll be intrigued to see if we have any large-enough intact Precursor systems to make that judgment call, though."

―――――

IT TURNED out that they did, and it was as much of a big, inexplicable machine as Harriet had expected it to be.

It was the next morning before the Marines felt they'd surveyed the device enough to call it all the way up the chain to her, but that meant that they actually had *some* idea of what they were talking about.

"We brought several engineers over from *Exoneration*," the human Battalion Commander explained once they had Harriet on the line. On a human ship, he'd have been a Major or possibly a Colonel, the commanding officer of the five hundred Marines aboard the *Vindication*-class superbattleship.

With the reinforcements from other ships, his five hundred men had become five thousand, and he'd used them to get a feel for the structure his fragment had contained.

"The machine filled the full height of the ring station," Battalion Commander Andikan Mbala continued. "Our best guess is that it's about two point five kilometers across. Roughly circular, with accessways all through it for drones and people."

"Were the Taljzi using it?" Harriet asked.

"No, they'd sealed it off," Mbala reported. "Not with any great effort; we're talking the equivalent of a sheet of drywall with a warning sign painted on it. No details on the warning, if you were wondering."

That had been Harriet's next question, so she gestured for the Marine to continue.

"The engineers aren't *entirely* sure, but they think this might have been some kind of cloudscoop," the Marine continued. "We know from Squadron Lord Sun's mission here that the Taljzi had attached several of what we'd call traditional cloudscoops to the structure, drawing hydrogen up from the gas giant."

"And this did the same thing for the Precursors?" Harriet asked. "Giant tubes are pretty distinctive, Battalion Commander."

"If the engineers are right—and they're hedging their bets with a couple of pages of technobabble and weasel words—this was a gas scoop based on energy screens," the Marine told her. "I know our shields couldn't do this, but that's what Commander Pilo thinks we're looking at."

"Our shields can't do that," Harriet confirmed. Commander Pilo —a female Pibo officer from *Exoneration*'s mixed-race crew—would know that as well as she did.

The shielding technology that every known galactic civilization used required a complete bubble around a central projector. Humanity had stolen the technology from the A!Tol, who'd stolen it from the Kanzi, which was pretty standard for how it had spread, from what Harriet could tell. The shields were ubiquitous and their limits were well known.

"I think that's why the Commander has so many weasel words in her report," Mbala replied with a grin, his teeth brilliantly white against his pitch-black skin. "But if she's right, they had something *similar* to but very clearly different that allowed them to open a channel of projected force screens right down into the planet and pull the gasses up. They got filtered up here, and the unneeded gasses were pumped right back down."

"That's damn impressive," Harriet murmured.

"Of course, Commander Pilo doesn't think it would have worked," the Marine offered. "Not just because of the shields. She said something about 'power conduits without actual conductors in them,' I think?"

That sent a chill down Harriet's spine.

"I think the team on Centauri said something similar," she told Mbala. "A bunch of the systems on that ship looked like they should never have so much as conducted electricity, let alone *worked*."

"That's what we're seeing, Fleet Lord," he agreed. "It's damned weird." He paused, as if swallowing a thought.

"Commander?" she asked sharply.

"I don't think it was a surprise to the Taljzi," Mbala told her. "They blocked off this entire structure, a piece of technology that could have made activating this place a few hundred times easier, and just...left it. They treated it like mildly dangerous garbage."

Harriet nodded slowly.

"That fits, Battalion Commander. I'm not sure what the pattern is yet...but that fits it."

CHAPTER TWENTY-FOUR

THE PATTERN OF THE TALJZI NOT EVEN TRYING TO USE THE Precursor systems was pervasive. As the troops swarmed through the wreckage of the station, they found it again and again. What systems were still in use versus abandoned was almost random.

"My guess is that we're looking at the systems that worked when the Taljzi powered them up versus the ones that didn't," *Ajax*'s chief engineer told Harriet after the Marines had spent a full day digging through the structures. The sentient was a Frole, a sentient fungus whose translator was working with some very *odd* signals to human ears. And noses.

Right now, Commander Kiffit was sharing a briefing room with Harriet and Koanest as they tried to make sense of what they were looking at.

They'd cleared many of the smaller fragments, but they'd barely scratched the surface of some of the bigger pieces. There were chunks of station out there that were the full hundred kilometers high and two kilometers thick, after all, and they weren't searching those in a day.

"The Taljzi knew how to power them up?" Harriet asked.

"Pretty clearly," the engineer replied. A pseudopod manipulated the hologram in the briefing room, bringing up a chunk of wall that the Marines had opened up with force-blades.

"This is a good example of what we're seeing," they continued. "At the top, you're looking at what we'd call a standard power conduit. Old Kanzi design, updated a bit but still recognizable. Fiber optics and high-capacity gold and copper cabling contained in a safety shell.

"Here"—a chunk of the image flashed—"you see a set of cabling come out of the conduit and go through this device before hooking into the Precursor systems here."

"They had an adaptor?" Koanest asked.

"Exactly. This was the power system for the active microbot walls and doors, based on a copper alloy. Low conductivity but still functional, which is what we're seeing in all still-functional Precursor systems. Linking power into it, they got the microbot chargers working.

"But *here*"—Kiffit highlighted a different section—"we see more Taljzi conduits—and a clear gap where Precursor systems were removed to install them. We've seen more and more of this as we dig through the station.

"The Taljzi know exactly how to power up Precursor technology, but they are clearly operating on the assumption that a significant chunk of it just won't work. So, they try and then they either remove or section off the systems that don't work."

"So...whatever this station was originally built for, the Taljzi weren't using it for that?" Harriet asked.

"I can't say and I don't think we're going to be able to," Kiffit replied. "Given the amount of raw hydrogen the one cloudscoop we examined could have pulled out of the gas giant, the station either was purely a power facility or *required* vast amounts of power.

"If we had an intact Taljzi shipyard, I suspect we'd be able to tell whether they were using Precursor systems. If there was any system in there that I would have expected them to make sure was functional if they could, it would have been any Precursor industrial modules or shipyard sections."

"Both of which the Mesharom would have almost certainly destroyed," Harriet concluded. "If nothing else, Tilsan knew we'd be following them, and *they* were going to make sure we couldn't retrieve any of this for study."

"It seems likely," Kiffit agreed. "There are still pieces of this I expect we could learn a great deal from. As with the other Gold Dragon systems, though, I suspect we would be duplicating concepts rather than reverse-engineering systems outright."

"Make sure anything we could use for that is flagged for towing into stable orbit," Harriet ordered. "We'll have to negotiate with the Kanzi for where it ends up, but we don't want it to fall into the gas giant before we can do that."

"I will make sure to inform the teams catalog—"

Alerts went off on all three of their communicators simultaneously, and Harriet grabbed hers to open a channel.

"Fleet Lord Tanaka here," she snapped, flicking the call onto the hologram in the middle of the room. She vaguely recognized the A!Tol as one of her Brigade Commanders, the handful of more senior Marine officers assigned to her fleet on the realization that she was carrying over half a million Marines and might want to use them in larger forces.

"Fleet Lord, we found it."

"Found what, Brigade Commander !Loka?" Harriet asked.

"The Precursor map."

THE RECORDED helmet footage showed the Marines, all Rekiki in this case, sweeping through a heavily decorated portion of the station. Statues and murals, familiar from the other Taljzi facilities the Imperium had seized by now, lined the walls.

Some of the murals were the same constellations that had been found in the DLK-5539 depot that had sent them on their search into Taljzi space. Others were of people and gods, familiar Kanzi myths—though often with bloodier twists than the usual Kanzi versions Harriet knew.

The corridor ended in one of the weird nanobot doors the Precursors had favored. By now, over a day into the search of the station, the Marines clearly had opening those down to a science. Two of the power-armored Rekiki stepped up to flank the door and made careful cuts through the walls to find the power cables.

Linking their own systems in, they charged up the door, then removed the cables. One of them rapped the center of the door, activating its systems.

Not only did the door ripple open, vanishing into the walls around it like it had never existed, the cuts the Marines had made in the walls healed as well. The Marines remained outside of the door, running a scanner over the wall.

"Power discharged, everything should be safe," the Rekiki reported. From their size, they were a Vassal-caste Rekiki, the smaller members of the race that both culturally and biologically tended to attach themselves to the larger Noble caste.

Pheromones were bad enough, but culture tended to double down on them in Harriet's experience.

"Move forward," the squad leader—the Marine whose helmet Harriet was watching footage from—ordered.

The Marines moved forward in pairs, sweeping into the room on the other side.

"Sir...I think we need more lights." The smaller infrared lights mounted on the Marines' helmets were highlighting objects in the air. Harriet had seen a *lot* of footage of the submerged map they'd found at the abandoned Precursor starcom and recognized the objects instantly.

"Send them up," the senior Marine ordered.

Moments later, half a dozen drones took off, stabilizing themselves in the lack of air and gravity and turning on their lights to high-light the entire room.

It was centered differently from the first map they had, but the design was the same. Small models hung from the ceiling on stiff wires, suspended against a gravity that was no longer there. An eyeball estimate put it at several thousand stars, so the map was bigger than the first one, too.

"Well done, team," the squad leader said. "Get the drones taking footage. This is *exactly* the kind of lucky feedstock we were hoping to find!"

Harriet paused the recording and looked at Koanest.

"Get me the three-dimensional model the drones will have made," she ordered. "That map looks bigger than the other one, so we'll want to update it for stellar drift and locate the systems we already know about.

"Once that's done, set up a conference with Cawl and Kanmorad. It looks like we have work to do still."

THE HOLOGRAPHIC MAP spun in the middle of the room as the three fleet commanders and their aides studied it.

"The map from the starcom had just over a thousand stars marked on it," Koanest noted. "This one has two thousand seven hundred and eighty. It's centered on this system and covers most of the stars in the first map we had.

"Stellar-drift calculations suggest that both maps are frozen at the same point in time." The Yin paused to let that sink in. "In fact, our best guess now is that they were being actively updated until the systems failed, and whatever caused the system to fail was *simulta-neous* across an approximately twenty-six light-year distance."

That was...not good.

"Do we have a time frame?" Harriet asked.

"We're narrowing it down," her operations officer replied. "Right now, we have it nailed to within a thousand long-cycles: a hundred and twelve thousand long-cycles to be exact, plus or minus five hundred."

Fifty-nine thousand and seven hundred years, plus or minus about two hundred and fifty. That fit with the roughly sixty-thousand-year timeline the Mesharom gave for the fall of the Precursors.

"How close can we narrow it?" Kanmorad asked. "An exact timeline of the Precursor's collapse would be...interesting."

"If we get a third one of these maps, we can probably narrow it down to within ten or fifteen long-cycles. A fourth...potentially down to the twenty-cycle or even the *cycle*, depending on how separate the maps are in distance."

"Could it have been that simultaneous?" Cawl asked. "Their entire empire collapsing in a single nightfall?"

"We would not be calculating the moment the Precursor empire fell," Harriet pointed out. "We would be calculating the moment all of their technology stopped working." She shivered.

"The ship we found on Hope had partially intact bodies," she noted. That was classified—most of what the Imperium knew about the Precursor courier they'd found on Hope was—but it seemed relevant. "They had implants in their brains...implants based on the same technology that we see here. Technology that should never have worked."

"And when those implants failed, they died," Kanmorad concluded heavily. "We have had similar discoveries, though the Mesharom took most of our notes and records each time—as they did with you."

"As you said about the cloudscoop, Fleet Lord, there is a pattern here," Cawl noted. "I don't see it all, but I don't like what I see."

"Neither do I," Harriet agreed. "For the moment, however, this map. Koanest, what does it show us?"

"Like the first map, most of the stars are marked in plain steel," the Yin told them. "We presume those are stars of no immediate interest to the Precursors. We overlap with all of the gold, silver and copper systems from the previous map except for PG-Three itself. That is now the central point of the map and, like the starcom system, is actually missing from the structure.

"We have identified one of the new silver systems, designated PS-Three, as the system we found the original map in. We can also confirm that there are no other silver or gold systems closer to our own territory than that one. This appears to have been an isolated province, well away from their main territory."

"I'm guessing there are more systems out here, though?" Harriet asked. "I don't suppose any systems flagged differently in the two maps?"

"Yes and no," Koanest replied. "There are two new copper systems relatively close to Kanzi territory that aren't on the original map, but otherwise, everything new is further Rimward. All of the flagged systems are labeled the same in both cases."

"What are our new possibilities?" Cawl said.

"There are another fourteen copper systems," the Yin reported. "Unfortunately, the track record suggests that the Taljzi located and exterminated the original populations in those systems. Scouting them with light forces to be certain could be useful, but we *also* have six new silver systems and three gold ones."

He highlighted them on the map.

"How close are the new systems to the routes of the task forces we already sent out?" Harriet asked.

"Some of them are close," Koanest said after a moment. Three green lines appeared on the map. "We can add PG-Six and -Eight to the routes for JTF Twenty-Three and Twenty-Four, respectively. Both of those can pick up a silver system as well, and Twenty-Five can hit two silver systems if they proceed past their gold target."

"That still leaves us with a gold system and two silvers that are well outside the area we were sending scout missions to," Harriet noted, reaching over to flag the three systems. They were the farthest out of the systems the Precursors had flagged, and the space beyond them was plain steel stars.

"We always knew this was a fringe area for the Precursors," Cawl noted. "It appears we may have reached the limits of even their empire. I suggest we assemble a fourth scouting task force and send it to those systems."

"They'll arrive at their first destination after most of the rest of the scouting is done," Koanest noted.

"If we feel we can't engage whatever we found without those squadrons, we can hold position for them to return," Harrict suggested. "I'd rather send out scouts and learn what we can. We need to know where the Taljzi bases and homeworlds are, and the Precursor bases are our best starting point."

"Agreed," Cawl said. "Though, I am left with one question that I do not like."

"And that is, Fleet Master?" Kanmorad asked.

"The Mesharom don't appear to have surveyed the wreckage at all, so they didn't have this map," the Kanzi said. "They had the previous map, but they had no more information on what that meant than we did.

"So the question I find myself asking, Pincer, Fleet Lord...is where did Grand Commander Tilsan go from here?"

CHAPTER TWENTY-FIVE

"SCANNING FOR HOSTILES."

Nidei's words were a bland announcement, but they were also a reminder that no one in JTF 25 had a clue what to expect in PS-Two. Imperial battleships were spreading out from the hyper portal in a glittering flower of steel and technology.

At the heart of that flower were the squadron of Kanzi superbattleships, a Laian war-dreadnought, and *Jean Villeneuve*. The twelve massive capital ships edged slowly toward the central star at a "mere" ten percent of lightspeed while the battleships and cruisers stretched out to get a better eyeball on the system.

It was a trinary system, with a large yellow F-sequence star playing anchor to a near-partner in a small G-sequence star and a clear child in an M-sequence red dwarf. Fourteen planets, only two of them gas giants, and several large, oddly shaped asteroid belts, filled the system.

"None of the planets are registering as habitable," Morgan reported. "Are we seeing *anything* here, Nidei?"

"Not yet," the Ivida replied. "No active interface-drive fields, no detectable power sources. Not seeing much of anything, sir."

Morgan nodded, turning her attention back to the display. No habitable planets. No liquid water anywhere in the star system—too many stars with odd orbits. One of the planets *might* hit a liquid-water range for part of its orbit...but it looked like that was for about five months of a forty-six-month year.

"See anything that looks familiar?" Tan!Stalla asked her. "As I recall, the first Precursor system we found also looked pretty dead."

"It at least had liquid water somewhere," she replied. "I'm seeing one place with a partial liquid-water cycle. We'll want to throw some drones at it."

"Squadron Lord Sun agrees," the A!Tol Captain replied. "*Horatio* is redirecting their drones to check out the planet."

Tan!Stalla shivered her tentacles in a shrug.

"I'm glad to see a lack of enemies," she admitted. "But we were hoping for some answers. It looks like this system is a dead end."

"That's why we're checking out two," Morgan said. "We knew the silver systems were a low-chance target, but we didn't know what the Precursors were flagging as silver."

She gestured at the hologram.

"I'm guessing 'astronomically interesting but worthless,'" she replied. "None of the planets or rocks we're scanning are even showing up with easily extractable minerals of value. Nothing worth hauling even an automated mining ship out here for unless you're *very* near."

It might have been worth it to send some mining ships there to feed *whatever* they'd been doing at PG-Three, but it didn't look like there'd been a permanent-enough presence for anything to survive.

THE MAIN FORCE came to a delicate halt still well clear of the conflicting gravity wells of the trinary system. Cruisers and destroyers dove deeper in, shepherding fleets of drones until they stopped and came back.

Even from the initial impression, Morgan wasn't surprised by Squadron Lord Sun's orders. There was nothing in PS-Two worth bringing ships in too close for. Whatever the Precursors had seen and done there, it was long gone. It was quiet enough that Tan!Stalla had left the bridge, leaving Morgan in active command.

"We're getting updated orders from Fleet Lord Tanaka," their communications officer reported as the last of the escorts turned around. "I'm passing them on to the Captain; they're mostly for the Squadron Lord."

"What about personal mail call?" Morgan asked. "I didn't see anything come through on the starcom."

"We had an encryption-key glitch on the personal mail download," the Speaker admitted. "Didn't really show up until we checked with the rest of the fleet after coming through the portal and realizing everyone *else* had mail.

"We had to bounce some stuff back by hyperfold to get it sorted out. You'll get about a five-cycle's worth of starcom mail sometime this evening, sir."

Morgan turned to level a sharp gaze on the Tosumi officer.

"You're telling me it took five cycles for us to notice that no one was getting personal mail?" she asked coldly, letting her full First Sword face drop down. "And even *I* am only hearing about this now? *In passing?*"

Feathers fluttered.

"We were getting the packages," Kira Alles told her. "There was no reason that it shouldn't have been decrypted and dispersed by the automatic processes. I was making sure the military dispatches were coming through and I didn't have time to check."

Alles wasn't, Morgan noted, even trying to make excuses. It just didn't seem to occur to the Tosumi that their screw-up was that big a deal.

"My office at the end of your shift, Speaker," she said flatly. If there'd been one important lesson that Jean Villeneuve had pounded into the head of the teenagers around him that were likely to end up in this fleet, it was that one: praise in public, condemn in private.

Bloody strips of feathers made for wonderful trophies, but it was never a good idea to extract them where an officer's subordinates could see.

Kira Alles was spared more immediate words—though the end of shift was only an hour away—by a sudden alert from the main hologram.

"The drones found something," Nidei reported. "Planet Six, the one we figure occasionally has oceans."

"Show me," Morgan ordered.

The hologram zoomed in on the planet. The orbiting drones were marked by green icons in orbit, each of them scanning the surface with a wide variety of exotic sensors.

Those scanners were showing that Planet Six clearly did have oceans some part of the year. There were definite continents and what looked to even be liquid water under the ice currently encasing the planet.

She doubted there was life down there, but she could be wrong. Life was *extraordinarily* determined, and if the planet's ice casing melted away for even a few months of the year, Morgan was sure that some form of bacteria or plant life could make it work.

Right now, however, the most important thing was what the sensors were picking up *in* that water.

"Processed metal and inactive nanobots, huh?" she said aloud. More of the drones were shifting around to concentrate on the debris field as she spoke. Different angles and more sensors provided more detail.

"What do you make of this, Nidei?" Morgan asked.

"Cluster of stations that were in orbit and fell," the Ivida replied. "They're all really close together, though."

"If you're setting up a way station rather than a major settlement, why wouldn't you keep them all together?" she said. Tapping a command, she zoomed in. "Well, at least we know the one thing that their silver icons marked."

"Sir?"

"That's a starcom station," Morgan told the tactical officer. "It's... about half the size of ours and broken in two, but there's no mistaking that outline once you know to look for it."

She grinned back at Nidei.

"When I was *Bellerophon*'s tactical officer, I missed it at Precursor-One," she told them. "Our communications officer caught it, so I was looking for it this time. The rest of this...is pretty hard to identify, really."

"Probably a transfer station and hydroponics facilities," Nidei said. "It doesn't look like this place was ever stable enough to grow food. There's no reason *not* to anchor around Planet Six—liquid water even some of the time is better than no liquid water ever, after all—but Six definitely wasn't what they were here for."

"Cloudscoops and fueling facilities could have fallen into the gas giants by now," Morgan concluded. "Six looks like it would be pretty easily accessed from any of the giants for most of its orbit. The asteroids wouldn't even get in the way."

"Anchor point, food, and water," Nidei concluded. "Refueling from the gas giants. Feels like the Precursors had a bunch of systems that just acted as fuel stops. It's weird. That's not really necessary."

Something fit there and itched at the back of Morgan's head, but it wasn't forming into a full-fledged idea just yet.

"It wouldn't be necessary for *us*," she pointed out. "But we don't know if the Precursors used the same FTL system we do. It's possible whatever they used was more fuel-intensive, in which case waystations like this would have been critical."

"From the map we have, I'd say they didn't want to go more than thirty light-years from a fuel stop," Nidei said. "Assuming that there's a bunch of similar stations and relays deeper towards the Core that aren't on these maps, anyway."

"We know this was the ass end of nowhere for them, too," Morgan agreed. She shook her head. "Last reports I saw from PG-Three say they had a new map. Run that thirty-light-year concept by those data points, Commander, then we'll present the idea to the Captain."

"More planning sessions, sir?" Nidei asked.

"Later this evening." Morgan shook her head and glanced over at the still apparently unbothered Kira Alles. "I'm going to go over those reports from PG-Three in my office. You have the con, Nidei."

CHAPTER TWENTY-SIX

"It is your responsibility to handle the ship's communications, Speaker Alles," Morgan told Kira Alles harshly. "Not your subordinates'. Not the people sending messages from the Imperium. *Yours*. Military coms are a priority, yes, but the ship's morale *depends* on mail call from home."

The Tosumi was trying to put on a brave face but her feathers were clearly starting to wilt.

"I checked that the package arrived and was downloaded," she pointed out.

"So did I," Morgan replied. "That's the kind of high-level double-check the First Sword does. It certainly shouldn't be where *your* double-check ends. A five-cycle, Speaker? Were *you* not expecting any personal messages in that time?"

Alles shifted on her seat, that piece of uncomfortable body language almost universal across species.

"Not...really," she admitted.

Morgan snorted. What was it with communications officers who didn't have anyone at home to communicate with? Victoria Antonova barely spoke to her surviving parent, and she'd been the communications officer on *Bellerophon* when they went out this way the previous year.

"I didn't exactly notice the lack of my own personal messages," she conceded. "It's been a busy few cycles. But it is your job to keep watch over just that, Speaker Alles. If the military communications were taking up all of your time, who did you delegate double-checking the personal communications too?"

The Tosumi was silent.

"Well, Speaker?" Morgan asked.

"No one," Alles admitted. "It slipped my mind."

"Well, make bloody damn sure it doesn't next time," Morgan snapped. "There are five officers under your command, Speaker Alles. A hundred spacers. While it wouldn't necessarily be optimal to have a freshly recruited Spacer Third Class on her first deployment double-checking that the personal mail was being delivered, they could certainly do a better job than you just did!"

"Yes, sir," Alles ground out. "It won't happen again, sir."

"No. It won't," Morgan agreed. "And so long as it doesn't happen again and the crew are getting their messages today, this is the end of it. Understood?"

Unspoken was that if it *did* happen again, Morgan would probably have the Speaker in front of the Captain. If the First Sword tearing a strip off an officer didn't work, there weren't many bigger sticks in the cabinet short of Tan!Stalla herself.

"I understand, sir," Speaker Alles conceded. "PG-Three was my first battle. I was...distracted."

Morgan swallowed a sigh.

"Half of the crew on this ship are inexperienced for their roles," she reminded the Speaker—a list that included Morgan Casimir herself. "But remember that we're all in this together. If you're over-whelmed, let me know and we'll see what we can do."

She grinned.

"You have five officers and a hundred spacers, Speaker Alles. I can call on *Jean Villeneuve*'s entire crew, all five thousand of them, if I need to. Don't let yourself or your people drown.

"We're all in this together," she repeated. It was a promise…and a warning. After all, if they were all in it together, Alles screwing up something major would hurt them all, too.

———

THE GRADATIONS OF "ON DUTY" for the executive officer were many and complicated. Truthfully, Morgan Casimir figured she was never really *off* duty while she was awake, but the least on-duty she got was spending time in her own quarters.

Of course, there was an office space in her quarters. It wasn't the full-size setup of her main office—even superbattleships were spaceships and only had so much room—but she had a desk and a wallscreen tucked into one corner of the living room of her two-room space.

Currently, that wallscreen was showing the latest scans of the debris field from Planet Six. None of the warships had gone any closer to the planet, but a closer sweep by the drones had got them as much data as they were going to get.

The drones were on their way back and the task force was scheduled to be in motion before Morgan was back on the bridge. To get more information than the drones could get would require burning holes in the ice and sending down submersible drones.

It didn't seem worth it to Morgan, and Squadron Lord Sun clearly agreed. The only thing that might be of any value would be a new version of the maps they'd been finding, and if Fleet Lord Tanaka decided she wanted that, a single destroyer would suffice to get it.

Morgan waved her hand through the holographic controls, closing the image of Planet Six. The other image she'd had open behind it was the updated regional map, drawing on the newly discovered Precursor map at PG-Three.

JTF 25's newly added destinations were systems the Precursors had flagged with silver icons, and Morgan was pretty sure she knew what they were going to find: either an orbital or planetary starcom, refueling facilities and some R&R facilities.

The silver systems appeared to be glorified truck stops designed for starships. She was more interested now in their next stop, PG-Four. They had no idea what that was going to be, since PS-Two had been the closest system to PG-Three.

PG-One and PG-Two were going to be swept in the next few days. That would give them a much better idea of what the Precursors had considered a gold-tier system—and then JTF 25 would reach PG-Four in another four days.

Hopefully. Hyperspace wasn't a neat and simple calculation like that.

With a sigh, Morgan minimized *all* of her work and flipped to the other set of icons. As Alles had warned, she'd got a five-cycle's worth of mail. Messages from her parents and two from Victoria.

For a moment, she wanted to hold off on the messages from Victoria. Part of it was wanting to leave the best for last—but part of it was also fear. She'd been dear-Janed by a recorded message before, after all.

But she *missed* the other woman, so she queued up the first message.

"Hey, you," the recorded image of Victoria Antonova greeted her. "I know you haven't reached anywhere you can send a message yet, but I wanted to record a note and let you know how things are going back here.

"The Militia is keeping things pretty low-key. We don't have much to do, what with the Imperials having stolen a bunch of our best people and our entire next generation of ships." Victoria's smile weakened some of the accusation there. "We're apparently talking about another transfer for me, this one to Admiral Rolfson's staff."

Morgan knew that communications officers sometimes had difficulty making a jump to more senior roles without making the switch to line command. A turn on the Admiral's staff as a squadron communications officer would be one of the few ways to make full Commander.

"No one has told me one way or another if it'll come with the bump to full Commander," Victoria continued, almost in answer to Morgan's thoughts. "Logically, if it doesn't right away, the bump should still come along pretty quickly. I can't have my lover outranking me forever!"

She smiled at Morgan and Morgan involuntarily smiled back. *Damn,* she missed the other woman.

"Speaking of which, I apparently have dinner with your sisters tonight that I need to get headed in the direction of. I'm assuming that they had business on Defense One *other* than buying me dinner...right?" She shook her head.

"I'm looking forward to hearing from you, love. Stay safe!"

Morgan chuckled as the message froze. She only gave it about a thirty-five percent chance that her sisters had gone into orbit *specifically* to have dinner with her girlfriend, but it wasn't out of the question. She wasn't entirely surprised they'd decided to pin down their big sister's lover if they were up there for business, though.

After a moment, she started the next message.

"Hey." Victoria sounded tired. "Got your message. Not sure you got mine, but that's the navy wife life, isn't it?"

She was in uniform and *looked* as exhausted as she sounded.

"I ended up on Rolfson's staff and today's the end of the first day. I don't think I realized just how many messages even a squadron at anchor produces! I'm glad Sun flew his flag somewhere other than *Bellerophon* now, since I think I'm going to break *Innocence's* communications officer by the end of the first week."

She shook her head.

"I think he thinks I'm utterly incompetent, but he'll learn," she said brightly. "My reports say that PG-Three was...weird. Now I'm on the Admiral's staff, I'm apparently cleared for the full reports for Tenth Fleet. Including what the Mesharom did.

"I couldn't believe it when I saw it." Victoria was silent for a few seconds. "I mean, I can see the purpose and the point, but billions of people…"

Morgan had gone through the same sequence when she'd seen it herself. Victoria had been a few days later, from the sound of it.

"Not much I can do from here, I know. You're in the thick of it and I worry. Send me an update when you can? I'm looking forward to hearing from you."

The message ended and Morgan sighed.

Humans, especially, had grown used to regarding the Mesharom as friendly semi-allies most of the time. Harmless caterpillar space elves at worst. Most Militia members knew that they'd threatened to bomb Hope, but looking back at that, no one seemed to take it seriously.

They'd been wrong. They'd been *so* wrong.

The Mesharom weren't harmless. They were *alien* and their priorities didn't align with the Imperium.

Morgan thought that Adamase wouldn't have ordered the destruction of the ring, but she couldn't be sure. The Interpreter-Shepherd was still technically the civilian authority for the Mesharom out here. She didn't know how that stacked up against Tilsan's Battle Fleet Grand Commander, though, and it was entirely possible they'd had to sign off on the attack.

Worse, though, was that the Imperium and the Kanzi now held the wreckage of at least one gold-tier Precursor installation. Just the scan data from the ring could easily birth entirely new generations of gas-giant extraction systems and metallurgical advancements.

Technology that the Mesharom would say was stolen. Technology that the Mesharom might well be willing to kill over.

CHAPTER TWENTY-SEVEN

"So, our current best guess is that we are approximately two cycles out from PG-Four," Cosa announced. "Hyperspatial density and variability in this region are low, so we are both moving slower than we expected and moving more consistently than normal."

"Could be worse," Tan!Stalla noted, the A!Tol looking around the meeting of *Jean Villeneuve*'s officers. "Casimir, what's the status of the other task forces?"

Morgan had spent the hour before the meeting with Speaker Alles, making sure they had collated all of that information. That had probably been overkill in the end, but there were a lot of moving parts to the allied deployment.

"JTF Twenty-Two is still en route to their designated target system," she noted first. "They'll arrive at PC-Three in just over two and a half cycles, plus-minus a tenth-cycle. However, as of our last update from Tenth Fleet, there'd been no contact from the pursuit force. That means that they haven't left hyperspace yet."

Or had been destroyed, but Morgan didn't need to tell anyone that. They could all do that math in their head.

"JTF Twenty-Three should have arrived at PG-One by now," she continued. "Their data has to be transmitted back to the Fleet by hyperfold com and then sent back to Sol by hyperfold com before it can be starcommed out to us. We'll get their initial reports in five to six hours, depending on the variability of their final approach.

"I plan on going through those as soon as they arrive myself," Morgan noted. "PG-One will be the first of the gold systems we've visited since PG-Three itself. I'm curious to see what else the Precursors thought was important."

Morgan brought up a holographic astrogation chart as she was speaking, marking in the green lines of the other task forces.

"JTF Twenty-Four dropped out of hyperspace to report that they'd hit an extremely low-density patch of hyperspace and lost some days unexpectedly," she noted. "Right now, the last estimate I saw is that they'll arrive at PG-Two within a couple of hours of our arriving at PG-Four. That's going to have been a long flight for Twenty-Four."

Four lines marked the map now, showing their route and the routes of the other JTFs.

"I suggest we all do the same as Commander Casimir," Tan!Stalla told them, her skin tone making it clear that the "suggestion" was definitely an order. "JTF Twenty-Three's survey of PG-One will be distributed to all senior officers on arrival. Just what the Precursors regarded as a Gold system is mission-critical data, people, and I want us all familiar with it."

"Are we expecting another ring station?" Alles asked.

"Right now, the extent of my expectation is that we have no idea what the Precursors were capable of," Morgan told the others. "The number of locations basically acting as fueling stops suggests a distinct range limit on their FTL systems, but they also appear to have been building starcoms far more casually than we do."

An orbital starcom like the one at Sol took *years* to build and couldn't be moved afterward. In terms of data-transmission rates, range, and time delay, the starcom was a vastly superior form of communication to the hyperfold communicator.

But a hyperfold communicator could be mass-produced in a size small enough to fit onto a specially built large drone. Starcoms still anchored the Imperial communication network, but the hyperfold coms now made up the bulk of it.

For random fueling stations to have starcoms, they must have either been easier to build or easier to move for the Precursors.

"I am reminded that this is the far edge of their empire," Tan!Stalla said calmly. "And yet we still see things like the ring station at PG-Three. I have to wonder what artifacts and terrors are forgotten closer to their core territory."

"Nothing that the Mesharom could find," Nidei noted. "We know there was *something* in the system where the Taljzi originally started, though. That's what led them to come out here in the end."

"If nothing else, they clearly had a map," Morgan agreed. "I suspect anything closer to Kanzi or Imperial space was swept by the Mesharom Frontier Fleet a while back. Anything obvious is long gone."

"And so, we are at the back of beyond by any standard, wondering what secrets they left behind," Tan!Stalla confirmed. "A few more hours and we'll have some clues, I suppose."

IT WAS easy to tell the moment when the first reports from PG-One arrived. Morgan was in secondary control, playing backup observer to Nidei's bridge watch, and her communicator pinged at the same moment as the tactical officer's.

"Ichri, you have the watch down here," she told the Indiri junior tactical officer holding down the sensor console. "I'm going to go see what we ran into."

The Captain's office was directly attached to the bridge, and the First Sword's office was directly attached to secondary control. Making it to her office and bringing up the central hologram was a matter of a couple of minutes.

PG-One was a surprisingly sparse system. Four rocky worlds, two gas giants. Only six planets in total and nothing that lit up JTF 23's scanners as a major technological installation. No asteroid belts, nothing for easy mining.

The answer to why the Precursors had cared about the system was easy enough to see, though. Two of the rocky planets were in the liquid-water zone of the system's G-sequence primary. One would have been uncomfortably warm for humans and one would have been uncomfortably cold, but both should have been habitable.

Neither was registering as habitable in the scans that Morgan was seeing, though, and she tapped a command to open the reports. The hologram itself continued to run through an accelerated version of JTF 23's sweep of the system, but the summaries would tell her what she wanted to know.

The inner gas giant was the first place the drones had reached and the first entry in the summary. There were no intact orbital installations, but the debris fields suggested the presence of significant industry that hadn't survived sixty thousand years of being ground between the gas giant's rings.

The drones were definitely picking up refined metals in that debris, but the installations were long gone. There were a few surface stations on the moons, including what looked like it had been a domed city before a *something* had nuked it. None of those stations were live and the city was in ruins.

A note on the report said that an eight-ship echelon of Imperial cruisers had been sent over to investigate the ruins anyway, but that their focus had been on the two once-habitable planets.

The continually updating hologram got to the outer habitable planet before Morgan reached the reports and she zoomed in on it and swallowed. Many Imperial worlds used different variations on the old concept of a skyhook or a space elevator.

They had a *lot* of safety functions built into them. Whatever safety functions had been built into this one had failed—potentially gone haywire and been the cause of the collapse themselves—and it had hauled its counterweight down with it. A perfect line of devastation wrapped around the planet, with an asteroid at the end.

The cable would have done terrible things as it came down, and the dozen stations built along its length would have made for nasty impactors on their own. The two-kilometer-wide asteroid at the *end* of the cable would have hit like the hammer of an angry god.

There was no atmosphere or water left on the planet now. A few decaying orbitals still drifted in space, but most of them had suffered the same fate as the fueling station in PS-Two. The planet was a dead rock, ruined by the very infrastructure that had probably enabled its rapid colonization and industrialization.

The summary reports told her that the second planet was at least in better shape. Shifting her view over to it, she could see that the main reason for that was that the Precursors hadn't really moved in there yet. There was no space elevator to choke the planet to death or deliver a tethered asteroid as a death blow.

There had been orbitals and they had fallen to smash into the planet below, but the planet remained an overly warm habitable world. Oceans covered its surface, and archipelagos of jungle-covered islands poked through the waters.

The odds were that some of the islands were more temperate than Morgan's assumption from the climate reports, but it certainly looked like it would make for a great beach getaway. It didn't look like there had been much there to begin with, and nature had probably eaten whatever was left.

The notes on her report said that JTF 23 was landing teams on the first world, looking for the starcom and the map. They wouldn't spend long, however.

The Precursors apparently had flagged their colonies in gold...but this colony was long dead and its death had destroyed anything the Imperium would find of value.

CHAPTER TWENTY-EIGHT

"Nothing."

Harriet shook her head at the report as she looked at the data Koanest was presenting.

"Nothing? Can we expand the scope again?"

Her operations officer shook her head and gestured to the hologram.

"We now have drones positioned one a light-year for ten light-years in every direction," she pointed out. "That's eating up a measurable chunk of our hyperfold com–equipped drones. The synthesizing benefits of a telescope twenty light-years across are significant, but we should really be thinking about pulling those drones back in."

"Not doubling down on them."

The Fleet Lord nodded. The two of them were locked in her office, discussing an aspect of the mission she wasn't even bringing the other two fleet commanders in on: the search for the Mesharom.

"We've transmitted on every band we can access, trying to reach them," Koanest told her. "But this isn't even them not responding, Fleet Lord. With this wide a catchment area and receivers as sensitive as we've got in the drones...if they're using hyperfold coms at *all*, we should be picking them up."

"They'd be going through relays, surely," Harriet pointed out. "We know they have an entire network back in Imperial and Kanzi space."

Koanest waved a blue-skinned hand and zoomed the map out. Even on this scale, the twenty-light-year-wide disk of drones remained visible.

"We know they have a relay network here," she said, highlighting a chunk of the map in purple. "That's Imperial and Kanzi space. We also know they almost certainly have networks over here and over here, but those are farther away."

Far enough away that she was highlighting directions at the edge of the three-dimensional map instead of areas on it.

"Assuming they left a trail of relays, like we did, they would almost certainly be on the line from Sol to PG-Three, here." The line lit up in purple. "Given where those relays all are, they would *have* to be transmitting through our Very Large Array to reach them.

"Relays or not, unless Tilsan turned around and went home after blowing up the ring world, we should be at least *detecting* their calls back to the Conclave," the Yin concluded. "Instead, we have silence on every bandwidth we can scan for hyperfold transmissions."

She held up her hand before Harriet spoke.

"And I've double-checked our old scan records. We most definitely *can* detect the Mesharom hyperfold coms towards their relays. We can't flag the directionality of the signals, but we can tell when they pass our receivers."

"So, either Tilsan isn't phoning home or..."

Harriet couldn't even finish the thought.

"Or his entire fleet is gone," Koanest said flatly. "We always knew it was a possibility that the Mesharom expedition would end in disaster, but no contact with the fleet and no sign of them even communicating with their own home command?

"I'd say we're looking at a significant probability that Tilsan is dead and their entire fleet with them."

Harriet nodded, looking at the hologram, then sighed.

"Recall the drones, Koanest," she ordered. "Whether Tilsan is alive or not doesn't change *our* mission. I just hoped that once we were all out at the sharp end of the stick, they'd see some sense."

"I don't get the impression that the Conclave Battle Fleet picks their Grand Commanders for anything we'd call sense, Fleet Lord," Koanest admitted. "The longer we spend out here, the creepier this whole chunk of the galaxy gets. The Mesharom just vanishing out here doesn't help!"

Vaporized stations. Fallen orbitals. Wrecked worlds. Irradiated and ruined cities—the latest reports out of PG-One were that the cities on the planets had suffered the same fate as the dome on the gas giant's moon. Their power stations had been decently separated from the cities, assuming any kind of safety precautions—but fusion power plants didn't usually *explode*.

Anyone who'd survived the failure of their implants had then had to survive the explosion of their city's power plants...and *then* the space elevator had hammered its counterweight asteroid into the planet.

They might still find the map, but Fleet Keeper Nordan Illrun wasn't counting on it. Harriet saw no reason to argue with the Kanzi officer's decision to move on after another cycle of searching.

From the sounds of it, PG-One was depressing to be present in. None of the Precursor systems were much better than that.

"The worst part to all of this is that if we find somewhere that *is* alive, it's going to be full of Taljzi," Harriet told her operations officer. "I'm surprised there isn't a Taljzi colony in PG-One. There's an intact surviving planet, after all."

"They might not have needed it yet, but they probably had it on their list for when they exceeded their carrying capacity of their existing colonies," Koanest replied. "Even that ring station could have easily held a couple dozen billion people, assuming they didn't mind living in an entirely artificial environment."

Harriet snorted.

"Most people can get used to that," she pointed out, gesturing at their own artificial surroundings. "You don't realize how much you miss *life* until you're back on a planet."

CLOSING down the privacy shield Harriet had kept active through the conversation with Koanest, she noted that there was a priority alert that had come in while she was sequestered. Kanmorad had sent out a request for a teleconference with her and Cawl.

They might want to prioritize the other two fleet commanders above everything else, but they were all swamped with the responsibilities of commanding their forces.

Kanmorad less so, perhaps, than Cawl or Harriet, since he only commanded a hundred and ten ships. Almost a third of his fleet was scattered across the various scouting forces, too, with half of his cruisers and four of his war-dreadnoughts out looking for the Taljzi.

Cawl had obviously been busy as well, as he pinged Harriet and Kanmorad as being available mere moments before Harriet did the same. A second later, the privacy shield resealed her office, leaving her alone with the holographic images of her counterparts.

"We have news from the scouting flotilla," Kanmorad said without preamble. "Our Taljzi friends make for uncomfortably squirmy prey."

"They eluded you?" Cawl asked.

"They clearly realized they were being pursued," the Laian officer confirmed. "They led my people on a multi-day voyage into deep space along a hyperspace current, far past PC-Three. They were headed for a black hole we hadn't surveyed into our charts yet."

"They like black holes far more than I find comfortable," Harriet murmured. "Are your people all right?"

"So far as they can tell, they were never detected with sufficient accuracy for the Taljzi to fire on them," Kanmorad replied. "They did lure my people into a dangerously close slingshot maneuver of the black hole and then broke orbit in three different fleets."

He clicked his mandibles in an irritated fashion.

"Between their speed edge and the interference in hyperspace, we lost two groups completely. The ship that transmitted the update has already reentered hyperspace in pursuit of the third, but the Captain suggested that the chances of a successful intercept are low."

"They know this space better than we do," Cawl observed. "We are lucky that they only tried to use the black hole to lose your fleet. Such phenomena are dangerous enough to make deadly traps."

"My ships were under orders to let the Taljzi go rather than take that risk," Kanmorad said calmly. "If they lose the third group, they are under orders to join JTF Twenty-Two at PC-Three. I'm not sure what value the pursuit will have now."

"It was a long shot," Harriet pointed out. "We always knew that. Cawl, has Twenty-Two arrived yet?"

"Three spans ago," he told her. Roughly forty-five minutes, Harriet translated. "We're waiting for a final sweep to present a complete report, but I took the liberty of virtually sitting on Fleet Master Rist's shoulder for the first sensor sweeps.

"Like we expected, there was a local sentient civilization in PC-Three. Looks like they were in a late industrial stage of civilization, but we'll never know for sure. No space infrastructure, and it looks like anything detectable from orbit was hit with kinetic strikes."

Cawl's voice was calm, but Harriet was starting to get used to Kanzi voices. That calm was fragile. His words sent a spasm of rage through her system, too...but the Taljzi were, at least biologically, *his people*.

"No active Taljzi presence, I presume?" Kanmorad asked.

The Laian really didn't seem bothered by the report. Harriet knew she was building her own emotional calluses against things like this, and she *hated* it. Kanmorad just...really didn't seem to care.

Given the Mesharom's actions in PG-Three, she was really starting to question the narrative of the Core Powers as more *morally* advanced than the Arm Powers as well as more technologically advanced.

"There may be a few sensor platforms, but no ships or infrastructure," Cawl replied. "The Taljzi appear to have swept the entire region around their new home and exterminated everyone they found—and thanks to the Precursors, they knew where to find them."

Harriet shivered. Based on what they'd seen so far, any Precursor map found near Sol would show the star in copper, home to a pre-technic sentient species. If the Taljzi had settled more Coreward, would Earth have suffered the same fate?

Probably. That was why they were there, after all.

"We'll want to hold the task force there until we hear back from my scouts," Kanmorad told them. "It's still possible that we'll find something worth sending JTF Twenty-Two after."

"It's a drain on their morale, but they'll hold up for a few days," Cawl agreed.

"And you question the necessity of the Taljzi's destruction?" the big Laian asked, his voice suddenly very soft. "There can only be one response to this kind of destruction."

"If you take an eye for an eye every time, sooner or later, everyone is blind," Harriet replied. "And if we wipe them out, how are we better?"

Kanmorad's mandibles chittered in laughter.

"In the only ways that matter in the end," he told them. "In that we didn't start it...and that we survived it."

CHAPTER TWENTY-NINE

ONE MORE SYSTEM. ONE MORE HYPER PORTAL. ONE MORE battle stations alert.

No matter where a crew member was in secondary control, the timer in the main holographic display was clearly visible. It was part of the design. No one there—or on the bridge, either—could miss the countdown to emergence.

Green icons flared across Morgan Casimir's display as she quickly ran through *Jean Villeneuve*'s systems. Captain Tan!Stalla would be doing the same thing, and her juniors would be running through the data at more and more granular levels of detail.

Morgan had been a tactical officer first, so she'd checked the superbattleship's arsenal first. Out of hundreds of weapons, not one was even reporting an excess delay. No yellows and certainly no reds in those reports.

From there, engines. Shields. Repair drones. Sensors. Part of it was to make sure that she was aware of everything aboard the big warship.

Part of it was simply to ease her nerves in the final moments before emergence. She didn't really need to know that three point four percent of Engineering's drones were overdue for maintenance but still on duty or that point six percent of the drones were downchecked for repairs.

The First Sword of the superbattleship, however, *did* need to not be seen being visibly nervous or impatient as the last few seconds ticked away on the timer. Going through everything made her *look* steady and calm and helped keep her focused.

Then the timer hit zero and *Jean Villeneuve* punched into PG-Four. JTF-25 wasn't large enough to require staged portals, and the entire task force punched from hyperspace into reality in a single massive portal.

"Scans active," someone reported.

There was a long, stunned pause as the first images of the star system appeared in the hologram. PG-Four was a gorgeous star system. A cool K-class dwarf anchored a system of large rocky worlds and glittering gas giants.

Five massive gas giants had clearly once provided the fuel for an immense industrial project. There wasn't anything visible left of the infrastructure that project must have required, but its results were clearly visible!

PG-Four had once had five rocky worlds, averaging about half again the size of Earth. None looked like they'd been habitable, but it was hard to say now.

All five of those worlds had been carved into pieces. They still hung in a shared orbit, but each of them had been cleaved into quarters and rotated to allow easy access to the dense metal core many worlds shared.

"Dear God," Morgan murmured. "What did they *do*?"

"Hard to say exactly how they did it," Speaker Ichri, the red-furred officer acting as tactical backup down in secondary control, told her. "*What* the Precursors did looks pretty obvious, though."

"Our entire *fleet* couldn't do that," Morgan said aloud. The

"Flag anything that looks like a permanent structure on the surface or in space. They can't have been running this entire operation with mobile ships."

"Well, they *could*," Ichri pointed out. "If they went to the effort to make the big platforms mobile..."

"With nothing else here, making the core modules mobile makes sense," she replied. "Not having any fixed infrastructure would be inefficient. And paranoid."

"And what makes you think they're not paranoid?" Tan!Stalla interjected, the Captain apparently listening to Morgan as well as running the bridge. "Get your team on analyzing the larger signatures, Casimir. Given the way they've done everything else, there's almost certainly warships out there."

"On it," Morgan confirmed. She flipped the command to Ichri and his team's consoles.

"Start at the largest units and run down by decreasing mass," she ordered. "My guess would be that there's at least some superbattleships here, so let's find them before they jump out at us!"

FOR A FEW MINUTES, Morgan was starting to wonder if there were actually warships there. No long-range missiles answered Joint Task Force 25's rapid approach. No warships stood out from the chaotic swarm of civilian shipping running away towards the big mining ships.

"There!"

Jean Villeneuve had some of the most sensitive sensors in the JTF, but she had to figure it was more than the systems that allowed Nidei to pick out the enemy formation concealed in the chaos of the civilians.

The two teams, on the bridge and there in secondary control, had been dividing the swarm into sections and cycling through targets as rapidly as possible, trying to find the ships that were intentionally keeping their power down—and they'd done it.

Villeneuve might be relatively new, but her crew was clicking like they'd served together for years.

"At least two squadrons of capital ships," the Ivida continued, highlighting the icons in the display on the bridge and its mirror in secondary control. "There's probably escorts in there somewhere, but they're hiding well."

"Pass it up to the Squadron Lord," Tan!Stalla ordered. "What's the range?"

At fifty-five percent of lightspeed, even light-minutes vanished with disturbing speed.

"We're well inside even their long-range missile range," Morgan cut in. "Permission to engage with HSMs?"

The Taljzi capital ships were in the middle of the mess of fleeing civilians, but twenty superbattleships was a serious threat to JTF 25. Even with *Jean Villeneuve*, they only had eleven superbattleships of their own.

"That's Lord Sun's call," Tan!Stalla replied. "There's too many civi—"

The Taljzi had calculated it perfectly. They lunged out of the mining ships in a perfect formation, closing the range at sixty percent of lightspeed and bringing JTF 25 into regular missile range in under ten seconds.

It wasn't twenty superbattleships. It was *forty*, with a screening force of a hundred cruisers.

Thousands of missiles blazed out at JTF 25 at eighty percent of lightspeed—and Morgan didn't even wait for orders to hit the command that surrendered control of *Jean Villeneuve*'s hyperfold cannon to the missile-defense systems.

"Return fire!" Tan!Stalla barked—and orders dropped into the tactical network at the same time.

Twenty-eight allied capital ships opened fire, the Laian war-dreadnought intentionally slipping ahead of the rest of the formation as her launchers spewed hundreds of missiles all on her own.

The Laian missiles were smaller and smarter than the Imperial missiles, which were smarter—though not smaller—than the Kanzi missiles. All of them had the same velocity, though, as did the Taljzi missiles.

Even the self-destructing interface drives used on missiles couldn't travel faster than point eight cee. That seemed to be a physical limitation of the interface, but it was fast *enough*.

Missiles crashed over JTF 25 in a wave of explosions. Hyperfold cannon started engaging them at ten light seconds. Plasma and laser defenses joined in at four light-seconds, and the missiles that made it through hammered into powerful shields energized by matter-conversion cores and antimatter power plants.

With forty superbattleships firing at the task force, missiles got through. The war-dreadnought *Hammerfall* was the primary target, her captain having pushed the Laian ship out in front with the intent of taking the fire.

Jean Villeneuve, as the second-largest ship in the fleet, came in for her own barrage. Unlike the rest of the fleet—including *Hammerfall* —though, *her* shields were powered by a pair of matter-conversion cores. She lacked the war-dreadnought's size and mass, but her shields were *more* powerful.

Dozens of missiles hammered into *Villeneuve*'s shields at eighty percent of the speed of light. A handful of sectors flickered down into the yellow on Morgan's displays, but they held up under the bombardment with aplomb.

For every dozen missiles that hit *Jean Villeneuve*, a hundred struck *Hammerfall*. The war-dreadnought's shields were almost as tough as the Imperial ship's—sheer size and number of emitters managed what an immense amount of energy achieved on the smaller ship—but the number of surviving weapons strained even those defenses.

But not enough. *Hammerfall* weathered the storm, and the rest of the task force went undamaged. Morgan probably imagined the moment of shock on the part of their Taljzi opponents, but it certainly didn't slow their second salvo.

"They're pushing for us hard," Ichri said aloud. "They have to know that getting into cannon range of us is death."

Morgan shook her head slowly, watching their own missiles die in the teeth of the active defenses of...the cruisers?

"That can't be right," she said.

"That they're pushing for us?" Ichri asked. "Check their vectors. They can break off anytime, same as us, but they're heading straight for the heart of our formation."

"Not that," Morgan snapped. "Ichri, Nidei—did either of you see counter-missile fire from the superbattleships?"

There was a pause.

"No," Nidei replied.

"Not here, either," Ichri confirmed.

"They're older ships," Morgan realized. "Ones they didn't refit with antimissile defenses after the First Return. They're pushing through our missile range because they don't *have* long-range missiles or antimissile defenses.

"They can't fight us at long range. They'll pay in blood to get to disruptor range, but..."

Even a cruiser's disruptors could kill a superbattleship. If the Taljzi managed to get any portion of their fleet through the killing zone of JTF 25's hyperfold cannons and plasma lances, JTF 25 was going to lose ships. A lot of ships.

"Get that up to the Squadron Lord," Morgan ordered. "If they don't have antimissile defenses, that changes a *lot*."

A Taljzi superbattleship had shields to rival *Jean Villeneuve's*—they were using singularity power cores, a technology the Imperium was only just beginning to build a usable form of—with even heavier compressed-matter armor.

But without antimissile defenses, they'd face a hundred missiles for every one that hit the Imperial ship's shields. A missile duel suddenly looked *much* more appealing.

It wasn't Morgan's call, though. She was trying to keep track of everything *Jean Villeneuve* was doing and supporting the team running the antimissile defenses.

"It's Squadron Lord Sun's call," Tan!Stalla's voice said in her ear, mirroring her own thoughts. "If we close, we'll get hammered by the disruptors. If we keep the range open, we lose the mining ships."

As they spoke, *Jean Villeneuve* shivered around them with the indescribable sensation of being *near* to a hyper portal opening. Hyperspace missiles sparkled momentarily on the display before detonating on the screen.

The orders coming down from Lord Sun were clear in the results of the HSM salvo. The cruisers had the rapid-fire defenses the Taljzi had built to defeat HSMs. The superbattleships didn't...but the salvo's target had been the cruisers.

An entire squadron of Taljzi cruisers just vanished, with at least twice that showing obvious signs of damage.

"We're pulling off course," Tan!Stalla reported as new orders came down the tactical network. "We're going to try and loop around and stay with the mining ships while keeping out of disruptor range of the warships."

Morgan ran the projections on her displays as another salvo of missiles slammed into *Jean Villeneuve*'s shields.

"It's not going to work," she pointed out to the Captain. "The mining ships are fast enough to keep the defense fleet between us and them. The only way to get to them before they're into hyperspace and long gone is to go *through* the fleet."

"Sun thinks we'll lose too many ships," Tan!Stalla pointed out. "He's...probably right."

Morgan couldn't see her Captain's skin, so she couldn't be sure, but she didn't think Tan!Stalla agreed with Sun's call.

She wasn't sure *she* agreed with it...but she didn't necessarily disagree with Sun's priorities.

There were a lot of ways to find the Taljzi's home base. Next time, they'd plan better and make sure they brought Laian escort cruisers that could follow their prey in stealth.

This time, they'd shatter a major Taljzi formation...and if they managed the maneuvers even remotely right, they had a decent chance of doing it without losing a single ship.

CHAPTER THIRTY

THE MOMENT THAT THE TALJZI REALIZED WHAT SUN WAS UP TO was obvious. The cruisers drew in more tightly around the superbattleships for mutual support against the hyperspace missiles, and the entire force found another few percent of lightspeed.

An entire fleet came charging out toward JTF 25 at sixty-five percent of lightspeed—and JTF 25 retreated in front of them at fifty-five percent. It wasn't a game that the allied force could win in the end, but that wasn't the point. The point was to extend the time that they were in missile range, and then in hyperfold cannon range and plasma lance range and...

Well, Morgan was sure there was something else the fleet was carrying that was longer-ranged than the Taljzi disruptors. Even *Jean Villeneuve* still carried proton beams, after all, even if they were unquestionably the poor sibling of her arsenal.

Hammerfall and the Kanzi superbattleships had more powerful proton beams. Neither species' ship had hyperspace missiles or plasma lances, after all, and Kanzi hyperfold cannon were a new refit.

"One hundred fifty seconds to hyperfold cannon range," Ichri reported. "They're down over half of their cruisers."

Morgan nodded silently. Fifty-five Taljzi cruisers were gone, but only six of their superbattleships had been taken out. The cruisers had understood their role in this fight far too well. They'd protected the bigger ships with their antimissile plasma cannons and lasers... and when that had failed, with their shields and their hulls.

Those same defenses meant that they were hard targets for the hyperspace missiles. Morgan wasn't sure she'd have focused her weapons on the cruisers, though they were responsible for easily half of the shattered cruisers.

More missiles hammered down on both fleets while she watched, and four more Taljzi cruisers vanished. Hyperspace missiles claimed another trio a few seconds later. The more cruisers died, the more vulnerable the remainder became. They weren't designed to face the focused fire of almost thirty capital ships.

The Laian war-dreadnought holding the closest position in the JTF's formation was starting to show the wear. Her shields had dropped three times now. So far as Morgan could tell, her armor was holding, but the big ship *needed* a break.

Morgan wasn't surprised when the order came down. *Jean Villeneuve* and six Kanzi superbattleships cut their velocity in half for a critical quarter-second.

It was enough to leave them eighty thousand kilometers behind the main body of the force, but the seven ships were big enough and tough enough to take whatever fire was flung at them.

The first salvo they ran into hadn't been expecting the shift in formation. Many of the missiles managed to adapt—more, Morgan suspected, than would have out of an Imperial salvo—but not enough. Hyperfold cannon and lasers swept the incoming fire again and again, the survivors sweeping past to try to engage *Hammerfall*.

None of them made it through, but the next salvo was more accurately targeted. After a few seconds of watching the missiles rearrange, Morgan realized they were all targeted at *Jean Villeneuve*.

"Well, it's nice to be loved," she muttered. "Watch your sectors, people. I'm taking control of the twenty- and thirty-series Buckler drones.

The antimissile defense system used by the Imperium were the Terran-built Sword turrets and Buckler drones. Originally entirely based on stolen obsolete Laian concepts and borrowed Imperial laser technology, it had proven a massive leap in survivability for the Imperial fleet.

Now, revised and redesigned over almost two decades, only half of her Sword turrets' and Buckler drones' weapons were lasers. The drone and the turret were basically identical except for one having engines, and they carried a mix of lasers and hyperfold cannon—targeted by a central tachyon scanner.

That tachyon sensor gave them real-time targeting data across multiple light-minutes. It didn't increase the range of either defensive weapon system, but it did vastly increase their accuracy.

The Kanzi had their own equivalent of the Sword turrets, and thanks to the tech transfers that had been part of the alliance, their defensive turrets were basically equivalent to hers. What they didn't have was the drones.

The forty Buckler drones *Jean Villeneuve* had deployed were the only secondary defensive nodes on the seven superbattleships, and Morgan spread them wide to clear her lines of fire. The Kanzi would help protect her, but there was a word for people who relied too heavily on their allies:

Dead.

Nidei focused on pounding their way through the Taljzi cruisers while Ichri and his team joined Morgan in running the superbattleship's defenses. Watching the salvo vanish under her defensive fire, the First Sword started to feel momentarily confident.

The Taljzi's losses were bad enough that if they'd been any bit less focused, none of their missiles would have made it through. As it was, fewer than thirty missiles smashed into *Jean Villeneuve*'s shields in the end.

A single sector flickered into yellow on her displays before returning to green.

"Rear guard is to hold position," Tan!Stalla told her calmly. "We get the first shot. Orders are to aim for the big boys."

She'd almost forgotten Ichri's time frame. Now she checked—and made sure that the battleship's heavy hyperfold cannon were returned to offensive fire control.

Ten seconds left. Another salvo hammered into her defenses, only a fraction of it penetrating to hit *Villeneuve*'s shields. This time, two sectors flashed yellow and stayed there...but there were sixteen separate sectors on the superbattleship's shields.

Cosa was rotating the ship before Morgan even drew attention to the weakened shield segments.

"Range."

Nidei's voice was soft, but everyone in the two command centers heard them. Not that it mattered. The firing patterns for the super-battleship's hyperfold cannon were already programmed in. Computers with far faster reaction times than any sentient acted on their orders.

Seven superbattleships activated almost four hundred hyperfold cannon, twisting space to deliver vast amounts of energy across seemingly infinitesimal distances. Two of their Taljzi counterparts bore the brunt of the fire...and simply vanished.

Barely two seconds later, the *rest* of JTF 25 followed suit. The Kanzi superbattleships only carried forty hyperfold cannon apiece. The *Bellerophon*-B-class battleships of the Imperial squadron were far smaller, but they each carried forty-*eight* of the guns.

Hammerfall carried almost three hundred.

Another twelve hundred hyperfold cannon blew five more Taljzi superbattleships to pieces. If there'd been any way for the Taljzi to go faster, Morgan suspected they would have. A fifth of their remaining capital ships had vanished in a few seconds.

The cycle time of the hyperfold cannon was long enough for the range to drop by almost half before they were ready to fire again.

Proton beams were starting to flash across the void as well, the heavy Kanzi beams focusing on a single Taljzi superbattleship.

The usual terrifying power of the "obsolete" weapon was demonstrated as the beams tore down the superbattleship's singularity-powered shields. The beams then collided with the antiproton curtain that defended the inside of the superbattleship.

There was enough firepower in play that Morgan expected the Kanzi ships to overwhelm their target's defenses—until a swarm of missiles smashed into the now-unshielded capital ship.

The superbattleship vanished and the Kanzi retargeted.

"We need to use those beams to bring down their shields," Morgan noted. "Too late for this fight, but it won't be the last time we fight alongside the Kanzi."

As she spoke, her hands were flying over her controls, making sure her Buckler drones were continuing to defend *Villeneuve* from the enemy fire.

The range dropped further, and *Villeneuve*'s last weapons systems came into play. The wingtip plasma lances ignored the superbattleships that the rest of the JTF was now hammering and targeted the cruisers. Four cruisers died in moments as the massive weapons vaporized the smaller ships.

Even with the JTF withdrawing away from the pursuing Taljzi, there was no way to keep the range from dropping now. *Jean Villeneuve* was being hammered by every weapon the Taljzi had. Missiles and proton beams hammered into her shields now, and Cosa kept rotating the ship to try to keep stronger shields in the line of fire.

"Shield failure!" Morgan snapped as the inevitable happened.

"Sprint, get us forward!" Tan!Stalla barked, her beak snapping the words off in a series of sharp clicks that underlay her translated voice.

Jean Villeneuve had a sprint mode of sixty-five percent of light-speed. She lunged forward, clearing herself from the enemy before more than a dozen missiles and a single proton beam had hit her hull.

Almost like the maneuver had been practiced, *Hammerfall* fell back into *Villeneuve*'s place. The Laian war-dreadnought's shields were almost back to full, which meant she now had more shielding than anything *else* in the fleet.

The proton beam hit had left an entire section of hull flickering on Morgan's display. It hadn't punched through the ship's armor, but it had come close. A few more hits like that could leave her seriously vulnerable.

The switch had been intended to keep the heaviest units bearing the worst of the fire, but Morgan realized their timing had been just barely right. They'd been out of the line of fire for less than five seconds before the rest of the superbattleships broke formation themselves.

They were scattering, trying to keep outside the one-light-second range of the enemy's terrifying close-range molecular disruptors. Over three-quarters of the enemy fleet was gone, and *Hammerfall* and *Jean Villeneuve* combined had taken every hit the Taljzi had landed without complaint.

This time, though, the superbattleships didn't go for *Hammerfall*. When their Kanzi cousins scattered, they broke formation in turn to pursue.

Every weapon in JTF 25 went to maximum rate of fire, trying desperately to keep the Taljzi from achieving what they were trying to do—but the Taljzi crews had probably known they were going to die from the moment the hyperfold cannon had fired.

They had spent blood and ships like water to get to this moment, and they did not fail. Four of the superbattleships closed with their Kanzi counterparts, and the twisted energy signatures of molecular disruptors tore through the screens.

Morgan forced herself to watch...but it was over in moments. A hundred and forty Taljzi warships had been wiped out.

One Kanzi superbattleship was crippled, leaking atmosphere as she lurched away from the fight on a barely functional interface drive that—thankfully—safely shut down as Morgan watched.

Three more were just gone.

"STATUS REPORT," Tan!Stalla asked after several seconds of silence.

"Shields are yellow in all sectors," Morgan replied instantly. "We have some nasty damage to the plating in sector B-Two, but Engineering already has the microbots reinforcing underneath. It won't be the same, but we can't fix compressed-matter armor in the field."

"Good timing on the fallback, Speaker Cosa," the A!Tol Captain said calmly. "Well done, everyone. We should be receiving formation instructions from the flag momentarily, so let's be ready to shift back into position.

"Ichri, Nidei, do we still have a bead on the civilian ships?" she continued.

"We're still picking up civilian shipping scattered around the system, but the big mining ships are gone," Nidei reported. "What other traffic I see seems to be heading for the outermost gas giant. There's either some kind of secondary facility there or they're under orders not to go into hyperspace if we can follow."

"Potentially both," Morgan pointed out. "We don't know much about what's going on in this system."

New orders flickered through from the flagship as they were talking. The Kanzi superbattleships were going to move in to evacuate and assess their crippled sibling. The Imperial capital ships and *Hammerfall* were going to investigate the carved-up planets.

A cruiser squadron was going to check out the civilian shipping.

"With civilian ships trapped in the system with us, we might actually get prisoners," Ichri said quietly. "Do we even have a plan for what to *do* with prisoners?"

Morgan snorted.

"Standard protocol," she replied. "Military prisoners are treated as POWs. Civilian prisoners are detained as necessary, preferably aboard their own ships with all engines disabled.

"There's no special orders. We should even be able to talk to them, though I don't envy the interrogator charged with getting any information out of them. Nothing I've seen suggests that even the civilians are going to be easy to talk to."

"That's someone else's problem later today," Tan!Stalla said calmly. "We may be called upon to provide brig space, but I'm not expecting to be putting up more than Marines.

"Right now, we're going to go check out where they were mining, and I want everyone's attention entirely on the waters we swim in." The Captain clicked sharply in concern. "*Something* was used to cut planets into pieces, and I don't want to find out it's still here by being its next target!"

CHAPTER THIRTY-ONE

MORGAN COULD HAVE CUT THE TENSION IN *JEAN VILLENEUVE*'S command centers with a knife. It was one thing to charge into battle all guns blazing, knowing the layers of defenses between them and enemy weapons and tied up in their own tasks.

It was an entirely different thing to slowly approach a section of space that clearly *had* contained something that could obliterate your starship in a single blast. The capital ships were well outside normal support distances, with nearly a hundred thousand kilometers between *Jean Villeneuve* and her nearest neighbor, Sun's flagship *Horatio*.

Even *Hammerfall* was keeping the same massive interval. Six Hundred and Fifth Sword of the Republic Mordak clearly agreed with his Arm Power counterparts: the odds said the mining device was no longer present, but anything that could cut planets up could wreck a warship.

"Just look at those gouges," Ichri murmured. The closest chunk of the planet zoomed in on the main display. "Two hundred meters deep and fifty kilometers long. Each of those was probably the better part of twenty *billion* tons of iron, and they're basically scratches in the exposed core."

The Precursors had split four planets open like a handy orange. There were elements of value in the crust, but the cores were nearly pure iron and heavy metals. Large portions of those cores had been molten when *whatever* hell-device the Precursors had used had cut them open, creating a fascinating geography on the new outside edges of the planet chunks.

Just one of the gouges Ichri was pointing out would have provided the raw materials for almost the entirety of the Taljzi fleets they'd faced to date, and just the one face of one piece of one planet they could see had a dozen of them.

"We're pretty sure the raw materials for the ring station in PG-Three came from here," Morgan said levelly. "Any sign of whatever cut the planet up?"

"Nothing," Ichri told her. "We've got a solid sweep of every planet now. If it was still here, I'd guess that the Taljzi took it home for examination."

"Because that's a reassuring thought," Morgan muttered. New orders came through the tactical net as she was muttering, standing *Jean Villeneuve* down to Status Two.

There were no hostile contacts left in the system. The remaining civilian ships were trying to hide inside the outermost gas giant, which was thankfully a problem for the cruiser squadron chasing them.

The battle, at least, was over.

"Get our sensor drones into space," Morgan ordered. "Let's get as detailed a close-up of that chunk as we can. I want to know if there's anything about these planets that's special, Speaker Ichri. If there was something that made these rocks more appealing to chop up—or even just *easier* to chop up—we want to know."

She shook her head.

"And if we can do anything to identify just what they cut it up *with*, that would be damn useful."

Especially if the Taljzi had taken it home to study. The *last* thing Tenth Fleet and its allies needed was for the Taljzi to have added a superweapon to the *rest* of their advantages.

"THE KANZI ARE GOING to have to write off *Voice of Glory*," Tan!Stalla informed the senior officers as they gathered the next morning.

A solid night's rest had restored most of the officers' calm, even if orbiting around a quarter of a planet was still nerve-wracking. Each of the planetary chunks now had an Imperial battleship orbiting it, with drones poring over every nook and cranny.

Jean Villeneuve was backing *Horatio* up on what appeared to be the most heavily mined piece. They weren't finding much of interest: the Taljzi had apparently mined the crystalline iron by carving huge chunks out with lasers and lifting them up to the refineries on the big mining ships.

The effort had been immense, but when each chunk was enough raw iron to build a battleship—with enough other elements mixed in to provide a large portion of the battleship's systems—it had to be worth it.

"Are they going to leave her or destroy her?" Nidei asked.

"They're setting antimatter scuttling charges as we speak," the Captain confirmed. "She just took too much damage. Those molecular disruptors are monsters."

"My biggest fear is that we're going to run into longer-ranged versions before this is over," Morgan admitted. "We don't know enough about how the things work to know if just building a bigger projector would increase the range."

"Currently, it appears that they have the same projector on their superbattleships as on their destroyers," Tan!Stalla pointed out. "We can assume some structural limitations there—and I understand that the Mesharom had the same range limitation."

"I'd agree," Morgan said, "but we're going after their homeworld, sooner or later. If the projector with a ten-light-second range is the size of a superbattleship, they can't mount it on a starship but they can sure as hell hang it in orbit of a planet."

The briefing room was silent as everyone processed that mental image.

"The good news, such as it is, is that I'm pretty sure that they can't use the device that chopped PG-Four's planets up as a weapon," Nidei said quietly. "All of our scans agree: it was basically a giant plasma saw. Cutting the planet up took weeks."

"And it says everything about how flexible my sense of reality is getting that that sounds almost reasonable," Morgan said. "I wouldn't want to run into a thirty-thousand-kilometer plasma saw, but at least we can probably avoid that."

Plasma saws were a derivation of the technology used for portable plasma weaponry, the mainstay of sidearms the galaxy over. Instead of firing a condensed projectile, they created a continuous arc between two projectors.

A worker had to create a hole to fit the projector in if he was working on a piece larger than the arc, but that arc could cut just about everything known to the Imperium except high-ratio compressed-matter armor.

"I'd hope we can dodge a giant-scale industrial element, yes," Tan!Stalla agreed. "The existence of such a device, with the construction scale and power levels required, is still terrifying."

Assuming it could be built and operated today. A lot of Precursor tech couldn't, which was something Morgan was still trying to wrap her head around.

"What about the civilians who were trying to hide?" Nidei asked. "I didn't see any reports of prisoners."

"We don't have any," Morgan told them grimly. "The civilian shipping dove too deep into the gas giant. Most of them won't have survived. Any that did...we can't get to."

Not without risking warships, and Squadron Lord Sun wasn't

doing that for a handful of civilian miners who wouldn't know anything. If they were willing to kill themselves to keep whatever they knew, the allies were more than willing to let them do just that.

"They suicided," Tan!Stalla said bluntly. "Some of them might be lucky enough to survive, but they plotted a suicide course rather than be captured. The Taljzi are insane."

"I thought the *Kanzi* were insane," Elstar rumbled, the big Rekiki engineer looking uncomfortable. "Slavers and rapists and fanatics all. These guys are something...else."

"Neither of them are insane," Morgan snapped. "Twisted, yes. Evil, definitely in the case of the Taljzi, but not insane. Insane would say they didn't have a choice in any of this. The Taljzi and Kanzi have a choice, they're just bound by the rules of societies that tell them what they have to do.

"And what those societies say they have to do; we think is evil." She gestured to the display showing the Kanzi superbattleships and their escorts. "The Kanzi are trying to be better, if only because they're realizing they can't fight *everyone*. When we have a chance to separate them from the worst of what their religion demands, we can deal with them. Talk to them. Understand them.

"It's no different with the Taljzi except that the society *they've* built embraces mass murder. If we were able to separate some of them, talk to them? We'd find out they're just Kanzi with ritual scars.

"But every one of them we've met, from the warship captains to the miners, has been a fanatic follower of a religion that says half the species in this room are unholy abominations that need to be destroyed."

She shook her head.

"They're not insane," she repeated. "If they were insane, we might be able to *help* them."

The briefing room was silent.

"And we can't," Tan!Stalla concluded quietly. "Maybe once we've beaten them. Maybe once we've smashed the structures and infrastructure of the Taljzi *state*, we can help the Taljzi *people*. But so long as the Taljzi remain what they are, they are our enemy and we must fight them.

"But Commander Casimir is correct. They are not insane. Everything they do seems perfectly reasonable to them." Her skin flashed dark purple in sadness and fear. "Including intentional mass suicide, it seems."

FROM *VILLENEUVE'S* BRIDGE, Morgan watched JTF 25 slowly gather back together above the wreckage of what had been PG-Four's fourth world. They'd flagged the system on their maps with the scans of the exposed cores. It wouldn't be worth it for anyone to fly this far out from Imperial and Kanzi space to harvest the massive chunks of crystalline iron, but once the Arm Powers' expansion reached there, the system would be of immense value.

For now, however, they had two more silver-flagged systems to explore. PG-Four hadn't been a bust, but the Taljzi were far too willing to die to preserve their secrets.

"Cosa? What's our ETA for getting out of here?" she asked the navigator. She and the Pibo were holding down what was expected to be a quiet watch while the task force reconvened, short four Kanzi superbattleships.

Hopefully, they weren't going to miss those ships.

"Looks like another half-cycle," Cosa told her. "There are still some sections of the mining sites that the engineers want a closer look at. The odds of finding anything are low at this point, but...well, why not?"

Morgan snorted. That would have been her deciding factor in Squadron Lord Sun's place, too. They weren't coming *back* to this system anytime soon. Making sure they knew everything they could learn was important.

"And the sensor network?" she asked.

"I'll have to check that," Cosa admitted. "It hasn't been in my field."

"I'll pull up the reports," Morgan replied.

Several hundred sensor drones, including six of the larger hyper-fold-equipped communication drones, were being left behind in PG-Four. The Taljzi might write the system off completely now, but Morgan doubted it. Exposed planetary cores were rare and valuable.

The reports from the cruisers laying the network were much what she expected. They'd be done six hours before the engineers were finished with their scans and tests, leaving a small but significant percentage of the system's comets and asteroids with concealed passengers.

If the Taljzi came back, Tenth Fleet would know. That might be what gave them the key to finding the enemy home system. Despite having taken two enemy systems, they still had no idea where the Taljzi's main centers were.

The next gold system on the list for them to get more data on was PG-Two, the target for the much-delayed JTF 24. By now, JTF 24 should actually be in the system, but hyperfold-com delays were what they were.

JTF 24 was eight light-years from JTF 25 and almost eleven from Tenth Fleet. That meant *Villeneuve* and her fellows would be the first to hear from the other Task Force for once.

"Sir!" The Anbrai Lesser Speaker holding down the communications console jerked away from her console in shock, Given the scale of the four-legged barrel-torsoed alien, that was an impressive gesture that risked breaking the seat.

"We have an alert from JTF Twenty-Four."

"An alert?" Morgan snapped. She'd been expecting a *report* from the other task force, not an alert. "What kind of alert?"

"It's from *Louis Pasteur*," the officer said quickly, massive hands dancing across the screen...and then freezing. "Commander...it's *Louis Pasteur*'s Tsunami Code."

The A!Tol had crawled from the water to the land relatively late in their evolution and remained partially aquatic creatures even now. The English word *tsunami* paled in comparison to what a major tidal wave meant to a species that lived in the shallows along the coastline.

It was a technically accurate translation...but a better *cultural* translation was *Armageddon*.

A starship's Tsunami Code was her final transmission, an automated black-box protocol enabled by the new hyperfold communicators.

"Anything else?" Morgan demanded. "Even...even Tsunami Codes from anyone else?"

Lesser Speaker Odon was still focused on her console, tapping in commands as she pulled data from the fleet's sensors.

"Negative, sir," Odon finally admitted. "We didn't even get the automated data dump that's supposed to be attached. I can confirm she was at PG-Two...and that's it, sir. She's gone...and it looks like JTF Twenty-Four went with her."

CHAPTER THIRTY-TWO

"WE HAVE CONFIRMATION FROM TENTH FLEET THAT THE Laians received an equivalent to the Imperial Tsunami Code signal from *Sickle Strike*," Squadron Lord Octavius Sun informed the virtual briefing of all of JTF 25's Captains and executive officers.

"Whatever hit JTF Twenty-Four hit hard enough that only the two most powerfully shielded units in the fleet survived long enough to even send a terminal transmission," the rotund little flag officer continued. "We have no reports of Tsunami Codes from any of the battleships or cruisers assigned to the Task Force from either the Imperial or Kanzi fleets."

The mass virtual briefing was dead silent.

"Twenty-six battleships, a superbattleship and a war-dreadnought," Sun noted. "Plus seventy-two cruisers and destroyers. Over a hundred and fifty thousand sentient beings...and as far as we can tell, they vanished before they could so much as send a message."

He shook his head.

"JTF Twenty-Four reported that their route from PG-Three to PG-Two was through an area of surprisingly low hyperspatial density," the Admiral continued. "Even evading that region, any force deploying from the main fleet will take a minimum of ten cycles to reach PG-Two.

"Assuming there's no similar region between PG-Four and PG-Two, we can reach JTF Twenty-Four's last known location in less than three. We haven't had time for a round-trip conversation with Fleet Lord Tanaka and Fleet Master Cawl yet, but they placed me in command of this task force, and I see no alternative.

"The last of our drones will be aboard within a twentieth-cycle," he noted. "They're going to be catching up, as movement orders have already been issued to all of your navigation departments. Within twenty minutes of those drones being aboard, this Task Force will enter hyperspace on course for PG-Two.

"We have no idea what to expect, but we know that it wiped out the entirety of JTF Twenty-Four. We may have more superbattle-ships than Squadron Lord Yone did, but remember: the *entire task force* was gone before they could send a message."

Sun looked at his subordinates grimly.

"My current intention is to exit hyperspace one full light-day from the star and carry out long-distance scans. From there, we will judge whether a rescue operation can be mounted to retrieve any survivors of JTF Twenty-Four or if there is anything in the system worth further operations.

"In either case, we will most likely need to wait for reinforce-ments from PG-Three. *Our* job is to make sure that those reinforce-ments don't walk into a trap."

Sun's words sent a chill down Morgan's spine. The best way to make sure that the main fleet didn't walk into a trap, after all, was to trigger it themselves.

"There will be time for questions later," the Squadron Lord told them. "For now, make sure your ships have everything they need from the logistics train before we get moving. This may be one of our most dangerous missions so far—but we need to know what happened to our comrades!"

SUN'S WORDS about "our most dangerous mission" echoed in Morgan's mind as she poked diffidently at the files in her office. The task force was underway, a timer in the corner of her displays telling her how long she had before she'd no longer be able to send messages home.

She'd traded a few more messages with Victoria, but she always found it hard to know just what to say. They couldn't even talk live, not without the fleet getting far closer to a starcom than they were going to get.

But...once again, she was going to be aboard a warship heading into action and didn't know how the next few days were going to end up.

Almost unconsciously, she started playback of part of the last message she'd got from the twins.

"Hey, sis, we pinned your girlfriend down for dinner in orbit last night," Leah's image told her from the screen. "I think we scared her; she seemed to think we had some dastardly plan."

"Well, we *had* a dastardly plan," Carol noted. "It was just pointed at Admiral Kurzman-Wellesley, not her. It was his birthday and I think he was hoping everyone had forgotten for once."

The pair of identical blonde women grinned with equal wicked mischievousness.

"Since we were there, we wanted to pick Victoria's brain," Leah said. "I mean, mostly we wanted to talk about *you* and see how she was handling having our sister out on the pointy end again, but we got onto half a dozen other topics.

"It's a damn smart cookie you've found yourself, big sis. We're probably going to pin her down again for dinner sometime just to talk shop."

"That said, she's got no fucking idea how to do the navy-wife bullshit," Carol cut in. "She misses you, wants to support you, but this is outside her experience set. 'Course, she's not the only one in the Duchy's uniform dealing with that, but, hey, wanted to poke *you* on this particular one.

"A little bit of reassurance might go a long way."

She paused the message. The message had gone from there into an accidental eleven-minute lecture on economic policy, followed by a seven-minute digression on boys and determined-lesbian-Carol's opinion of her bisexual older sisters' interest in them.

The important piece had been the reminder that as awkward and hard as the messages were for *Morgan*, they were still valued and appreciated by the woman she was sending them to.

She checked the time. Still twenty minutes before hyperspace and she wasn't on watch for hours yet.

The recorder turned on at the touch of her hand.

"Hey, Victoria, it's Morgan," she told the camera. "We're about to hit hyperspace again, early. I can't tell you much, Admiral's staff officer or no, but we're definitely heading into trouble."

Morgan paused, swallowing.

"I think this one might be *big* trouble. I think we'll pull through—we always have before—but it's at least as likely to be the end of me as that first run into PG-Three. There's not much of an update, really, but I wanted to let you know that."

She was silent, looking at the camera while she tried to find words.

"I love you," she finally said. "I want you to know that, no matter what happens. If fate wills it, I'll be back home soon enough. If not... remember that I love you."

It was a terrible message, but it was what she had in her today. A few tapped commands dropped it into the queue for the message stack home. Hopefully, it was the right thing to say, or at least close enough.

Morgan was pretty sure Victoria was going to run out of patience with her sooner or later, but she was at least going to *try* to be a good girlfriend!

CHAPTER THIRTY-THREE

"WE DIDN'T GET ANYTHING MORE FROM SICKLE STRIKE THAN you got from *Louis Pasteur*," Kanmorad admitted on the private call.

They'd settled into a schedule now. All three fleet commanders and their operations officers met once a day to make sure they were up to date on everything going on.

At least in PG-Three, that wasn't much. The joint task forces were doing all of the work...and all of the dying.

"That's the scariest part of this for me," Harriet admitted as she looked at the astrographic display all six of them were sharing. "I can accept something that can one-shot a battleship. We know perfectly well that molecular disruptors can do that, for example, if they get close enough. I'll accept that something can one-shot a *Galileo*-class superbattleship or a war-dreadnought, because the evidence shows something did...

"But we're talking something that one-shotted an entire *task force*. A task force that, if it wasn't a subdivision of the monster we've gathered here, would qualify as a significant fleet in its own right. A hundred ships, led by thirty capital ships."

She sighed.

"Only two even got out a terminal warning code," she said. "*Two*. The two most powerful ships in that fleet. If the Taljzi have some kind of superweapon, why haven't we seen it already?"

"Most likely, whatever it is, it's stuck in PG-Two," Cawl pointed out. "A fixed defensive installation of some kind, I presume. Which leads *me* to wonder if we've found the Taljzi home system— and if so, whether or not we actually have enough firepower to take it."

Harriet shivered, studying the chart again.

Two of the JTFs were continuing their scout missions. It seemed likely, still, that one of the gold systems was going to hold the Precursor installation responsible for the Taljzi's cloning technology. That was the target, really. The home system that held the cloning facilities.

They were down to four gold-flagged systems now. JTF-23 was still on their way to PG-Five and PG-Six. JTF-26 was headed to Seven and would pick up Eight as well now.

Hopefully, those missions would get them some answers.

"So far, every gold-marked system on the Precursor map has contained as much horror as wonder," Harriet noted. "Is it possible that we're looking at an actual Precursor weapon system in PG-Two? In Taljzi hands..."

"Well, that's going to feature in my nightmares," Fleet Master Cawl said after a long moment. "Though some variant of that has certainly been present in my worst-case planning."

The old Kanzi sighed.

"The longer the main fleet sits here and does nothing, the worse the politicking in my ranks becomes," he admitted. "The loss of JTF Twenty-Four is at least going to shut some of those idiots up, but we are going to need to do something."

"The last of my escort cruisers arrived at JTF Twenty-Two's position a few twentieth-cycles ago," Kanmorad pointed out. "They should be able to get to PG-Two more quickly than we can, even if they'll arrive well after Squadron Lord Sun. They'll need to exit hyperspace even further out than Lord Sun. We can't risk losing that entire force."

They couldn't really risk losing JTF 25, for that matter. JTF 22, though, was three hundred and sixty capital ships to the other task forces' twenty-eight.

The loss of JTF 24 meant over a hundred thousand dead. The loss of JTF 22 would mean over a million.

Those kind of numbers of dead were still all too possible once they finally launched their attack.

"We'll order Fleet Master Rist to exit hyperspace a light-week out," Harriet said firmly. "He is not to deploy his fleet into PG-Two until and unless he knows what happened to JTF 24."

JTF 25 would have to test the system to see what had happened. JTF 22 would do no such thing.

"Agreed," Cawl confirmed. "We need to make certain our people are safe, Fleet Lord Tanaka. The more horrors we find out here, the more I am concerned that we may have underestimated our enemy.

"They have, after all, had access to all of these Precursor systems for centuries. If it *can* be learned from, they have had the opportunity to do so."

TO HARRIET'S SURPRISE, Cawl remained on the call after Kanmorad dropped off. His aide, Karal, had been in a different room and dropped off with the Laians.

"My apologies, Captain Koanest," he addressed Harriet's operations officer. "May we speak in private?"

The Yin looked to Harriet for permission. The Fleet Lord was confused by what Cawl wanted...but also curious. She nodded her permission to her subordinate, and she bowed her way out of the office.

The privacy shield engaged, and she leveled her best "command glare" on Fleet Master Cawl.

"Well, Shairon?" she asked. "What's so important that you have to speak to me in absolute privacy...without drawing attention to it?"

Cawl snorted, the old Kanzi leaning back in his chair and stretching his blue-furred hands.

"You noticed that," he concluded. "Karal is aware and covering for me. So far as my fleet is concerned, we are still speaking to Kanmorad."

Even without orders to that effect, Harriet was quite sure that Koanest would at least be implying the same to everyone.

"Meaning everyone thinks this is a regular fleet command meeting and you wanted it to be a private one," she concluded. "So, I repeat myself. What's so important?"

"I underestimated certain elements of my own government," he said bluntly. "I can't be certain, but it looks like there's been a coup back home."

Harriet felt like she'd been punched in the gut. The entire Imperium had been operating on the assumption that, while the Kanzi Theocracy was a disgusting, slave-holding mess, their leadership was trying to make things better.

High Priestess Reesi Karal had convinced Annette Bond of that... and that meant she'd convinced the Empress, since A!Shall trusted Bond completely. Or at least, if the Empress didn't, she wasn't telling such unworthy peons as the commander of the largest fleet the Imperium had ever assembled.

"The High Priestess?" Harriet demanded.

"The forms and formalities are being run as they always have," Cawl replied. "Karal lives, but...you know my eldest daughter is one of the leading priestesses of the reformist movement, yes?"

"I've been briefed," she confirmed. Priestess Asiri Cawlstar wasn't the *leader* of the official reformist movement, such as it was, but she was apparently recognized as one of its greatest philosophers and speakers.

"She's been forced into hiding," Cawl said. "Orders came down from the Church's hierarchy for her to go into a meditative isolation.

That's a punishment but one that usually comes with a direction as to what they want you to meditate on—generally, it means your superiors think you've fallen away from God's guidance."

He shook his head.

"The orders didn't come from any of her direct superiors...and then Streya learned that Grand Priestess Altara was dead."

That was two mores names that Harriet recognized. Grand Priestess Ella Altara *was* the recognized leader of the reformists—and Guard Keeper Streya Cawlan was Fleet Master Cawl's youngest daughter.

"I take it that your daughter's hiding is *not* the meditative isolation that was ordered," Harriet presumed aloud.

"No. Streya's troops penetrated that monastery in time to intercept a contingent of Mahalzi sent to kill her."

Mahalzi. Harriet knew that name, though she'd mostly heard it in the context of "Uncle" James Wellesley-Kurzman talking about the Kanzi commandos who'd hunted them across a pirate station at one point.

The "Sons of God," they were elite Kanzi special forces that she'd thought reported directly to the High Priestess.

"Aren't those Karal's personal troops?" she asked.

"They're the *First Priest*'s personal troops," Cawl corrected. "An odd post, the only one in the high ranks of the Church for a male. The First Priest acts as the voice of the High Priestess and runs much of the day-to-day of the government while the High Priestess sets the agenda."

"And this First Priest is compromised?"

"If the Mahalzi are hunting reformers, I think the First Priest may have taken control," the Fleet Master admitted flatly. "The commandos at the monastery are all dead. My daughters took the monastery staff with them when they left. There are no witnesses to Asiri's fate left to be found, but questions are already being asked of my other daughters.

"And other reformists." He shook his head. "We are not a free and open society as you call it, Fleet Lord, but we have our rights and privileges. They are being trampled on by soldiers bearing writs in the High Priestess's name. From what my daughters tell me, the Golden Palace has been locked down but there is an attempt to make everyone think things are progressing normally."

"You are at risk of being recalled?" Harriet asked. The Golden Palace was the city-sized government complex that ran the Kanzi Theocracy.

"The Gloried Armada is not," he told her. "*I*, on the other hand, am at risk of being replaced if the worst interpretations are true. The Companions of the Divine Chosen are traditionally soldiers, warlords linked to the High Priestess's cause by"—he coughed— "being taken as her lovers.

"It would fall to the Companions in the past to protect the High Priestess against this kind of revolt. I think it will fall to us to protect it again—and the First Priest will fear us doing just that."

The First Priest was a kind of chancellor or prime minister, as Harriet's briefings understood, but a weak one in comparison to the executive power of the High Priestess.

"There are other Companions?" Harriet asked.

"And they are closer and, in a perfect world, would deal with this situation before it reached us," Cawl said calmly. "There are situations I can see arising that will impact you directly, Fleet Lord Tanaka, and I need your word as to how you will respond to them."

"I am bound by the orders of my Empress and the dictates of my own laws," Harriet pointed out. "Beyond that, my own honor asks that I help you."

He closed his eyes in a wince.

"That is exactly what you must not do," he said quietly. "The most likely situation is that I am relieved of command or potentially assassinated. My successor in either case will be bound by their orders to see the Taljzi defeated.

"If I am struck down, you must do *nothing*. The mission we have undertaken is far too critical, far too dangerous, for you to act."

"You expect me to stand by while an allied flag officer is murdered?" Harriet demanded. "To watch your own people kill you and do *nothing?*"

"If I am wrong, then they have the authority," he pointed out. "Our ways are not your ways, Fleet Lord. Judicial assassination is not unknown to us or even necessarily illegal. If it happens...the alliance between the Theocracy and the Imperium is too valuable to risk it over the life of one over-aged flag officer."

He was deathly serious, but Harriet shook her head.

"I will consider the situation if it happens," she told him. "But *our* ways are not your ways, either, Fleet Master. Our alliance with the Theocracy was born of mutual need, yes, but also of the understanding that Kanzi like you and High Priestess Karal were going to make changes.

"If those changes aren't going to happen and if the few Kanzi we've started to trust start showing up dead...my Empress may well reevaluate the agreement."

CHAPTER THIRTY-FOUR

Joint Task Force Twenty-Five's emergence into normal space was a slower affair than usual. With a trio of the *Bellerophon*-B battleships holding the portal open, a trio of destroyers led the way.

Their sensor data was being fed back to every ship in the JTF, and Morgan joined *Jean Villeneuve*'s tactical department in going over it with a fine-toothed comb.

Nothing attacked the destroyers and nothing was showing up on the close-range scans, so she was unsurprised when Squadron Lord Sun sent the order for the next wave to head through the portal.

That wave was a mix of every size of ships available to the fleet, from the Kanzi destroyers like the ones that had led the way through a *Bellerophon*-B-class battleship and a Kanzi *Righteous Sword*–class superbattleship.

Sixty seconds after those ships had made it through, the JTF continuing to be unscathed, *Jean Villeneuve* and *Hammerfall* passed through the portal. The two largest ships in the task force came through without escorts, and Morgan was holding her breath as they made the transition.

Nothing.

"I think we're clear," she said aloud. "Any blips, Ichri? Nidei?"

"Nothing," the tactical officer replied from the bridge. "We're clear out to at least a light-hour. There's nothing here. I expect Lord Sun to declare the rest of the Task Force clear..." The Ivida made a sharp barking noise, probably a chuckle.

"Now," they concluded their sentence, a moment after the order for the rest of the JTF to transition into normal space had come through.

At a full light-day clear of the star labeled PG-Two, they were still inside what would generally be regarded as the star system. The usual cloud of comets and icy planetoids—called the Oort cloud in Sol—was still several light-days farther out, but the main system mass of star and planets and main asteroid belts was still well within them.

"What are we looking at with the system, officers?" Tan!Stalla demanded. The A!Tol sounded nervous.

That was fair. Morgan *was* nervous.

"We're getting general geography data on the system," she told her boss. "Looks...looks surprisingly light. I've got an outer belt at eight light-hours and a pair of gas giants that look like the outer satellites but then..." She shivered. "*Nothing.* Innermost gas giant is at forty-two light-minutes, and I'm not seeing anything on a planetary scale inside that."

"There's something strange going on with the star," Nidei said. "I'm getting some weird interference patterns. Nothing we can pick up yet; we're still resolving sensor data."

From this far out, there was only so much resolving they *could* do. Spreading the fleet out would let them do more, though.

"Orders from the flag," Kira Alles cut in. "New coordinates are being sent to every ship for both direct location and drone deployment. ELA formation," she summarized.

"Extremely Large Array" formation meant that the fleet was going to spread out across a disk roughly a light-minute in diameter. Spreading the ships and their drones across that much distance would vastly improve the amount of data and resolution they could get and, with the speeds available to the fleet, would only take a few minutes.

"Cosa, get us in position," Tan!Stalla ordered. "Ichri, get the drones into space. Nidei, Casimir...keep watching what we resolve as we spread out.

"Something *very* strange is going on here, and past experience suggests that the Precursors are to blame!"

MORGAN RAN the numbers three times.

"Ichri, can you double-check this?" she asked after the third sequencing came back with the same impossible result. "The ELA isn't fully formed, so I might have missed something."

The Indiri pulled the data over to his own console and stared at her conclusion.

"I... This can't be right," he replied.

"I would say the same, so double-check my numbers," Morgan ordered.

Once the task force completed its unspooling, she'd know for sure, but the calculations she'd run were pretty conclusive.

"I have the same," Ichri said after a few seconds. "A minimum of a hundred thousand orbital platforms, each somewhere between a hundred and a thousand kilometers on a side."

The reason the star in PG-Two was looking weird was because it kept getting blocked. A *hundred thousand* stations, all roughly square constructions presumably covered with solar collectors on the under-side, orbited the star at approximately thirty light-seconds.

"I make it two layers," the Indiri noted as more data continued to come in. "It's hard to pick up without the extra data from the full ELA, since they're clearly set to orbit without interfering with each other."

"A Dyson swarm," Morgan concluded. Hundreds of millions of square kilometers of solar collectors, supporting *something*. Hell, for all she knew, this was just a power station and it was beaming power to installations in other *star systems.*

"Sir, if you look here...I think we found what's left of the inner planets," Ichri told her, highlighting a large object that drifted into sight around the star.

It was in a stable but fast orbit at one light-minute, and if Morgan hadn't seen the wreckage in PG-Four, she might never have recognized it. Entire planets had been chopped up—and then chopped up again and again and fed into what looked like a foundry a thousand kilometers across.

The machine had, presumably, spat out the bases for the plates that formed the Dyson swarm. The Precursors had carved *multiple planets* up for raw materials.

"You know, I never thought that the ring station in PG-Three would turn out to be the *least* intimidating thing in the region," Morgan said slowly. "More and more, I'm wondering just what the hell they were using that for when they had things of this scale."

"They definitely seem to have spread their operations out over more systems than we would have," Tan!Stalla noted. "PG-Three was a shipyard, we think. PG-Four was a raw materials source. PG-One was a colony...and it looks like PG-Two was the power source for all of that. They certainly didn't need this much power *here.*"

Nothing in the technological databanks available to the Imperium could transmit power on this scale—but there was one thing, Morgan realized, that could consume it.

"Or maybe this was where they built the singularities for their power cores," she said softly. "Finding either natural singularities or the energy to build artificial ones is the biggest impediment to *our* attempts to build singularity power plants, after all."

She couldn't see the bridge very well, but Ichri turned his attention back to the Dyson swarm. Morgan was moderately familiar with Indiri body language, but she was mostly unfamiliar with their scent signals...and the one Ichri was emitting was unknown to her.

At a guess, it was either terror or wonder. Morgan wasn't entirely sure which she was feeling, but she was realizing that she was looking at an entire system turned into a glorified factory.

"Wait." Nidei cut into everyone's moment. "Take a look at these grid coordinates. It's not a Dyson swarm but..."

The full Extremely Large Array was complete now, giving them solid resolution across the entire star system, and Nidei had flagged something far smaller than the plates of the Dyson swarm...something that looked *very* familiar.

"You're the expert, Commander Casimir, but I think..."

"You're right," Morgan confirmed shortly. "That's a Mesharom war sphere."

Or, more accurately, it was *half* of a Mesharom war sphere.

CHAPTER THIRTY-FIVE

THE DATA CONTINUED TO FLOW IN, AND *JEAN VILLENEUVE*'s bridge and secondary command center were silent as the wreckage of ship after ship was plotted on the displays. Over thirty Mesharom war spheres, none even remotely intact, were plotted onto the screen.

There was no sign of any of the smaller Mesharom battlecruisers. As the sensors expanded, though, they did manage to find at least *one* other ship.

"That's *Sickle Strike*," Ichri concluded after his team had gone through the scans. "Or, well, approximately thirty-six percent of her. *Something* hit her with enough force to vaporize the front two-thirds of the ship."

Morgan whistled silently, looking at the image on secondary control's big holodisplay. The solid slug of metal of a Laian war-dreadnought was a familiar sight now, but this one was now missing most of its lines and mass.

"Any chance of survivors?" she asked.

"Hyperfold communicator is in the front half of the ship," Ichri told her. "The shield held for long enough for the death alert to be sent, but then the communicator was destroyed. Any survivors wouldn't be able to call for help by any means but radio...and wouldn't know we were out here yet."

So, potentially, there were survivors. The war spheres were much the same, though the sheer lack of living hands aboard a Mesharom warship and the time frame since they had to have been struck meant the odds were low.

"What do we *do*, sir?" Nidei asked.

"I see two choices," Tan!Stalla replied. "The first is that we send a scouting force in farther to see what happens to them. The second is we pull back to the point where we can get the light from what happened to JTF 24."

Morgan shivered.

"All of the wrecks are inside the gravity zone of the star," she pointed out. "Even the Mesharom couldn't open a hyperspace portal in there. Not one big enough and sustained enough for a starship, anyway."

The Mesharom would have been able to launch hyperspace missiles there, but they wouldn't have been able to escape. Not once they'd entered whatever hell trap this was.

"Orders from the flag," Alles said into the conversation, as if in answer to Tan!Stalla's suggestions. "We're staying here, but—"

"Squadron Lord Sun is ordering a test salvo of hyperspace missiles into the region near *Sickle Strike*," Nidei interrupted as the tactical officer read the instructions. "Why us?"

"We have the biggest HSM magazines in the fleet," Morgan replied instantly. "The *Thunderstorms* only have half our magazines per launcher, and even the *Bellerophons* are only up to about eighty percent. Plus, we have the most powerful shields, and even HSMs will need us to get a *lot* closer.

"If we're firing missiles to see what happens, better us than anyone else."

"Makes sense, I suppose," Nidei replied. "Setting it up. What's everyone else doing?"

"Escorts are falling back through hyperspace to set up a second

ELA to catch the sequence of events when JTF 24 arrived," Alles said. "Couldn't we also grab the Mesharom's emergence?"

"We don't know when they came here," Morgan pointed out. "We'd need the drones to sit at six light-months for weeks, at least. Might be worth it...but we could also pull that data from the war spheres if we can safely board them."

"That's a significant depth of 'if,' Commander," Nidei noted. "We're ready to fire the test salvo. I have eighteen missiles targeted in a sphere around *Sickle Strike*. Sphere is exactly one light-minute in diameter. Fourteen shots will be inside the gravity zone, four outside it."

Sickle Strike wasn't deep inside the zone where she couldn't have brought up a hyper portal to escape...but she was inside it. And moving, Morgan noted. Usually, the collapse of interface drive took away all of the ship's velocity. A catastrophic failure, such as a missile impact, released that velocity violently as thermal and kinetic energy. Normally, though, it was just shunted back into hyperspace where it came from.

Strike appeared to be drifting toward the star at several hundred kilometers per second.

"You've factored the velocity across the time delay of the light?" Morgan asked.

"Yes, sir. Targeting the expected location after a twenty-four-hour delay," Nidei confirmed. "It looks like the wreckage was partially expelled from the interface-drive field before the field failed."

Morgan shivered again. That would have been...unpleasant for anyone inside the surviving chunk of the Laian warship.

"Commander Cosa. Take us in to the designated firing point."

Even targeting an un-evading target, they couldn't fire a full light-day.

"We emerge at our maximum range from the target," Tan!Stalla continued. "We will keep the hyper portal open and return as soon as the missiles are fired. Ichri—I want three hyperfold drones deployed alongside the missiles, because *we* are not staying in those waters long enough to see what happens."

Hyperspace settled around the superbattleship in a reassuring blanket as they dove deeper into PG-Two.

"Emergence will be in forty-five seconds," Cosa announced. "If I do this right, we'll only be in real space for two and a half seconds before we get back out of the hot waters."

Seconds ticked away and Morgan concealed her clenched hands in her lap. She trusted both Nidei and Ichri to do their jobs, but even the First Sword had to stand by and watch for this kind of maneuver.

"Emergence in ten seconds."

The programs were laid in. The organic sentients now got to wait and see if they lived or died.

"Emergence."

It was a blur. The portal tore open in front of them, and *Jean Villeneuve* lunged forward into normal space. She was already turning in space as she emerged, the seconds of acceleration required for the interface drive potentially enough to be a danger in this system.

"Firing," Nidei snapped.

"Drones away," Ichri responded.

"Portal entrance!" Cosa said.

"Dodge!" Morgan ordered, seeing the danger before anyone else did. "Energy signature!"

Something was following them *through* the hyper portal. A blast of unfocused energy surged through the portal before Cosa closed it —but the Pibo had been listening, and the superbattleship danced sideways as a blast of solar plasma shot through the two-kilometer-wide portal.

They all stared grimly at the gray void where that blast had been.

"That's...not good," Ichri finally said.

It was one *hell* of an understatement as far as Morgan was concerned.

THANKFULLY, the rest of the task force was still around when they dropped back into real space back at the light-day mark. They'd only been gone a few minutes, but Morgan had still been concerned after watching the blast of energy that had nearly caught them.

"Pulling the update from the hyperfold drones," Nidei reported, then paused. "Sir...they're gone."

"That's not a surprise, I suppose," Tan!Stalla admitted. "Alles, get us linked back into the tactical net. I need to know what everyone *else* got from the drones before they died."

It only took a few seconds...and it didn't even take that long to watch the footage.

The drones hadn't survived long enough to see the missiles' fate. They'd died in the same moment that *Jean Villeneuve* jumped into hyperspace. They had enough data for Morgan to be sure they hadn't been hit by the same blast as *Villeneuve*, but they'd died fast enough that they may as well have been.

"They weren't hit simultaneously," Nidei said after they went through the recorded sensor data for the third time. "The gap is miniscule, but it's there. Whatever it was hit us, then each of the hyperfold drones in sequence." The Ivida made a sad choking noise. "That sequence lasted one hundred thirty-six milliseconds, to be clear. To make four shots."

"All of equal power, too," Morgan replied. "That's overkill for a drone."

Even the portion of the blast that had made it through the hyper portal would have been enough to cripple *Jean Villeneuve*. It probably wouldn't have vaporized her—but it would have overwhelmed the shields.

"Sirs," Alles said. "I have a request from Squadron Lord Sun for Captain Tan!Stalla and Commander Casimir on a closed conference."

Morgan looked at the visual link to the bridge and shrugged.

"No one argues with the Lord," she observed. "I'll move to my office?"

"I'll drop the privacy shield here," Tan!Stalla replied. "I don't think I should leave the bridge just now."

A few moments later, both of them were on the link with the Squadron Lord. Tan!Stalla's holographic form looked somewhat... squished. The privacy shield was a physical tube that dropped around the command seat. It was sized for any officer that could hold command, but the larger Imperial species—like the Anbrai or the A!Tol themselves—could find it cramped.

Morgan found the privacy shield on the bridge claustrophobic, and she was much smaller than Tan!Stalla.

"Squadron Lord Sun," she greeted the human flag officer.

"Captain, Commander." Sun looked perfectly calm and ordered, but there was a hint of Morgan's current fear and nervousness behind her eyes. "We've received the initial reports from the second ELA with regards to JTF 24's fate.

"I'm keeping them under wraps until we have the full scan, but the destroyers dropped a pretty deep field of drones. We have an initial scan I'd like to show you both."

"No one argues with the Lord," Morgan echoed her earlier comment.

Sun smirked at that, but the expression vanished as quickly as it appeared. A moment later, a new image added itself to the holographic gallery. It was an empty piece of space, but that didn't last long.

Hyper portals appeared across that empty chunk of space. Standard doctrine in the face of most enemies was to get as much firepower into real space as quickly as possible, and JTF 24 did just that.

In one maneuver that was over in under ten seconds, every one of JTF 24's hundred starships were in the system. Nothing reacted to them initially, and they were clearly scanning the system.

Presumably, they'd seen much the same things with the Dyson

swarm and the Mesharom wrecks as JTF 25 had. They brought their drives up and headed in-system...and then it happened.

In the blink of an eye, massive blasts of plasma appeared out of nowhere on top of every ship in the task group. *Louis Pasteur* and *Sickle Strike* lasted a few fractions of a second longer, thanks to their shields, and *Strike*'s sheer mass meant a portion of the warship's two hundred million tons survived.

"Less than a second," Sun observed. "A hundred warships obliterated in less than a second—but whatever it was ignored them for the first minute or so. I wanted to talk to Casimir specifically. You're our Mesharom expert—would this weapon have done the damage we see on the war spheres?"

"Unquestionably," Morgan confirmed. "The only thing I find odd is how much deeper in the system the Mesharom were when they were destroyed. Plus, well..." She considered. "Can you replay the moment before they were attacked?"

Sun did.

"JTF 24 had their drives on minimum after emerging from the portal. It was only when they brought their drives to full power that they were attacked—and they were attacked as *soon* as they passed the point one cee mark.

"Our hyperfold drones were maneuvering at point five cee when they were shot. *Villeneuve* wasn't moving particularly quickly, but we were changing velocities and our drive signature was out of proportion with our velocity at that instant."

"Something's targeting interface drives," Sun agreed. "Which means your missiles are probably going to get vaporized the moment they emerge from hyperspace. God *damn* it."

"Sir?"

"Even in a worst-case scenario, there could be as many as a thousand Laians alive aboard *Sickle Strike*—and even assuming all of the Mesharom are dead, their computers could give us critical intelligence about what they know about this region that we didn't.

"Tilsan certainly seemed to feel they knew perfectly well what to do out here," the Squadron Lord concluded. "What a bloody mess."

Morgan considered the scans again.

"What do we do, sir?" she asked.

"I don't know," Sun admitted. "I see no reason not to wait for the data on your missiles' emergence...but I also don't see how that's going to change anything. I don't know how the Mesharom ended up here, but whether it was intended as such by the Precursors or turned into it by the Taljzi, this entire system is one giant trap."

CHAPTER THIRTY-SIX

SLOWLY LEAPFROGGING DESTROYERS AND DRONES TESTED THE limits of the range of the weapon. Twelve hours after the test launch of the hyperspace missiles, they were close enough to pick up the results.

Twelve light-hours was as close as *Morgan* would have been comfortable coming at this point, but she understood where Sun was coming from. If there was any way they could get to the damaged ships to attempt contact with any survivors, they had to do it.

Sitting in her office, *Jean Villeneuve*'s First Sword watched the footage of their test-missile salvo's arrival. The hyperspace missiles had a far lower maximum velocity in their terminal mode than a regular interface-drive weapon, and she wondered if that was enough to keep them safe.

It wasn't.

The portals opened. The missiles shot through. Plasma teleported onto them and they died. Sixteen missiles vanished in a handful of seconds.

But not instantly. The missiles had been in real space for entire seconds before they vanished, and Morgan ran the sensor data again at an even more delayed speed.

There was definitely a minimum threshold in play. It wasn't a very high threshold. There was enough data now for Morgan to run the numbers and at least make a guess as to how much power an interface drive needed to be running at to draw the attention of whatever angry god ruled PG-Two.

A starship literally *couldn't* get its drive low enough to elude notice and still move. Even their shuttles would be moving so slowly that they might as well be using reaction engines.

Morgan snorted and tapped a command on her communicator.

"Commander Elstar," she greeted the ship's chief engineer. "Question for you."

"No, I have no idea how to get past a hell-weapon that is apparently teleporting pieces of a star onto anyone who steals its water," the Rekiki replied. "Other than that, I might have an answer."

"Do we have any non-interface-drive engine systems in storage?" she asked.

He was silent.

"Nothing...significant," he said. "A few thruster packs for work suits and pods designed for use on the exterior of the ship. But we have schematics. Give me raw materials and I could build an engine that could move *Jean Villeneuve*...if not very fast or for very long."

Morgan chuckled.

"What about one of our assault shuttles?" she asked. "Could we refit one of them with a set of fusion thrusters without having to hunt down asteroids for you?"

"Probably," he agreed. "That's at least a two-day project, sir. What are you thinking?"

"I'm not sure," she told him. "Don't start anything—we'd need the Battalion Commander's okay before we started carving up her spacecraft, anyway—but I needed the data."

"To help the one can help the herd," Elstar replied. "Let me know if you need anything more. We're sitting quietly at the moment." The crocodilian alien snorted. "That never lasts, though."

The channel closed and Morgan turned back to her numbers. A low-enough-power interface drive might be okay, but it was *definitely* the interface drive that was causing the problem. The hyper portal wasn't drawing attention on its own, and the wrecks were just sitting there.

A fusion thruster was almost certainly fine, but its range was inherently limited. An interface-drive ship could cross the twelve light-hours from their closest approach in a day. A fusion rocket ship was looking at weeks, even months.

They *could*, she supposed, use a starship to open a portal at the edge of the gravity zone and send the shuttles through. It looked like interface drives were safe enough on the other side of the portal.

Even the closest approach was still millions of kilometers from even *Sickle Strike*, though, and Morgan doubted they even carried the parts for Elstar to rig up the massively overpowered artificial-gravity systems the old United Earth Space Force had used to allow their ships to accelerate at several dozen gravities.

At two or three gravities, even a few million kilometers would be hell.

It was a shame that the portal generators contained inside *Jean Villeneuve*'s hull could only be opened from regular space. They could punch through the gravity well, but they were only half the system—they could only open into hyperspace, and the drives built into the missiles could only open into real space.

Her train of thought ground out as she stared at the frozen image of the hyperspace missiles being vaporized.

It was time to talk to Commander Elstar and Battalion Commander Petrina Damyanov. In person, because the idea was beyond merely *questionable*.

PETRINA DAMYANOV WAS a blonde and blue-eyed woman with a hooked nose and piercing stare. She waited calmly for Morgan to finish explaining her brainstorm, then looked down that nose at the shorter Commander.

"Are you fucking insane?" she asked bluntly. "Hooking a *missile* system up to my shuttles? And that's after you gut their existing drive systems?"

"We wouldn't be gutting their drives," Elstar pointed out. Even Morgan, who'd grown up with Rekiki bodyguards, had some problems reading the expression on the engineer's long face...but she thought he was thinking hard.

"There isn't really a purpose in modifying the shuttles themselves," the engineer continued. "There are modular equipment bays on the craft. They are mostly only used for fuel tanks, guns, or missiles, but they are present and make the task easier.

"We can strip the portal system from a hyperspace missile and install it in the modular bays. We'd need the projectors from two missiles per shuttle, but that should suffice to open a large-enough portal for long enough."

The engineer was doing math on his communicator. Morgan chuckled.

"You can hook up to the holoprojector, Lesser Commander," she suggested. They'd taken over one of *Jean Villeneuve*'s dozens of small meeting rooms designed for just this kind of meeting.

Elstar did so, and Damyanov was surprisingly patient while he ran the numbers, slotting and removing virtual objects from a three-dimensional model of the Imperium's standard assault shuttle.

"Clear plains," Elstar finally concluded. "Need the projectors from *three* missiles, but that provides a twenty-five percent safety margin. Three is too much, two is too little, may as well use three."

"When my people's lives are on the line, I agree," Damyanov said. She was studying the design. "I see. We strip the missiles, leave two autocannon. Limited ammunition, but better than unarmed." She nodded.

"The engines will need to be a bolt-on," Elstar told them, gesturing to the second item taking shape on the holoprojector. "We have a standardized harness for adding extra gear to the shuttles that I can repurpose. It's designed for heavy-duty delivery."

The Rekiki shrugged, an impressive gesture on a sentient the size of a small horse.

"If it can haul a tank or a self-contained hospital, it can hold a rocket," he concluded. "We'll triple-secure the connections. We'll use these modular bays on the shuttle here and here for fuel.

"It'll depend on what we can pull off for the engines, but I think I can give you about five hundred KPS of delta-v."

"That's not much," Morgan pointed out. "I mean, we can deliver them to the right place in hyperspace so they only have to maneuver a few dozen thousand kilometers at worst, but that still leaves my biggest concern."

"Five hundred KPS leaves my people a *long* walk home," Damyanov said, clearly picking up on Morgan's concern. "I'm reasonably comfortable assuming we can find hydrogen aboard the wrecks to refill the tanks, but just getting clear of the gravity zone for someone to open up a hyper portal for us could take a damn long time."

"Three hours from *Sickle Strike*," Elstar said. "Twenty light-seconds isn't much. Will take you about as long to get up to speed, but that just makes it easier for whoever is playing catcher."

"Damyanov has a point," Morgan said quietly. "We'll want to tag *Sickle Strike*, and knowing we can just fly the Marines out from there is handy, but if we're doing this...we need to get to the Mesharom ships."

"And while I see the value, I'm not sure it's *enough* value to justify sending my people on a one-way trip," Damyanov agreed grimly. "So, Commander Elstar, Commander Casimir, what miracle do you have to suggest?"

"If we could open a ship-sized portal that deep in the gravity zone, I'd say send a ship," the engineer admitted, studying the shuttle design on the map. "As it is, though...I don't know."

"What about the portal emitters for the missile launchers?" Morgan asked. "Can we refit one of those to fit on a shuttle? They only open from regular space, but if we send three shuttles and one is just carrying the way home..."

"That won't work," Elstar replied. "The assembly is too large, for one thing, and it needs to be fully contained to work. It's too large to fit through the portal generated by the missile system, let alone fit through the portal it creates."

"There would be Mesharom hyperspace missiles aboard their ships, though, wouldn't there?" Morgan noted. "They use a two-portal design that can enter hyperspace from that deep in the system. If we do the same thing to their missiles that we're doing to ours, would they be able to bring the shuttles back into hyperspace?"

"It's...possible," the Rekiki said slowly. "I don't know anyone familiar enough with Mesharom missile technology to do the work, though. You'd be hoping to find Mesharom gear...and a Mesharom *technician* on the other side."

"And in the worst case, Battalion Commander, you're still only looking at a twenty-six-cycle flight out," Morgan pointed out. "If we make sure the shuttles have, say, a fifty-cycle food and air supply, that should be safe enough. Every third unit already carries a hyperfold com. No one gets left behind; they just get stuck with a long, boring flight. Even in the worst-case scenario, the task force can leave a destroyer or cruiser behind to pick the Marines up."

Damyanov looked at the hologram of the shuttle on the screen.

"Twenty-six cycles on a shuttle," she repeated. "That's a hell of a thing to ask of my Marines, but I see the point. Is it really worth it, though?"

"Best-case scenario, there are Mesharom survivors and we buy some goodwill with the Conclave," Morgan pointed out. "I'm not overly concerned with their goodwill if they're closer to Tilsan than Adamase, but I won't pretend it doesn't have value."

She shook her head.

"There may even be information that survivors could give us or that we can pull from their computers that will help us track down where we need to go to deal with the Taljzi. In the worst case...well."

Morgan looked around the room at the other two officers and smiled sadly.

"If the Mesharom are all dead, then we get a chance to loot one of their ships for tech and information in a way no one will ever blame us for," she said quietly. "I'm not going to turn that down, even if it feels ghoulish."

Damyanov snorted.

"Easy for *you* to say," she pointed out. "It's not like you're going to be on the shuttles making that twenty-six-cycle flight home."

"I'm the task force's Mesharom expert," Morgan replied, realizing the situation even as she said it aloud. "It's...entirely possible I will be."

CHAPTER THIRTY-SEVEN

"The engineering team has run all of the tests they can short of actually modifying a shuttlecraft," Morgan explained to Tan!Stalla and Squadron Lord Sun twelve hours later. "All of the models say that it's going to be one hell of a rough ride on the Marines, but the system will work to deliver an assault shuttle safely into regular space inside the gravity zone."

"If that works, it's going to make for some interesting options down the line," Squadron Lord Sun noted. "I'm guessing you want the okay to proceed with tests in live space?"

"It's as much time as anything else," Morgan told them. "If we're doing this, we want at least a day or two to run tests with an actual rig before we try and make the insertion. Plus, well, if we make the deep insertion to board the Mesharom ships, we'll need to leave a starship to wait for the Marines to make their way out with a fusion rocket."

"Fortunately, it's not like the shuttle will need to slow down," Tan!Stalla observed. "Any interface-drive starship would easily be able to match velocities and scoop them up."

"We still haven't even established how close an interface-drive ship can safely get into the star system," Sun pointed out. "I cut the testing off at ten light-hours. That would be a two hundred and fifty-seven cycle flight for the Marines."

"We're not expecting anyone to pick them up in normal space," Morgan replied. "With enough vector data from drones positioned at the ten light-hour line, we should be able to open a hyper portal just outside the gravity zone and have the shuttles fly right through.

"Then whoever is left behind picks us up in hyperspace."

"Us, Commander?" Tan!Stalla asked. "You are, may I remind you, the First Sword of an Imperial superbattleship. This isn't your job."

"Has anyone else in this fleet dealt with Mesharom face to face?" Morgan asked quietly. "If there are survivors aboard the war sphere, we need to speak to them. Work with them—those survivors would be our best chance of getting the Marines back within cycles instead of twenty-cycles."

"You're aware, Commander, that we can test all of this and still be wrong, yes?" Squadron Lord Sun asked. "I'm not entirely sure I'm comfortable with risking Marines on a long shot like this, but the First Sword of one of my superbattleships..."

"It's a dangerous mission, but it's not a suicide mission," she replied. "If I thought it was a suicide mission, I wouldn't even be suggesting that we send the Marines. If the one-way hyper portal system for the shuttles works, then we have a chance to rescue people who have no other chance of survival—and to access the Mesharom databanks and see if they knew more about the mess out here than we do.

"I think the risk is worth it. I'm not going to argue that I *have* to go, but I think my presence would help." Morgan shrugged. "Plus, I'd feel like an ass putting together an ops plan this risky and asking someone *else* to do it."

"That's the nature of command, *Commander*," Sun said pointedly. "Nonetheless, you're right. Captain Tan!Stalla?"

"I'd rather not lose my First Sword," *Jean Villeneuve*'s Captain replied. "I see the value in assigning her to this mission if we're going to do it. I would volunteer *Villeneuve* to wait for them, but..."

"That's not happening," the Squadron Lord chuckled. "What I'm leaning towards right now is launching the mission, checking to see if we can rig up hyperdrives from the Mesharom gear, and then heading out to scout our two new silver systems while the Marines make the long flight out."

"You're approving the operation, then?" Morgan asked.

"The risk is worth it," Sun concluded. "We owe the Laians that much, and while the Mesharom may be a giant pain in the ass, I'm not leaving *anyone* to die in deep space if we can save them."

He grimaced.

"And I'm cold-blooded enough to be swayed by the opportunity to go through their tech databases if they're dead," he admitted. "You'll have orders to cover you from any potential backlash on that one, Commander Casimir. It's ghoulish but it's arguably necessary. Let the blame lie on my head if needed."

***

"REMOTE LINK ESTABLISHED TO SHUTTLE FOUR," Damyanov reported from *Jean Villeneuve*'s flight control center. "We are in full control of the shuttlecraft."

"Just to triple-confirm: there is nobody aboard her, right?" Morgan asked from her own seat in secondary control. The superbattleship currently hung in hyperspace, just on the other side of an immaterial and near-impenetrable barrier from where the rest of JTF 25 waited one light-day from PG-Two.

"No one has been assigned to her, and bay scanners say she is empty of life signs," the Marine CO confirmed. She didn't even seem surprised by the question. "There might be some cockroaches aboard, but we'd pick up anything down to a stray rat."

There was almost certainly insect life of several varieties aboard

Jean Villeneuve, but those same life-sign scanners meant that Morgan would be *very* surprised if someone found a rat aboard.

"Take her out, Battalion Commander," Morgan told the other woman. She was watching the ship's sensors. Shuttle Four, refitted with Lesser Commander Elstar's new systems, was their new test project.

"Taking her out."

The shuttle drifted out under interface drive at a sedate few hundred meters per second. Then, still under remote control, it shot out to exactly three thousand kilometers from *Jean Villeneuve*.

The small craft was still well within the one-light-second "visibility bubble" where sensors could see much as they would in regular space. Beyond that bubble, only gravitational-anomaly scanners could pick anything up.

That was enough to track starships and roughly estimate mass, but it didn't give them details. For this project, they needed more detailed data and a short-enough range for remote control by a light-speed-limited radio link.

"Safe distance established," Damyanov said. "Do you confirm, Commander Casimir?"

"Should be plenty," Morgan agreed. "Elstar?"

The engineer was in secondary control with her, watching the test with sharp eyes. His actual work would come once they were finished, either adjusting or duplicating what had been done to Shuttle Four.

"It's only opening a sixty-three-meter portal," he pointed out. "Anything more than a kilometer is overkill."

"There's no such thing as overkill," Morgan replied. "Only 'open fire' and 'I need to reload.'"

"Then you're clear," the Rekiki replied with the thump of his hind leg that was equivalent to a human chuckle.

"Battalion Commander?" Morgan said.

"Passing this over to Lesser Speaker Istil!," Damyanov replied. "Better to have an actual pilot for this part."

The A!Tol chuckled on the channel.

"This is probably the easy part," he noted. "All of the modules look green. Interface drive is down; fusion rocket is standing by. We're good to go on your click, Commander Casimir."

"Go."

Morgan didn't say the word particularly loudly, but she didn't need to. Moments later, new energy signatures flared as the systems they'd torn out of a trio of hyperspace missiles flared to life.

She wasn't entirely clear on the science behind why these projectors could only open a portal from hyperspace into regular space. She *did* know that building them that way had saved sixty-three percent of the mass and volume required for the system compared to projectors that could open a portal into and out of hyperspace.

By using the projectors from three missiles, Shuttle Four tore open a hole into reality. The fusion rocket lit off and flung the spacecraft toward the portal.

The entry into real space was slightly larger than Elstar had projected, just over a hundred meters, but that shouldn't be a—

The portal snapped closed with Shuttle Four only halfway through it, severing the shuttle cleanly in two. With the fusion rocket live and hydrogen flooding through the conduits, the rocket flickered...and then exploded.

It was a small explosion, only the equivalent of a few hundred kilos of TNT. Enough to wreck the half of Shuttle Four still in hyperspace.

Her channel was silent for several seconds.

"You know, I'm the best pilot *Jean Villeneuve* has," Istil! said conversationally, "but I think that was at *least* half my fault. I didn't have enough velocity going in. Not used to the rocket."

"The portal should also have stayed open longer," Elstar replied. "We can adjust for that, but only by opening the portal while already at velocity along the vector. Is that doable?"

"Entirely," Istil! said. "I think I need to sit down with your team as we do the next iteration, though. Even if that blip is all we're getting, I think we can work with it. Might need to take the organic out of the equation, though."

"You're talking shop," Morgan pointed out, trying not to feel *too* disappointed. This was, after all, why they had been experimenting. "Pull together that meeting, Lesser Speaker, Lesser Commander."

She smiled calmly.

"You have six hours to get the next shuttle ready."

If she had to burn half of *Jean Villeneuve*'s assault shuttles to get the other half where she needed them, well, shuttles were a *lot* easier to replace than Marines!

IT TOOK them seven hours to rig up the second shuttle, Shuttle Seventeen this time, with the new loadout and the software solution for the problem.

Once again, the spacecraft hung three thousand kilometers from *Jean Villeneuve* as the Marines went through remote checks.

"All right. All systems are green," Istil! reported. "Bringing up the fusion rocket."

New icons and data streamed across Morgan's display in secondary control. The main holoprojector was zoomed in on the one small shuttlecraft as it began to accelerate.

"Velocity up to one KPS. Initiating insertion program."

There was no visible change from the moment Istil! was directly controlling the engine to when the computer took over. The point wasn't that the computer was a better pilot.

The point was that the computer had better *timing*. The portal appeared without any notification to the organics after the pilot's report of the program initiation, a hundred-meter hole back into reality flashing into existence in front of the shuttle.

It was open for less than half a second—four hundred and thirty-six milliseconds, according to Morgan's scans—but it was enough when the timing and the velocity were perfectly matched.

"Insertion complete," Damyanov reported. "Commander Casimir?"

"Everything looks fine from this side. I'll have Cosa drop us back into normal space so we can check that it came out without issues."

The program would have had the shuttle accelerate away from the portal for five minutes, then decelerate to a stop. That would leave it with plenty of fuel to make it back to *Villeneuve*, assuming there were no problems.

"Speaker Cosa?" Morgan linked to the bridge. "First phase was successful. Take us back into regular space, please."

"On it."

Jean Villeneuve's exotic-matter arrays cut a far larger hole through reality than the shuttle's projectors had. A four-kilometer gap opened in front of the warship and she gracefully glided through.

Shuttle Seventeen was waiting for them, exactly where it should have been—about halfway through its circle.

"*Horatio*, this is Commander Casimir on *Jean Villeneuve*," Morgan said into her com. "Please forward the data on the shuttle emergence. Any problems you saw?"

"*Villeneuve*, this is Commander Shepard," the other battleship's XO replied. "We're forwarding the data now, but the second emergence looked fine." She paused. "The first one...not so much."

"The back half blew itself up," Morgan replied. "I'm hoping it looked a bit better on this side."

Commander Jennifer Shepard laughed.

"I guess it did, then," she admitted. "We just saw half an assault shuttle go flying across the fleet. You sure about this whole plan, Casimir?"

"It worked out here," Morgan said. "We'll run a few more test flights, then we need to do the *really* messy test."

"Sending a remote shuttle through inside the range of the weapon?" Shepard suggested.

"Exactly."

CHAPTER THIRTY-EIGHT

THERE WAS NO FAST WAY FOR THEM TO GET THE RESULTS OF THE final test. *Jean Villeneuve* had dropped the automated shuttle in hyperspace and triggered its program, then stuck around long enough to watch it disappear into real space near the stricken Laian war-dreadnought.

Then it was a long twelve-hour wait until they knew whether the hell-weapon at the heart of the PG-Two System found something offensive in their reaction-drive shuttle.

It at least let them take some time to study the data they had on just what the weapon *was*. Attending that virtual briefing was part of Morgan's day-to-day workload, making sure *Villeneuve* was represented in the discussion.

"Officers, welcome. I am Lesser Commander Benedicta Wong, the senior engineer aboard *Horatio*."

Wong was a petite Asian woman and clearly in charge of the briefing. There were several other engineers on the virtual stage being shared across the Joint Task Force as well. In the absence of a ready team of scientists, working out the science behind things fell to a mix of tactical officers and engineers.

Whoever had time, really.

"Among my many past sins is a masters in astrophysics from the University of Hong Kong," she told them. "When someone needed to head up our investigation of PG-Two's teleportation-plasma-cannon, Squadron Lord Sun apparently noticed that in my file."

She smiled readily.

"I call the system a teleportation-plasma-cannon because that is basically what it does," she noted. Sensor data splayed across the screen behind Wong as she spoke. "Upon locating a vessel with an interface drive, it teleports a packet of plasma—approximately half a million tons, give or take—from the convective zone of PG-Two to the destination.

"Basically, any vessel that the system detects ends up being ground zero for a major solar flare," Wong concluded. "Worse, the targeting appears to be FTL and live. Nine times out of ten, the flare is going to emerge *inside* the vessel's shields.

"It represents a terrible and deadly weapon, which is why it took us so long to work out what exactly the system *is*," she told them.

"Which is?" someone asked.

"It's not a weapon," Wong replied calmly. "It's a malfunctioning refueling system."

The entire briefing was silent, and Morgan looked at the repeating datafeed of the destruction of JTF 24.

"That seems unlikely," another officer replied. "Refueling systems don't fire hundreds of thousands of tons of superheated plasma at you."

"And this system was never intended to do so," the engineer said. A schematic of the star and the Dyson swarm appeared behind her. "The key factor to understand is that the presence of the Dyson swarm and the *many* malfunctions of its systems have warped the star. Most important to our current discussion, the star has expanded by approximately a hundred thousand kilometers.

"When the system activates, it is attempting to link to a Precursor facility that was originally orbiting *inside* that hundred-thousand-kilometer line. To be clear: if this inner layer of the Dyson swarm existed, the entire layer would now be inside the star by our estimate.

"Presumably, the first layer was the primary layer of power-generation platforms. The device was supposed to link with an existing network and draw energy from it. It would then link to a specifically designed receptor on the target vessel and recharge batteries and other power capacitors."

Morgan could definitely see the value. It wouldn't cover all of a ship's needs—even the Precursors, she was sure, required physical fuel for some things—but running off beamed power while in the system would definitely save on resources.

"Could they beam it interstellar distances?" she asked. If the other systems were drawing their power from PG-Two...

"We can't be sure," Wong admitted. "It seems likely, but it's hard for us to say, since we're not looking at anything resembling a functional system."

"How does a beamed power array become a plasma teleporter?" *Horatio*'s Commander Shepard asked.

"Something has clearly gone wrong with both its origin and destination calculation," Wong replied. "But the teleporter system itself is running off power collectors on the Dyson swarm. It's targeting *inside* the star, so it picks up plasma instead of making a link with the systems on the inner layer of platforms...and even if we had the right receptors for what it's *supposed* to be sending us, it would still be sending us a coronal flare instead of a stream of power."

"But how did the Mesharom get lured as deep into its range as they did?" Morgan asked.

"Here." Wong zoomed the image back out to the star system and highlighted a region away from the Mesharom but still inside the gravity zone of the star.

"That, officers, is a debris field we missed on the initial scans because none of the ships are intact," she said bluntly. "Knowing what the weapon impact looks like, we went looking for recent debris that followed the pattern.

"It appears that a fleet of several hundred Taljzi warships was destroyed at the same time as the Mesharom Expeditionary Fleet," Wong told them. "My guess would be that at some point in the past, the Taljzi disabled the teleporter system.

"Faced with the Mesharom Expeditionary Fleet, they sacrificed a fleet of their own to lure Grand Commander Tilsan into the lethal radius of the teleporter and turned it back on. If they expected to survive, they miscalculated."

She shook her head.

"It might not have been designed as a weapon, but the PG-Two Dyson swarm is powering a system that will destroy any interface-drive ship that enters the star system. Thanks to Commanders Casimir and Elstar, we believe we can reach the damaged ships...but that's all we're ever going to do.

"Without the time to either send ships in ballistic or the free resources to build specialty reaction-drive vessels, PG-Two is going to be immune to *our* investigations for a very long while."

Morgan studied the Dyson swarm still visible around the star in the zoomed-out view. There'd probably been people living on the swarm, the personnel to operate the terrifying version of a refueling and power station the Precursors had developed.

Precursor tech failed and warped in weird ways. A beamed-power system was only so distant from a weapon at the best of times.

She could only hope that whatever mechanism had allowed the system to beam across stars was permanently offline!

———

DROPPING out of the virtual conference, Morgan checked the time and realized that they should finally be getting data on their test. Only in space combat, she reflected, could the speed of light be considered obnoxiously slow.

Getting up to go check on the results, her admittance chime sounded before she even reached the door to secondary control.

"Enter," she ordered, pausing her own course out of her office. She was unsurprised to see Ichri open the door and step inside.

He'd managed to find a chance to soak his fur relatively recently, and the frog-like sentient's red hair was slick and glistening with moisture.

"We have our scans of the test," he told her. "As of twelve hours ago, Shuttle Seventeen was entering an automated orbit of *Sickle Strike*. She exited hyperspace without any problems and followed the preset protocol."

"Good," Morgan agreed. "The second test?"

"We'll see in an about an hour," Ichri replied. "I don't see any reason why we'd be any worse off near the Mesharom ships than near *Sickle Strike*."

"Neither do I," Morgan agreed. "But since I will personally be riding one of the shuttles investigating the war sphere wreckage, I'm perfectly happy to spend a few more hours making sure it's safe."

"Of course, sir," Ichri said. "Everything is looking good, though. I'm surprised the JTF has waited this long."

"Because we owe the Laians that much," she said quietly. "The Mesharom, too, though Tilsan managed to burn a *lot* of goodwill."

Her wallscreen had gone back to showing a tactical map of the star system once the conference was over. She considered what Commander Wong had been saying as she studied it, then stepped over and tapped a specific section of space.

The screen zoomed in and her request brought up the data on the debris field the engineer had located.

"Sir?" Ichri asked.

"The Mesharom left Sol a hundred cycles ahead of us," Morgan told him. "We assumed that their final fate here was around the same time—or longer, since the Mesharom can modify hyperspace to travel faster and we can't. *This*, though, is the Taljzi fleet that lured them into this system. They were only destroyed sixty-two cycles ago."

A fleet that had to have known *exactly* what they were doing. Or had the Taljzi command told the crews of those hundreds of superbattleships—and the escorts that hadn't even left enough debris to identify—that the teleporter had an Identify-Friend-or-Foe system so they'd be safe?

For that matter, it was entirely possible the Taljzi had thought they *had* built an IFF system into the teleporter, only for the flailing Precursor system to ignore it. It was, after all, a broken, malfunctioning tool.

"So, it took the Mesharom forty cycles longer to get here than us?" Ichri asked. "That seems odd."

"I'd agree...except for why they were here." Morgan tapped the wreckage of the Taljzi fleet again. "They were chasing the Taljzi fleet. There's two options I see: either there's another Taljzi system we haven't found yet that the Mesharom did, and this fleet ran here from there—or the Taljzi punched Tilsan in the nose and led them around like an angry pig for forty cycles."

Morgan *hoped* that someone would have reined the Grand Commander in if they'd fallen for that, but it was entirely possible no one had been able to. She'd have expected, after all, for Adamase to be able to prevent the Battle Fleet officer from burning the Mesharom's bridges with the Imperium.

"The important part about the fleet only having been hammered sixty-two cycles ago is the sheer *scale* of a Mesharom war sphere versus its crew," Morgan continued. "Even with completely non-functioning life support, half a war sphere should still have had enough air aboard to support two dozen Mesharom for sixty-two cycles."

Two dozen Mesharom was about half the crew of a war sphere. The Mesharom did not like other people, not even their own species. Mesharom spacers were a rare breed, willing to be in relatively enclosed spaces with each other—and those "relatively enclosed spaces" consisted of thousands of cubic meters with each Mesharom in charge of hundreds of servitor droids.

Those robots didn't need air or food. The Mesharom crew did and probably wouldn't have survived a hundred cycles.

"It's all a question of odds, either way—but the probability of there being survivors goes up several orders of magnitude if they've only been there for sixty cycles, Speaker." Morgan shook her head.

"We weren't actually expecting survivors, Ichri. We were hoping, but we were expecting to be tearing into their tech and their computers. Now...now it looks like we might just save a few lives along the way."

The Speaker nodded his understanding, looking over her shoulder at the data.

"May I suggest that we leave Grand Commander Tilsan there if we find him?" he suggested.

Morgan barked laughter before she managed to swallow it.

"No, Speaker," she told Ichri firmly. "I understand the temptation, but if there's anyone left out there, we are *not* leaving them behind."

Even if the Mesharom Battle Fleet Grand Commander was one of the most aggravating sentients her nation had ever had technically friendly interactions with.

CHAPTER THIRTY-NINE

"FORCE ALPHA MAKING INSERTION IN SIXTY SECONDS."

Damyanov's announcement echoed through the shuttle, making another shiver run down Morgan's spine. She intentionally had the helmet for her armored vac-suit on her lap, covering her hands as they clenched and unclenched nervously.

"If anyone's got some last words for Company Commander Tret and the rest of Company Delta, now would be a good time for them," Damyanov continued. "Declarations of unrequited love are discouraged, though. We *are* expecting to see them all again."

A series of chuckles ran through the shuttle. There were forty Marines of two different species in the shuttle with Morgan.

That was a pretty standard setup for a mixed-species ship like *Jean Villeneuve*. No Marine CO would ever stand for a mixed-species *squad*—though Morgan had heard stories of the mixed-race Special Space Service troops that had saved her mother a few times—or more than two species to a platoon.

Two squads and a command section filled a fifty-sentient shuttle, assuming a reasonable average size between the sentients. A!Tol or

Anbrai Marines ended up needing larger shuttles, for example, but *Villeneuve* didn't carry any Marines of their size.

Four shuttles carried all of Company Delta toward *Sickle Strike*. Morgan watched their path on the headset she was wearing. At thirty seconds, they switched from interface drive to fusion rockets.

At zero, the portals sliced open in front of them and they vanished.

"We're showing clean penetration for all of Force Alpha," Damyanov announced. A moment later, her voice sounded directly in Morgan's ear.

"That's one company in, three to go in with us," the Marine CO told her. "Are you ready for this, Commander?"

Morgan coughed, softly enough that the Marines probably didn't hear her through their power armor. She *really* envied the humans and Tosumi troopers around her their power armor.

"It's search and rescue, Damyanov," she pointed out. "I'm not going to pretend I'd be ready for a forced boarding of an enemy warship, but the Mesharom are at least theoretically friendly—and even if they're not, we're their ride home."

The Marine chuckled.

"You'd be surprised how little that means sometimes," Damyanov said. "Your file says you're qualified on that gun. How *comfortable* are you with it?"

The plasma rifle leaning against Morgan's leg was designed for use by an unarmored sentient. It could be set to fire the same intensity as the standard blast from the armored Marines' weapon, but that was its maximum setting and she'd be replacing power cartridges like candy at that setting...and on the default setting, a cartridge held forty shots.

"I qualify twice a long-cycle on it," Morgan pointed out. "I take one to range every twenty-cycle or so. Any of your people will outshoot me with it, but I can carry it, I can aim it, and I can fire it."

"Believe me, Commander, firing it at a living target is a very different affair," the Slavic Marine said gently. "That said, your qualification scores are *better* than ten percent of my troops, and they practice a lot more than you do. They, on the other hand, have shot at real enemies."

"I haven't," Morgan agreed. "And if this goes according to plan, that isn't changing today."

"Oorah," Damyanov replied—a phrase that seemed to be unique to human Marines but that every human Imperial Marine seemed to have picked up somewhere. "Force Bravo is making insertion in eighty seconds, Commander.

"Last chance to chicken out."

Even from the phrasing, Morgan knew that Damyanov wasn't actually expecting her to.

"This is a private channel, Battalion Commander," she pointed out sweetly. "So, I *can* tell you to go fuck yourself."

She could still hear the laughter in the Marine CO's voice when she sounded the sixty-second warning on the main channel.

<hr />

MORGAN HADN'T BEEN aboard a shuttle under actual thrust since she was three years old. She suspected that the Tosumi half of the platoon sharing a shuttle with her *never* had—and enough of the human Marines were young enough that it was probably a foreign experience to them, too.

The fusion rocket hammered the shuttle's passengers back into their seats as the ship struggled to get up to the velocity the insertion program called for.

And then the passengers got a foretaste of hell.

Every calculation and model they'd run had told Morgan that the transition through the missile-style portal punched into the gravity well would be uncomfortable. The exact details hadn't been entirely certain, but she'd figured it would be unpleasant but it would also be over quickly.

Instead, that fraction of a second seemed to stretch out into eternity. A couple of pieces of equipment that hadn't been *quite* properly secured against thrust gravity broke free just before transition, and Morgan got to watch them fly toward the back of the shuttle for what felt like at least an hour.

Time wasn't frozen, but it moved with a treacly slowness unlike anything she'd ever experienced—except for her body, which reacted to an unfamiliar twisting of space and time by revolting violently. Pain wracked her torso, on par with the worst period cramps of her teenage years, and she gagged against a rising sense of nausea.

She heard several Marines vomit through their helmets, the sound strange and drawn out by the impossible nature of the space and time they were cutting through. The transition lasted less than a tenth of a second, she *knew* that...but they endured it for *hours* before it finally ended.

Everything snapped back to normal in an instant that sent the nausea spinning completely out of control—and several more Marines to vomiting. Morgan swallowed her own gorge and snapped her helmet back on.

The headwear and the vac-suit had systems for that, after all. As did the power armor—not that that made throwing up in a helmet any less unpleasant.

"We're through," Damyanov said in a breathless voice. "That was..." She paused, then swallowed. "That was a hell of a ride, right, Marines?" she snapped in a forcefully cheery voice.

"Oorah!"

It seemed the Tosumi aboard had been working with humans for a while.

Morgan waited in silence, checking data through her headset as she waited for an update from the shuttle pilots.

They'd emerged as close to on-target as was possible, drifting a hundred and twenty thousand kilometers from the wreck of one war sphere and a hundred and fifty thousand from the next closest.

Whatever formation the Mesharom had been maintaining had

been wrecked by the additional velocity imparted by unexpected point-blank solar flares.

Curiosity led her to check a different piece of data, and she inhaled sharply.

"If you ever suggest we do that again, I may hurt you," Damyanov's voice said quietly in her ear.

"It worked," Morgan pointed out. "It's probably going to end up in the Imperial Marines' list of options now." She shook her head. "If it makes you feel any better, the systems agree with our perception of that bullshit. The shuttle says transition took eleven minutes."

"Are you fucking *kidding* me?" the Marine demanded. "I thought I was imagining it."

"I thought it took about three hours, so I'll trust the shuttle's systems," Morgan replied. "We can probably work out better tools with proper experimentation back home, but I doubt it's ever going to be a fun ride. I can see it being a damn useful one."

"So can I," Damyanov agreed. "So long as I get to send someone *else* on that trip."

Morgan could hear the other woman shake her head inside her armor helmet.

"All right, Casimir, this is at least partially your show. What do you need?"

"First off, I want an ID on the closest war spheres if we can manage it," Morgan ordered. "I'm planning on going to the closer one, but there's at least one more inside a practical range. Depending on what ship that is, it could change my mind."

"I'll get the pilots on it," Damyanov promised. "Just one question."

"Of course?"

"If we do manage to find a way back into hyperspace from here, is it going to be that bad?" the Marine asked.

"From what the techs tell me..." Morgan paused, considering how to phrase it. Then she figured *blunt honesty* was probably the best plan. "It'll be worse."

"Great. Just great."

<hr />

"WELL, that does change things, doesn't it?" Morgan asked softly as she looked at the two war spheres on her heads-up display.

The closer ship was *Deception*—well, the name actually translated as something like *A Disagreement on Lying*, but that was a mouthful, so they'd put in an override on the translator—and was slightly less intact than the farther ship.

That wouldn't have been enough on its own, though. Forty-two percent of *Deception*'s mass remained, while forty-eight percent of the farther ship remained. They were still going to find intact hydrogen tanks on both ships, and the computers would contain much the same information.

The farther ship, however, was *Blade*. More accurately translated as *Honorable Edged Weapon*, that war sphere had been Grand Commander Tilsan's flagship. Just as important in Morgan's mind, however, was that Interpreter-Shepherd Adamase had been aboard *Blade*.

"It's only six minutes' difference in the flight time," Istil! pointed out from the cockpit. "Five gees the whole way. I'm not going to say it's going to be *comfortable* or anything, but we accelerate for an extra few minutes and get up to a peak velocity of an extra ten KPS.

"We won't even use up half our fuel."

Morgan nodded slowly.

"Battalion Commander?" she asked. "It's a pretty small difference, and one of the Mesharom I've actually met was aboard *Blade*. I'm inclined to make the longer jump."

"It's your mission," Damyanov pointed out.

"My mission. Your Marines. Your shuttles," Morgan pointed out genteelly. "And I'm asking your opinion."

The Marine snorted.

"I can't tell one giant caterpillar from another, but if you say we're more likely to find friends on *Blade*, then let's go to *Blade*. It's still your call."

"It is," the Commander agreed. "But it's so much easier to give orders when everyone agrees with you. Set your course for *Blade*, Lesser Speaker Istil!."

"Yes, sir!"

CHAPTER FORTY

OVER AN HOUR AT FIVE GRAVITIES WAS A PUNISHING experience, but Istil! thankfully reduced the acceleration as they came into position around *Blade*. Three companies had brought twelve assault shuttles, and their scanners were giving Morgan a spectacular and complete view of the wrecked starship.

War spheres weren't quite the perfect sphere the name implied. Twelve kilometers across at their "waist," they were "only" eleven point eight kilometers tall. *Blade* had even been larger than that, Morgan noted as she reviewed the video footage.

There was apparently more left of the Grand Commander's flagship because there'd been more of it to survive in the first place. It had been an extra three hundred meters wider and taller than its siblings, presumably a different class if the Mesharom bothered to define their ships that way.

"The plasma flare started inside her hull," Morgan observed, thinking out loud on a channel only Damyanov could hear. "Looks like it was equidistant between her primary drive emitters."

It wasn't *quite* the exact center of the ship, but it was close enough.

"From there, it cut along a line directly away from the star, vaporizing everything in its path." She shook her head. "The flare itself was about two hundred meters wide. On a smaller ship, the flare itself would have consumed everything.

"On the war sphere, a lot of what we're seeing is secondary damage from it vaporizing a kilometer-wide path from the center of the ship through the outside. Then we're seeing secondary explosions and antimatter containment failures. The flare itself did about...two-thirds of the damage we're seeing.

"The rest was...well, it was the consequence of vaporizing thirty-five percent of a ship's hull, Morgan concluded bluntly. "It *looks* like the microbots had enough power to seal off the damage, but she's cold now."

"What does a war sphere even *use* for power?" Damyanov asked. "Shouldn't they have some kind of secondaries?"

"The antimatter cores *were* her secondaries," Morgan pointed out. "Her primary power supply was a pair of singularity power cores. Both of *Blade*'s were...huh."

She traced a line in the air.

"Both of *Blade*'s singularity cores were outside the vaporization zone," she noted. "That meant they survived long enough for safe shutdown. The singularities themselves would probably have been fired into space at near-lightspeed, but their capacitors could have kept the ship running for long enough to seal the wounds and stabilize affairs.

"There's too much damage for them to get the interface drives back online." Morgan shook her head. "That was probably lucky. If the Taljzi activated the Dyson swarm's teleporter while they were in combat, they might not have realized what was being used as a targeting beacon."

"What would have happened if the cores had been inside the vaporization zone?" Damyanov asked carefully, her voice sounding slightly ill.

Morgan made a sucking sound.

"You can't vaporize a singularity, so it would suck up all of that mass and energy...and without any safety constructs or controls, it would suck up the rest of the ship. We're talking unstable singularities with multiple planets' worth of mass."

She shrugged.

"They'd consume the flare. Then they'd consume the ship. Then they'd explode." Morgan waved towards their contacts. "There's a reason not all of Tilsan's ships are still here. I suspect the rest made it to PG-Two...but didn't survive the teleporter."

"Okay. So, that's *terrifying*, but how do we board the Mesharom ships?" Damyanov asked.

"Emergency access protocols are in the shuttles' databases," Morgan replied. "I suggest we head for as close to the center of the ship as we can get and dock over the automatic sealant. Form a seal, pump electricity in according to those protocols, the microbots will open an airlock for us.

"They'll be running off power from the shuttle, but that's why we have those protocols. We feed them energy, and they let us in."

"All right." Damyanov still sounded more than a bit sick. "Let's go knock on the scary alien super-warship."

Morgan didn't argue the classification. If nothing else, a Mesharom war-sphere massed well over a *billion* tons.

Scary alien super-warship was a perfectly accurate term.

***

"CONTACT. BOARDING DOCK LINKED IN."

Morgan had felt the moment the shuttle had touched the alien starship. So had everyone else in the shuttle.

"Power is feeding and the hull material is drinking like it hasn't seen the ocean in a month," Istil! continued. "Other shuttles are reporting the same. How long does this ta—"

Morgan grinned as the video feed told her the answer. The microbots recognized emergency protocols as soon as they woke up.

She'd told Damyanov that the microbots would "open an airlock," but that was a bit of a misstatement.

The microbots *built* an airlock. A complete, two-door airlock sized to match the boarding dock extended by the assault shuttle. The dock itself could also act as an airlock, but that wasn't going to be necessary.

"We should be getting some data feedback telling us what the air is like on the other side," Morgan told the pilot. "What have you got?"

"CO_2 levels are high but oxygen is breathable levels for us and Mesharom," the pilot replied. "Seriously? How did they manage *that*? The ship has no power!"

"You're looking at half of a sphere with an average twelve point two kilometer diameter," she pointed out. "That's a *lot* of air to work with, and even if the entire crew survived, there's only fifty or so of them. I was worried about how much atmo they'd lost before the hull sealed itself, but if they had power to keep even one life support plant running for a *week*, they'd buy themselves another month."

"Well, the doorway is open and the airlock protocols are integrated," Istil! told them. "I'm not letting their air into the shuttle, but we can move a combat section in each transfer."

"The Commander doesn't go first," Damyanov said calmly. "Section Alpha-Two-Two, move up and into the ship."

Morgan grimaced but didn't argue. The Marine was right.

The airlock cycled four times before she joined platoon Alpha-Two's command section—and the Battalion Commander—in the airlock.

"Our job is to keep you alive and find any survivors," Damyanov told her over a private channel. "I *know* your stepmother's reputation."

Morgan snorted and checked the strap on her plasma rifle.

"So do I," she agreed. "And I've seen the scar on her face from when she was wrong. There shouldn't be any hostiles on *Blade*, though. What reports are we getting?"

"Empty white corridors with minimal lighting and no computers," the Marine CO summarized as the airlock cycled around them. "If there are survivors, where would they be?"

"You should all have the standard map of a war sphere," Morgan replied. "It's not reliable, not with how everything in the ship can change, but a lot of things are permanent. The major physical infrastructure can't move much, after all."

The degree to which the Mesharom ship could relocate entire modules like, say, hyperspace missiles, inside its hull was still weird to her.

"It looks like the computer core is intact and near us," she continued. "I suggest that we and Alpha-Two head there and haul a cable to hook it up to the shuttle's power.

"Other teams should sweep for survivors, fuel and hyperspace-missile magazines." She grimaced. "Hopefully, the engineers we brought with us can work miracles if we *don't* find any survivors."

She wasn't hopeful. Without Mesharom help, Morgan knew they were making the long flight back outside the gravity zone.

The good news was that it looked like there *should* be survivors. Hopefully, even Mesharom could talk to aliens when their very lives were at stake!

WITH THE LIGHTING NONFUNCTIONAL, the stark white corridors of a Mesharom ship looked less "sterile" and more "haunted." The lights from the Marines' armor and Morgan's own vac-suit cast stark shadows on walls unmarked by decoration or even doors.

"How are we supposed to know when we're near our destination? Or, hell, near *anything*?" Damyanov asked.

"Scan for heat signatures," Morgan suggested. "Mesharom run warm, over thirty-five Celsius. Penetrating radar should give us the structure as well. The doors open on the same emergency protocols as the exterior hull, without needing a seal."

"Wonderful."

Morgan concealed a chuckle. All of this had been discussed in advance. Damyanov could be forgiven for forgetting—her people were the ones doing the scans. On the other hand, her people *were* doing the scans as they went.

"We've got a heat signature," one of the Marines announced a couple of minutes later. "Not warm enough to be a Mesharom, but I think we're looking at live hardware. Through there." The Tosumi pointed with one of her lower arms.

"Set up the terminal and tickle the wall into opening," Morgan ordered. "That's the first sign of life we've had so far."

It was hard to tell where the door had been *supposed* to be. The microbots would, normally, have had a specific spot acting as a door that would automatically sense when a Mesharom or a servitor robot was approaching.

Without main power, though, the microbots couldn't even move. A trickle of extra power from the portable batteries the Marines were carrying, accompanied by the right data signals, opened a neat two-meter-wide hole in the wall.

"You don't go first," Damyanov repeated to Morgan, managing to short-stop the Fleet officer's advance without blatantly knocking her away.

A fireteam of four Tosumi Marines went in first instead. Cameras and lights swept the space, the feeds coming back to Morgan's helmet and heads-up display.

"I've got what looks like a battery hooked up to an air circulator fan," the team leader reported. "The battery is almost dead, but it looks like they were running the air from here to somewhere else."

"Makes sense," Morgan said. "With life support down, making sure the unused air is heading to where the people are is essential. Can you see where it was going?"

"I can send a drone down the piping," the Marine suggested. "It's not going where we were going, though."

"That's fine," Damyanov said. "Put the drone in on autonomous mode and link it to the rest of the teams. Whoever is closest can follow it home.

"We need to get Commander Casimir to the computer core."

Morgan nodded and gestured for the Marines to keep leading the way. Knowing that *someone* was alive aboard the ship was worth the stop, but they needed those computers. Survivors would make this trip worthwhile—but the computers could make this trip *game-changing*.

THE TERMINAL CHIRPED ONCE MORE and the wall dissolved into a doorway. It felt weird to Morgan that they were leaving the holes they were opening behind them, but there wasn't much reason to *close* them, either.

"Air in here isn't great," the lead Marine reported. "And...these are computers? They don't look like any computers I've ever seen."

Morgan pushed her way past the Marines to enter the computer core. It was about what she expected.

"That's because we can only build molecular computers in crystals the size of your arm. Not the size of your house," she told the Marine as she stared up at the immense blocks of crystal that controlled the systems of the war sphere.

"How long is this going to take?" Damyanov asked.

"A while. First step is getting the interface set up," Morgan replied. "That's those crates you Marines have been hauling. Open them up."

"Should we be getting some of the engineers up here?" the Marine asked.

"Eventually," Morgan agreed. "Right now, we're better served having them sort through fuel and missiles and see if they can tell us which way we're going home. Once we know that, we'll pull them into this project."

Most of the interface setup was pretty self-explanatory, anyway.

Or at least, Morgan found it self-explanatory, but from the way some of the Marines were easing away from the setup like they'd break it... well, she *had* helped design it.

It took a few minutes to get the holoprojector and computing hardware set up. Once that was done, it was a matter of setting up the memory crystals—a far smaller version of the massive spikes filling the chamber she was sitting in and dedicated purely to data storage without any processing power—and then linking the whole affair to the computers.

And giving the computers power.

"Bring that cable over here," she ordered as she grabbed the interface connectors. "There should be a set up for us to plug all of this in...somewhere."

She stood at the base of the block of crystal circuitry, staring up at it for several seconds before she shook her head and started poking around the base of the structure.

"Sir, this is Speaker Talzon," a Tosumi officer interrupted her thoughts. "We've located a group of survivors...including Shepherd Adamase."

Morgan froze.

"Adamase asked who was in charge...and when I told them it was you, they demanded to speak to you. In person.

"Immediately."

CHAPTER FORTY-ONE

APPROACHING THE AREA THE SURVIVORS HAD RETREATED TO answered a question it hadn't yet occurred to Morgan to ask: if the war sphere had a hundred thousand servitor robots aboard, where were they?

They were there. Slumped against the walls where their internal power sources had failed or been cannibalized to buy more operating time for the robots with the programming the Mesharom needed.

Morgan could tell she was getting closer as the stacks of dead robots grew denser. The servitors didn't look like any sentient race she'd ever encountered—including the Mesharom. The serpent-with-arms structure was based on a semi-sentient creature on the Mesharom homeworld that they'd used as a beast of burden for most of their history.

As she understood it, the species still played a major role on the Mesharom homeworld but wasn't capable of the level of intelligence necessary to be useful in technological production and starship crews.

Hence the servitor robots that did so much of the physical labor aboard Mesharom ships.

They might not look like any sentient creature she knew, but they still looked like people to Morgan's eyes. Seeing them stacked up like spare parts was unnerving.

Finally, she and her escort—she'd left most of the Marines in the computer core—reached an opening in the microbot walls that was large enough to admit a Mesharom. There were actually lights there, and her vac-suit told her that the air was getting warmer around her.

Stepping through the door, she was thankful for the fact that the helmet concealed her face. She'd *never* seen multiple Mesharom at once. The room she'd entered was huge, and its subdivisions were only half-walls. From the entrance, she could see fourteen Mesharom. Each of them was a multicolored three-to-five-meter-long caterpillar.

Many of them wore strange-looking long helmets that covered their eyes, likely hooked up to a VR sim of some kind to help them deal with the "crowd."

Near the entrance, there was a single Mesharom who'd exited their cubicle to speak with her Marines. Spotting her, the dark-green Mesharom waved the Marines away with several of their dozens of feelers and moved toward her.

"Interpreter-Shepherd Adamase," Morgan greeted the alien. She recognized their patterns from pictures and video her stepmother had shown her from their many interactions.

"Commander Morgan Casimir," Adamase said, bending their entire body in thirds to achieve a strange bow. "I never expected to see the Imperium here...let alone you."

"I am the closest thing Tenth Fleet had to a Mesharom expert," she replied. "I'm in charge of the expedition. Rescuing any survivors is the top of our priority list. What's your status?"

"May we speak in private?" they asked. "The situation is...complex."

"It's your ship, Interpreter-Shepherd," Morgan pointed out. "We're still fumbling our way around, trying to find people."

"Of course. Follow me."

Gesturing for her Marines to join the team watching the survivors, Morgan did just that. If she couldn't trust Adamase in this situation, well...if things were somehow that bad, they were all going to die.

"UNFORTUNATELY, I cannot rearrange this space to your comfort," Adamase told her as they entered a smaller chamber off the big area the Mesharom had created. "We have limited power resources remaining at this point, and I have reserved them for keeping what limited life support we have running."

"Why wasn't the ship equipped with emergency power plants?" Morgan asked.

The alien made a grumbling noise as they arranged themself on a bench and gestured for her to make herself comfortable. The bench might have been designed for a massive caterpillar-esque alien, but it could at least support her.

"Because a war sphere is invulnerable," the Interpreter-Shepherd explained. "Even if a ship were somehow to be badly damaged enough to be non-combat-capable, the core working compartments for the Mesharom crew and the singularity power cores are secured behind an entire secondary layer of compressed-matter armor. We should always have power—and a war sphere is never alone."

"But the damage here was too great for the singularities to be safely contained," Morgan said.

"So, we safely ejected them." Adamase shivered. "And the anti-matter cores had to be shut down for similar reasons, and suddenly all we had was batteries and capacitors. They...sufficed for a while. They would have lasted multiple orbits as long as we concentrated ourselves." The same grumbling sound followed.

"Convincing ourselves to concentrate was not easy. But we started running low on power and could no longer charge even the fraction of the servitors we were operating. Even our walls and doors require power."

They shivered again.

"We managed to bring together the survivors in time, I think, but you asked our status. Our status is *dying*." A hundred shoulders shrugged.

"We have nearly exhausted the food supplies near us, and over half of the survivors are using personal VR sets to slip into a fugue state that they cannot be recovered from without medical training none of us have."

That grumbling sound again.

"The surviving doctor was the first to be lost," they admitted. "Without aid, Commander Casimir, we are doomed. I expect you came expecting to find a dead ship you could loot, but I must request your help."

Adamase paused for several seconds, then bowed their head.

"I must *beg* your help. There are thirteen others here. Seven of them are in a near-helpless fugue state, but they *can* be saved. There will be others on the rest of the fleet. You owe us nothing. Tilsan burned all debts away.

"But we will die without your aid."

"I was sent to find survivors," Morgan told them. "Tilsan may have burned a lot of bridges, Shepherd Adamase, but we will abandon no one to death in the cold dark. *No one.*

"I don't have the resources I might wish, but I also know what I can and cannot do without triggering the Precursor teleporter. Have you communicated with the other ships?"

She wasn't sure how many Mesharom she could squeeze onto her shuttles, and she was pretty *damn* sure they wouldn't survive the twenty-five-day flight out to the fleet. There were, though, other shuttles aboard the Mesharom ships. If they could load the Mesharom onto their own ships and retrofit fusion rockets for those...

It was a hell of an *if*.

"Not...all," Adamase said. "We did not have communications for long, and our hyperfold communicator was destroyed in the blast. I know there are fifteen other war spheres intact enough to have survivors. Can you get us out?"

"We don't have a way back into hyperspace from here," Morgan admitted. "It's a twenty-five-day flight back to where the fleet can open a portal for us."

She grimaced.

"We used the emitters from our hyperspace missiles to get here, but they can only go from hyperspace to regular space. We were hoping to use *your* missiles to go back, but I'll admit that we have no idea where to even start."

"Twenty-five days aboard a shuttle would be outright dangerous for some of my people," Adamase admitted. "Plus, I presume your shuttles are already carrying people?"

"We brought sixteen shuttles for twelve shuttles of Marines, but I don't think we can fit fifty of your people aboard one of our shuttles," Morgan told him. "Do your people have shuttles capable of transition inside the gravity zone?"

"No," the Shepherd admitted. "What we can do depends on the threat environment, I suppose. Aren't the Taljzi gone?"

"They are, but you weren't shot by a Taljzi weapon," Morgan pointed out.

The Mesharom paused, seeming to gather their thoughts.

"Yes, you mentioned a Precursor teleporter. Can you clarify?"

"The system appears to have been built with a long-range power-beaming system used to recharge starship batteries," Morgan told them. "I'm assuming there was some system originally to control what ships were receiving the power, but right now it is malfunctioning and transporting portions of the star to any ship with an interface drive."

Adamase closed their eyes.

"Our hyperfold technology is a caveman's attempt to duplicate the science of gods," they said bluntly. "The space-folding technology of the Precursors is still beyond us, for many reasons. But...the Taljzi?"

"They may have been told they would be safe from the weapon," she said. "Most likely, though, the entire fleet you pursued sacrificed themselves to destroy you."

"That would...make sense," Adamase admitted. "Especially if they realized that we'd finally managed to penetrate their starships' systems."

Morgan paused. That was a very calm way to admit that they'd hacked an enemy starship in the middle of a running firefight.

"And?" she prodded.

"We followed their fleets from PG-Three to a system that isn't on the Precursor map," Adamase told her. "There, we found what we believed to be a secondary colony of some billion Taljzi."

The Mesharom shivered.

"The Taljzi fleet faced us to defend it, but they retreated after taking heavy losses. To try to convince them to turn around, Tilsan ordered the planet burned from orbit."

"You didn't stop him," Morgan said flatly.

"My people do not value the lives of other races highly," Adamase said slowly. "It is a flaw I have struggled with my entire career as an Interpreter—and a flaw that Grand Commander Tilsan saw as a virtue.

"I did not challenge him, though. I did not *like* what he was doing, but the authority was his. My own position as Shepherd was—is, I supposed—at risk due to his assessment of my interactions with the Imperium."

Adamase shivered, but Morgan didn't think it was the cold bothering the old Mesharom.

"We followed their fleet from the colony here and finally cracked their surface electronic defenses," they concluded. "Tilsan didn't even intend to follow them from here: he had learned what he needed to know.

"We know where their homeworld is. It wasn't on the map you

found before, but it was a major Precursor installation. We don't know what the Precursors *did* there, but presumably it is the location of the Taljzi cloning facility."

"We need that location," Morgan told Adamase.

The Mesharom chittered their amusement.

"And you don't already have my ship's computers half-open to let you steal our archives and maps?" they asked. "I will even help you access all of those files...assuming you tell no one you ever had them and help rescue the survivors of the fleet."

"If you can see a way to get your people out of here, I'll gladly help," Morgan replied. "Right now, though, that twenty-five-day flight is the only option I see."

"You already have the answer, Commander Casimir," he told her. "You just hadn't thought quite large enough. I am no engineer, but I am familiar enough with our systems to say that two of our hyper-space missiles should be able to carry one of your shuttles back into hyperspace.

"This ship's remaining magazines contain three thousand such missiles. The other surviving ships likely contain similar numbers. I will need to refine my numbers, but my initial impulse is that thirty thousand missiles, properly synchronized, will be able to create a portal large enough for the entirety of *Blade*."

The sheer scale of Adamase's suggestion stunned Morgan, but there was one very clear problem with all of it.

"Those missiles are interface-drive weapons," she pointed out. "The Precursor system is targeting anything that brings a drive online. We've been moving around on fusion rockets. That's not going to let us haul tens of thousands of missiles into place. Not with less than twenty shuttles."

Adamase wilted.

"This is true," they admitted, and began to rise. "I need to speak to my engineers, to see what we can manage. If we can recharge some of our servitors from your power supply, that will let us multiply our feelers and examine our missiles. Trust the Precursors to have created a system that caused problems to echo across a hundred thousand orbits."

"I've noticed," Morgan said dryly. "Does anything of theirs work right anymore?"

"No," the Shepherd told. They were studying her now, the massive black eyes glittering in the light like faceted gems. "I see your second-bearer never told you that. Her honor does your Imperium credit."

Morgan had to pause and process just what the Mesharom meant. Mesharom reproduction involved seven different genders, including *three* embryo carriers. *Second-bearer* was the middle... which meant Adamase probably meant her stepmother.

"My mother never told me what?"

"I think it is necessary that you understand," Adamase said slowly. They folded themself back into the couch again, the language of their four-meter bulk suddenly thoughtful.

"Understand *what?*" Morgan repeated.

"The Precursors," they explained. "How they died. What they did. Why none of their systems work anymore."

That was enough to silence her, and she gestured wordlessly for them to continue.

"None of their technology works as it was built to," Adamase told her. "None of it. When they built their technology, the universe worked *differently*. Their star travel was different: they used a drive that jumped instantly between the stars at a vast cost in energy."

"So, they needed fueling stops every thirty light-years or so," Morgan said softly. "As we've seen out here."

"Exactly." The Mesharom shivered. "Tell me, Commander, have you ever seen a starkiller?"

This time, *she* shivered.

"There are two Imperial ones with the Allied Fleet," she said quietly. The deadly weapons were about the size of a destroyer and were carefully disguised to look just like the warship. Get one within a light-minute of a star, however...

"Then you have seen a Precursor jump drive," Adamase told her. "Our attempts to make our former masters' interstellar drive work again destroyed an entire star system. Thankfully, we had already developed the early forms of the hyperdrive and didn't destroy our *home* system."

They paused.

"One point two billion Mesharom died regardless. There is a reason we are afraid of the Precursors' technology. We study and duplicate concepts, but we never attempt to duplicate their actual systems."

"But much of it would *never* have worked," Morgan pointed out.

"The universe worked differently then," Adamase repeated. "Materials that would not carry electricity now formed the underpinnings of much of their technology. We have limited options as to what is conductive enough now, so our more-powerful cabling is simply more of the same.

"The Precursors had far more options and used them. Only their highest-energy systems still work now, and with the lack of the controls and AIs that once ran them, well, they are broken."

The power transmitter would definitely have been one of their "highest-energy systems."

"I don't understand," Morgan admitted. "The laws of physics can't change. The universe doesn't just start working differently!"

"No, Commander, it doesn't," Adamase agreed. "It took the Precursors a *lot* of effort to make the universe work differently...and they got it wrong."

There was no easy word for what Morgan felt in response to that. Terror? Awe? It felt like her back was turning to ice.

"How do you even *do* that?" she asked softly. "Let alone get it wrong."

"We only know parts," they said. "We were one of their subject races, the only ones to hold out against mass integration with their computer networks. Our psyches handled it poorly enough that they didn't force us.

"There was a device of some kind built at the galactic core. Using the singularity there as a power source, they created an instantaneous pulse that...well, changed the laws of physics. It was a *targeted* effort, intended to change very specific laws. Electrical conduction, the principles underlying their jump drive, the rules around their space-folding technology..."

Another sixty-shoulder shrug.

"It was supposed to make their ships faster. They got it wrong," Adamase repeated. "Conduction levels for metallics were cut by a massive factor. Their jump drives stopped working. Most of their space-folding self-destructed."

"Some still worked?" Morgan asked. "We're seeing that."

"Some still works, yes," he confirmed. "Some of the teleporter tech, some of the nanotech—even their singularity power cores survived for a while. But the change in conductivity level fried every cybernetic implant they'd ever built.

"And every one of them and every member of their other subject species had a network implant in their head linked to vast portions of their autonomic nervous systems. They died."

The two words hung in the air.

"Instantly, I'm guessing," Morgan said quietly.

"Or near enough. They might have been able to undo what they did. Certainly no one else. The change is permanent and universal. It created the universe we live in today, but it broke all existing technology.

"Precursor technologies are at best useless and at worst a dangerous trap. This system is a perfect example of the latter."

"And we need to find a way out of it," Morgan replied.

"I still think the answer is in our missiles," Adamase told her. "Our chief engineer died along with Tilsan and the command crew. I need more engineers, engineers I don't have, Commander Casimir."

"But might be alive on other ships?" Morgan asked.

"We have had some intermittent communications. I know *Deception*'s chief engineer, Idoni, lived through the battle," the Shepherd told her. "If we retrieve them, they will be able to assist us with the answer."

"If we get them, who is in charge?" Morgan said. "I wasn't under the impression that you were military anymore."

"I am the Shepherd of this region," Adamase said firmly. "In the absence of a Battle Fleet Grand Commander, the officers of both Frontier Fleet and Battle Fleet answer to me—and I am well aware that you and your people are our only hope, Commander Casimir.

"So far as I am concerned, *you* are in charge."

The Mesharom shifted to look at her very directly.

"Shall we proceed?"

CHAPTER FORTY-TWO

THE SHUTTLES HAD DRAMATICALLY MORE GENERATION capacity than they needed for their own systems. They were designed to be able to charge everything from plasma rifles to power armor to, if necessary, localized surface defense shields and tanks.

Even sixteen of them couldn't provide enough power to bring major systems online aboard the war sphere, and Morgan had already sent half of them over to the wreckage of *Deception* to collect the survivors.

The eight that were left were enough to stabilize the life support of the Mesharom's impromptu survival pod inside *Blade*. There was also enough power for Adamase and his conscious people to *move* the entire pod through the ship to where the Imperial craft were docked.

Once that was complete, they were running power cabling for only a few dozen meters instead of over a kilometer. The connection to the war sphere's computer core was still roughly twelve hundred meters, but they could at least more easily make sure their survivors *stayed* alive.

The fugue state of half the Mesharom was terrifying to Morgan. Of the fourteen survivors, eight had locked themselves into VR simulations and…shut down. Even turning off the sims didn't trigger a reaction. They still ate if food was put in front of them, but that was it.

"It's an extreme stress reaction," Adamase told Morgan. "The people we select as Interpreters are much less prone to it." They glanced around at the other five Mesharom dealing awkwardly with the Imperials.

"There are three Interpreters in this room, including me," they noted. "The other three are just…stubborn."

"And everyone, including them, is going to benefit from that," Morgan replied. Now that there was power, some of the servitor robots were being turned on.

As a set of ten of them turned on, the Mesharom working on them made their way over to Morgan and Adamase.

"Lead Feeler Calorite," they introduced themself. "Power systems. I can use servitors and Imperial hands. Bring power online."

The Mehsarom's phrasing was hard to follow, but Morgan thought she understood.

"You can boot one of the reactors?" she asked.

"Possible. Thirty-one out of sixty. One reactor minimally damaged. Servitor power ran out. Repairs incomplete."

Even a single antimatter plant would outstrip the microfusion plants aboard her shuttles by a few orders of magnitude. It would make their plans a lot easier.

"How many Marines?" Morgan asked.

"Twenty. Ten if power system knowledge. Armor required."

Morgan glanced at Adamase, who made an affirming gesture.

"I'll arrange it. Wait a few minutes."

She stepped away from the two Mesharom and opened a private channel to Damyanov.

"Battalion Commander, how much power-system experience do your people have?" she asked.

"My Marines are cross-trained for damage control in combat,"

Damyanov replied. "They also run maintenance support for our tanks and shuttles and aircraft. Why?"

"I need ten troops in power armor with power-system experience to support a Mesharom noncom who thinks they can boot an anti-matter plant with a few more repairs."

There was a pause.

"I can give the caterpillar two full squads with at least *some* experience with our antimatter plants," Damyanov replied. "I can spare forty sets of hands now for the chance of real power supply later!"

"I thought so too," Morgan agreed. "Send them my way; I'll hook them up with the Lead Feeler."

THE SHUTTLES she'd sent over to *Deception* reported in as the newly designated power-plant-repair team headed off.

"Commander, this is Istil!," the pilot leading the flight reported in. "Our Marines have made contact but *Deception* is in terrible shape."

There was only a single platoon spread across the eight space-craft, primarily intended to scout through the vessel for survivors and bring them back to the shuttles. Whatever happened next, they were going to be best served having everyone in one piece.

"How bad is *terrible*?" Morgan asked.

"They've had no power since the beginning," Istil! reported. "They didn't have enough people to take care of the fugue cases. Most of them died, and they didn't have many survivors to begin with."

The pilot audibly swallowed.

"I'm sending two shuttles back with the survivors we've extracted," he reported. "There's three of them."

Morgan winced. Each of the war spheres was supposed to have a crew of fifty. Three survivors was bad, but she also needed to know *who* they were.

"Did Commander Idoni survive?" she asked.

"We have Commander Idoni. They are aboard the shuttle." Istil! paused. "I don't think Idoni is in very good shape mentally, but I'm not qualified to provide therapy for a Mesharom."

"I don't think anyone here is," Morgan replied. "And I'm not sure anyone *would* be in good shape after that. Is there anything else worth staying on *Deception* for?"

"We're doing a radar survey so we have current maps if we do come back for the missiles or the shuttles," Istil! reported. "I'm not sure we're going to find much else of value here. The flare gutted this ship pretty badly. I'm surprised anyone lived."

"It turns out that our Mesharom friends are bloody stubborn," Morgan replied. "Are your teams up for a second search? Scans are showing that *Insistence* is a hundred thousand kilometers further along the vector from *Blade* to *Deception*."

There was a pause.

"It's not like coming back to *Blade* is going to be any less depressing, I suppose," the pilot said. "We'll make the swing to *Insistence* and scan for other ships. I'm guessing we're sweeping until we've got them all?"

"There were over three thousand Mesharom here," Morgan said quietly. "If we pull even a hundred of them from this mess, that will be a miracle—but no one gets left behind that we can find, Speaker. You understand me?"

"To the dark and the sky beyond, Commander," Istil! replied. "Nobody freezes on our watch. We'll bring them back to *Blade*, sir, but we can't bring them home. There just isn't enough space on the shuttles."

"You get them here, Speaker. I'll get us all home," Morgan promised.

She wasn't sure how she was going to do that yet.

She was just *damn* sure she was going to.

COMMANDER IDONI WAS on the small side for a Mesharom, a black-and-purple sentient just under three meters long. Morgan was only vaguely aware at best of Mesharom body language, but even she could read the exhaustion in the way Idoni dragged themself across the floor.

Much of their fur was ragged and patchy as well. It had clearly *not* been a good two months for the engineer, but they perked up at the sight of Shepherd Adamase.

"It's true," they breathed. "You live. The Grand Commander?"

"Dead. Tilsan was vaporized with the rest of the command crew," Adamase told them. "I am in command now. Your status?"

Idoni shivered back into silence.

"*Deception* is nonfunctional. You knew that. Crew...dead. Couldn't save those entering dream. No feelers, no robots. Two other survivors. A!Tol subjects brought us."

"I know," Adamase said. "We don't have any doctors left aboard except the Imperials, and they're not trained on our physiology or psychology. Can you serve, Commander Idoni? We need your skills."

Idoni closed their massive eyes, shivering again. Morgan gestured for the non-Mesharom to back away, to give the sick sentient even more space.

"What purpose?" they asked, even their translated voice sounding lost. "The drive is the target. The Imperials told me. No way out, not in time."

"One way out, Commander Idoni," Adamase corrected. "Few of us could handle the shuttle flight, even if we refitted our shuttles to run on fusion engines. But there is still one way out: hyperspace."

The engineer stopped shivering.

"Impossible. Too deep in gravity zone," they snapped. "False hope."

"The Imperials used their *missile* portal generators to pierce the gravity zone with shuttles," Adamase said calmly. "The portals on *our* missiles can also open into hyperspace from within the gravity zone.

"We're going to bring all of the survivors aboard *Blade,* and then we're going to bring every hyperspace missile left aboard our ships here, too, and then we're going to tear open a portal into hyperspace *through* the gravity zone of the star and take *Blade* through it."

Idoni was silent for several seconds.

"Not false hope," they said slowly. "Hard. Difficult. May be impossible." Their attention suddenly dropped onto Morgan.

"Commander Morgan Casimir," they greeted her. "I have heard of you. Missiles." They paused, trying to find both words and the emotional energy to speak to her. "Their drives. Safe / not safe?"

"Not safe," Morgan said gently, wondering how the engineer had heard of her. "They're high-enough intensity to attract the teleporter's sensors. Any use of an interface drive is too dangerous. Anything big enough to be able to operate at low-enough velocities is big enough to put off a target signature at any speed—and anything small enough to drop below targetable levels can't go that slow."

"Problem, yes." Idoni wavered. "Need...food. Liquid. Then... computers, servitors. May need Imperial hands."

"Adamase?" Morgan said.

"We'll take care of it. If we need anything from your people, I'll let you know."

"Time is everything," she told the Mesharom. "I need to report in." She looked at Idoni. "What are the chances, Commander Idoni?"

"Fourteen feelers," he said vaguely.

Roughly twenty-five percent—a Mesharom had sixty feelers that could operate as legs or hands as needed, each of them capable of a level of fine manipulation humans needed tools for.

Adamase started to usher Idoni away—and the next survivor made their way off the shuttle and stopped.

"Commander Casimir?" the Mesharom asked haltingly.

Morgan was *extremely* well trained to be able to distinguish between members of alien species. It still took her a moment to recognize the Mesharom.

Until this mission, Interpreter-Lieutenant Coraniss had been the only Mesharom she'd met in person—and Coraniss's help had been key to saving the human colonies from the First Return.

She hadn't even known the young Mesharom officer was with Tilsan's fleet!

INTERPRETER-LIEUTENANT CORANISS WAS a three-meter-long Mesharom with orange and blue markings on their fur. They looked just as ragged as Idoni, and Morgan had to resist the urge to try to hug the alien.

Even if she could work out *how* to hug a three-meter long caterpillar roughly seventy centimeters across with sixty arms, it would have freaked Coraniss out even more than they already were.

"I didn't know you were with the fleet," she confessed to Coraniss as the Mesharom came carefully close. "I'm glad to see you're all right!"

"That...may be overestimating my condition," the young Mesharom replied. "I am alive, but twice now, I have seen my ship destroyed and the rest of my crew killed. I am...not all right."

As Adamase had said talking to Idoni, there was no one aboard *Blade* qualified to deal with Mesharom physiology or psychology. She had no idea, really, what to do with a stressed-out Mesharom navigation officer.

"How can we help?" she finally asked. Coraniss was a friend, but cross-species friendships were always messy. Even before you were looking at someone who unquestionably had a severe level of PTSD.

"I need...I need to help," Coraniss finally told her. "Tilsan decided to go to war without you, and we have only regretted it since. If we can escape, it is only through you."

Morgan shook her head...and then remembered that Coraniss was a *navigation* officer.

"When your people pulled the coordinates for the Taljzi home system from their computers, did they share them to every ship?" she asked.

"Yes," Coraniss replied after a long pause to think. "I don't remember them, though. My files are aboard *Deception*...and probably destroyed."

"Do you think you can help me find that information in *Blade*'s systems?" Morgan asked.

Adamase had given her a set of access codes but then had been absorbed by the process of rescuing his people. Probably intentionally, really—he could pretend he didn't know what they'd done that way.

"I don't have access," Coraniss told her, the Mesharom shifting uncomfortably. "But if you do, I'm afraid to report that I am badly traumatized and I *clearly* won't remember whatever I help you with."

Morgan grinned as she parsed through that mouthful.

"As it happens, my friend, I *do* have access to *Blade*'s systems. Just no familiarity with her data infrastructure—and I need those coordinates."

"I need to do something," Coraniss told her. "I have sat helplessly and watched comrades die and my ship freeze around me for a quarter-orbit. I *must* act."

"Then follow me," Morgan instructed. "We have a *lot* that's going to need doing."

CHAPTER FORTY-THREE

"It's good to see proof that you're alive, Commander," Squadron Lord Sun's image noted sardonically.

Morgan had taken over one of the command pods on the shuttles docked with *Blade*. Each was designed to manage up to an entire battalion of Marines, which meant that Damyanov could easily spare one to let the Commander phone home.

"You should have been getting the updates," Morgan replied, glancing between Sun and Tan!Stalla. "Should I be expecting anyone else to arrive on the call?"

"We're recording it for our allies, but we wanted to get a chance to check on you first," Sun told her. "Text updates every hour let us know you aren't dead, but they don't really give us an assessment of the morale of the team."

"Morale is battered but steady," she said. "Wandering around dead ships is never reassuring, but we at least found survivors." She shook her head. "I'd have been happier with more, but I wasn't expecting *any*."

"*Sickle Strike*'s crew was less lucky, though there were more of them to be unlucky," Sun admitted. "We pulled six hundred Laians off her." The Squadron Lord paused. "She had a crew of ten thousand three hundred and fifty."

Morgan hadn't known the exact number, but she had known the range.

"How's our Laian allies' morale?" she asked.

"Homicidal," Tan!Stalla noted. "I wouldn't want to be the first Taljzi fleet that ends up in their sights."

"My sympathy for the Taljzi is limited," Morgan admitted. "It's more present now than it was a few days ago, but...still limited."

Sun winced.

"We saw the summary of Tilsan's operation," he said. "Text... always leaves something to be desired. You spoke to Adamase. Did they agree with the orders?"

"It's hard to tell," Morgan said. "I don't think so, but I also know that Adamase is perfectly capable of playing my emotions. Even Adamase doesn't value sentient life to a level I'd regard as acceptable, but they seemed perturbed by Tilsan's wanton murder of a billion people."

Sun shook his head.

"What a mess," he concluded. "And then the Taljzi sacrificed themselves to lure them into range of this system.

"I suppose that leaves us one question, Commander: how quickly are you going to be getting out? Am I waiting for sublight shuttles or...?"

"We think we could reconfigure Mesharom shuttles for fusion rockets, but the Mesharom don't think most of their survivors could survive twenty-five cycles in close confinement with each other," Morgan admitted. "Or close confinement in general. They are somewhat claustrophobic on average, and that's a hell of a trip."

"I can't imagine any of them are in great shape, either," Tan!Stalla noted. "Sixty-plus cycles trapped on a dead ship?"

"A lot of them are lost," she told her superiors. "A fugue state—Adamase called it *the dream*. They'll eat if given food, apparently, but without someone to take care of them, they starve." She winced.

"*Deception*'s survivors didn't have enough crew left to save the ones that slipped into it.

"So far, *Blade* does...but we couldn't put those Mesharom on a shuttle for twenty-five cycles."

"That's not a great situation, Commander," Sun pointed out. "Do you have a solution yet, or are we going to have to try the long flight anyway?"

"The Mesharom are working on a plan to use their missile hyperdrives to transit the entirety of *Blade* into hyperspace," Morgan explained. "If that works, we'll still need to evacuate onto the rest of JTF 25, but we won't need to put anyone in shuttles."

"You reported you were concentrating the survivors onto *Blade*," Sun murmured. "That has more than one possibility, especially if you do manage to get part of *Blade*'s power systems online."

"Sir?"

"There has to be enough food aboard that ship to last them for years," the Squadron Lord pointed out. "Without an interface drive, you can't adjust the ship's course much, but *Blade*'s orbit is unstable. You might be able to adjust her into a slingshot course around the star and the Dyson Swarm."

Sun was running numbers on a screen Morgan couldn't see, and sighed as they came up.

"I'll forward you the numbers, Commander," he told her. "Your shuttles probably won't be able to create enough delta-*v* and it would be a sixteen-month—two point five long-cycles—voyage before they were outside the gravity zone, but it's an option if they can manage it.

"I'll hope that they get the hyper portal option sorted out," he concluded quietly. "Because if it comes to that, we need you and your Marines back with the JTF.

"You have seventy-two hours, Commander," he told her, then blinked and translated into A!Tol time. "Three cycles. Seventy hours. At the end of that, I need a solid timeline for either a hyper portal or a slingshot maneuver on the Mesharom's part.

"Because in three cycles, if we *don't* have a hard time frame for the portal, your shuttles are coming home. Am I clear, Commander? We'll go a long way for the Mesharom...but there's a limit to how long I can sit here with a hundred warships."

"If nothing else, sir, it will take me at least a cycle to confirm that we've got the Taljzi homeworld coordinates," Morgan said quietly. "I'll try to upload the Mesharom database in chunks via the hyperfold com as we can, but it's a lot of data. We're going to be filling a shuttle with data crystals and hoping the Mesharom don't notice or turn a blind eye."

"How likely is that?" Tan!Stalla asked. "That data is valuable, but I need my First Sword back."

Morgan snorted.

"Adamase gave me the access codes and Coraniss is helping us dissect their data infrastructure," she told them. "None of that's in the reports because, well, it didn't happen. If you understand me, sirs."

"So, we're getting that blind eye," Tan!Stalla concluded. "Good."

"One way or another, we're going to save them, sir," Morgan promised.

She wasn't sure what would happen if Sun gave her orders to leave before they were sure they could save the survivors, though. She didn't have to decide in advance, though.

She could always burn that bridge when she came to it.

"THE MISSILES WON'T WORK."

Idoni had clearly improved in the twenty-odd hours since Morgan's people had brought them aboard *Blade*. They looked less strained, their fur was more neatly groomed if still patchy, and they were clearly less bothered by being around non-Mesharom.

They also had clearly never learned to soften their words at all.

"Clarify," Adamase ordered, slipping into far more clipped phrases speaking to another Mesharom.

The two Mesharom were sitting in a room with Morgan and

Damyanov. The room had adjusted to provide proper seating for everyone and had a comforting soft glow coming from the walls—clear reminders that Lead Feeler Calorite had succeeded in bringing an antimatter power plant online.

They had *far* more power than they needed to keep up lights and power now. The Mesharom were recharging servitor robots now. Soon, the serpent-like machines would sweep the rest of ship for food supplies and start working on repairing the nearby life support plant.

Morgan had some hope at their ability to actually survive a sixteen-month slingshot around the star and out of the PG-Two System. It would be messy, but they could survive.

Her people were still bringing over survivors, though. Once they'd searched all of the surviving spheres for Mesharom, they'd be going through the closer ones for food supplies. The Mesharom only carried their own species aboard their ships, so they didn't even have the tofu-like Universal Protein the Imperium relied on.

If the slingshot was needed, JTF 25 would probably have to send a few shuttles full of UP to make sure the Mesharom made it. It sounded more and more like that was going to be the plan, too.

"No reaction engine," Idoni finally answered Adamase's order. "Could refit. But each missile, one by one. No time."

Adamase had figured they could make the needed portal with thirty thousand missiles. Refitting each of those missiles, manually, with a fusion rocket...Morgan had figured that was going to be the big problem.

"Can we manage something with the missiles aboard *Blade*?" she asked.

"Two thousand eight hundred forty-six," Idoni replied. Presumably, that was how many missiles were aboard *Blade*. It seemed sparse for the arsenal she'd have expected for a war sphere, but *Blade*'s specifications hadn't been shared with the Imperium.

"Not useful," the Mesharom concluded. "Not useless."

Morgan closed her eyes to swallow down a harsh response.

"Clarify?" she asked, echoing Adamase's earlier word.

"Strip emitters from missiles. Place on hull. Allow for calibration. Can't carry enough power."

Morgan blinked, wrapping her brain around what Idoni was suggested. Stripping the exotic-matter emitters—the portal projectors —from the missiles would be a project, but placing them around the war sphere's hull...could work.

"Where do we get the power from?" she finally asked. The problem was scale. The emitters were meant to open a circular portal ten meters across. She couldn't easily do the math in her head, but she doubted three thousand or so missiles could open a portal large enough for *Blade*'s twelve-kilometer diameter.

"*Blade*'s emitters are intact but wrong calibration," Idoni told them. "Designed for sustained use. Not one burnout: Combine with missile emitters. Calibrate frequency. Overload emitters."

Morgan exhaled as the sheer audacity of what the engineer was planning sank in. One of the main differences between the emitters everyone used for starships and the emitters the Imperium and Mesharom used for missiles was that the missile emitters only needed to work once, twice at most.

A starship's portal emitters needed to work indefinitely. They were far more carefully calibrated, created with solid spikes of exotic matter instead of the fragile lattices of missiles, and designed for far higher overall energy levels.

But the reason missiles could penetrate the hyper barrier inside the gravity zone of a star was because their power was far greater relative to the size of the portal they were opening. Running that much power through a portal projector was an inherently destructive process. Imperial designers weren't even sure how the Mesharom managed to make an emitter that could do it twice—they'd built a two-portal hyperspace missile by the simple method of having two sets of emitters.

"Will it work?" she finally asked.

"Will hurt," the engineer told her. "Large time-dilation factor.

Very large. Will work." Idoni paused. "Forty-one in sixty. If fails?" The Mesharom gave a sixty-shoulder shrug. "Will never know."

A sixty-eight percent chance. That was better than Morgan had expected, but it was also a thirty-two percent chance that *Blade* and her passengers wouldn't survive.

"What do you need?" she finally asked.

"More power," Idoni replied. "One more plant on *Blade*. Not enough. Extract plants from other spheres? At least three more."

That sounded painful. Antimatter cores weren't easily extracted from ships, even when nonfunctional. On the other hand...

"Would a conversion core cover the power needs?" she asked slowly. The Imperium did *not* trust their matter-conversion power plants just yet, which meant that *Jean Villeneuve*'s plants were designed to be easily ejected.

And replaced, which would be relevant if this worked.

"Yes," Idoni said, their massive black eyes blinking. "We don't have one."

"I can get one," Morgan promised. "And extra engineers. *If* you can get that sixty-eight percent up a bit."

"With conversion core...maybe forty-five in sixty?" Idoni promised.

She sighed. It might be enough. It might not. In either case, it sounded like borrowing one of *Villeneuve*'s conversion cores was a better plan than trying to carve power systems out of dead war spheres.

CHAPTER FORTY-FOUR

MORGAN COULDN'T HELP BUT GRIN AS THE NEW SET OF PORTALS tore open, less than thirty thousand kilometers from *Blade*. She hadn't expected anyone to go for it, but the proof that her superiors trusted her was right there in the single two-kilometer-wide portal opened by another flotilla of sixteen shuttles.

Those shuttles were flying in close formation, each of them linked by a set of immense cables both to each other and to the assemblage at the heart of the formation.

Tapping commands on her temporary console in the command pod, she opened a channel.

"This is Commander Casimir calling Force Charlie. What's your status?"

"This is Lesser Commander Elstar," an unexpected voice responded. "My status is wishing that someone had warned me just what *time dilation* meant in this context."

"About eleven minutes of pure hell," Morgan told him. "I wasn't expecting *you*, Commander Elstar."

If nothing else, she was still figuring a one-in-four chance that they'd all get vaporized when they tried Idoni's stunningly reckless stunt. Having both the First Sword and the chief engineer of the most powerful Imperial unit in the JTF aboard when they tried it seemed unwise.

"I'm the best expert in the JTF on conversion cores *and* hyper-space-missile portal emitters," Elstar pointed out. "Captain Tan!Stalla said you didn't tell her the odds, so she figured they were terrible.

"My job is to improve them."

"I'm pretty sure you can do that," Morgan admitted. "How much help did you bring?"

"A hundred of the best engineers from the entire Task Force," Elstar replied. "Mostly power-core people from *Villeneuve*, but we grabbed HSM techs from across the squadron. If we don't make it back, the JTF is going to be short some of their best hands for their biggest guns."

Morgan found herself grinning again.

"Well, I'll need to introduce you to Commander Idoni once you're aboard," she told the Rekiki. "They're the Mesharom respon-sible for this entire ridiculous idea. *Blade* isn't their ship, but she's the one we've got most of the survivors aboard."

"Most, huh? Guessing that's why we brought another sixteen shuttles."

"Exactly," Morgan agreed. "If we're going to make this jump, we're not leaving anyone behind."

Unspoken between them was that several of the shuttles were also packed to the gills with data crystals. The Mesharom war sphere's databases were *huge*. Coraniss was helping them find data related to their current location and situation, but Morgan couldn't ask her Mesharom friend to outright betray their government by handing over technical files on the Mesharom singularity reactors and hyperspace-compression fields.

While Coraniss was helping them find data they *could* ask a Mesharom to help them find, they were also quietly copying the war sphere's entire database to a set of offline cold-storage data crystals.

They wouldn't change anything today...but they might open all *sorts* of doors for the Imperium in the future.

"COMMANDER IDONI, Shepherd Adamase, this is Lesser Commander Elstar, Chief Engineer aboard *Jean Villeneuve*," Morgan introduced the Rekiki to the Mesharom. In a space with those three sentients, she couldn't help but feel very small and vulnerable.

Fortunately for her equanimity, she could tell that both Mesharom were equally uncomfortable being this close to non-Mesharom. Idoni's fur was starting to fray again as they lurched forward and studied Elstar.

"Conversion core yours?" they asked. "Missile emitters?"

"The core is mine, yes," Elstar confirmed. "And I'm well versed in our missile emitters—including the ones we used for hyperspatial entry from inside the gravity zone before we went on a different path."

Idoni made a strange grunting sound.

"Your emitters bulky, crude. Removing entry emitters from the missiles clever, though. Power-conversion protocols needed. Come with."

Elstar glanced at Morgan, who nodded.

"I *think* the Squadron Lord is going to wait for us to at least try this now," she told him. "But we only have a cycle left on his original deadline. The sooner you and your people are working, the sooner we're in hyperspace."

And the sooner they all got off this ship of the dead and damned.

The engineers left, Elstar already barking orders into his communicator for his people to follow along, and Morgan turned a wry smile on Adamase.

"Is Idoni as strange for your people as Elstar is for mine?" she asked. "Engineers seem to be a breed of their own."

"I am...intrigued by how well Idoni is handling working with your people," Adamase replied, not really an answer to her question. "Testing suggested they would have severe problems with aliens. They were far from the levels we would have expected for an Interpreter...though few engineers would reach that level of ease with others."

"Needs must when the devil drives," Morgan quoted softly. "I suspect that one is going to have extreme problems once they are no longer busily working. Until then, all else is pushed aside."

"Humans do that as well, do they?" the Shepherd asked. "None of the survivors of Tilsan's fleet are going to do well. My entire district is shattered as well. With the losses here, there no longer *is* a Frontier Fleet for this arm of the galaxy.

"We will go home after this, Commander...and I fear it will be a long time before the Mesharom are seen in this corner of the galaxy again."

She chuckled.

"We've seen more of your people in the last few years than this corner of the galaxy had seen in the prior few hundred," she pointed out. "Most wouldn't notice your absence."

"You will," Adamase told her. "More than you think right now. For now, though, we must survive." They shook themself. "Once we are in hyperspace, I must request as rapid an evacuation back to PG-Three as possible. I have called for a ship, with appropriately trained medical crew, to meet us there...but it is an unarmed vessel, a mobile administration center. Not a warship.

"Thanks to your assistance, I have also exchanged messages with the Conclave." The Mesharom shivered. "My instructions are to activate the self-destructs on the other war spheres before we attempt the transition. Under no circumstances are Tilsan's vessels to be left for even the Imperium to scavenge from."

"And that applies to *Blade* once we've evacuated you as well, I presume," Morgan noted.

"I will wait for you to remove your conversion core, I promise,"

Adamase noted with a soft rumble of amusement. "But yes. *Blade* will serve us one last time, and then she will join her sisters in fire."

There was another warning hidden in there, Morgan knew. Adamase was almost certainly aware that they were draining *Blade*'s computers. But if he had to take *official* recognition of that, there would be trouble.

"In case the transit goes wrong, I will provide you with the coordinates of the Taljzi home system now," he finally said. "We will not be able to deal with them ourselves now, but...I have faith in the Imperium. Even if others did not."

Grand Commander Tilsan had been vaporized, after all. There was no point in speaking ill of the dead.

───────

IT WAS ALMOST fourteen hours later before Elstar entered Morgan's impromptu office aboard the shuttle she'd landed on. The Rekiki looked more cramped in the space than any of the humans did, but that was normal for Rekiki, in her experience.

"How are we doing, Commander?" she asked.

"We'll be ready in half a cycle," Elstar told her. "We won't make the Squadron Lord's original deadline, but we'll only miss it by a few twentieth-cycles."

She sat upright and studied the tired-looking engineer.

"That's better than I expected," she admitted. "You're sure?"

"Idoni knew the power was coming, so they focused on the emitters. We hooked up the power, and Idoni and I found a few ways to tweak the alignments and calibrations of the emitters, too.

"Once the last of the missile emitters are placed—and we've got teams and robots out on the hull by the dozen right now—we'll be ready for a few test runs, and then...it'll be time to charge or break."

Morgan shivered.

"Idoni put the odds at seventy to seventy-five percent," she noted. "Your guess?"

"About the same," Elstar admitted. "I *think* we've built in an emergency break protocol that will protect us if the portal isn't stable enough, but I only give *that* a half-chance of holding up."

"So, seventy percent chance of success, fifteen percent chance of being stranded here still and a fifteen percent chance of never knowing anything went wrong?" Morgan asked.

Elstar stamped a hind foot in amusement.

"Exactly," he agreed. "I have faith in my work, and Idoni is a *genius*...but yeah. One in seven chance we're vaporized when we hit the portal."

A hundred and sixty Mesharom. A thousand Imperial Marines and engineers. Fifteen percent chance of instant death—and the decision was Morgan's.

Of course, she'd already *made* that decision, and everybody knew it.

"I'll let the JTF know the timeline," she told him. "They'll have a ride waiting for us."

"Reattaching the conversion core will take about a cycle, then what?" Elstar asked.

"Straight back to PG-Three. We know where the Taljzi are now, so there's no need to scout random systems from the map. There'll be a ship waiting for the Mesharom, too."

Elstar snorted.

"And we don't tell them you have a complete copy of *Blade*'s databanks, I assume?" he asked.

"Coraniss helped us locate the Taljzi home system and will swear we touched nothing else," Morgan noted. "Of course, they're not in the greatest mental health."

"None of them are," the Rekiki warned her. "Idoni...I've never met a Mesharom in person, but I've worked with a few by email and recording before. Idoni is a very broken sentient. Once this jump is complete, I'm not sure they'll be good for anything for a long time."

"That's why we're rushing them to their ride," she pointed out.

"That ship will have their doctors and counselors aboard. They're loading up and heading straight back to Mesharom space."

The ship in question, from what Adamase had said, was the center of Mesharom frontier operations out there. Without it, there would be no Frontier Fleet. No Shepherd. No Mesharom watching for Precursor tech or treaty violations.

It was going to be a weird galaxy once this was all over.

"First, though, we need to get them—and ourselves!—to safety. Half a cycle, huh?"

"I suggest you let everyone who can, rest," Elstar told her. "You remember the time dilation of coming *out* of hyperspace?"

"Yeah," Morgan admitted with a shiver.

"I *think* the pain will be better...but the dilation is going to be ten times worse. Expect a subjective two-hour transition, Commander. It's going to be the longest hundred and seventy-five milliseconds of your life."

CHAPTER FORTY-FIVE

HARRIET TANAKA HUMMED SADLY TO HERSELF AS SHE STUDIED the reports from JTF 25. She couldn't help feeling that Sun should have argued harder against letting the stepdaughter of a planetary duchess stick herself in the situation Commander Casimir had put herself in, but she couldn't argue with the results.

Her own inclination to treat Morgan Casimir as one of her own children—or at least a beloved niece—wasn't something a Fleet Lord of the A!Tol Imperium could afford, in any case.

Casimir's dancing around the expected success rate of the stunt she was about to pull told Harriet everything she needed to know. Her own estimate of their chances was about fifty percent.

For the Mesharom, it was this or a cold and unpleasant death. For Casimir and the rest of the Imperial personnel aboard *Blade*, it was this or a twenty-five-day flight.

Harriet wasn't going to try and micromanage with an eighteen-hour conversation loop. All she could do was sit aboard *Ajax*, watch the pieces of the Precursor ring station go by, and hope for safety.

Then she reached the end of Casimir's last report and realized she had a *lot* more work to do.

It wasn't much. A pair of sentences and a set of coordinates, but it changed everything.

We have found the coordinates Adamase mentioned and verified the authenticity of the ones he provided directly. Coordinates for the Taljzi home system to follow.

There were a thousand people in the Allied Fleet who would need the coordinates, but Harriet plugged them into her console immediately and opened up a three-dimensional astrographic chart across her office.

The hologram already had the gold, silver and copper icons from the Precursor maps loaded into it, and she dropped a diamond icon on the coordinates Casimir had sent.

Precursor Gold Six. The farthest out of the gold-flagged systems they'd found on the map there in PG-Three. So far as she knew, the farthest-out Precursor installation, period.

Just what had those incredibly advanced, clearly mind-bogglingly arrogant people done there at the end of the universe?

What was starting to sink in for Harriet was that PG-Two, PG-Three, and PG-Four were a combined multi-stellar construction facility, with Two and Four providing power and materials for building starships—probably warships—around singularity cores.

Three entire star systems dedicated to a single purpose. PG-Three's construction was on a smaller scale than Two and Four as well, and she wondered if that was intentional. Had the shipyard been separated from its resource supply to protect it from the possible side effects of work on that scale?

The colony at PG-One definitely had been. For all of the immense scale of the Precursors' work in systems they didn't live in, there had been no planetary-scale construction projects in a system they'd actually colonized.

Shaking her head, she opened a channel to Koanest.

"Captain, I need a meeting set up with the other fleet commanders immediately," she told Koanest. "We have Casimir's report from *Blade*—and that means we have a target."

"I'll set it up," her ops officer promised. "But I was about to contact you as well. We have the first report from JTF 26."

"They reached PG-Five early?" Harriet asked. They hadn't been scheduled to arrive for another ten hours at least. Hyperspace was hyperspace, though, and always unpredictable.

"They did. I'll forward you their report, but it's pretty straightforward," Koanest admitted. "There's nothing there."

"No installations? That's odd," she murmured.

Koanest barked a sharp, bitter laugh.

"No, Fleet Lord," she corrected. "There's *nothing* there. Someone blew up PG-5 with a starkiller. Given our own traipsing around the region, we can even estimate when."

That was...unexpected.

"When?"

"It's in the report. Between five and six hundred long-cycles ago."

Two hundred and sixty to three hundred and twenty years ago, give or take.

"That would have been less than two hundred long-cycles after the Taljzi got out here," Harriet said. Probably less, she realized. The Taljzi had been driven out of Kanzi space about three hundred and fifty years before, and they knew the Kanzi renegades had spent years at multiple sites along the way before they found their new home.

"They didn't have starkillers then," she said slowly. "If they had starkillers *now*, I'm sure we would have seen them. How did they blow up a star?"

"I don't know, Fleet Lord," Koanest confessed. "But given everything else we've seen out here, I'm guessing they pushed the wrong button in a Precursor installation."

IT WAS the same six beings who had been in most of the operational meetings since Tenth Fleet had rendezvoused with the Gloried Armada. Two Laians, two Kanzi, one human and a Yin.

For the first time in a while, the meeting didn't even feel like an administrative necessity. There was actual *work* to do.

"PG-Five is a dead field," Cawl noted. "I wonder if its destruction was intentional or not."

"Given what we've seen of Precursor technology out here, I'm not taking that bet," Harriet replied dryly. "Captain Koanest thinks accidental. Certainly, the lack of starkiller weapons in the Taljzi's known arsenal suggests they didn't replicate whatever happened there."

"My people have gone over the data the scouts found," Kanmorad told them. "There is no question that it was a starkiller weapon. The energy patterns and debris fields exactly align with the use of one."

Harriet concealed a shiver. It wasn't reassuring to hear her ally discuss comparing the wreckage of a star system against what was clearly a set of existing samples. She didn't know how many times the Laians had used starkillers, but she knew it was more than once.

There was a dead zone of shattered star systems marking the old border between the Laian Republic and the Wendira Great Hive. They'd both decided never to do that again after the *second* time, which was part of why that border was now at least a hundred light-years closer to the Wendira homeworlds.

"It seems unlikely that the Taljzi would not have deployed starkiller weaponry if they had it," Cawl pointed out. "And yet...it seems equally unlikely that a malfunctioning Precursor device would have the exact same effect."

Harriet shook her head.

"And since the star died five hundred long-cycles ago, the potential for misreading data is high," she reminded them. "Equally, now PG-Five is irrelevant to us unless it turns out that the Taljzi can duplicate it.

"Right now, it matters that PG-Five is definitely not the Taljzi home system. That leaves PG-Six as our most likely target, which I would leave for JTF Twenty-Six to validate, except that I don't need to."

"Fleet Lord?" Kanmorad said slowly. "News from your people aboard *Blade*?"

"Casimir's full report will be distributed shortly," she told the others. If nothing else, the other fleet commanders' people could easily steal it or acquire updates from their people with JTF Twenty-Five. "But yes.

"The Mesharom penetrated the electronic defenses of the Taljzi fleet while they were pursuing them. Not fast enough or deeply enough for them to realize what was about to happen in PG-Two, but they located the Taljzi home system."

"PG-Six," Cawl guessed.

"The furthest out of the Precursor's major installations," she agreed. "A backwater facility at the far side of a backwater sector. But the Taljzi found something there, something that allowed fifty-odd thousand refugees to become a threat to our nations."

"Are we certain?" Kanmorad asked. "If we are..."

"Then we don't want to let JTF Twenty-Six spoil the surprise," Harriet said. "We've validated it as best we can. We know the *Mesharom* think it's the real thing, and we've run out of major Precursor installations to scout. The rest of JTF Twenty-Three and Twenty-Five's targets are silver systems, and we're pretty sure what we're going to find there."

"So, we recall all of the task forces," Cawl suggested. "Pull everyone back here and launch one massive attack."

"We give up any chance of a preliminary survey," Kanmorad warned. "Surprise may make up for that, but if we're talking about their home system. It will be well defended."

"We can scout the system from a light-week or so out," Harriet countered. "It won't be as detailed, but if we spread several thousand ships out, we can get decent resolution. Unless they're paranoid enough to keep significant fleets under stealth screens in their home system, we'll know what we're getting into."

"It's decided, then," Cawl concluded. "We recall our subsidiary forces—leaving JTF Twenty-Five time to complete their rescue mission, of course—and then we head for PG-Six."

The Kanzi shrugged and smiled, baring brilliant white teeth.

"If nothing else, just *moving* the main fleet will shut up some of the grumblers!"

CHAPTER FORTY-SIX

"We're ready."

Elstar's calm words echoed in the impromptu shuttle bay the Mesharom had assembled around the Imperial craft once they had power. Morgan had been operating out of one of the shuttles since they'd arrived, but she didn't think anyone in the Imperial party had done more than catnap since arriving.

"Are you sure?" she asked the Rekiki, glancing past him to where Idoni was fiddling with a console.

He raised a forward hoof in a questioning gesture and lowered his volume.

"Unless there is something you think I've missed?" he murmured.

Translation: *Do you need me to create a delay?* It was an opportunity to slow things down if Morgan still needed more time to copy the entirety of the Mesharom database.

"Well, I'd *love* a ninety percent chance of success," she told him with a smile.

Translation: *We've ripped the entirety of their database, and it's stored in the shuttles.*

She knew Adamase, at least, expected her to have done just that. They'd been intentionally turning a blind eye, an unofficial repayment of the Imperium's rescue of the one hundred and sixty survivors of Tilsan's fleet.

Coraniss had been right there as Morgan's techs had copied the entire database, but the Interpreter hadn't been entirely kidding about their level of trauma. Those same techs were telling Morgan that Coraniss's short-term and medium memory were a mess right now.

They might realize it had been done at some point in the future, but even then, they'd likely go to Adamase, who'd tell them to keep quiet. Right now, though, Coraniss only seemed to realize they'd pulled the data the Mesharom had stolen from the Taljzi.

For the first time ever, Morgan found herself wishing that the Mesharom were better at tearing into other people's computers. They had rough navigational data of the Taljzi sphere and the location of their homeworld. All of that was worth its weight in gold, but they had no data on the defenses of the Taljzi home system.

Elstar thumped his leg in laughter at her comment—and blinked his acknowledge of what had gone unspoken.

"We're drifting toward the star at about fifty kilometers a second, so at least we don't need to worry about getting *Blade* moving," Elstar noted. "It's just a matter of opening a large-enough portal in the right place through the gravity zone barrier of a good-sized star."

"'Just,'" Morgan quoted back to him. "*Just* something that only three or four militaries in the galaxy have worked out how to do on the scale of a missile...and we're doing it on the scale of the largest warship in existence."

"I never said it was easy," the engineer replied. "Just that it could have been *harder*."

"I leave that chaos of interpretation in your hands, then," Morgan told Elstar. "Let everyone know before you pull the trigger. My understanding is that this is going to be rough."

"There is one piece of good news, I suppose," the Rekiki told her.

"What's that?"

"If the failsafe fails, we'll never know."

"PORTAL PROCESS INITIATING. FIFTEEN SECONDS."

Idoni's voice echoed across the speakers the Imperials had set up. Morgan's earbuds heard it, translated it into English, and then played it into her ears at a tone that covered up most of the Mesharom's original buzzing voice.

If only the translator would have let the Mesharom know that they should have given people more than fifteen seconds' warning!

Morgan was standing in the middle of the shuttle, about to shout out to Damyanov, when the announcement came. It took her several precious seconds to realize that she couldn't make it to the command pod she was using as an office.

Fortunately, the main section of the shuttle contained the acceleration seats for the Marines, and it took less than ten seconds to get seated and strapped in.

From her seat she could see the rush as the Marines and crew tried to make it to *somewhere* secure after Idoni dropped their warning. They'd been expecting it, but clearly Morgan hadn't been the only one who was counting on at least a minute's actual warning.

She had just enough time to open a holoscreen from her communicator to keep her updated before Idoni threw the metaphorical switch.

Blade's outer hull now had over ten thousand individual exotic-matter emitters. She'd had almost two thousand to begin with, massive things that made even *Villeneuve*'s individual projectors look like toys, and then they'd stripped thousands more from her missiles.

The smaller ones from the missiles triggered first. Their calibration and frequency were the key, and Morgan could feel the world start to shiver as they stabbed their beams of energy into the gap between reality and hyperspace.

The gap between the small emitters and the big ones was barely long enough to be noticed. Those larger beams followed the lines the thousands of smaller projectors had drawn with phenomenal power.

Alerts flashed across Morgan's display, even the shuttle's sensors able to tell that the power surging through *Blade*'s emitters was more than the structures could ever withstand.

She flinched backward in her seat as the first explosion rocked the entire war sphere. A primary emitter had failed—but Idoni kept pouring power through. The failsafes hadn't engaged. The full energy of an Imperial matter-conversion power core was being thrown through portal emitters designed for half that at most.

For an eternal three or four seconds after the explosion, *nothing happened*. Massive amounts of power were being run through the thousands of exotic-matter emitters, but the gravity-zone barrier refused to open.

And then reality tore. Idoni had run their calculations perfectly. Even with the lost emitter, the portal appeared directly in front of *Blade*, less than twenty kilometers away from the war sphere.

Half a second later, the sphere hit the portal—and everything went mad.

IT STARTED by feeling like her head was in a vice. A few seconds later, stars started to sparkle across Morgan's vision as she struggled to breathe. To lift a hand. To move at all.

Her entire body felt like the air around her had turned to concrete, and trying to breathe didn't dispel that illusion. Every breath was a struggle against the immense weight on her body and the fact that the air felt made of rocks.

After what felt like several hours but her communicator showed her was only thirty seconds, the worst of that lifted. The world still felt wrong. It wasn't even the pressure of gravity—that pressure would have been directional.

This pressed in on her from every direction. Her head felt compressed. Her chest felt compressed. Her *feet* felt compressed.

Coughing against the pressure, she managed to reach her communicator.

"Report," she ordered. "Any casualties?"

The holodisplay was fascinating. It had frozen with the war sphere halfway through the portal.

There was only silence from her communicator, and she swallowed a curse. She couldn't even move enough to unstrap herself. The personal computer was responding to her, but it didn't seem to be connected to anyone else.

She tried to look out the end of the shuttle and then shivered. It was *exactly* like staring into hyperspace. The effect was short-range enough that she couldn't see it without looking out of the spacecraft, but at about three or four meters away, visibility fell off *fast* into the familiar gray haze.

Her communicator said it had been almost five minutes since they'd hit the portal when a second wave of full-on compression hit her, hammering her back into herself as she gasped for air.

This could not be good for the already-ill Mesharom. It wasn't going overly well for *her*. She struggled to breathe as she surveyed the shuttle, checking in on the trio of Marines in the command pod through the open door.

None of the Tosumi troopers looked great, but one clearly saw her looking. As the current wave of pressure faded, he managed to weakly raise a feathered arm and give her a thumbs-up.

The Tosumi Marines aboard *Jean Villeneuve* were clearly spending too much time with the human Marines—but Morgan returned the gesture as best she could.

Her communicator's clock was enough to warn her that she was drifting in and out of awareness of time. Over fifteen minutes had passed in the weird limbo when the third wave of pressure crashed down on her.

This time, she blacked out. When she struggled back to consciousness, one of the Tosumi had somehow made it over to her and was holding an oxygen mask to her face.

"Thanks," she muttered, hoping he heard her.

"Fifteen minutes left, minimum," the Marine said grimly. "Nobody's dying where I can reach them."

What a nightmare.

Another wave of pressure crashed down on them, and Morgan grabbed desperately for the mask. The Marine helped her cover her mouth with it before he froze, an immobile statue except for his eyes for several minutes.

Then the oxygen bottle shattered, its automatic pressure adjusting failing to account for the changes in reality around it, and Morgan was once again gasping for breath.

And then, as suddenly as it had all begun, it was over. There was no need for a report. Morgan could *tell* the instant they'd finished transiting the portal.

She could breathe. She could move.

Carefully controlling her breathing to avoid hyperventilating, she gave the Tosumi Marine a firm nod and grabbed her communicator again.

Fifty-six minutes. A transition that had probably taken less than two hundred *milliseconds* in objective time had taken fifty-six minutes per the clocks of the ship making it.

"Casualty report," she barked into the communicator. "Everyone, link in and confirm. Medical help will be en route, and we need to know who needs it most."

Even as the exhausted and terrified voices started answering her, the device pinged a minor notification, a completely normal and mundane icon that meant *everything* today.

The device had established a link with *Jean Villeneuve*'s internal network. Since the scroll-like communicator didn't have a hyperfold com—it was less than a hundredth of the size of the smallest of those devices—that meant they were within fifteen thousand kilometers of the superbattleship.

They had made it.

CHAPTER FORTY-SEVEN

SHUTTLES SWARMED *BLADE* WITHIN MINUTES OF THEIR emergence, medics of half a dozen Imperial races rushing onto the Mesharom ship. No one had expected the transition to be easy on anyone, though Morgan was grimly aware it had been worse than they'd expected.

After the initial rush, she found Adamase pulling away alone. Even knowing how Mesharom thought, she couldn't help herself reaching out to them.

"Are you all right?" she asked. She was still keeping her distance, leaving a lot of space to allow for the Mesharom's psychological quirks.

"Six of my people did not survive the transition," they told her. "Several more hang in the balance. I trust your people to do all that they can, but they need Mesharom doctors and Mesharom care. They will not get that here."

"I can't say how quickly we're going to be on our way back to PG-Three yet, but it will be soon," she promised. "We're going to get them to help as quickly as possible. When will your people be there?"

The Mesharom gave a many-shouldered shrug.

"They confirmed they were on their way, but hyperspace is not *that* much more predictable to us," they admitted. "They should be there by the time we arrive...but nothing is certain in life. I may still lose people, and to have come this far beyond what I had dared hoped for..."

"It hurts," Morgan agreed. "We're doing all we can."

"Your people were an unexpected miracle," the Interpreter-Shepherd told her. "An *undeserved* miracle. Your mother long ago earned *my* trust. The debt the Conclave now owes the Imperium..."

Adamase shivered.

"My people are not used to debts," they admitted. "Ask A!Ana about that sometime." They paused, then made a strangely delicate grumbling noise.

"Ki!Tana," they corrected, then sighed. "And so I break another confidence. May ashes scour my way home, I am lost to any hope of competence."

Morgan paused, carefully digesting the piece of information the Mesharom had just let slip. Ki!Tana was an old family friend, the ancient Ki!Tol one of the reasons humanity had leapfrogged as far ahead as they had.

But A!Ana was a *very* different matter. A!Ana had been the A!Tol Empress three hundred and fifty years earlier. She'd been the one and only Empress to order a starkiller fired, destroying the home world of one of the Kanzi factions in the ugly three-way war between A!Tol, Kanzi and Taljzi.

!Ana was not *that* uncommon an A!Tol name. If Morgan had even thought about the name's similarity to Ki!Tana, she'd have assumed it was coincidence.

But if Adamase implied it was *not* coincidence, then it was not. Her old family friend—her unofficial giant-squid aunt—was apparently even older than she thought. And the life she'd lived before she was Ki!Tol had been even more...eventful.

"I don't know if you're lost to competence just yet," Morgan finally told the Interpreter. "As you say, you have learned to trust my family. I will not betray the trust you have shown in me; I swear."

Well, she was going to hand over the entirety of *Blade*'s files to the Imperium, but she was pretty sure Adamase knew she was going to do that. She suspected, though, that that database was lacking many of the Mesharom's secrets.

There was no need for a military database to contain all the details of a four-century-past covert operation, after all.

"We'll get you home," she promised.

"I know it," Adamase replied. "I doubt it less than I doubt that I will take another breath. Remember, Commander, that I *know* who pushed for the rescue operation. I know who suggested a reckless scouting mission that could have gone so wrong in so many ways—and who convinced her superiors to send us one of *Jean Villeneuve*'s power cores.

"The Conclave owes the Imperium, yes, but we also owe *you*, Commander Morgan Casimir. *I* owe you." The Mesharom shivered.

"That will not be forgotten. By my people or by me."

SOMEHOW, Morgan was unsurprised that Tan!Stalla was waiting for her when she exited the shuttle. She'd been gone, when all was said and done, for over a week. Eight and a half cycles. Less time than if they'd taken the long flight back in normal space, but still long enough.

"Well, Commander?" the big A!Tol Captain asked. "Do I get my First Sword back now, or are you determined to permanently darken the shade of my skin?"

Dark skin was a sign of fear and stress. An A!Tol with pure black skin was a terrified sentient, one running for their life.

Morgan didn't think that repeated emotions permanently etched themselves on A!Tol skin, but it was possible? Maybe?

The red flash and beak-snap of an A!Tol chuckle interrupted her sudden train of concerned thoughts.

"It's a saying, Commander Casimir," Tan!Stalla told her. "It's no more likely than for a human's hair to turn gray from stress."

"That *does* happen," Morgan pointed out. "My mother's hair is a very different color now than it was twenty years ago." She shook her head. "I can't think of any other tasks requiring me to head out on reckless independent commands, though, sir, so I think you get your First Sword back."

"Good. Your second task is going to be double-checking all of our arrangements for our new passengers. I know there's no way we can meet all of their needs, not really, but the closer we get, the better this trip will be."

"And my first task, sir?" Morgan asked.

"Debrief in my office," the A!Tol ordered. "Two hundredth-cycles. Go clean yourself up first; I'm guessing that sanitation facilities were rather lacking on a dead war sphere."

"Just a bit, sir," Morgan confirmed. "I won't pretend I wouldn't prefer showering before anything else, but—"

"It's going to take a twentieth-cycle for us to finish evacuating the ship," Tan!Stalla told her sharply. "Even the Mesharom aren't going to blow her up until everybody's off and we've removed our power core.

"We can spare the time. Go clean up."

From the flush of Tan!Stalla's skin, Morgan realized she probably smelled worse than she'd thought. On *Blade*, surrounded by members of a dozen races who *also* hadn't managed to clean up in a week, no one had noticed.

Aboard *Jean Villeneuve*, however, that wasn't an acceptable look for the First Sword.

"Yes, Captain."

A SHOWER, a fresh uniform, and a new lease on humanity later, Morgan reported to Captain Tan!Stalla's office. The A!Tol had a holographic display of *Blade* hanging in the middle of the room, rotated to show the gaping wound that had been over half of the starship's volume and mass.

"Hard to believe that this was an *accident*," she said as Morgan took a seat across the desk from her. "To hit anything with an interface drive with that much power."

The A!Tol shivered.

"I think it's pretty obvious the Taljzi turned it off," Morgan told her. "They probably worked out the key to it much the same way we did. And faced with a Mesharom Expeditionary Fleet, they realized it could be turned into one hell of a trap."

"I have to wonder if the crews knew what was going to happen to them," Tan!Stalla asked. "You'd think they'd have thought to shut down the drives, if nothing else."

"I think they were afraid the Mesharom were going to get the information out of their ship's computers," Morgan said quietly. "I mean, the Mesharom *did* get the location of their home system and a general map of their territory. They had to have known the Expeditionary Fleet was attacking their firewalls."

"So, some officers knew, some didn't...and the commanders chose to sacrifice the entire fleet to make *sure* they got Tilsan?" Tan!Stalla suggested.

"How far would we go to get someone who blew up a billion people, sir?" Morgan asked.

Tan!Stalla was silent. She was the one who'd warned Morgan that the Mesharom would embrace the deaths of billions in pursuit of their cause.

"I suspect that if Tilsan had survived, there would have been a lot more hesitation to let you take the risks you did to save them," the Captain finally said. "That's not a sentient I'll turn purple for."

Purple was the color of A!Tol grief and mourning. The human

crew wouldn't shed any tears for Grand Commander Tilsan—and the A!Tol wouldn't waste any moments of purple on the being.

"It worked out for us in a few ways," Morgan said. "There's a stack of data crystals on the shuttles we're going to want to lock in a secure vault somewhere. Maybe copy them, but we can't risk letting their contents into *Villeneuve*'s mainframe.

"We know damn well our firewalls can't keep the Mesharom out, so let's not put the fact that we have those crystals in our systems. Not until we have a much more secure location to put them."

"How much did you get?" Tan!Stalla asked.

"All of it. Adamase gave me their access codes," Morgan replied. "And the only record that they did so is aboard that ship." She gestured to *Blade*. "Have they given us a detonation timeline yet?"

"Commander Elstar tells me it will be at least another tenth-cycle to remove the conversion core. Shepherd Adamase has promised they won't trigger the self-destruct until everything is clear." Tan!Stalla shivered her tentacles.

"*All of it?*" she asked.

"All of it," Morgan repeated. "Historical archives, military status, the full specifications of their entire battle fleet...everything."

"That's a dangerous prize," Tan!Stalla noted.

"And one we will need to be extraordinarily careful in how we use," Morgan agreed. If they started building war spheres, for example, that would inevitably draw the Conclave's attention. "From what Adamase says, though, we're probably going to be looking at an across-the-board withdrawal of Mesharom assets in our arm of the galaxy. Potentially in several arms of the galaxy.

"I think Tilsan's fleet may have represented a larger portion of their resources than they want to admit. They're going to need to pull Frontier Fleet battlecruisers back to their core territories to maintain their security against the other Core Powers."

"Leaving the Arm Powers to their own devices." Tan!Stalla flushed blue in concern. "How long, do you think, before the treaties and laws that limited us start being ignored? The

Mesharom were always the most active in things like the Kovius Treaty."

"It depends on the more powerful Arm Powers and the other Core Powers," Morgan said. "If we and the Kanzi determine that the Kovius Treaty will be respected, there's no one else in this arm of the galaxy that will argue with us."

The Kovius Treaty declared that all stars and—especially—habitable worlds within forty light-years of the homeworld of a newly discovered race belonged to that race. None of the dozen or so minor powers scattered around the Imperium and the Theocracy were going to violate it if they thought the Imperium or the Theocracy would come down on them.

Right now, though, it was the Mesharom Frontier Fleet that provided that fear. A future with the Mesharom withdrawn to their own affairs...that was a scary thought.

It was one Morgan had been getting used to, but Tan!Stalla was clearly going through the same progression she had.

"Once we have our core back, are we returning to PG-Three with our passengers?" Morgan asked.

"Everyone has been recalled," Tan!Stalla replied. "All of the joint task forces. Every ship, every scout. No one is even scouting PG-Six until we're all assembled into a combined force."

"That's what the whole alliance is for," Morgan said with a small sigh of relief. "We don't know what the Taljzi have gathered to protect their system."

"Given everything we know about the Precursors' use of the area, I'm expecting to see some of *their* warships," the Captain admitted. "Those are...an unknown headache."

From what Adamase had told Morgan, that was basically impossible. She wasn't sure how much of that discussion she could share with Tan!Stalla, though. Until the database was fully cracked open and some of that information became more common knowledge, she was going to err on the side of caution.

"PG-Five, though...that suggests they have starkillers. I don't *think* they'll blow up their home system to spite us, but given everything else they've done..." the A!Tol shivered.

Several pieces snapped into place in Morgan's head and she inhaled sharply.

"Commander?"

"Something Adamase said," Morgan said slowly, realizing that she had to share this bit at least. "They said that the first time the Mesharom blew up a star, it was because they tried to activate a Precursor jump drive and something went very wrong."

The office was quiet for a moment.

"I don't think they have starkillers, sir," Morgan concluded aloud. "I'm also not sure about Precursor warships...but I would bet money that what happened in PG-Five was that they refitted a Precursor ship and tried to take it home."

"And when they turned on the FTL drive..."

"It blew up the star system," Morgan finished.

CHAPTER FORTY-EIGHT

"We have a new hyper portal," the sensor tech reported behind Harriet.

Tenth Fleet's commander nodded silently and flipped what information they had to her seat's screens. The big holodisplay at the center of the flag deck was tracking ships only by squadron at best, tens of millions of tons of warships or freighters reduced to single icons.

If she needed to, Harriet could order the display zoomed in to focus on the Allied Fleet. Right now, as the JTFs came home, she needed the wider view of the PG-Three System.

She ran through the timelines as she looked at the details of the portal and realized something was wrong. JTF 22 was already back, the largest of their detached forces already on their way before the recall order had come out. JTF 23 had been early and arrived that morning.

That left 25 and 26, and neither of those was due back for forty-eight hours. JTF 25 was going around the region of low-density hyperspace that JTF 24 had found, but they'd had to reinstall *Villeneuve*'s power core before they could get underway.

Even in the most optimistic of scenarios, they weren't due for another arrival for at least another day. An unexpected arrival out there was dangerous.

Especially one with a hundred-kilometer-wide hyper portal!

"Koanest, we may have a problem," she realized aloud, watching the portal for *any* sign of what was coming through. "Take the fleet to battle stations."

The portal snapped shut with *nothing* having come through.

"We have stealth ships in the system," she continued. "I want a full sweep of probes through that sector and maximum post-processing. Even if it's 'just' Taljzi battleships, the last thing we need is their ships swanning around this system!"

Her staff was already leaping into action, and the icons on the big display were changing color as her orders went out. Ships that were still at ready status were blue. Orange meant they'd confirmed receipt of the order. Green icons were entire squadrons reporting battle stations.

New icons appeared on the display, marking multiple swarms of hyperfold communicator– and tachyon scanner–equipped probes. Each of those icons was fifty probes spread across at least a light-second, flashing out toward the unexpected portal at seventy-five percent of the speed of light.

"Post-processing is engaged," Koanest reported, the operations officer seeming to appear out of nowhere at Harriet's right hand. She *had* a station, Harriet knew, but until they were actually in combat, her main job was to act as the Fleet Lord's filter, making sure the call she *needed* to hear out of the hundreds coming her way made it to her.

"If it's the Taljzi, we'll know in two thousandth-cycles," The operations officer told her. She nodded. Three minutes. It would have to do.

"Is Cawl in the net?" she asked.

"Should be." Koanest checked the tablet she had leaned against her arm. A larger version of her communicator, it was almost certainly linked to her primary console and mirroring all of its functions.

"He's linked in," the Yin confirmed.

Nodding her thanks, Harriet pulled on a headset and linked into a private channel with the Kanzi.

"Fleet Master. Which of us is supposed to be in charge today?" she asked. The day-to-day operations of the combined fleet really were being run jointly—mostly by each of them handling their own people.

"You are, Fleet Lord," Cawl replied. "I'm moving the Gloried Armada out into Formation One-Twenty-Seven, but we can adjust if you have a different suggestion."

One-Twenty-Seven made sense. It was a pretty simple formation, one that formed the Gloried Armada into a hemispherical outer shield around the Imperial ships with their hyperspace missiles, along with the freighters and tankers the combined fleet couldn't survive without.

"I concur," she said calmly, gesturing to Koanest. "Captain, pass the order for us to drop into Formation One-Twenty-Seven.

"The portal wasn't large enough for the Taljzi to have sent a sufficient force of their stealth ships," she concluded to Cawl. "Worst-case scenario is that we're looking at several hundred battleships. They're not going to want to fight us, so they'll make a scouting pass.

"We're attempting to localize them, at which point I'll happily take a few hundred random HSM potshots and see if we hit anything."

The Taljzi had shown stealth on only battleships and destroyers to date. They probably *could* build superbattleships and cruisers with stealth fields, but for all that they'd updated their defenses, they'd kept to the same four ship types.

"The hyper portal was only eight light-minutes out," Cawl pointed out. "At point six cee...they're well on their way to weapons range."

"Even the *Mesharom* can't fire without losing their stealth shields," Harriet replied. The Mesharom relied on lightspeed delays to help conceal their presence until their fire arrived. She'd seen it done once.

It hadn't ended well for the people on the receiving end.

Thinking about the Mesharom made her pause, and she sighed.

"Worst case is Taljzi battleships," she repeated. "The most likely scenario is the Mesharom administration ship that Adamase called for. If that's the case, I am going to be *very* grumpy at them for staying in stealth."

Cawl was silent for several seconds before he released a half-snarl, half-chuckle.

"You've dealt with them more than I have," he noted calmly. "Adamase was being quite open in their fleet's presence in Sol for that battle. Would that be...normal for them?"

"Yes," Harriet admitted with an exasperated sigh. "Which means that random potshots are a terrible idea before the probes manage to validate *who* is out there."

Cawl repeated his bitter chuckle.

"I'll hold my fleet at the base position for One-Twenty-Seven, then," he told her. "Stealthed or not, even the Mesharom can't sneak a ship through that formation to threaten the freighters. I can't do much if they decide to fire HSMs at our logistics train, though."

"Nobody could." Harriet sighed. "Best plan is to secure the logistics train against the possibility. I don't *expect* the Mesharom to fire at our tankers, but I can spare a few squadrons of destroyers to make sure."

She waved Koanest back over to her.

"Koanest, we need at least five squadrons of destroyers to fall back on the logistics fleet and take up interspersed defensive formations. Anti-HSM doctrine."

The Yin paused, then nodded slowly.

"Mesharom?" he asked.

"Seems most likely," Harriet agreed. "I don't think they're going to shoot at us if so, but I can spare eighty destroyers to be sure."

Even with their losses, she still had over nine hundred Imperial destroyers, after all.

———————

AFTER AN HOUR, Harriet was about ready to go back to shooting random chunks of space to see what happened.

"It's definitely *not* a Taljzi ship," Koanest told the channel with the fleet command officers on it. "We know how long it takes us to find a Taljzi ship in our post-process sweep. With this ship, whoever she is, we're barely even managing to confirm that there is *anything* there, let alone locate or ID her."

Kanmorad snorted.

"And would you have located and IDed a Laian ship by now?" he asked.

"Four thousandth-cycles for a Taljzi stealth screen, eleven for a Laian one," Koanest replied instantly. "About the same for a Wendira, but they have some odd frequency glitches that make it easier to actually ID the underlying ship."

The Laian Pincer of the Republic's mandibles clicked in a mix of surprise and disbelief, and Harriet covered a chuckle.

Koanest had *overstated* how long it took them to ID a stealthed Republic warship significantly. Eleven thousandth-cycles was roughly fifteen minutes. The actual time frame was about eight minutes—or *five* thousandth-cycles.

They were allies with the Laian Republic today and on generally good terms with them—but it hadn't been *that* long since then– Echelon Lord Harriet Tanaka had led an Imperial formation into battle with a Laian war-dreadnought.

"So, our guest is almost certainly Mesharom, then?" Kanmorad asked.

"Or a Precursor ship," Cawl said softly, striking the entire channel to stunned silence. "We don't *know* what happened to them, not with certainty. Even if they are all truly dead, it appears that the

Taljzi were able to reverse-engineer several of their technologies, leaping them ahead centuries on shields, power, and interface-drive technology.

"It's not beyond the realm of reason that they have a functioning Precursor ship to use as a stealth scout."

"I'm not convinced the Precursors *believed* in stealth," Harriet pointed out. She gestured at the wreckage of the PG-Three ring station. "This system held a space station that they wrapped around a gas giant, and that's been one of the *smaller* Precursor projects we've encountered.

"Small stealth ships don't seem to be in their idiom."

Kanmorad's mandibles chittered in laughter.

"There was the ship in Alpha Centauri that we all caused each other such problems over," he pointed out. "That was a small courier ship, from what we saw of it. It fit inside a Mesharom battlecruiser in the end, if nothing else."

"On the other hand, whatever this is, it needed a hundred-kilometer-wide hyper portal." Harriet shook her head. "I'm pretty sure we're looking at a Mesharom mobile administration center. I just have no idea what that actually entails. I don't think Arm Powers are supposed to see those."

"If it makes you feel better, Fleet Lord, the Republic has no record of ever seeing one of their mobile starbases either," Kanmorad told her. "If and when our friend finally drops her stealth screen, it will be a first for everyone here."

"If we don't know when that's likely to happen, we need to consider how long to keep the fleet at battle stations," Cawl noted. "It's your command today, Fleet Lord Tanaka. One hour is fine. Two days, until JTF Twenty-Five gets here with their Mesharom passengers? Not so much."

"Agreed." Harriet hummed to herself in thought for a moment. "Move the combined fleet to rotating battle stations. One third at battle stations, one third at readiness one, one third at readiness two.

"I think we can be reasonably confident that, whatever is out there, *five hundred* capital ships should suffice to buy time for the rest of the fleet to get to battle stations!"

CHAPTER FORTY-NINE

THE FLIGHT BACK FROM PG-TWO HAD BEEN A LOT LONGER THAN anyone would have preferred. In theory, a straight flight from PG-Two to PG-Three would have taken only a day. In practice, the area directly between the two star systems was one of the lowest-density areas of hyperspace the Imperium had on record.

JTF 24 had tried to push through it, assuming that the area would be relatively small. They'd ended up stuck in the middle.

Carefully skirting around it had turned a voyage of a single day into a voyage of five days—still shorter than JTF 24's trip through the hyperspace shallow, but long enough to leave Morgan concerned about their Mesharom passengers.

"Everyone is still with us," Adamase told her from the screen at her seat. "It was a concern for some, but so long as the admin ship is waiting for us, everyone will be okay."

"We'll be portaling into PG-Three in about twenty minutes," she told him. "Starcommed update from a few minutes ago said *somebody* showed up in a massive stealth ship."

Adamase blinked.

"That will almost certainly be the ship, yes," they confirmed.

"Protocol is to keep the admin ships as covert as possible. It won't matter as much out here for a while. Once my ship returns to the Conclave with our survivors, it will be some time before another one is sent."

"How badly will the loss of Tilsan's fleet impact the Conclave?" Morgan asked.

Another long blink.

"I cannot give you details," they said slowly. "But you can assume the worst and may still be too optimistic for my people. I must ask a promise of you, Commander Casimir. One that you will likely need your second-bearer's help to complete, but I must ask it regardless."

"I am bound by duty and law, Interpreter-Shepherd," Morgan warned. "Outside that, I will help my friends as best as I can."

"This should line up well with duty and law, then," Adamase told her. "Everything that I have told you of the Precursors and their fate...I trust your mother to have kept much of it to herself. I trust *you* to do the same.

"I am now asking you to tell your Empress," they said flatly. "Your people, humans and the Imperium alike, are too curious. You will end up with your hands in Precursor technology and systems, and we will not be there to guide you or warn you."

They closed their eyes and kept them closed as they continued.

"We have perhaps done so in the worst possible of ways, but we have at least *tried* to protect you," Adamase said. "Your Imperium must be aware of the dangers and threats along that path. Entire *star systems* have died for these mistakes, Commander Casimir. You must avoid those mistakes. If you *must* dig where gods have tread, do so carefully. Do so wisely.

"This is the message you must take to your Empress. Take *all* that you have learned from us and go forward without us—but remember that the paths of the Precursors were dangerous enough *before* they broke the universe."

The emphasis on *all* did not go unnoticed. Adamase was telling her that they *were* aware that she'd stolen *Blade*'s databases before the ship had been annihilated in antimatter fire.

"I will try," Morgan said quietly. "You're right in that my mother should be able to carry the message if I cannot. We will not forget, Adamase."

Her smile was grim.

"And if nothing else, I swear to you that *we* will not break the universe."

They laughed, a grim, near-choking sound.

"I wish I could promise that of my folk with such certainty."

JOINT TASK FORCE Twenty-Five blasted through the portal into regular space in a single moment. The likelihood that something had happened to the entire Allied Fleet was low, but the report Morgan had seen suggested that there was, if nothing else, a very large stealth ship in the PG-Three System.

"Looks like everybody is still here," Nidei reported from the bridge. "Even looks like Twenty-Six beat us back. We're the last ones in."

"Someone must always be the last to the waters," Tan!Stalla replied calmly. "Orders from the flag?"

"Standing by to receive orbital slots from Allied Fleet," Speaker Kira Alles said.

"The Fleet is in combat formation," Nidei noted. "Looks like one-third battle stations. I would presume the ghost never showed themselves."

"If they were going to show themselves easily, they wouldn't have entered the system under a stealth screen," Morgan pointed out. "From what Adamase said, if it is their admin ship, those ships are under strict orders not to reveal themselves."

"How are they planning on getting our passengers off, then?" Nidei asked.

"We'll find out," she told the Ivida officer. "I suspect it's going to be something I'd call bloody stupid, though."

"New orders from the flag," Alles interrupted. "Each of the squadrons has been assigned an orbital slot. Passing the location to Speaker Cosa. We're to join the escort around *Ajax*, as before."

"Do you have a course, Speaker?" Tan!Stalla asked.

"Yes, Captain."

Morgan concealed an approving nod. It was the most likely place for *Jean Villeneuve* to be sent, so preparing a course for that option made sense. Not having it ready wouldn't have been a black mark *against* the Pibo officer, but having it was a solid checkmark for the Speaker.

"Twenty-one minutes to arrival at a steady point five cee," Cosa continued. "Permission to execute?"

"Take us in, Speaker," Tan!Stalla ordered. She turned her eyes to focus on Nidei and Morgan. "Commander Casimir, Lesser Commander Nidei. I want the ship at readiness one. We may think we know who's hiding out there, but JTF Twenty-Five is a lot more vulnerable than the entire Allied Fleet. If our ghost is actually a Taljzi fleet, jumping us would make for a decent slice of the Fleet's overall strength—and while they don't know it, *we* know we're carrying the survivors of Tilsan's Expeditionary Fleet.

"Nothing's happening to them. Understand?"

"Yes, sir."

Switching the ship from readiness two—the minimum for transit —to readiness one was the push of a button on the Captain's seat. It sent the crew into motion, calling another shift into their duty stations, but it was easy enough to *start*.

"Stations reporting in at readiness one," Morgan said several minutes later. "No concerns or issues."

Buckler drones were ready to deploy. Internal hyperspace portals were charged, ready to be opened and have missiles flung into them.

Jean Villeneuve hummed around them, a single set of orders from being ready for war.

"Sir, we're receiving a hyperfold transmission from an unknown source," Alles reported. "Formatting and data identifiers are Mesharom." She paused. "They're sending us a new set of coordinates, on the far side of the outermost gas giant. It's...quite clear we are to come alone."

Tan!Stalla's skin gave the quick flash of an A!Tol sigh.

"Get me a channel to Squadron Lord Sun," she ordered.

PROPER AUTHORIZATION for the detour only took a few minutes, and then *Jean Villeneuve* dropped away from the rest of JTF 25. Despite the Joint Task Force already effectively being dissolved, Morgan still suppressed a shiver of loneliness and fear as the distance increased.

"They do realize that we've blanketed the entire star system with sensor probes, right?" Nidei asked. "And that everything we see is being sent to the Fleet in real time via the hyperfold coms?"

"I suspect it's the principle of the thing," Morgan replied as the superbattleship rounded the gas giant. They no longer had direct line of sight to any of the other ships in the star system, though the bridge's big holodisplay showed at *least* thirty drones at various distances that could see them perfectly well.

"This is a ship that no one is supposed to know exists, but if they want to send over shuttles or anything like that, they need to drop the stealth field," she continued. "They're not leaving Adamase or the others behind, but they need to show at least a surface allowance for the protocol that their mission requires them to viola..."

The Mesharom dropped the stealth field. One moment, *Jean Villeneuve* was alone in the "hidden" area in the lee of the gas giant.

The next, she was utterly dwarfed by her companion. Morgan had thought that the war spheres were the largest mobile spaceship she would ever see. They had overshadowed the Laian war-dreadnoughts and even the massive and slow Taljzi mining ships in PG-Four.

This was the war sphere's big brother. The "admin ship" was a rounded disk at least sixty kilometers across. She had to blink away surprise as she processed the numbers.

"She's sixty-one point six two kilometers across, four point oh five kilometers thick at the edges, and sixteen point one three kilometers thick at the center," Nidei said slowly. "That isn't a ship. That's a *space station.*"

"The Laians have similar vessels," Morgan pointed out as she swallowed her shock. "The only one we've ever seen is Tortuga, but they exist."

Tortuga was a pirate port run by Laian Exiles, the losers of a civil war fought around the same time as Earth's World War One. Originally intended to provide mobile maintenance to ships roughly the size of a modern Imperial superbattleship, it was still bigger than their modern war-dreadnoughts.

Tortuga's modern siblings were designed to take entire war-dreadnoughts into their maintenance bays and were larger than Mesharom war spheres. They were also mind-bogglingly slow and never went anywhere they couldn't flee into hyperspace from.

"She's moving at point two cee towards us," Nidei noted. "No communication yet. Energy levels suggest multiple singularity cores." The Ivida shivered. "I don't think she's a warship, but even her *defensive* weapons can probably obliterate us."

"Commander Casimir, please check in with Shepherd Adamase," Tan!Stalla ordered. "Are they expecting us to dock with them or..."

"On it," Morgan promised, dropping a partial privacy shield as she pinged the channel for the Mesharom official.

"Adamase."

"We found your ride. They're being damned untalkative, even for your people, but that is a very large ship for us to let near us without coms."

The channel was silent.

"Very well," Adamase said slowly. "May I have access to a radio transmitter?"

Morgan dropped the privacy field and turned to Alles.

"Alles, hook up one of the transceivers to Adamase's quarters," she ordered. "Let's let our caterpillars talk to each other."

"Do it, Alles," Tan!Stalla confirmed. "Cosa, keep us at least a hundred thousand kilometers from that thing until we've confirmed *some* kind of plan!"

The icon for *Villeneuve* on the display shifted, flitting away from the oncoming Mesharom construct. Morgan brought up a report that confirmed that Adamase had made contact with his people. She wasn't eavesdropping—she suspected Adamase would have engaged some kind of encryption to keep the conversation private anyway— but it was reassuring to know for sure that the Mesharom ship *was* talking to them.

"Wait, we're receiving another transmission by hyperfold," Alles reported. "More precise coordinates, a number of different time stamps and what looks like code for an automated docking protocol?"

"Casimir?" Adamase's translated voice sounded in her ear.

"I'm here," Morgan confirmed. "Your friends have sent locations and what looks like a docking protocol."

"We had to strip the base of Interpreter personnel to provide Tilsan with enough people to talk to yours," Adamase told her. "There's no one aboard *Region Six* really able to politely talk to you.

"If you proceed to the coordinates, they will be sending several waves of shuttles. You have time stamps for each scheduled arrival. Our docking protocols are close to yours, but our pilots will be happier dealing with your computers.

"Pick a shuttle bay for us and I'll get my people moving."

Morgan looked up at Tan!Stalla.

"What shuttle bay do we want them coming to?" she asked. "I'd suggest Bay Two; it's the least crowded."

"You're the First Sword, Commander. Bay Two it is," Tan!Stalla confirmed.

"Move your people down to Bay Two, and we'll have flight control load the software," Morgan told Adamase.

"Your assistance and care in getting us out of that trap and to safety will be remembered, Commander Casimir," Adamase told her. "May the fates and the universe lead you to the goal you seek."

"May they lead *you* to safety," Morgan replied.

Her current goal, after all, was going to involve a major space battle in the very near future.

MESHAROM SHUTTLES WERE SLEEK, needle-like things. They swept away from *Region Six* in groups of ten, each arriving exactly at one of the time-stamps *Six* had sent ahead.

Morgan made sure the bay was waiting as they arrived. Coraniss was on the first wave out, the young Interpreter having slipped into the dream fugue state in the last day or so. There was no chance to even say goodbye.

Each shuttle loaded four Mesharom aboard and then danced back out of *Jean Villeneuve*'s bay.

"They're the same size as our shuttles, really," Nidei said quietly as they watched the maneuvers. "Longer and narrower, but that's all. Not even that much more maneuverable."

"Variable geometry," Morgan replied. When the Ivida looked back at her, she grinned. "Like the interiors of their ships, except it's the entire outside hull as well. Whatever shape they need, they can be in. Medical transport needs to be long and narrow because they're stacking in multiple Mesharom basically nose to tail.

"If they're in assault mode, it's a broader shape designed to carry attack units of their servitor robots. Another mode allows for them to mount an array of interface-drive or even hyperspace missiles."

She shook her head as she watched the second group of shuttles swoop in.

"There's footage of them changing in mid-flight, even," she told

Nidei. "Growing wings when they hit an atmosphere, basically. They're quite clever little ships...but as you say, they're not much more impressive than our own."

Adamase, it appeared, was going out on the last flight. The second and third flights picked up their passengers and left while the Interpreter-Shepherd watched.

"Aren't we working on similar mobile hull tech?" Nidei asked as the fourth and final flight of shuttles swept in.

"So I'm told," Morgan demurred, unwilling to reveal Dragon-Works secrets. The Mesharom archives concealed in cold storage aboard *Jean Villeneuve*—with four backups on the superbattleship and several more sneaked over to *Horatio* and the other ships of Sun's squadron—would let them duplicate the Mesharom systems too.

The last shuttles dodged free and the Mesharom were away. Far too few for how many of that ancient race had headed out with Grand Commander Tilsan.

"We're receiving a communication from *Region Six*," Alles reported. "Just text. Two words: *thank you*."

Before Morgan could even suggest a reply, the stealth field descended again. It cut both *Region Six* and the last shuttles off from view, leaving *Jean Villeneuve* apparently alone again in the lee of the gas giant.

"All right, people," Captain Tan!Stalla said sharply. "Taxi service is over. It's time for us to go rejoin the fleet and get ready for action.

"We gave the Fleet Lord a target. Now it's time to go hammer it flat."

CHAPTER FIFTY

"Officers. We have a target."

It was entirely redundant for Harriet Tanaka to announce that, really. The information that Casimir and her team had pulled from the Mesharom war sphere had been spread widely throughout the fleet over the days since they'd pulled off their perilous jump out of PG-Two.

This was still different, though. Once again, she was facing a virtual conference of every flag officer, starship captain and executive officer of three fleets and over four thousand warships.

A hundred fewer ships were represented there. The handful of battles fought over the weeks since they'd arrived hadn't cost much in the grand scheme of things, but the trap at PG-Two had killed a lot of people.

Now the entire Allied Fleet was back together. There would still be surprises, but they wouldn't lose any more detachments on their own.

"We came out this far with a mission," Harriet reminded everyone. "The Taljzi came to our worlds with fire and death. Millions of civilians were killed. Millions of our fellow spacers died when we fought them at Sol.

"We drove them back from our worlds, but we knew we couldn't leave them alone," she said quietly. "We *had* left them alone, from sheer ignorance if nothing else, for hundreds of long-cycles. It would have been hundreds more before we ever reached their stars, and we would have freely negotiated and traded with them then."

Well, the Imperium would have. She couldn't speak for the Kanzi, several of whom her conferencing software was flagging as looking quite rebellious at that description. The Laians, she was sure, wouldn't have given a damn either way.

"But they chose to Return." She let the capital the Taljzi had used for themselves roll off her tongue, lending emphasis to the single word.

"So, we knew we couldn't leave them. We knew there was a base here at PG-Three, so we came to deal with it." She shrugged. "The Mesharom came before us. We now know what happened here: they fought the reinforced survivors of the fleet that attacked Sol. They won. They destroyed the ring station and pursued those survivors deeper into Taljzi space.

"Grand Commander Tilsan burned a colony world, and then the Taljzi led them into a trap, sacrificing an entire fleet to make sure that Tilsan's war spheres would never again be a threat to them."

She smiled.

"But it turned out that there was one last threat Tilsan could deliver to the Taljzi. One final piece of aid the Mesharom left us: they learned the location of the Taljzi homeworld. Our own scouting would have found it shortly, but this way, our branded friends don't know we're coming. They don't know that the secret they have fought so hard to protect has been betrayed.

"The Allied Fleet is ready," Harriet concluded with a glance at Cawl and Kanmorad. "We have been bled by this enemy. They have burned our worlds and shattered our ships, and this was a war they brought to *us*. The Taljzi chose to start this war.

"We are going to finish it."

She let that sink in. None of her audience was going quite so far as to start a standing ovation, but even across the thousands of virtual presences, she could sense their eagerness to end this. Their anger over what had happened.

"Our current ops plan calls for us to emerge one light week from the Taljzi system, what we had previously labeled PG-Six. There, we will take a cycle to prepare based off what the old light there tells us.

"After that day, we will launch our final assault and *end* the threat the Taljzi represent to our nations." Harriet's smile turned grim and cold. "We estimate it will take us twelve cycles to reach that jump-off point.

"If you have any preparations you need to make before that trip, I suggest you make them now. Our pause at the jump-off point is going to be *very* busy."

THERE WERE a thousand different administrative tasks necessary to get a fleet of thousands of warships heading in the same direction. The logistics fleet alone had over a thousand ships. The Allied Fleet was a monster in any sense of the word.

It took hours, even with the staff and support available to Harriet, but they made it inside the deadline she'd set. When the final orders were given, the last instructions and priorities were decided, she was able to sit back in her chair on *Ajax*'s flag deck and watch everything unfold.

The Laians moved first. There was no question in anyone's mind that the war-dreadnoughts were the toughest units in the fleet. If something went wrong, Harriet wanted the problem to collide with Kanmorad's ships.

Behind the massive Laian starships, the three-part formation unfolded. Battleships and superbattleships spread out in a series of walls half a million kilometers across. The lighter ships inserted themselves into those walls, filling the gaps between the immense capital ships.

There was no way any force in the galaxy could open a single hyper portal large enough for the entire Allied Fleet. The portals went by squadron, hundreds of them opening in the space of a few seconds.

For a moment, Harriet's display resembled nothing so much as a neon-tinted block of swiss cheese...then *Ajax* was through.

The rest of the Fleet followed. Over five thousand starships transited through about five hundred hyperspace portals, the formation remaining completely intact through the maneuver.

"The virtual exercises have paid off," Harriet noted aloud. She was actually impressed—with this many starships in play, she'd expected more than the handful of errors she was seeing.

"They look good now," Koanest agreed. "But it's when we come out of hyperspace in PG-Six that it will 'pay off,' I think."

She nodded.

"Mail transmission went out before we left?" Harriet asked after a moment.

"Everything was confirmed and double-checked," Koanest confirmed. "Everyone *should* even know to have their last responses recorded before we make the final jump."

Twelve cycles to the surveillance zone. A cycle of surveillance and then a tenth-cycle, at most, to make that final jump.

"Just a few more cycles," she murmured. "Then we get to finish this."

Harriet was far from alone in missing her family, she was sure. Everything the Taljzi had done had led to the days to come. Her orders and her nature called for mercy...but they also demanded that when the Allied Fleet was done, the Taljzi would no longer be a threat.

Finding that balance...well, that was why Fleet Lords got paid so well.

CHAPTER FIFTY-ONE

"I GOT YOUR LAST MESSAGE," VICTORIA ANTONOVA'S IMAGE SAID. "Between you trying *not* to sound like a fatalist walking to her execution and the briefings being given here in Sol, my read is that you're about to kick off the final offensive."

The blonde woman smiled grimly.

"You would not *believe* the rumors flying back here," she continued. "Or the number of people who think that I know everything because my girlfriend is with Tenth Fleet! I know Admiral Rolfson is getting pretty detailed briefings, but even his staff is standing in a bit of shadow."

And at that, Victoria knew more than most people in the Militia Morgan knew. She *was* the primary communications officer for the second-ranked officer of the Duchy of Terra Militia, after all.

"So, yeah. I'm still back home, flying a desk that happens to be on a superbattleship," Victoria told her. "The Militia has finished most of their repairs since the battle. We're understrength, what with your new employer stealing all of our new construction, but we're ready if things go wrong."

She reached out to the camera, a gentle caress that Morgan couldn't feel.

"At least I know you're going into battle," she said quietly. "A lot of people have family or loved ones with Tenth Fleet, and we're not talking much about what's going on. I'm not sure which is worse, but at least I *know* I have reason to be worried.

"Come back to me, Morgan Casimir. I'll be waiting."

Morgan sighed as the message ended. There wasn't much more she could tell Victoria that the woman didn't already know. There were days she hated that she was asking the other woman to wait, but she also knew she wasn't giving up the Imperial Fleet anytime soon, either.

They had to find a way to make it work, or they had to accept it wouldn't. She really didn't know which one it was going to be.

She checked the clock. Three cycles to hyperspace emergence, and a twentieth-cycle—a bit over an hour—until she was back on duty. She had time to record a message back, but it wouldn't be sent until they dropped out for the final surveillance.

Morgan stared at the console in her quarters for several minutes, trying to sort out what she would say or how to say it. Then she sighed.

She needed to record a message back, but she did have three days. Right now, she would be better served by showering before she took over the watch.

HYPERSPACE WASN'T NECESSARILY PERFECTLY safe—especially not when flying in formation with five thousand–odd other starships—but it was safe enough to almost guarantee quiet watches. Morgan made it through two watches and a duty period in her office before she was even remotely sure of what she wanted to say to Victoria.

That was...enough to get started at least, and she settled down in her quarters with a mug of hot chocolate, still thinking it through as she turned on the camera.

"Hey, Victoria," she said cheerfully. "Obviously, I'm not going to tell you whether you guessed right. If you did, you'll be getting briefed with everyone else on the results a few days after you get this.

"If you didn't, well, you'll get briefed with everyone else whenever we actually find the blue-furred bastards." She chuckled.

"Regardless, well, I don't know when we'll be coming back," she admitted. "Barring us crossing a few lines I don't think the Fleet Lord is going to cross, there's going to need to be an invasion and an occupation before this is all over.

"We could easily end up being out here for months, even years." Morgan sighed. "I love you," she told Victoria. "But I don't know how long I can ask you to wait. We joke about the 'Navy wife' problem, but that's what we're looking at, and you and I haven't even been together that long.

"I've been *on this mission* for almost as long as you and I had together in Sol. I *want* you to wait for me. I want to come home and find you there looking for me, but I can't pretend my life is going to change anytime soon.

"In the Ducal Militia, it was a given that most of both of our postings would be in Sol. We knew that we'd only be apart for so long, and that's what we were both thinking when we started this. Now... well, now I'm part of the Imperial Fleet and I could end up being sent a thousand light-years from home."

Morgan paused, rallying her thoughts.

"I'm *not* breaking up with you," she said firmly. "Not just because I won't dear-Jane anyone, but because I really *do* want to come home and be with you. But it's been sinking in just how much I changed the situation on you when I took Fleet Lord Tanaka's transfer offer. I know you said it would be okay, but I have to wonder if you were thinking I'd only be in the Fleet for this mission."

She hadn't even realized she was clenching her hands together and she took a moment to separate them and inhale a deep breath.

"I want you to know that if this *is* too much, I understand," she said quietly. "I don't want you to feel trapped by us. I want you to be waiting for me when I get home because you *want* to be, not because you feel you *have* to be."

Morgan brushed stubborn tears away from her eyes and chuckled hoarsely.

"And the funniest part is that I have no reason to think you're even doing that," she admitted. "But I'm hundreds of light-years from home and about to go into battle. I want you to know I love you. But I also want you to know that I don't want you to feel trapped."

She blew a kiss at the camera and smiled.

"Hopefully, I'll see you soon," she told Victoria. "Either way, I won't hear from you before this is over." She realized she'd given up on pretending Victoria *hadn't* guessed correctly. No one was going to be overly surprised, she supposed.

"If I don't make it...remember me. But whether I make it or not, don't be *trapped* by me. Okay?"

She ended the recording and laughed at herself. How many demons was she borrowing? Did Victoria really need to deal with them all?

Morgan wasn't sure of the answers to those questions...but she was sure she wasn't going to get around to recording another message before the surveillance dropout, which meant this one would have to do.

CHAPTER FIFTY-TWO

"And here we all are," Harriet murmured to herself as *Ajax* punched through another hyper portal. The flight had been half a cycle longer than anticipated, roughly normal for any trip in hyperspace, and the Allied Fleet was now one light-week from PG-Six.

She wanted to call it the Taljzi home system, but that was inaccurate. The Taljzi's home star was Arjzi, their homeworld Kanarj. It was easy to forget that there was no biological difference between the Taljzi and the Kanzi who made up half of her fleet. Their schismatic sect of the Kanzi faith had been born in the Syah System, an early Kanzi colony that had served as the capital of the Taljzi rebellion... until the A!Tol had blown it up with the only starkiller her service had ever fired.

"Extremely Large Array positions have been calculated and distributed," Koanest ordered. "*Ajax* is launching probes for her own component, but we're staying right here."

With, Harriet noted, all three remaining *Galileo*-class superbattleships hanging out around her to keep the flagship safe. She couldn't complain particularly loudly, though—Fleet Master Cawl's flagship was similarly secured at the heart of the ELA formation.

There were enough ships in play that the fleet had to move slowly for interface-drive vessels. The expansion of the ELA was taking place at barely a third of the speed of light. With four thousand warships and thousands more sensor probes, though, they could establish a telescope just over a light-minute across.

Hyperfold coms fed all of the information being picked up from those thousands of individual sensor platforms back to *Ajax* and her escorts. The *Galileo*'s computers were a generation more advanced than even the *Bellerophon*-Bs like *Ajax*, which meant the collation was taking place on *Jean Villeneuve* and her sisters.

That was then fed to *Ajax* and into the main holographic display. There, in front of Harriet Tanaka's eyes, a new star system slowly took shape.

It was nearly a mirror of Sol in many ways. Four rocky worlds surrounded by a major asteroid belt, three gas giants outside the asteroid belt. The gas giants were larger on average than Sol's, probably bringing the entire system to a very similar mass to humanity's home.

"We're still resolving energy signatures," Koanest said quietly, watching the image taking shape beside Harriet. "No megastructures, at least. Even the PG-Three ring station would have shown up already."

"Looks like the third planet is smack-dab in the habitable zone," Harriet replied. "Fourth might be, depending on atmospherics. Prime terraforming candidate."

Terraforming wasn't something the Imperium did very often. There were enough habitable planets around to cover most of their territory needs—and one of the Imperium's biggest problems was population growth.

With Imperial tech and medicine available, human lifespans were expanding dramatically. The birth rate was dropping in roughly equal proportion. Most Imperial Races were functionally *below* replacement rate for births, a demographic crisis postponed by the long lives enabled by their technology.

Even reduced as the current human birth rate was, humanity was accounting for one tenth of the Imperium's new births. Humanity had been annexed for their *numbers*, not any great special talent or quality.

Of course, that annexation had worked out rather well for everyone involved—though Harriet would admit she was at least a little biased there.

"Energy signatures should be layering in n..."

Harriet didn't even ask what Koanest had been shocked to silence by. She could see it herself.

There were no megastructures in the system, but the Taljzi might as well have built a ring around the third habitable world. Layer upon layer of space stations encircled the planet, with what had to be ship-yards and orbital industry and a thousand other stations all piled on top of each other.

A!To approached that level of industry but had moved most of it to the planet-star Lagrange points to keep it out of orbit. Earth was following the same logic now, not only moving industry into orbit but moving it away from the planets and the routes ships traveled.

The Taljzi had just kept building on top of earlier stations. There had to be fortresses in there, but there was no way that Harriet's people would be able to distinguish them at this distance.

Worse, from her perspective, was that they *could* distinguish the warships that weren't around the third world. With all of the losses that had been inflicted on the Taljzi so far, she'd really believed that they had to have lost most of their fleet. That they had to be reaching the end of the resources a rogue colony on the far end of nowhere could muster.

The hundreds of capital ships scattered across the system gave the lie to that. Cruisers and destroyers escorted cargo ships while battleships and superbattleships orbited in defensive clouds.

"Look there, Fleet Lord," Koanest suggested, pointing to a cluster she hadn't noticed. "It looks like the fourth planet is inhabited."

The Taljzi had clearly done some equivalent of terraforming on the planet on the edge of the liquid-water zone. The energy levels radiating off the world suggested a prosperous colony, if far from the industrial monster they'd turned the third world into.

And four hundred capital ships, half of them the twenty-megaton monsters of Taljzi superbattleships, orbited above that world.

"CIC makes it just over two thousand capital ships total, with a fifth of their strength around the third world," Koanest said after a few more minutes of study. "Approximately thirty-five hundred cruisers and destroyers. They're not...as much of a concern."

"No," Harriet agreed, studying the holodisplay. "Especially not with these guys."

Her hands sank into the display, haptic feedback systems recognizing her gesture and zooming in on the four massive structures positioned around the main planet.

Two were in orbit ahead of the world and two were in orbit behind. Each of them acted as the anchor for two hundred capital ships, representing almost a quarter of the capital's defenders. They were spherical constructs, each at least eighty kilometers in diameter.

"Defensive fortresses," Koanest agreed. "They may be vulnerable to hyperspace missiles."

"Do we want to bet that they didn't upgrade their home-system defenses when they upgraded their strike fleets?" Harriet replied. "If they were going to upgrade *anything*, it would be those stations. Plus..."

She studied the data codes attached to the icons.

"Get CIC to double-check that, because those energy signatures are way off from Taljzi or Kanzi systems," she told him. "If that's the case, that leaves me with a really ugly thought on just *who* built those fortresses."

She heard Koanest snap her beak shut with a hard click and knew she'd followed Harriet.

If the Taljzi hadn't built the spherical battle stations themselves... then they were inherited Precursor tech.

Somehow, Harriet doubted the resemblance to a scaled-up Mesharom war sphere was a coincidence in that case.

HARRIET LEFT the data-gathering mostly to the analysts after that, convening with the other two fleet commanders after they'd been out of hyperspace for just over two hours.

"That is going to be a risky plain to run," Cawl said bluntly as they linked together, all three of them and their aides studying the same hologram of the star system. "Twelve hundred superbattleships and nine hundred battleships? Plus thirty-five hundred escorts?

"How did my estranged kin even *build* this?"

"They took over a mostly nonfunctional Precursor shipbuilding facility, found its source of raw resources, and fed a trillion tons of raw iron into the shipyard in PG-Three and the stations here," Harriet replied. "So long as they had the *people*, I can see where they got the resources."

"Your best guess is that they fled the Theocracy with, what, fifty thousand people?" Kanmorad asked. "I would expect something more like the descendants of the Ascendancy and *Builder of Sorrows*."

Harriet concealed a smirk. Kanmorad was relatively open to talking about the Exiles, though she noted he rarely mentioned that a good half of the Exiles—those "descendants of the Ascendancy"—now lived on Earth.

But he was also right. *Builder of Sorrows*—mostly known in Sol as Tortuga—and her forty thousand or so crew and refugees represented a logical comparison point.

They'd become the premier criminal bankers for this arm of the galaxy...and that was it. They certainly hadn't taken over multiple star systems and assembled fleets of thousands of capital ships.

"Energy signatures suggest the main planet has a population of over twelve billion," Cawl noted. "The fourth planet is another billion, at least. All Kanzi. No slaves here. I...don't think that level of population growth is even physically possible."

"Previous estimates put the population of the ring station at about two billion, and the colony Tilsan bombarded had another billion," Harriet added. "So. Sixteen billion people. In five hundred long-cycles."

"And that's why we're all here looking for a Precursor cloning facility," Kanmorad said with a chitter of his mandibles. "Those fortresses and perhaps an intact warship or two would explain the tech level of their starships."

"Those 'fortresses' may well be Precursor warships," Cawl replied. "The one thing I think has been clearly established is that their FTL drive is completely unusable by any other race. Who knows about their sublight engines?"

"That's true," Harriet agreed. "They are probably *less* dangerous, in many ways, than if they were of Taljzi construction." She shook her head, studying the system. "Unfortunately, it doesn't look like whatever cloning facility the Precursors left behind is registering on our scanners."

"I'm not surprised," Kanmorad admitted. "To produce as many clones as we have seen, we're almost certainly looking at hundreds or thousands of individual facilities. Hospital-sized, most likely. Maybe city sized."

"I'll concede I was hoping for a nice, neat space station I could vaporize," Harriet said.

"You face an enemy that may well be able to mass-produce soldiers to defend their planet," the Laian reminded her. "I admire your commitment to your Imperium's principles, Fleet Lord, but you must realize that you do not face a foe you can readily conquer or intimidate.

"The Taljzi must be destroyed. You brought starkillers, did you not? *Use them.*"

The virtual conference was deathly silent.

"I must object," Cawl finally said, his voice recognizably tired and sad. "These are *my people*, Pincer of the Republic. Their leadership may be lost, and their ancestors may have been fanatics, but they remain Kanzi in their blood and their bone.

"I am not yet prepared to condemn them all."

"And I am not yet prepared to become the second Imperial commander to ever fire a starkiller in earnest," Harriet added. "The challenge in front of us is impressive, but we have gathered one of the largest fleets in the recorded history of any of our nations."

There were two of the destroyer-sized starkillers hidden among her own Tenth Fleet. She suspected—and Cawl's words and reactions implied she was correct—that the Gloried Armada had access to the weapons as well.

A starkiller was extremely vulnerable right up to the point of terminal delivery—and whoever escorted it to that point would find the odds and the physics against them as they tried to outrun the blast wave and escape the target system.

From terminal delivery to final nova would be only about fifteen minutes. Only the fact that the shockwave "only" propagated at light-speed would allow any of Harriet's ships to escape.

"We have better options, in any case," she continued. A gesture highlighted the fourth world. "This is PG-Six-D. Clearly a secondary terraformed colony and a major industrial site. Hardly world-shattering in importance, but still guarded by a defensive fleet of four hundred capital ships.

"It is also at the opposite side of the star from PG-Six-C *and* closer to the edge of the gravity zone," she reminded the other two fleet commanders. "We can assault PG-Six-D, destroy its defending fleet, and secure control of the orbitals long before the forces at Six-C can engage us.

"Unless those fortresses have some kind of super-long-range weapon we don't know about, we can smash a fifth of their forces in one strike—a strike in which will we have overwhelming force.

"From PG-Six-D, we will have a better position to get a direct view of PG-Six-C and see if we can localize targets for a more precise assault."

"It makes for a solid opening move," Cawl agreed. "If we're lucky, we may even be able to lure their warships out from Six-C into an open-space engagement out of range of Six-C's defenses.

"In those circumstances, I will happily match our fleet against sixteen hundred Taljzi warships. A mere two hundred extra ships in their hands? We have crushed them at longer odds."

Harriet nodded agreement fiercely. Of course, when they'd fought the Taljzi at those "longer odds," the enemy hadn't had antimissile defenses other than their shields. The losses the First Return had taken were quite clearly the reason *why* those defenses had been deployed.

"This is your war to fight, Fleet Master, Fleet Lord," Kanmorad conceded with a wide gesture of his claw. "I am here to assist, not to command. My advice is given. Your plan is a reasonable one, in any case."

He studied the fourth planet for several seconds.

"If nothing else, with civilian prisoners in hand, it seems that we may well learn more about our enemy at last."

CHAPTER FIFTY-THREE

THERE WAS A TIME FOR GAMES. FOR FANCY TACTICS AND LURING enemies into traps, for deception and sleight of hand and subtlety.

When the enemy was divided into two forces and the Allied Fleet knew where both those forces were wasn't that time. This was, in Harriet Tanaka's mind, a time for the largest available hammer, applied *very* carefully...but still a hammer.

The Allied Fleet exited hyperspace at fifty-five percent of the speed of light through five hundred portals. The logistics train had been left behind, sent on their way to a rendezvous point several light-years away.

Here and now, there were only warships, led by fourteen hundred and ninety-six capital ships of the three nations present.

Cruisers and destroyers swarmed through the formation, keeping pace with the leviathans at the core of the fleet as antimissile drones spilled out into space in their thousands.

Sensor probes joined them. There was no point in risking the escorts to expand the Allied Fleet's vision of the system when hyper-fold-com-equipped drones could serve just as well.

Harriet hummed to herself, smiling as the fleet unfolded like a well-oiled machine. Their weeks at PG-Three hadn't gone to waste, and now the Taljzi would understand just how bad an idea screwing with the Imperium had been.

"Two minutes to hyperspace-missile range," Koanest reported. "All Imperial ships report ready."

"And their long-range missiles?" Harriet asked.

"Ninety-three seconds after that. We hit general interface-drive missile range at four minutes, fifty seconds."

"With whatever's left," Harriet said in tones she *knew* were predatory. "All firing solutions programmed in?"

"Yes, Fleet Lord."

She leaned back in her chair. The PG-Six-D defensive force had been exactly where they'd expected. The ships were clearly scrambling, only the size of a star's gravity zone giving them any chance to prepare.

That in itself was strange, she had to admit. A similar strike on Sol would have been detected at least a tenth-cycle ago. The Taljzi's technology continued to have...odd gaps.

Right now, however, she'd take whatever surprise she got. The orders had been issued and there wasn't much the fleet commander could do at this point. The rest of this battle would ride on her squadron commanders and captains, not her.

"Keep an eye on the fleet at Six-C," she ordered quietly. "I want to know the moment they twitch in our direction."

"Probes are already on their way," her ops officer confirmed. "We'll see how they jump soon enough."

ICONS SPARKLED on the big display as the Allied Fleet entered HSM range. The lead formation of Laian and Kanzi capital ships crossed the line before the Imperial warships did, but that was the point. Once the Taljzi opened up with their missiles, the Imperial ships with their precious hyperspace missile launchers would be protected.

"All ships have fired," Koanest reported. "Impact...now. Scanning for results."

The Imperium's Tenth Fleet had almost seven hundred capital ships and over seven hundred cruisers, all of them carrying at least one hyperspace missile battery with a built-in launching portal. The icons that exploded over the Taljzi formation like confetti were almost beyond counting. There were enough tachyon jammers in play to protect the entire Tajzi fleet from detailed targeting, and that also meant that the missiles were hard to detect.

Their results were much easier to pick out.

"Looks like about half of the capital ships and all of the escorts have been refitted with new defenses," her operations officer reported. Blinking icons marked where Taljzi ships had disappeared, new numbers appearing in the display as Harriet's staff totaled the losses.

"It's not going well for the ones without the antimissile guns," Koanest said with satisfaction. "Thirty-two battleships and fifteen superbattleships destroyed."

"See if we can adjust fire to focus on the undefended ships," Harriet replied. "Every one of those we kill now can't shoot at us later."

A second salvo of glittering, deadly confetti lit up the display.

"I'm updating priorities in the tactical network," the Yin replied. "But I suspect...yes. Most of the ship tactical officers are already making that prioritization."

"Flag the ones that didn't," Harriet noted. "No censure, but we'll quietly arrange for some extra training for them."

Koanest clicked her beak in a soft chuckle.

"Understood. Results incoming." Koanest whistled, sounding almost exactly like an exasperated crow Harriet had once met. "*Seventy* superbattleships destroyed. Sixteen battleships. I think that's all of the un-refitted superbattleships gone, Fleet Lord."

"Good." She checked the range. "Because they're in range now."

Now the small icons appearing on her screen were in bright red, and the data notes attached to them were accompanied by warning notes. Her systems and staff hadn't bothered to precisely enumerate the number of HSMs the Allied Fleet had launched.

The count of Taljzi LRMs coming their way was *far* more important in many ways.

"Looks like none of the escorts are carrying LRMs," Koanest reported calmly. "The surviving un-refitted battleships just fired two hundred missiles apiece—which is strange, given that the *refitted* ships are only firing fifty from the battleships and a hundred and twenty from the superbattleships."

"Watch to see if the un-refitted ships fire again," Harriet suggested. "I suspect we're looking at externally mounted weapons."

"Second salvo launching...and you're right," he told her. "Only the refitted units are firing LRMs now."

Their own third salvo of HSMs smashed into the defenders, hammering the rest of the un-updated units and a chunk of the refitted warships into debris.

"They're down to ninety superbattleships and eighty-three battleships," Koanest reported. "Twenty-two thousand missiles incoming in that first salvo. They'll hit the outer perimeter in ten seconds."

"Focus on coordinating the offensive fire, Koanest," Harriet said quietly. "The missiles are Cawl's problem."

And Cawl was *very* good at his job. The Kanzi fleet had deployed almost ten thousand antimissile platforms and moved them forward. They hung almost a million kilometers ahead of the Gloried Armada and were utterly expendable.

The Taljzi salvo had to make it past that gauntlet before they ever reached a starship of the Armada, and there were only two missiles per defensive platform—and the new hyperfold cannon mounted on all of Cawl's ships could reach out that far.

None of the first salvo reached the Kanzi fleet. The follow-on salvos were even smaller, vanishing in the teeth of the Gloried Armada's defensives like snowflakes in a furnace.

"Regular range in thirty seconds. All ships report weapons ready," Koanest told Harriet.

She nodded.

"Proceed as planned," she replied. There was no question how this battle was going to end—there never had been, but it was *very* clear now. Two-thirds of the Taljzi capital ships were already wreckage and debris, and a hundred and thirty superbattleships were no threat to the Allied Fleet.

Harriet's attention shifted to the other planet, studying the main Taljzi fleet. Twenty-one light-minutes away, they would only now be registering the arrival of her fleet.

Even with the probes, her data was six light-minutes out of date. Newer than the Taljzi's information was going to be, but old enough that she wouldn't know how they jumped just yet.

"Tilsan burned an entire world," she murmured, more to her enemies than anyone else. "You know I'm not them, but do you know *who* I am? Will you risk it? Will you leave a world to me?"

They could do the math. No one was going to send four hundred capital ships against fifteen hundred and expect to get them back.

So, the question was: knowing that they couldn't save PG-Six-D's defenders, what would the Taljzi commanding the main fleet do?

REGULAR INTERFACE-MISSILE RANGE saw the space between the two fleets overwhelmed with thousands upon thousands of missiles. If the flag-deck holodisplay had tried to keep everything represented with an individual icon, there would have been nothing *else* visible in the hologram.

Instead, missiles were represented by icons with numbers attached. A thousand missiles. Ten thousand.

A hundred thousand.

"Hold fire after the next salvo," Harriet ordered as she watched the Allied Fleet's first massive volley enter space. "I don't think we're going to need them."

The Taljzi were clearly thinking the same thing. They were spitting missiles out at their maximum rate of fire, a hundred-plus super-battleships trying to get enough fire into space to threaten a far larger force.

It was never going to be enough. The second salvo blasted clear of the Allied Fleet, and then *Ajax* seemed to calm around Harriet. The HSM launchers were cooling down, their portals contained and closed. The regular missiles were loading into the launchers but waiting.

Waiting to see if any of the enemy survived.

"Enemy salvos are hitting the perimeter," Koanest reported. "There's a lot more missiles this time, with less flight time for tracking." She paused. "Some are going to get through."

"That's why we have shields, Captain," Harriet replied. "Keep an eye on it."

The Taljzi got five salvos off before the first Allied missiles hammered home, a rate of fire that had to have burnt out power conduits and probably wrecked loader systems.

It didn't matter. The entire first salvo, hundreds of thousands of weapons, was targeted on the superbattleships. Each of them was a leviathan of deep space, twenty million tons of technology, armor and weapons.

Their defenses slaughtered missiles by the tens of thousands. Their shields absorbed missiles by the hundreds.

It was never going to be enough.

One hundred and eleven Taljzi superbattleships died in a single cataclysmic moment of flame.

"We still have eight superbattleships on the scopes," Koanest reported. "Secondary salvo is spreading to target all escorts as well. Just cleanup now."

Even as she said that, a new alert flashed up on Harriet's screen.

The first Taljzi salvo had battered down the shields of the lead units of Cawl's fleet, focusing their fire on his battleships.

The replacement cycle had been planned in advance, but it wasn't fast enough to account for how readily the Taljzi fleet had burned out their systems to get their weapons into play.

Four of the battleships hadn't retreated fast enough, and their shields were still flickering as the second salvo crashed down on them.

Shields failed, and Kanzi compressed-matter armor was still a work in progress compared to Imperial or Laian defenses.

Two battleships lurched in space, damage codes flashing up on the display as Harriet zoomed in on them.

The other two simply ceased to exist.

"Cleanup," Harriet echoed softly. "Why does cleanup always end up feeling so damned expensive?"

CHAPTER FIFTY-FOUR

"Occupants of the orbital platforms above the planet we are approaching, this is Fleet Lord Harriet Tanaka of the A!Tol Imperium," Harriet intoned calmly into the camera. "You have one twentieth-cycle to evacuate the orbitals. After that, they will be destroyed by long-range fire. I will not approach the stations sufficiently to fire with accuracy and cannot guarantee the safety of any residential sections.

"You must evacuate the stations completely inside the given time frame."

She made a cut-off gesture and turned to her communications officer.

"Set that on repeat and auto-update the time available," she told the young-seeming officer, a Japanese woman from Harriet's own hometown of Tokyo. "There will be no negotiation."

"What about the planet itself?" Koanest asked from behind her.

"If they reach out, we'll talk to them," Harriet replied. "Otherwise, I want anything capable of firing into orbit identified long before we enter orbit. We'll launch a precision bombardment from half a million kilometers unless we flag something longer-ranged."

That was roughly the maximum range of a precision bombardment—and a hell of a lot closer than she was letting any ship in her fleet get to the planet until the orbitals were debris. At five hundred thousand kilometers, even her superbattleships' shields would fail under proton-beam fire.

They'd brought overwhelming force and good tactics to the fight against PG-Six-D's defenders, but they'd still been lucky to lose only two battleships. The forces around PG-Six-C still had them outnumbered but not by enough to truly concern her.

Assuming the Taljzi had no more surprises—a risky assumption, but not entirely invalid—she figured she could easily wreck several hundred capital ships with hyperspace missiles before they brought her into range.

That would even the odds handily. Of course, if the Taljzi found some way to get into disruptor range of her fleet, they'd swing the odds back in their direction—but with fifteen hundred capital ships' worth of hyperfold cannon, she could probably prevent that.

Probably. But she was back to assumptions.

"Any response from C's defenders yet?" she asked. They now had probes close enough to the Taljzi fleet to get real-time information—and the main fleet hadn't done anything yet.

"They're moving," Koanest replied. "But it's mostly just formation changes. They're settling in around the big fortresses. It looks like they're going to wait for us to come to them."

Harriet shook her head, rising from her chair and zooming the hologram in on the planet ahead of them with a gesture.

"Orbitals look mostly like shipping facilities," her ops officer told her. "No space elevator, but a bunch of sky-tether hooks. They should fly off into space if we hit them right."

"Make sure we do," Harriet said. "Those are dangerous enough, even if they're not as bad as the elevator at PG-One."

A sky-tether was a disconnected space elevator, a long line of hypertensile material lowered into atmosphere. High-altitude transports would fly into position, carrying cargo pods for the tether hook to catch on to as it swung by.

From there, the process was much the same as a space elevator, but the tether was slightly easier to build with lower risk to the ground. Not least because, as Koanest was pointing out, a tether's failure state was usually "up and away," as opposed to an elevator wrapping its cable around the entire planet.

"No response as yet from anyone. Think they're going to talk to us at all?" Koanest asked.

"I don't give a *kuso*," Harriet snapped. The translator would probably catch her mixing languages, but the Japanese still made her feel better. "So long as they evacuate. And if they don't..." She shook her head. "I'm not going to burn worlds or commit mass murder, but I'm not going to cry over Taljzi who don't get clear before we nuke the orbitals."

"What do we do if the other fleet doesn't move?" her ops officer said, looking back at the main map of the star system.

"Sooner or later, we go to them," Harriet said. "I'm hoping that we outrange whatever those fortresses have for weapons with the hyperspace missiles. It seems most likely that they'd have duplicated any particular system for the rest of their fleet, though."

"That depends on how big it is, doesn't it?" Koanest asked.

She sighed and nodded.

"We don't have much of a choice," she admitted. "Once we've cleared the orbitals and defenses here, we'll have to take the fight to them and find out. When this is over, there can be *nothing* left in this system that can carry or build a weapon."

It was one hell of a task, one that was probably going to require at least part of the Allied Fleet to remain for years...but when they were done, the Taljzi could *not* be a threat.

"I almost wish they thought they could take us," Koanest said. "Open space, with the chance to retreat to draw out the range...we'd rip them to pieces."

"They're not much better off if we advance on them," Harriet reminded her. "So long as they let us control the range of the engagement, we will empty our HSM magazines before we close in their weapons range."

"And the planet?" her ops officer asked.

Harriet gestured a command through the big display, zooming it on PG-Six-C.

"How good an image do we have?" she replied. "We're not getting precise hits without getting into orbit, but I want to know what I'm looking at."

"Let me see what I can resolve from the probes," Koanest said. "We were focusing on the fleet but there should still be... There."

More detail flickered into existence across the globe Harriet was looking at. Swarm after swarm of orbitals occluded the image of the ground, but they were moving enough that the probes had managed to get solid imagery of the system's other inhabited planet.

With a gesture, she blanked out the icons and imagery of the orbital platforms. She'd do the same thing to C as she was about to do to D. Those platforms represented over two hundred years of work, but she wasn't going to weep at vaporizing them.

Too many people had died at the Taljzi's furry hands for her to mourn them, even if she was unwilling to embrace their annihilation.

The continent in front of her on the model of PG-Six-C was even more densely populated than she'd expected. Glittering lights and structures marked a megalopolis that covered a landmass the size of South America. There were probably breaks and divisions, but they weren't visible to the probes orbiting almost a million kilometers away.

"Is that their only continent?" Harriet said to herself. "There's got to be at least six billion people crammed into that city, maybe more."

She gestured, rotating the globe and picking out a second continent. Slightly larger than the first and slightly less densely populated, it "only" had four megalopolises that between them covered eighty percent of its landmass. The vast majority of the landmass she'd seen so far had been covered in city. Two continents, roughly equivalent to Earth's Americas, home to at least ten billion people.

A third, smaller continent turned out to be close enough to the second to allow for easy boating, with the two continents creating a sheltered basin similar to Earth's Mediterranean Sea. Several large islands formed the core of an archipelago, and the scans suggested that the three-quarters of the planet she'd skimmed past held the entire calculated population.

She was guessing that the rest of the planet was like Earth's Pacific, a vast expanse of mostly empty water, when she saw the first floating weapons platform.

"Koanest, get me an ID on that," she ordered.

It would be visible from orbit with the naked eye, an artificial island at least thirty kilometers across. As she continued rotating the globe to see what she found, more of them showed up. There was an entire circle of them, hundreds of the platforms...surrounding the planet's fourth continent.

"The platforms appear to be primarily missile defense systems," the Yin reported, rejoining her. "Lasers, plasma cannons, surface-to-orbit weapons. Since interface missiles can't enter an atmosphere at full velocity...well, they could defend themselves against just about anything we'd throw at them."

Studying the globe himself, Koanest shook his head.

"That ring might well be impenetrable from orbit," he admitted. "What the hell are they guarding..."

Harriet was already studying the last continent and its occupant.

"I need the probes to focus on that," she said, her voice very calm. "As close a look as we can get—and yes, Koanest, that means flying one right into those defenses and letting them vaporize it if we can."

The scanners were showing the entire continent was covered by a single massive structure—and that the structure in question was *alive*.

SHUTTLES WERE FINALLY BEGINNING to swarm out of PG-Six-D's orbitals as Harriet watched. Her time limit was counting down rapidly—the Taljzi had let more than thirty of their seventy minutes disappear before they started moving—but she'd give them a little extra time, so long as they were actively evacuating.

Right up until the moment the Taljzi fleets did something she needed to respond to, in any case. Her mercy had a hard limit at the point where it would threaten her people.

Even as shuttles began carrying people down to the surface of one planet, though, her attention and that of most of the senior staff of the Allied Fleet were focused on the other.

One probe made it down into a thunderstorm passing over the target before the defenses destroyed it, giving them their clearest direct visual of the...*thing* that had brought everyone to PG-Six-D.

Her display was zoomed in on the fourth continent, and numbers ran across the screen as Harriet studied her enemy and hummed thoughtfully to herself.

Five thousand, eight hundred and sixty kilometers wide by six thousand, two hundred kilometers across. It was a continent larger than Africa, nearly approaching the size of Asia, and it was covered almost in its entirety by a single dark green...blob.

Three massive dock complexes with attached floating spaceports marked where the Taljzi interacted with the creature. Each of the complexes seemed associated with...well, with an orifice.

"We're seeing massive quantities of raw biomatter stored at this complex," Koanest told her on the closed link with the other fleet commanders. "It looks like they're harvesting Six-D for crops and fish to feed this thing as well as their population."

That made sense. Six-C *looked* self-sufficient on food, but Six-D had definitely been mostly set up for agricultural production. If they'd been feeding a continent-sized beast, then they would have needed more food.

"It's complex three where our deep-dive probe got the visual that

I think matters most, though," Cawl interjected. "Take a look, Fleet Lord. Pincer."

The Kanzi Fleet Master highlighted a single zoomed-in image from the probe's descent. Lights had been turned on, giving a partial view inside the cavernous opening nearest the dock. A heavy hauler vehicle of some kind was stopped and a cargo was being offloaded.

"Those are clothes," Harriet said slowly. "Why are they offloading..."

She finally saw what Cawl had been drawing attention to. Walking out of the shadowy orifice were people. A *lot* of people.

In the half-second of video they had, it was hard to be sure, but it looked like they were identical. At least several thousand *identical* Kanzi marched out of the giant creature, naked as the day they were born.

An...accurate phrasing, she realized, since today *had* been the day they were born.

"Raw biomatter goes in here," Koanest said slowly, highlighting one port. "Looks like people are coming in here. Not in...huge numbers, but we're definitely looking at personnel transports carrying hundreds of people.

"And then...well, the thing shits out people over here."

"We found your cloning facility, Fleet Lord," Kanmorad said. "Not a machine, though clearly still a creation of science. I wonder how many copies of a given individual it makes."

"I have to wonder whether or not the *original* survives," Harriet replied. "It, what, eats people and makes duplicates of them?"

"Clearly on an immense scale," Cawl agreed. "Thousands per cycle. Potentially hundreds of cycles per day. This one...creature has provided the population growth we were all wondering at."

"It's not a creature," Harriet objected. "It's biotech instead of nanotechnology, but we're still looking at a Precursor creation. One of their terrible wonders."

The call was silent and so was Harriet's flag deck. She had a partial privacy shield up so only the fleet commanders could hear her, but the entire fleet was looking at the same images.

"What do we do?" Kanmorad finally asked. "I imagine your people have had the same assessment of the defenses as I have: we have no long-range bombardment weapons that can penetrate them."

"We could destroy the defensive ring," Cawl replied. "It is—"

"Functionally impossible," Harriet cut him off.

Interface drives interacted weirdly with atmosphere. At a given velocity, relative to the density of the atmosphere, the drive ceased to work—and it vented its excess energy into hyperspace. It was a useful natural safety measure when you *didn't* want to hit a planet, but meant that no interface-drive bombardment weapon had a terminal velocity above roughly two hundred kilometers per second.

That could be bad enough in terms of impact energy, but it meant that there was no way they could reasonably get a weapon of any kind down to a defended planet. Conventional bombardment munitions were disposable launchers, moved into position by an interface drive but relying on a railgun and gravity to hit their targets at speeds of around one percent of light.

The defenses around the cloning creature would obliterate them before they could launch.

"A saturation bombardment with antimatter weapons would work," Kanmorad suggested.

"And exterminate every living thing on the planet," Cawl replied. "I refuse to embrace genocide as an option here, Pincer."

"Then you embrace futility," the Laian flag officer replied. "Even if you take the orbitals, those defenses will defy you. A hyperfold cannon can't be targeted that close to a planet. There are limits to that technology."

"And our hyperspace missiles lack the precision," Harriet admitted. "They carry multigigaton warheads. We're back to the antimatter-bombardment option there, just with a greater range."

"Your hesitation will doom you," Kanmorad said calmly. "You do not even know the capacity of those Precursor fortresses. A conventional assault will see millions of lives lost, and we will end in orbit with no more answers on dealing with this *thing* than we have now."

"Once we secure the orbitals, we can call for ground forces," Cawl suggested. "Those defenses are focused entirely on air and space. If we can secure a beachhead over the horizon, ground assault troops can attack by boat or low-flying aircraft.

"Control of several of the fortresses should open the way for more options," he concluded.

"You want to fight a ground war against an enemy with infinite reserves?" Kanmorad replied. His mandibles chittered in disgust.

"Most of my fellows would have opened this attack with a starkiller," he told them. "I am less willing to go that far than others in the Republic, but if there was ever a target, ever a situation, that called for the destruction of a star system, this is it."

"Thirteen billion people," Cawl said quietly. "Yes, clones. Yes, almost certainly indoctrinated. But the vast majority of them cannot be soldiers or spacers. Only a tiny portion of them have any responsibility for the war waged against us.

"I will not murder thirteen billion people to make my life easier."

"Nor will I," Harriet agreed. Kanmorad was correct that it was the *easiest* option. That just didn't make it the *right* option. "You said you would follow our decision on this, Pincer Kanmorad."

"I did and I *will*," he replied, his mandibles snapping hard as he spoke. "I just think you're both mad!"

Harriet chuckled bitterly as she turned her attention back to the near-invulnerable fortress ring around her ultimate target.

Kanmorad was right in one thing: even if they won the space battle, they'd have no more answers for what to do with the cloner or the Taljzi.

"We'll prepare a plan for the assault," she told them. "I think we should be able to arrange things so everyone on our ships gets at least a half-cycle of rest before we go into action. Once we move, I think our priority has to be engaging the Precursor fortresses with hyperspace missiles..."

The discussion went on, but underneath it all was the one chilling decision Harriet realized she'd already made: she'd do everything within her power to avoid it, but if it looked like the Allied Fleet was about to be driven from PG-Six, she would order the starkillers into action.

It would be a failure...but if things got that bad, she would have already failed.

CHAPTER FIFTY-FIVE

"BOMBARDMENT ROUNDS AWAY."

Nidei's words were quiet, hanging in the silence on both the bridge and secondary control as *Jean Villeneuve* orbited PG-Six-D, shields pushing aside the debris left of the planet's orbitals. The *Ivida*'s report was the only sign that anything had happened for a moment, then new icons appeared on Morgan's main display in secondary control.

At this stage, the bombardment weapons looked like regular missiles. Despite the number of ships in the Allied Fleet, only *Villeneuve* and a dozen other apparently randomly selected capital ships had been tasked with engaging the surface defenses.

Four hundred weapons sliced into orbit at eighty percent of light-speed. Once they passed the hundred-thousand-kilometer line, the weapons they were aimed at returned fire. Defensive missiles rose out of the atmosphere, rapidly accelerating toward their own maximum speed.

As soon as they cleared the atmosphere, the fleet opened fire. They couldn't hit the defenses with hyperfold cannon or lasers, but they could easily hit missiles barely half a million kilometers away.

Most of the interceptors were shot down. Some made it through. Some of the planetary defense centers had massive railguns and lasers that the fleet couldn't guard the bombardment launchers from.

Fifty-two missiles were lost, but almost three hundred and fifty reached orbit untouched. Calmly, driven by electronic brains that didn't register the deaths of their fellows, the railguns they carried aligned with their targets and fired.

Each round hit with the force of a hundred kilotons of TNT. There were no explosives or warheads—none were *needed* at the one percent of lightspeed left after losing the interface drive's velocity.

"Probes are scanning for target results," Nidei said quietly. "We'll probably need at least another... new targets received. Captain?"

"Proceed as per Fleet firing plan," Tan!Stalla ordered.

New icons popped up on Morgan's holodisplay. This salvo was less than half the strength of the first, but it also faced much less opposition. The first rounds had shattered the defenses.

The second finished them. Result data flowed across Morgan's seat displays, and she found herself feeling a little ill. Every PDC, gone. Every spaceport, gone. Military bases, gone.

Even major transportation hubs had been the subject of the Allied Fleet's very carefully targeted attack. A handful of the transport hubs had been too close to major population centers and been spared.

Despite that, they'd just shattered the planet's long-distance transportation capacity—and completely destroyed Six-D's ability to get into space for a long, *long* time without rescue.

"It's not a preparatory bombardment," Tan!Stalla said quietly in her ear. "It's a *smash the harbors and move on now they're not a threat* bombardment."

"It's not a terror bombing, either," Morgan agreed. "We still just killed a lot of innocent people."

"They started this war, Commander," her A!Tol Captain said fiercely. "We'll minimize the deaths—because that's what *our* code demands—but we will do what is necessary."

"Because they would have burned the entire world." Morgan understood. It still went against the grain.

"And we won't let them do that again," Tan!Stalla concluded.

MORGAN'S DESIGNATED ten hours of sleep turned into a fit of insomnia. She should have been exhausted from the adrenaline, but she was still wired. She could get meds for it, but she didn't necessarily trust that they'd be cleared out of her system in time.

No matter what, she wasn't going into battle with sleep drugs in her system.

Her brain kept circling around the cloning center on PG-Six-C. The massive biotech monstrosity that was clearly producing thousands—if not millions—of clones every day.

Its destruction would probably end the war. The Taljzi's disregard for death had to be at least partially fuelled by the realization that there were always going to be more of them. So long as that green lump of flesh, organs and machines continued to breathe, the Taljzi could never truly die.

She got up and crossed to the mini-office in her quarters. A few commands brought up the hologram of the cloner and she looked at it.

From what Adamase had said, the Precursors had been very careful when they built their physical-law-changing device. Reckless as building the device in the first place had been, they'd apparently made *very* certain they weren't touching any of the processes required for life.

Adamase hadn't said anything about Precursor biotech, and she'd generally assumed it was more advanced than anything available today but nothing entirely out of scope.

She'd clearly been wrong. And if the Precursors had left biological processes alone, then their *biotech* constructions would still be entirely functional.

That was a terrifying thought. She doubted the cloner had originally covered a continent. It had been left alone for over fifty thousand years, years in which it had clearly sucked up sunlight and soil and grown bigger.

Then the Taljzi had worked out what they'd found and started feeding it biomass. She doubted the cloner even cared what its raw biomass was, so long as it had roughly the right proportions of carbon and so forth.

She couldn't be certain, but it was entirely possible that the Taljzi had encouraged it to grow larger to produce more clones. They'd probably put a lot of effort into learning how to be good stewards of the thing.

And now it had to die. Regardless of a ring of defensive stations that could stand off the entire bombardment capability of the fleet, they had to find a way to take the cloner out.

Morgan stared at the screen for several long minutes, then brought up the specifics of the bombardment munitions. Scans of the fortresses had been pretty clear that they could take down any system before it could launch, but there had to be a key.

The note on her files that the launchers could be loaded into an assault shuttle's modular weapons bays sparked...something. There was something there, but fatigue was finally starting to take over.

Sleep, hopefully, would get her ready for the battle to come—and help shake out the idea part of her mind was saying could change everything.

THE TALJZI CAVALIERNESS with regards to their own lives clearly spread to the civilian population of PG-Six-D. Even after a full cycle of the Allied Fleet orbiting near D, the fleet defending C hadn't moved.

Someone in the Taljzi command had clearly decided the fleet couldn't engage the Allies without the massive Precursor fortresses.

Cold-blooded as the decision was, Morgan could understand it. If the Taljzi engaged them in open space and were destroyed, the fortresses probably couldn't defend C on their own.

Combined, though...they were going to find out very quickly whether the Taljzi fleets could stop the Allied Fleet with the fortresses in support.

"Navigation orders from the flag," Alles reported. "Transferring them to Cosa."

"We're to fall in on *Ajax* again," the Pibo navigator reported. "Fleet is moved towards PG-Six-C. Estimated time to HSM range... half a twentieth-cycle."

Thirty-five minutes.

Morgan leaned back in her chair and glanced around secondary control. Her people there were support right now. In the absence of some kind of disaster, they'd stay that way. It didn't mean they weren't doing *anything*—a lot of the detailed analysis that required more time than the bridge could spare would be down there.

It duplicated the tasks of what humanity would normally call the combat information center, but secondary control's main purpose was to be the backup bridge. Morgan's job was to be entirely aware of everything going on, both to be able to step into the Captain's role and to warn the Captain of anything they missed.

There wasn't much to say right now. The situation was...straightforward enough. There were a thousand superbattleships, seven hundred battleships and three thousand cruisers and destroyers in front of the Allied Fleet. Four Precursor superfortresses and an estimated five hundred Taljzi-built battle stations.

The fleet would turn once they entered HSM range, orbiting at the edge of their weapons range, and pound the Taljzi until they either ran out of missiles or the Taljzi came out to meet them. It wouldn't be the most efficient use of their weapons, but the opportunity to engage unopposed couldn't be given up.

"Elstar," she pinged the engineer as part of her idea fell into place. "Got a sec for a question?"

"Everything on this ship has been checked three times and we're about to check it a fourth," the Rekiki engineer replied. "I can answer questions, at least, for the next few thousandth-cycles."

"We brought the shuttles from the PG-Two hyper insertion back," she said. "Are they still rigged up to open a hyperspace portal?"

"No, we stripped them and reset them for regular ops," he told her. "Wouldn't matter if they were still rigged up, either. Those emitters are a one-shot deal; they were fried."

"Fair," Morgan shook her head. "I had a thought, but I'm not sure it would make a difference."

Elstar was silent for a second.

"Your thoughts are those of an eager colt that flees the herd to meet the howls of the pack," he replied. "But they have worked before. I...*may* have rigged up a few extra sets of hyper emitters for our shuttles. A pre-built modular setup, one we can insert into any ship."

"I'm not entirely sure what I've got rattling around my brain just yet," Morgan said. "But if you can spare the hands before we light up this fight...rig up a shuttle for me. Stick a bombardment launcher on it, if you can."

The Rekiki inhaled sharply.

"I begin to see, Commander Casimir. Surely, we'd need to have dropped the shuttle off outside the gravity zone, though?"

"Probably," she confirmed. "We're not getting a shuttle, a missile, or a bombardment platform close enough to the cloner in real space. Clever ideas are our only hope. While we're at it...how good's the AI on those birds?"

"Not good enough to fly it through hyperspace and deploy a bombardment munition, if that's your question," Elstar told her. "You'd need a pilot."

"Fuck. That *would* be a suicide mission," Morgan glared at the display on her chair arm showing her the cloner. "Set up the shuttle anyway," she said. "I'm not sending someone to their death, but we might come up with a cleverer idea before this all comes apart."

"You're the sideways thinker, Commander," Elstar replied with a foot-thumping chuckle. "But I'll poke at some of the angles as I have time." He paused. "Is this worth bouncing up the chain for more minds, Commander?"

"I don't know," she admitted. "I think even you and I are going to have better things to think about very, *very* quickly, so it's probably best left to the back of our minds."

A timer had appeared on her main display, counting down the thousandth-cycles to hyperspace-missile range.

"I'll let you know if I have any sparks of brilliance," Elstar told her. "Hopefully before they start grassfires!"

The channel dropped and Morgan looked back at the screen. Ten thousandth-cycles—fourteen minutes—to range. That wasn't enough time to work out what her back-brain was bugging her with.

It was enough time to double-check—well, quadruple-check, at this point—that her ship was ready for war.

"ALL HSM BATTERIES are standing by. We are slaved to fleet fire control."

Morgan trusted Nidei implicitly. She double-checked their statement anyway, confirming that all of the hyperspace-missile batteries had opened their portals and loaded the launchers.

The portal in the battery was the other half of the system to make the Imperium's hyperspace missiles work. The emitters on the missiles—the ones they'd "borrowed" for her shuttle trick—could only open a portal back into normal space.

The system in the battery was the reverse. Fully contained in a physical structure, it wasn't disposable like the missile portal systems, but it could only open a portal *into* hyperspace.

Thanks to those systems, however, *Jean Villeneuve* was

approaching weapons range of the enemy with sixteen hyperspace portals open inside her hull.

"Orders from the flag are to target the smaller fixed fortifications first," Nidei explained after a few seconds. "They're the easiest targets, and Intel calculates less than a one-third chance that they've been upgraded with active defenses.

"Range in...one thousandth-cycle."

The plan made sense. The Taljzi-built fortresses were slow to maneuver, easy targets at any range that depended on powerful shields and armor to protect them. Those would do only so much against full salvos of hyperspace missiles that wouldn't miss.

Despite an effort that almost qualified as miraculous in its success, the Taljzi hadn't even managed to refit all of their capital ships with the active defenses that could shoot down a hyperspace missile in its terminal phase. Most likely, the fortresses lacked those defenses as well.

Which meant that the massed batteries of interface-drive missiles on those stations were going to die long before the Allied Fleet entered their range. There was nothing else in play that the Allies could destroy as easily to take out as many launchers.

But the four immense Precursor fortresses mocked Morgan's logic. They knew nothing about those stations. It was possible that they were just shells of Precursor materials refitted with Taljzi weapons—bad enough, given the sheer scale of the fortresses.

There was no way they were fully functional, after all. Morgan knew that better than anyone. But it *was* possible that there was something aboard them. Something the Allied Fleet hadn't cons—

"*Firing.*"

A shiver ran through *Jean Villeneuve* as every one of her hyperspace missile launchers activated at once.

Over fourteen hundred ships—all of the Imperial capital ships and cruisers—had fired at once, and thousands of missiles slashed through hyperspace at their targets. They were spread across exactly one hundred of the fortresses, each the target of over four hundred hyperspace missiles.

The skies above PG-Six-C lit up with antimatter fire. Nothing so far suggested that there'd been active defenses in place, though as the explosions cleared, there were definitely more of the fortresses remaining than expected.

"Nidei?" Captain Tan!Stalla asked calmly.

"It looks like we were right in projecting that they didn't have active defenses, but we badly underestimated their passives," the Ivida reported. "All of our targets are damaged, but only ten were destroyed." They paused. "New targeting orders are reducing the next salvo to thirty targets."

Morgan let her attention slip away from the immediate engagement as the next salvo blasted out. The Allied Fleet was continuing to maneuver along at just under five light-minutes from the Taljzi forces.

They could do this for over an hour. It would be a twentieth-cycle or more before the Imperials started to run out of ammunition—and while they were shooting at the defensive fortresses, anything that missed was likely to make a mess of the orbital infrastructure.

Even with hyperfold com–equipped drones with tachyon sensors orbiting closely enough to provide real-time targeting data, the range was hurting their accuracy. *Jean Villeneuve*'s crew could usually manage at least seventy percent accuracy at any range, but right now...they were below sixty and most of the rest of the fleet was doing worse. A lot of missiles were being "wasted" on the rest of the orbitals.

The Taljzi fleet wasn't moving yet. Morgan didn't think that was going to last—those fortresses had as much firepower and crew as half again their number of superbattleships.

The Taljzi were going to have to do *something*, even if it involved moving out of the protective shadow of the Precursor superfortresses.

One step removed from the active process of targeting and firing on the defense, Morgan was watching those superfortresses when the probes recorded the first energy spike.

"What the hell was that?" she snapped. "Energy spike on the Precursor fortresses. Anyone got an iden—"

"*Freedom's Claw* just blew the hell up," Alles report came across hers. "The Kanzi lost two ships, too, and *Hammerfall's* shields are flickering."

Three capital ships—all superbattleships—were gone. A fourth was reeling and a chill ran down Morgan's spine.

"Ichri!" Morgan barked at the Indiri assistant tactical officer with her in secondary control. "There was a pulse at all four super-fortresses, right? What was the timeline?"

The tactical officer was running through the data and looked up at her with a dark look in his massive eyes.

"Exactly right for them to be firing HSMs back at us," he reported. "But...HSMs aren't one-hit kills on superbattleships!"

A second sequence of energy pulses flickered across the fortresses as Ichri finished speaking, and Morgan grimly watched the report. The Taljzi had clearly decided to focus their fire this time, and *Hammerfall's* survival had clearly been declared unacceptable.

Six Hundred and Fifth Sword of the Republic Mordak and his ship vanished in a ball of fire as four of *whatever* the hell the Taljzi were firing converged on *Hammerfall*.

CHAPTER FIFTY-SIX

"WHAT THE HELL AM I LOOKING AT, KOANEST?" HARRIET demanded. About the only *good* thing she could say was that the Taljzi's latest surprise was slower-firing than their hyperspace missiles. In the time it had taken the new system to fire twice, they'd sent three salvos toward the defenses and wrecked over a fifth of the fortresses guarding the Taljzi capital.

"It looks like a successful weaponization of the same concept as we saw in PG-Two," the Yin replied. "There's a massive energy surge at each superfortress, which is then teleported to the target. Despite the range, they're hitting a hundred percent accuracy so far—and only our most powerful units can take even one hit."

Another salvo of hyperspace missiles headed toward the defenses —and another energy surge answered it. Harriet winced as four of her *Vindication*-class superbattleships just...vanished.

Those were the second-most powerful Imperial units in play, and the Taljzi had a weapon that was destroying them like they were *toys*.

"Why haven't we seen this before?" she demanded. "What kind of power draw are we looking at?"

"Huge," Koanest said simply. "Whatever it is, I think it might be bigger than their capital ships. From the breadth of the energy signature, the system takes up at least a third of the volume of those superfortresses."

So, it was all down to those four immense stations.

"Switch the targets," she ordered. The orbital fortifications were still mostly intact, the range and their heavy shields keeping them alive through the hyperspace missile salvo, but they couldn't shoot her right now.

"Focus all fire on *one* of those stations," she continued. She paused. "Get me Cawl."

Technically, Cawl was in command of the Allied Fleet today. The hyperspace missiles were all on her ships, so she'd change their targets on her own whim, but they needed to work together.

"Fleet Lord," he greeted her as the channel opened. "It seems my estranged cousins have one more surprise for us."

Ajax shivered around her as a new salvo of missiles flashed out.

"It's the Precursor fortresses," she told him. "The weapon is too big to be mounted on any of their ships."

"I agree. I see you've already changed the focus of your fire."

She checked the holodisplays. Part of her was expecting the fortress to be gone—even with the losses so far, she was still flinging forty thousand hyperspace missiles in each salvo.

The rest of her knew better, and she wasn't surprised by the end result. The Precursor superfortress wasn't equipped with active defenses...but it *was* equipped with shields more powerful than anything she'd ever seen, and the Taljzi had moved over four hundred escorts into a close position to provide antimissile and tachyon jammer coverage.

They'd *hit* the station, but they hadn't even brought down its shields...and as she watched, a new energy pulse lit the platform up.

And four Kanzi superbattleships died.

"We can't keep this up, Shairon," she told the Kanzi. "With less than half of our fleet engaged...I'm starting to think they're more likely to finish this at range than we are."

"And if whoever is in command over there thinks like I do, those platforms have quite a bit of range they haven't shown us yet," Cawl conceded. "I agree, Fleet Lord. We have to advance. All the way to hyperfold-cannon range."

Harriet took a look at her fleet. The icons that remained were a solid burning green, marking that her entire command was practically undamaged. Once they advanced into long-range-missile range, let alone regular-missile range, that would change.

If they advanced to engage the Taljzi fleet, they were going to lose ships by the dozens and people by the thousands.

If they didn't, the fortresses were going to rip them apart from beyond the range of most of their own weapons.

"You're in command today, Shairon," Harriet told him, her voice far calmer than she'd expected it to be. "The order is yours."

The old Kanzi nodded his head.

"Inform your fleet, Lord Tanaka," he replied. "We advance immediately."

PLANS DIDN'T ACCELERATE from "advance in a twentieth-cycle once we've expended the HSMs" to "advance *now*" instantly. Not with four thousand warships in play.

Another Laian war-dreadnought died, followed by two Imperial and two Kanzi superbattleships. In exchange, they'd pounded the closest superfortress with over a hundred thousand missiles. Its shields had failed several times and several dozen of its escorting ships had been caught too close to the cataclysm, but the station itself seemed unharmed.

Then the orders were out and the Allied Fleet moved. It was the same plan as before, with the Kanzi and Laian capital ships moving out in front while the Imperial ships continued to hammer the super-fortress with HSMs.

Against the Taljzi's teleporter weapon, having two thousand warships in front wasn't enough, and Harriet forced herself to a mask as the latest salvo claimed three of her ships, leaving *Albert Einstein* reeling in space at a blow that shattered her shields and blasted a hundred-meter-wide hole into her bow.

The next salvo focused on *Einstein*...and Harriet suddenly only had two *Galileo*-class superbattleships.

"The Taljzi are adjusting their formation," Koanest reported. "They're leaving escorts around all of the superfortresses, but their capital ships are moving to intercept us. Expecting LRM launches in the next sixty seconds."

"Tell me we're doing *something* to that damn fortress, Captain Koanest," Harriet demanded.

"We're hitting it," the Yin told her. "We've landed tens of thousands of missiles on its shields. Punched hundreds, at least, *through* the shields. Scans say we've vaporized thousands of cubic meters off its outer hull, probably even detonated a few warheads deeper inside...but it's eighty kilometers wide."

And Harriet Tanaka once again had a choice. The LRMs could be shot down by their own active defenses, but seventeen hundred capital ships were going to challenge those defenses. Missiles would get through. People would die.

The only answer the Allied Fleet had to those long-range missiles was her hyperspace missiles, but they were the only weapon she could threaten the Precursor superfortresses with. She hadn't expected one fortress to absorb several hundred thousand missiles... and keep firing the same godawful weapon at them.

"I don't think Fortress Alpha has any surface weapons left, Fleet Lord," Koanest said quietly. "I think the only thing left aboard it is the teleporter."

"Which is bad enough," Harriet replied, but she nodded. "We don't have a choice. Target the lead capital-ship elements and hit them. I don't care what that fortress is made of; once we get hyperfold cannon and plasma lances on it, it's history."

"Issuing new target orders," the Yin replied. Four more icons flashed red on the display. A Kanzi superbattleship and three of hers.

They were older ships, she noted, not her *Vindications*, *Galileos* or even the *Majesties* that Earth had built their economy on refitting. Part of her hated herself for being grateful for that.

The rest was grimly aware that those older ships had been smaller and harder to refit. They didn't have as many HSM launchers, which meant their loss didn't hurt as badly as a new ship would have.

Even if they'd still been crewed by over four thousand people apiece.

"HSMs away...LRM launch detected."

The two reports blurred together and Harriet looked at the display to see...exactly what she'd expected. None of the fleets they'd faced outside of PG-Six had used externally mounted LRMs, but those fleets had either been made up entirely of refitted ships or completely lacking in LRMs.

Mounting them on the hull was a brilliant solution to a weapon too large to launch without specialty launchers. It also meant that there was a red *wave* on her display instead of any red icons.

"There's too many to resolve into individual contacts at this distance," Koanest said quietly. "It does give us some clues, though."

"Explain," she ordered, watching as another salvo of HSMs hammered into the Taljzi formation.

"If we correlate the ships launching external LRMs with the regions where we're seeing less active defense, we should be able to flag the un-refitted vessels," her ops officer told her. "They're less of a threat at this range, but they're easier for us to take out at any range."

"And?"

"Got it," Koanest said with satisfaction as the ops officer's console beeped. "Looks like we have four hundred un-refitted superbattleships and only a hundred un-refitted battleships. Highlighting on the display."

"Hit the superbattleships without antimissile defenses," Harriet ordered. "We can take the LRMs, but every ship less when we reach regular-missile range is a better chance for everyone to survive."

The LRMs were hammering into the forward formations of the Kanzi fleets. Thousands of antimissile drones waited for them, backed by hundreds of destroyers and superbattleships. There was no way to stop them all this time, but the shields and armor of the Kanzi shield had been designed before they'd had the defenses.

Without the defenses, Cawl's fleet would have been savaged. Even with them, three dozen superbattleships had to be pulled back, their shields battered into near-uselessness.

Another dozen superbattleships didn't live long enough to *be* pulled back—and even while the battle was joined in earnest, the Precursor fortresses' teleporter cannons continued to work their way through the fleet.

"Standard interface missile range in sixty seconds," Koanest reported. "Neither the LRMs nor the teleporter cannons are targeting our battleships. We're losing superbattleships and Kanmorad's lost three of his war-dreadnoughts, but they're ignoring our lighter capital ships."

The weapon was overkill on most of her superbattleships! No wonder they weren't shooting at lighter ships when they had a near-guaranteed kill on the biggest ships in her fleet.

That meant her surviving two *Galileo*s were facing a countdown clock—and Harriet wasn't sure quite what she could do about that.

"Wait, Fleet Lord—what are the Kanzi doing?" Koanest demanded.

Harriet blinked away her fears for the near-future and focused on where the Yin was indicating. Two squadrons of battleships had broken free of the flank of Cawl's formation and were heading away from the battle. Twenty capital ships might make the difference in what was happening next, and she doubted Cawl had ordered them away.

"I don't know," she admitted. "I don't see... Wait... What do they have for escorts?"

"Looks like a single squadron of destroyers."

Harriet swallowed against the chill than ran down her spine.

"Get me Cawl," she barked. *"Those aren't destroyers."*

CHAPTER FIFTY-SEVEN

"WE BROUGHT FOUR STARKILLERS AND THEY ARE ALL IN THAT formation," Cawl confirmed the moment the channel reopened. "They've all separated themselves from the tactical network and are refusing to respond to communications."

The old Kanzi closed his eyes for a moment as another four of his superbattleships vanished to the teleporter cannon.

"I'm almost tempted to let them go," he murmured. "We're not winning this battle right now, Fleet Lord. I don't *like* it, but a starkiller might be our only way to win this."

"Maybe," Harriet conceded. "But that's a decision for *us* to make, not whoever the hell is in charge over there. What is going *on* in your fleet, Fleet Master?"

"They have orders from the First Priest, I suspect," Cawl admitted. "I knew there were plants in my fleet, Tanaka. I warned you."

He had. She hadn't expected it to turn into *this*.

"We're nine light-minutes from the star," she said quietly. "They'll be there in fifteen minutes. If they're not responding to our coms, I only see two choices: we break off or we fire on them."

More LRMs were pounding the front wave of their formation. The Kanzi fleet was losing ships.

Dropping the privacy screen on her call with Cawl, Harriet turned to Koanest.

"Get our capital ships forward," she ordered. "Reinforce the Kanzi. We're going to need every ship we can get."

The logic for spreading out the formation had made sense only when the Taljzi didn't have a weapon that matched the range of the Imperial HSMs. Now that the teleporter cannon was wreaking havoc through their formations, they *had* to close the range.

They may as well do it as a single formation.

"We can't break off," Cawl told her when she turned back to him and raised the privacy screen again. "They'll chase us out of the system now. We'd lose almost as many ships running as if we try to finish this. Maybe more."

"And we might just finish it," Harriet concluded. "Do we fire on the rogues?" she demanded. "They're your people, Shairon. I won't make that call for you."

Something in the light brought out all of Shairon Cawl's scars and the streaks of white fur across his face as he closed his eyes.

"I... I have to hope that they'll turn back if they realize we're not withdrawing," he whispered. "And at the worst...well, with hyperfold coms, we'll know to start running when they fire it."

"Fleet Lord!"

Koanest had an override on the privacy screen, and she *trusted* the ops officer to know when to use it. If she'd interjected herself into the conversation between the two fleet commanders, there was a reason.

"The Taljzi fleet," she reported. "They're moving. They're going after the starkillers!"

TWO OF THE rogue Kanzi battleships vanished as the teleporter cannon retargeted along with the rest of the fleet, leaving Harriet to breathe a sigh of relief. The entire formation of hundreds of capital ships was accelerating to full speed now.

Before, they'd been trying to control the range. Once they'd entered range of their LRMs, they'd been playing the range as much as the Imperials had originally planned to. Now, though, they were moving at a full sixty percent of lightspeed in pursuit of the starkillers.

"I see *they* remember what happened to their original base," Koanest noted. "Fleet Lord, the way they're moving, we may have an opening to punch part of our force through to the superfortress."

"We also can't let the main fleet go unengaged," she replied. "If they're focusing on the starkillers, let's take advantage of that to ram a few hundred million tons of starships past them."

"We have a number of squadrons held back for long-range HSM fire," her aide noted. "The *Galileos* and *Bellerophons*, primarily. We can send the main fleet after the Taljzi and detach the new ships to deal with the fortress."

"Take *Ajax* and her squadron along with the main fleet; leave the rest under Fleet Lord San Pozan," Harriet responded, thinking out loud. The Indiri Fleet Lord, a high-ranking scion of one of the Indiri's wealthiest Great Houses, had been poached from their Militia along with his squadrons of *Bellerophon*-class battleships.

"That will leave us short nine squadrons of battleships...but it might be our only chance to take out the superfortresses, and they can handle what's left of the orbitals as they do it."

She knew that half of the reason the rest of the *Bellerophons* were clustered around *Ajax* was to protect the flagship, but the Taljzi had been focusing their fire on the starkiller formation. Destroyers, it was turning out, *were* maneuverable enough and small enough to throw off the teleporter cannon.

"Pass the orders," she told Koanest. She took one final look at everything. "And one more order," she said quietly. "If the starkillers are about to reach activation range and I have not *specifically* countermanded it by then, *Ajax* and her escorts are to destroy them with HSM fire.

"No other squadron is to be informed of that order. Pass it by tightbeam, not hyperfold. Understand me, Captain Koanest?"

"Yes, Fleet Lord. It will be done."

Another one of the battleships around the starkillers was obliterated, but three clear misses lit up the space around the destroyers and starkillers.

Even Harriet didn't know which was which. Like the Imperial version of the weapon, the Kanzi built their starkillers to exactly match one of their destroyer classes. They didn't have the destroyers' offensive weaponry, but so long as none of the ships were firing, there was no way for the starkillers to be picked out from the destroyers.

The Taljzi fleet was now a curved line through space, focusing their fire on the formation escorting the starkillers. They weren't making themselves *much* more vulnerable...but it was enough.

"Secure stations. Standard missile range in ten seconds," Koanest reported. "It's down to the *Bellerophon*s now, Fleet Lord. If they can take down the superfortresses and we can even the odds with the main fleet..."

That was a lot of *if*s.

Ad triarios redisse.

"It comes down to the triarii." Everything was committed. Once the newly separated formation of the *Bellerophon*s—a formation that was well over seventy-five percent human and Indiri, given that a solid majority of those ships had been poached from the Ducal Militias—engaged the superfortresses, Harriet's role in this battle was almost over.

There were no more reserves. No clever games. Only one final decision for the fleet commander to truly make:

Whether or not she was prepared to kill an entire star system to end this war.

CHAPTER FIFTY-EIGHT

"NEW FORMATION ORDERS," TAN!STALLA READ OUT AS *JEAN Villeneuve* twisted in space. "We're joining the *Bellerophon*s and *Isaac Newton* in a flanking maneuver under Fleet Lord Pozan. Our target is the fortresses...all of them. *Starting* with that big dark-waters-born monster right in front of us."

Grim determination rippled off the A!Tol's translated tone, and even Morgan felt her spine stiffen as Tan!Stalla spoke.

"Pozan's orders are simple," the Captain continued. "Full sprint mode, straight for the superfortress. We pound the orbital fortresses with HSMs as we close, but it's plasma lances that are going to finish the Precursor station!"

Morgan wasn't sure she agreed. They'd hit the station with dozens of multi-gigaton antimatter warheads. The plasma lances on each of *Galileo*'s wingtips were only good for about a quarter-gigaton. That was a quarter-gigaton per *second* per lance, but...

It was going to take every weapon they had at maximum rate of fire at point-blank range to take down the Precursor station. The superfortress was just too big and too heavily built for anything less to carry the day.

"We also have to deal with the escorts," Morgan pointed out after a moment on her private channel with the Captain. "Do we have a plan for that?"

"We're still establishing the tactical network, but it looks like we're going to target them with the regular missiles first. We have ninety seconds before we're in range for those." Tan!Stalla snapped her beak in concern.

"Our course to the third superfortress is going to take us within bombardment range of PG-Six-C," she pointed out. "Nidei is going to handle dealing with the superfortress. I want you and Ichri to link with the rest of the fleet on the HSMs and keep pounding the platforms in orbit.

"While Ichri is doing that, I want you to prep a bombardment pattern. The way they're reacting to the starkillers..." Tan!Stalla trailed off, then started again a moment.

"They're reacting like they've seen one fired," she finished. "If the clones have all of the memories of the original, it's... They might have fleet commanders who remember the last one."

Morgan wanted to say that was impossible—except that producing fully adult clones was a difficult task and the Precursor creation was doing it on a massive scale. If they started with any skills at all, then they probably came with memories, too.

It made all too much sense and explained the sudden movement of the Taljzi fleet. Three-hundred-year-old PTSD kicking in when they realized what was happening.

"And if their memories go back that far, they might think of themselves as immortal," Morgan said. "Their final duty to report back and transfer their memories to ten thousand new Taljzi. My god."

She shook her head.

"Breaking the cloner is the key," Tan!Stalla concluded. "I need us set up to hit the fortresses. There has to be a way through that ring."

"We keep running scenarios, sir," Morgan replied. "Nothing conventional is going to manage it."

New icons flickered onto her screen, informing her that the new tactical network for the detached formation was online.

Morgan turned away from her link with Tan!Stalla for a second.

"Ichri, link in and take over the HSMs," she ordered. "Target is those orbital fortresses, but we're a lot more helpful with a hundred and fifty friends!"

Tan!Stalla was snapping her own orders and linked back to her after a moment.

"Standard missile range." Nidei's report held off the conversation for a second as both of them checked the displays.

One hundred and forty-four *Bellerophon*-B-class battleships and two *Galileo*-class superbattleships put a *lot* of missiles into space. It was nothing compared to the firepower of the massed Allied Fleet, but it was enough that Morgan wouldn't have wanted to be on the receiving end of it—and neither did the four hundred cruisers and destroyers guarding the superfortress.

"I have an idea," Morgan told her boss. "For the cloner. But it might only be one shot and it might be a suicide mission."

"My idea is to ram a battleship into it," Tan!Stalla admitted. "'*Might be* a suicide mission' is an improvement. Grab whatever resources you need, Casimir. You and your mother have a knack for mad ideas that work out.

"Make this one work."

Morgan swallowed and nodded.

"Yes, sir."

No pressure.

ICONS FLARED across the main holodisplay as *Jean Villeneuve*'s component of the main battle continued. The escorts around the superfortress were doing their damnedest, but they only outnumbered the attacking force two to one, and they were individually outmassed over twelve-to-one.

It wasn't winning odds for the smaller ships, but they stuck to their guns. Not a single destroyer or cruiser broke off while the Imperial force smashed through their defenses, grimly closing to the range of their energy weapons.

As they got closer to the fortress, it was very clear that this one, at least, no longer had any major weaponry left. Its shields were gone. Its outer hull had been turned into a blasted moonscape by the continued battering of the hyperspace missiles.

Only the teleporter cannon remained, and the crew was blatantly prioritizing trying to shoot down the starkillers over their own defenses.

It cost them. The plasma lances didn't match the sheer destructive power of an antimatter warhead, but the detached fleet had over a hundred and fifty of them...and plasma lances used a seeking magnetic tube to control their fire line.

They didn't miss. Hyperfold cannon joined in, but despite it all, the massive station seemed invulnerable for a few more seconds.

Then it just started coming apart.

While the fleet was cutting the first superfortress and its defenders to pieces, Morgan's focus was on the smaller yet more critical mission Tan!Stalla had assigned her.

They had three shuttles that Elstar had rigged up. They could exit hyperspace and had two bombardment launchers apiece. Six missiles hitting at point zero one cee would destroy the cloner—but there was no way out for the shuttles, and even emerging within one second's flight time of the target wasn't going to guarantee all six hits.

The shuttles would die. That was probably something Morgan had to accept. The problem was getting them into hyperspace...and as the fourth set of reports came in from the hyperspace-missile bombardment of the orbital forts, she realized she was an idiot.

"Elstar, how big are the shuttles with everything fitted?" she demanded.

"About a hundred and sixty tons?" the engineer replied.

"Not mass, Elstar. *Width*. Height. Hell, *radius* is probably critical."

The engineer was silent.

"I might actually have to go measure that," he admitted. "How much time do we have?"

"Five minutes," Morgan told him. "So, here's the real question: will one of them fit through a twelve-point-five-meter radius hyper-space portal?"

"Sun fall and burn the plains," Elstar swore. "The HSM batteries."

"Twelve-point-five-meter portal," she repeated. "Will they fit?"

"If they don't, I'll make them," the engineer replied. "Battery Hotel-Seven is closest to where I have the shuttles. We need the launchers shut down and the secondary access systems opened. Can we afford to give up six launchers?"

"We can't afford not to," Morgan told him. "I'll make the call."

She turned around.

"Ichri!"

"First Sword?" the Indiri officer spun, his red fur rippling as he turned bulbous eyes on Morgan.

"Shut down Battery Hotel-Seven," she snapped. "Launch what-ever missiles are in there and safe it for crew access. We need it for our final trick."

"Understood."

Ichri didn't even argue. He turned back to his console and passed the orders, adjusting his next salvo without even a pause.

Morgan had more calls to make. The next was to Battalion Commander Petrina Damyanov, the Marine officer currently standing by with her people to assist with damage control.

"Damyanov, I need volunteer pilots for three shuttles," she told the other woman as the channel opened. "It's..." Morgan choked off, then continued.

"It's a suicide mission," she said bluntly. "We're sending them into hyperspace to make a point-blank insertion inside PG-Six-C's atmosphere to take out the cloner. We've got three shuttles rigged up and they're on their way to Battery Hotel-Seven's hyper portal right now.

"But I need pilots willing to make the shot, knowing they're not coming back."

"My pilots are Marines, Commander," Damyanov said levelly. "They'll answer the call. You'll have your pilots."

"I'm sorry," Morgan whispered. "I didn't see another way."

"That's when you call the Marines, Commander," Damyanov told her. "When you don't see another way."

"THIS IS ISTIL!" the A!Tol reported in. "We're at Hotel-Seven and looking at three shuttles that appear to have been turned into an upgraded version of the last shadow-box the First Sword put me in.

"Battalion-Commander Damyanov said the mission was ground bombardment via hyperspace," he continued. "Shuttles are here. Portal is here. Pilots are here. Briefing, sir?"

Morgan forced a chuckle at the pilot's forced humor.

"The target is the Taljzi cloning facility," she told them. "If you've missed it, it's a continent-sized monstrosity of Precursor biotech that appears to eat people at one end and shit out ten thousand copies of them at the other. It's the only thing that let the Taljzi become the threat they are, and I can't imagine they're going to take lightly to losing it.

"To make sure they *didn't*, they wrapped it in the tightest ground defenses I've seen or heard of. The only way to guarantee we take out the cloner would be to wreck the planet or blow the star, both of which are war crimes, according to the Imperium."

"So, y'all sent for us," the second of the three pilots responded in a thick Texan drawl. Morgan's system flagged the speaker as one

Lesser Speaker Kenneth Donnelly. And confirmed that he was, yes, Texan.

"Marines down the middle. How's this gonna work, ma'am?"

"The shuttles are small enough to fit through the portal created by our HSM launchers," Morgan told them. As she spoke, another salvo flashed through the superbattleship's other fifteen HSM batteries.

"The emitters we stole from several of our missiles will let you open a portal back into real space wherever you want. We've calculated your emergence points, and you should come out within three thousand kilometers of the surface, directly above the cloner.

"You'll fire your bombardment units and high-tail it back to the fleet." Morgan paused. "I won't lie. Your odds of making it out of the fire zone of the defensive ring are basically zero."

"The Battalion Commander was clear that this was a suicide mission," Istil! confirmed. "But I agree that destroying the cloner may well break the Taljzi morale and end this damn war."

"Sounds like a hell of a ride," Donnelly drawled slowly. "And I figure I can beat any odds, and if I can't, I go out in style...but I got one question."

"Now's the time," Morgan replied. "We're running out."

"The bombardment units on our shuttles fire the slug, not the launch assembly as a big ship's gotta. There's no maneuvering after the rock goes out. Why don't we jus'...fire the rock *through* the hyper portal?"

There was a long silence.

"Out of the mouths of Americans," Morgan snapped. "Get in your shuttles and prep for flight, people. I'll know if the rock can cross the portal before you leave."

"THE INTERFACE DRIVE isn't required for the transition, but it definitely helps," Cosa told her after she asked the navigator the question. "There's enough resistance to the transition that I would normally argue that some kind of engine is required, but ballistic at one percent of lightspeed is..."

They paused.

"It should be enough. If they get the angle right. You'll lose velocity and you'll lose some of your projectiles even if you get the angle exactly. A ballistic transition of something that small is going to be rough."

"But we'll get, what, two-thirds of the projectiles through three-quarters of the velocity?" Morgan demanded. She was guessing on the numbers, but they seemed to fit.

"In an optimal scenario, yes," Cosa confirmed. "Velocity might be as high as eighty percent or as low as seventy. Losses might be as *high* as two-thirds."

Two shots at twenty-one hundred KPS weren't the certain kill she'd been planning for, but they didn't have a lot of other options.

"I'll let the Marines know."

"It's going to be a difficult maneuver regardless," the Pibo told her. "At maximum projection and minimum interface-drive velocity, they're only going to have one point one seconds to fire the bombardment projectiles and divert."

"They have computers and they know the drill," Morgan replied. "Thank you."

She dropped the link and connected with Istil!.

"I'm downloading Cosa's calculations to you all," she told the pilots. "Remember that you don't get a second hyper portal. The angle for entry for the projectiles has to be *perfect*. Even then, the impact velocity is lower.

"Once you've burned the portal emitters, head for the rendezvous point with the logistics fleet."

"The Fleet won't pick us up?" Istil! asked.

"If this goes wrong, there may not be a Fleet to pick you up," Morgan admitted. The orbital fortresses had been smashed, but the detached fleet was only now entering weapons range of the second superfortress—and *that* one hadn't been hammered flat by HSMs.

Plus, there were still Kanzi starkillers heading for the star, and that was looking uglier by the moment.

"We're out of time," she told the Marines. "Go."

"Oorah!"

She shook her head as the shuttles blasted into the portal. The human recruits to the Imperial Marines were being a bad influence.

THE SECOND SUPERFORTRESS was fully operational, and as soon as its surface weapons opened fire, Morgan started to worry that they hadn't brought enough battleships.

Twenty-five thousand interface-drive missiles tore into space from the surface of the massive installation—and then lunged for the fleet at seventy percent of lightspeed.

That number surprised everyone, and Morgan stared at it as she mentally calculated the increased flight time. If the weapons could reach the Imperial formation, they had to have an increased flight time over the point eight cee weapons the main Taljzi fleet was using.

It wouldn't matter. That ten percent of lightspeed was enough to render the weapons almost laughable in the teeth of the Imperial ships' defenses. Missiles made it through and several of the lead battleships had to rotate back in the ranks, but no one was lost while the detachment stripped away the superfortress's defenders.

"We're going to be in trouble shortly," Alles reported. "The main fleet says the starkiller formation is just about wrecked. They're verbally crawling back to Fleet Master Cawl as we speak, which I suspect means the starkillers are gone."

"They just got a lot of people killed for not bloody much," Morgan said. She shook her head. "I guess they gave us an opening."

Villeneuve shivered around her as a dozen missiles slammed into her shields. She and *Newton* were the biggest targets in play, and the superfortress was now specifically targeting them.

Unfortunately for the superfortress, while the *Bellerophon*s were the most shielded battleships in the Allied Fleet, the *Galileo* class had even heavier shields for their mass. Like the Laian war-dreadnoughts, they could take the worst the Precursor station could throw at them.

Except the teleporter cannon. Morgan was mentally gloating over their security in the face of the station's weapons when the three surviving teleporter cannons hit *Isaac Newton* as one.

Her shields vanished in an instant, and a massive ball of energy obliterated the rear third of the superbattleship. The forward two-thirds lurched as her interface drive flickered, but then she resumed firing at the Taljzi fort.

"What happened to the bombardment?" Tan!Stalla asked. "It's hyperspace; they shouldn't have taken this long."

"They needed to get it right," Morgan replied. "It had to be *exactly* the right angle—"

An alert flared across the main holodisplay as three hyper portals opened *inside* PG-6-C's atmosphere. They were even closer than they were supposed to be, and the missiles flashed through before they were even visible.

Two missiles hit. They'd never know how many failed to make it through the portal or were shot down, but two of them hit. They blew massive holes in the cloner, but the sheer size of the thing suggested they might not have been enough.

Sixty-kiloton impacts blew craters thirty kilometers wide into the monstrosity, but it was the size of a continent. Morgan wasn't sure it was going to be enough, and a chill started to settle into her stomach... and then she realized something *else* had come through the portal.

One of the pilots had either missed their turn or decided to be *damn* certain the thing went down. The shuttlecraft came through the portal at fifty percent of the speed of light. The usual trick of an interface drive and an atmosphere hammered their speed to nothing in fractions of a second, but the shuttle smashed through the top of the cloner with enough speed that none of the defensive weapons could hit it.

And then the pilot overloaded their fusion core.

Sixty kilotons had blown neat holes in a continent-sized monster.

Six hundred megatons *vaporized* its heart.

CHAPTER FIFTY-NINE

"Fleet Lord! They hit it."

Harriet's attention was focused on the battle around her, the clash between the Allied Fleet and the Taljzi having turned into exactly the kind of slugging match her instincts said to avoid. The Taljzi's focus on the starkillers had let the Allies level the odds, but the price was looking ugly.

Tenth Fleet was down over two hundred capital ships and a million sentients missing or dead—and they were in the best shape. The Gloried Armada had been devastated with almost four hundred capital ships lost—and she wasn't sure how many of the four hundred survivors were fully combat-capable!

Kanmorad's ships were the toughest vessels in the fight, but he was down to only four war-dreadnoughts, with the fifty or so escort cruisers clustered around them.

"I know they got the superfortress," she told Koanest, turning to address her operations officer—and then saw what she meant.

The explosion in the cloner would have been clearly visible from several light-seconds away. The image of PG-Six-C in her display was out of scale with the map of the star system, roughly the equivalent of the view from half a million kilometers away—and she could see the flash.

"The cloner?" she asked.

"I'm not sure how," Koanest told her, "but they hit it with multiple bombardment rounds and what looks like an assault-shuttle self-destruct. It's...it's *gone*, Fleet Lord."

Harriet's gaze snapped back to the main display. Calculations flashed through her head. She'd left a hundred and forty-eight battleships and superbattleships to attack the superfortresses. With that and her losses, she was down to barely three hundred capital ships... most of them superbattleships.

The Kanzi superbattleships had suffered more heavily than their smaller siblings, but there were still a hundred of them leading three hundred battleships.

Seven hundred capital ships on her side, plus the *Bellerophons* who could engage with HSMs.

The Taljzi had about eight hundred left, but the Allied Fleet had focused on their superbattleships. Five hundred of the Taljzi capital ships were battleships. The tonnage was almost equal—except for the superfortresses, but she trusted San Pozan and the fleet she'd given him to handle that.

"Cawl, it's time," she snapped at the channel they'd left open and public. "Their morale has to be pushed by the loss of the cloner. We can be in hyperfold-cannon range in twenty seconds and they know it.

"We have to push."

"General order, Fleet Lord Tanaka," the old Kanzi told her calmly, starting to speak before she'd even finished. "Full advance. Stay out of disruptor range, but hit them with everything we've got."

"Pass that order," Harriet snapped to Koanest. "Take us right at them."

"Only this squadron and the *Vindications* have capital-grade plasma lances," Koanest said after a moment. The fleet was moving around them, and Harriet could *feel* the Taljzi waver as the Allies charged. "Hyperfold-cannon range is greater and may be more effective."

"I don't think they have the nerve left to last to lance range," Harriet told her. "We push until they break."

Koanest said nothing, simply waiting as the massed fleet crossed into hyperfold-cannon range. Every capital ship in the Allied Fleet carried one version or another of the weapon. Despite the Imperium's efforts, the Laian version was more powerful—but it wasn't any longer-ranged.

More Taljzi superbattleships started to die. They returned fire with everything they had, and the Allied Fleet was still losing ships... but something was missing.

"The superfortresses. They stopped firing?" she asked.

"Two are gone, the third just...stopped firing entirely and the fourth is targeting Fleet Lord Pozan," Koanest reported. "I think we got a lucky HSM hit."

"Leave Pozan to it, then," she told the Yin. She'd been considering calling for long-range HSM fire, but that would have required the detached force to come after her. Saving her from losing four capital ships every minute was more than worth giving up those ships.

She looked back at the screen—in time to see *every* Taljzi capital ship vanish.

"What the *hell?*" she snapped.

"Last of the superbattleships were destroyed," Koanest reported. "I think...I think the battleships all went into stealth."

"Find them," Harriet ordered. That was unexpected and dangerous...but it might also be something *else* entirely. "But hold fire on any escort that stops shooting."

"Fleet Lord?"

"I think they might just be done," she said quietly. "So, let's not kill anyone we don't have to."

IT TOOK several more minutes for the chaos to resolve. It turned out that most of the destroyers had followed the battleships into stealth, but Harriet hadn't been paying that much attention to the escorts.

The cruisers didn't stop firing immediately. Some did and ran, and the Allies let them go.

Once the first handful had broken free of the fight, more and more followed. First it was handfuls. Then dozens. Then the last remaining ships broke and fled.

"Are we sure it's wise to let them go?" Cawl asked. Despite being officially in command, he hadn't argued with Harriet's order.

"The shooting's stopped, Fleet Master," Harriet pointed out. "We have the edge in numbers now, especially if we get the time to finish internal repairs on our damaged vessels and rejoin with Fleet Lord Pozan's force.

"I suggest we make our way to PG-Six-C. *Someone* in this system gave the order for the battleships to give up the fight, and they're either in a stealthed fleet or on the planet. Either way, orbit around their capital sounds like where I want to dictate terms from."

Kanmorad's mandibles chittered softly.

"Are you sure it's over?" the big alien asked. "My people are... Well. It has been a long time since a Republic detachment took these kinds of losses outside Wendira space."

"I give it fifty-fifty odds its really over," she admitted. "Keep your people in check—but I want all of our people focusing on repairing our ships, and I want the entire fleet reconvened."

Of course, they also couldn't fully abandon the battlespace. There had to be survivors in the wreckage of the hundreds of destroyed Imperial, Kanzi and Laian ships.

"We'll need to leave somebody behind to search for survivors," Cawl said, echoing her thoughts. "Fleet Lord Tanaka, I suggest we each detach two hundred or so cruisers. Say twenty of my squadrons and fifteen of yours? We owe our crew the effort."

"We owe them more than that, but that should suffice," she agreed. Four hundred-plus cruisers could field five thousand or so shuttles. That many craft *should* be able to find everyone who was still alive.

Should.

"What about Taljzi survivors?" Cawl asked.

"I suggest we tag them with a beacon and drop oxygen supplies for any of them in truly dire straits," Harriet said. "Make it as clear as possible that we won't engage Taljzi ships that move in to retrieve their own survivors.

"We may as well assume the situation is a truce until they prove differently...but let's hold that truce from the high ground above their capital."

"Even my estranged cousins should get *that* message," Cawl agreed. The channel to Kanmorad dropped, and once again, Harriet was on a call with just the Kanzi Fleet Master.

"Thank you, Harriet," he said, his voice very quiet. "For letting me *try* to talk my idiots down. And for your mercy. There is an argument that the Taljzi must die, yes...but they are my people under it all.

"I *must* give them a chance."

"The Imperium burned one star system around them already," Harriet pointed out. "We learned. And there's *nobody* offering me supertech for burning this one, either."

THERE WERE planetary defense centers on PG-Six-C still. Not just the ring around the ruins of the cloning facility but also launchers and fortresses scattered across the planet.

Many of them observed the hesitant truce over the star system as the Allied Fleet approached. Others did not.

The missiles didn't survive clearing atmosphere, and for several moments, Harriet considered ignoring the attack.

But the official commander of the fleet right then was still Cawl.

"Target the installations that fired and destroy them," he ordered calmly. "*Precisely*, if you please. No unnecessary damage...but if a base fired a missile at us, it burns."

Hundreds of bombardment launchers flashed into space from the Kanzi fleet. By the time the Allied Fleet slowed into an orbit eighty thousand kilometers above PG-Six-C, no one was shooting at them.

"I think you have to talk to them, Cawl," Harriet suggested as they relinked. "No one is saying anything to us; they've just stopped shooting. We'll stomp all over every military base on the planet with rocks and storm whatever their equivalent of the Golden Palace is with Marines if they keep playing the silent game, but we may as well *call* them."

"I'd prefer to keep kicking the enemy until they stop twitching," Kanmorad inserted. "This measured approach is starting to make me nervous."

"I will summon them to surrender," Cawl agreed. "I have one request."

"Of us?" Harriet asked.

"Of you, Fleet Lord Tanaka." Cawl shifted uncomfortably, clearly trying to adjust around his maimed leg. "I do not fully trust my own people not to agree with Pincer Kanmorad. And unlike Pincer Kanmorad, I also do not trust them to hunt with the pack.

"If unauthorized bombardment munitions are fired, I need them to be shot down." He paused. "And I also need you to do nothing *more* than that. I will deal with my own internal difficulties, but I must ask you to make sure that they do not interfere with the mission."

"You Kanzi make no sense to me," she admitted. "But we'll do it."

"Good. Now I need to decide just what to say to the people who hate everything I stand for." Cawl smiled sadly. "I'm sure this will be easy."

CHAPTER SIXTY

SHAIRON CAWL CERTAINLY CLEANED UP NICELY, HARRIET HAD to admit. With his leg brace concealed beneath a carefully tailored uniform and some camera tricks, he faced the recorder in his white dress uniform and looked every inch the conquering warlord.

The image was undermined, at least for his human audience, by him being covered in blue-and-white fur and being roughly a hundred and thirty centimeters tall. Kanzi might be enemies turned allies, slavers and warlords, but it was still hard for humans to find them intimidating.

"I am Fleet Master Shairon Cawl," he said calmly. "Commander of the Gloried Armada. Companion of the High Priestess of Kanarj. I am charged by my High Priestess to bring an end to the attacks by the Taljzi upon our worlds and the worlds of our allies in the Imperium."

No mention needed or wanted of the fact that the Imperium *hadn't* been the Theocracy's allies until the Taljzi showed up. That was an unnecessary complication in her mind—and Cawl's too, clearly.

"Your fleet has retreated. Your refitted Precursor fortresses have been disabled or destroyed. Your Precursor cloning device has been wrecked. This battle is over. It is within my power to end you, to sear this world and even this system clear of life."

Harriet shivered. She was glad Cawl wasn't directing the cold, flat gaze in his eyes at *her*.

"Those are not my orders," he finished softly. "A High Priestess proscribed the Taljzi once. We could see a way past that, except that you have followed that genocidal call to its conclusion and the deaths of millions.

"There is mercy in my High Priestess's will. There is mercy in the codes of my allies, for the Imperium has enough blood and fire on their hands to last them an eternity.

"But we will do what we must."

His words were iron boots on cobblestones, the unquestioned and unbending will of a warlord without peer among the Kanzi.

"I will not negotiate terms. You will surrender or be destroyed."

The transmission ended and Harriet shook her head, glancing at the main holodisplay.

"That's a bit harder of a current than I expected him to take," Koanest admitted.

"The only acceptable terms are complete disarmament and a permanent joint Imperial-Kanzi occupation," Harriet admitted. "At that point, we may as well demand unconditional surrender.

"Speaking of disarmament, though, have we localized their fleet?" she asked.

"Yup. They're in orbit of planet A, licking their wounds," her operations officer replied. "Their cruisers are doing search and rescue, same as ours. So far, everyone is being cautious, but they've been returning the favor on the locator beacons. We've picked up a few hundred people they found first—and vice versa, of course."

"From planet A, they can intercept us if we try to deploy more starkillers," Harriet guessed. "Not a bad plan. It won't be enough if we decide to go that route, but it's not a bad plan."

The Imperial starkillers were intact. If she decided that PG-Six needed to be destroyed, she'd escort them to their firing points with the entire fleet.

She didn't think it was going to come to that. The question now, though, was how were the Taljzi going to jump.

"Keep up the scans and analysis of the planet," she ordered. "If they keep playing the waiting game, *my* patience is limited. I want multiple priority lists for valid targets."

"We're already on it," Koanest confirmed. "Taking the time to do it right."

Harriet nodded and turned her attention back to the world beneath her. At this point, she was certain they could finish this if the fighting resumed. She'd burn everything from PDCs to power plants if she had to actually invade, though.

Not least because any actual invasion force was at least twenty to thirty cycles away!

"FLEET LORD. There's a transmission coming from the surface," Harriet's communication officer reported. "It's a directed tightbeam, targeting Cawl's flagship." The A!Tol officer paused. "Cawl's people are now forwarding it to us."

"Play it for me," she ordered.

A holographic image of a male Kanzi appeared in front of her. Like Cawl, the being was short and clad in a pure-white uniform that contrasted with their deep blue fur.

Unlike Cawl, this Kanzi had ritualistic scars branded into his fur. White lines of varying widths drew patterns across his fur that the Imperium had yet to manage to translate.

"I am the Grand Master of the Guardians of the Taljzi," he recited. "My name is irrelevant. I speak for the fleets of the Taljzi, and today I speak for the people of Jaltal."

Light of Mind, Harriet translated the planet name. The translator was surprisingly good at picking out proper nouns.

"I knew your ancestor, Shairon Cawl. In another life, Disten Cawl and I fought a dozen battles. Like you, he was a fool who never questioned his High Priestess."

The Taljzi was alone in the hologram, the recorders intentionally not picking up anything except him.

"It is not my place to decide the will and mind of God," he continued. "Our religious leaders have gone into seclusion in a safe place, where they cannot be harmed by your bombardment and they can decide what all of this means as to His Divine Purpose.

"You and I, Shairon, we are not priests. It is not for us to seek the truth of God's will or the messages He hides in darkness and light alike. It is for us to deal with the facts and the world He gives us."

The Grand Master bowed his head.

"I will not forswear my people to the Greater Interdict," he told Cawl. "To die or be sterilized. I will not do it. But until today, my people were immortal. I have a billion brothers and sisters who remember the fall of Talvar, yet only twenty-two of us fled that system before the star claimed all."

He smirked.

"You don't understand. You can't. Time and discussion will allow you to *know* but never to *understand*. And it doesn't matter, does it?"

The Taljzi, it seemed, could be just as irritatingly mystical as anyone.

"If you will swear upon the word of your High Priestess that we will face only the Lesser Interdict and not the Greater, then I will forswear one oath to serve another," the Grand Master said bluntly.

"Swear this, and I will deliver the Conclave into your hands and yield the Guardians without further terms. I am of the Taljzi. I am a child of God. But I must live in the world I live in, and this battle, this war...is already lost."

THE TRANSMISSION ENDED and Harriet breathed a long sigh of relief. She wasn't entirely sure what the distinction between the Greater Interdict and the Lesser Interdict was—she was only really aware that the original proscription of the Taljzi had required the members of the schismatic cult to recant their "heresies" and accept sterilization...or die.

Presumably, that was the Greater Interdict.

Her channel to Cawl pinged for her attention and she switched to it. It took her a moment to realize he was on his flag deck with a full privacy shield around him.

Before, he'd been using a semi-transparent screen like her own privacy shield. Now there was a solid white background behind him.

"Fleet Lord," he greeted her. "If I grant their one term, I am breaking the proscription by a High Priestess."

"And?" Harriet asked bluntly. "You're not getting sole occupation of this system, Fleet Master—and the Imperium will not stand by while you force them to recant their faith or die."

In many ways, the codes and laws that Harriet operated under as an Imperial officer would be more accepting of her detonating the star than they would be of her standing by while the Kanzi imposed this "Greater Interdiction."

"I know that," Cawl conceded. "I'm not arguing against it. I'm just warning you that the moment I accept their surrender, everything is going to go to hell over here. It will need to be Imperial troops that secure the Grand Master and take the Conclave into custody. If there was one single act that I expected to break open the fractures in my fleet, it was this."

"You knew this had to be the end result, didn't you?" Harriet asked. It couldn't be a *surprise* to Cawl that the Taljzi wouldn't blithely surrender themselves to forced sterilization.

"I did," he said levelly. "And once the pack fractures, matters will be resolved. But without letting the traitors *act*, I don't know how all of my Captains are going to jump."

"I'm not in this for your civil war, Shairon," she warned him.

"I don't need you to do anything for my civil war, Harriet Tanaka," he told her. "The plans for that have been in hand for some time now.

"I need you to make sure that bringing the Gloried Armada into line doesn't keep *this* war burning or see unnecessary deaths. *I* will deal with the First Priest and his treason, but I need this fleet to do it. So, I'm going to push it to the edge and see what happens."

She shook her head.

"I understand," she admitted. "Everything is ready to make sure no one bombards the surface without my permission."

Cawl bowed his head.

"I thank you, Fleet Lord Harriet Tanaka," he said formally. "I know that I have asked more of you than our alliance could ever justify. I owe you and your Imperium above and beyond what my nation owes yours."

"You want something more," she said quietly.

"My people may attack yours," he admitted, equally quietly. "You have to let me deal with it. I have no right to ask this of you, but I must. Please. Do no more than defend yourselves."

"And if you lose?" Harriet asked.

"Then I die...and the Kanzi Theocracy is no longer your ally," Shairon Cawl admitted calmly. "And then you must do what you must."

CHAPTER SIXTY-ONE

"You have got to be *kidding me*."

Morgan stared at the orders that had come through the secondary squadron tactical channels. Disconnected from the main network that was still linked to the Kanzi, those networks were short-range and heavily encrypted.

The orders carried the right stamps, along with instructions to relay them to another squadron by tightbeam. Once there, the codes would load them into the squadron tactical network and spread out again.

It was as fast a way as existed to get the orders out through the Imperial Fleet without notifying the allies who were still linked into their main network, but the *orders* were unbelievable.

"We are to stand by to prevent any Kanzi bombardment of the surface, and we are *not* to intervene if any fighting starts amidst the Kanzi fleet," Tan!Stalla confirmed. "I assume you checked the codes?"

"Three times," Morgan confirmed. "They're legit orders from the Fleet Lord. Including the part you *didn't* read."

The part about not returning fire if the Kanzi fleet opened fire on the Imperial fleet.

"I see the logic. The Fleet Lord is expecting internal conflict in our allies' forces, and we are to stay uninvolved." The A!Tol Captain flashed green with determination.

"Our focus is to deal with the Taljzi. The Kanzi can handle their own problems."

Morgan shook her head but starting laying in targeting parameters.

"We'll have the Bucklers standing by to launch the moment there's trouble," she told Tan!Stalla. "They won't do much, not at these ranges. If they open fire with proton beams, we're not going to have very long to decide whether we return fire."

"The Fleet Lord knows that," her Captain replied. "We follow our orders, Casimir. Right now, *Villeneuve* can take a heavier hit than anyone else in the fleet—so if they *do* start throwing proton beams around, we're going to start getting in the way."

"Makes sense, I suppose," Morgan admitted. "I passed Damyanov's part onto her as well. We may be short a few shuttles, but we should be able to drop the entire contingent without a problem."

One of their shuttles was gone, probably with its pilot. Two more would be winging their way back to the rendezvous point, unable to cross back into normal space to discover that their efforts had saved the day.

"Alles, warn us the moment Fleet Master Cawl sends his message," she told the communications officer. "If I have to sit here and take the Kanzi's best shot, I'd like to know it's coming."

"He just sent it," the Indiri replied. "Copied to the fleet. You want to see it?"

"No." Morgan shook her head again. "I know what it says. We accept the poor beaten bastard's solitary term—not least since I can't see the Imperium *letting* the Kanzi impose the Greater Interdict."

"So how long before it all goes to the darkest waters?" Nidei asked, the tactical officer's voice just as calm as ever.

"I don't know," Morgan admitted. "If you had a prearranged mutiny, how long do you think it would take *you* to trigger it?"

"THEY'RE STANDING DOWN. We have confirmation and drop locations for the Marines," Alles reported as the information traveled through the fleet.

The only thing faster than rumor appeared to be relief. New icons started appearing on the globe in Morgan's secondary control: the target locations for the first ground drops. Planetary defense centers, military bases, the capital where the Grand Master was currently communicating with them—and what looked like a secluded monastery tucked away in the mountains.

"What about the fleet?" Morgan asked.

"If they're following instructions, they're going to move outwards to planet B and abandon ship in shuttlecraft to return to C," Alles said. "I can't say if they *are* following instructions, but..."

"They just dropped the stealth screens," Nidei cut in. "I'm picking up a slow—point three cee—course towards planet B. So far, so good."

Morgan nodded. The Taljzi were falling into place as ordered. She wasn't sure if it was just sheer exhaustion—her own best guess was that they'd blown something like five thousand Taljzi *capital ships* to dust bunnies over the last two long-cycles, with a likely body count in the tens of millions—or if it was the loss of the cloner and their illusion of immortality.

Details on how the cloner worked were going to be *fascinating*, she suspected, even if there was no one in the galaxy who could duplicate Precursor biotech.

"How's what's left of the cloner doing, Ichri?" she asked, suddenly curious.

"Collapsing," the Indiri officer replied. "*Deflating* might even be the best term. Looks like there's a lot of fluid and air escaping now." The froglike sentient shook himself. "I'm not sure I *want* to know what that's going to do to their air and water, but it's pretty clear the thing is very, very dead."

"That's what I wanted to hear," Morgan said with a chuckle. *Villeneuve* shook around them as shuttles blasted away. Every ship in the Imperial Fleet was dropping shuttles like they were shaking off raindrops.

"Any movement from our Kanzi friends?" she asked. "They should be grabbing some of these targets, right?"

"The plan was always for Imperial troops to make the first landings if we could manage it," Tan!Stalla reminded her. "Kanzi troops were only going down in the first wave if we were actually launching an assault. With a surrender, it's better not to have the cousins they *really* hate in their faces."

Morgan wasn't sure that was the best plan. The A!Tol, after all, were the ones who'd blown up Talvar—and a good chunk of the rest of the Imperial troops were bipeds of the type even the regular Kanzi called false images of god.

But then, she was watching the Kanzi for an active attack on her fleet and—

"I have shuttle launches in the Kanzi fleet!" Nidei barked. "Unauthorized shuttle launches!"

"And so it begins," Morgan murmured.

"Maneuver us into formation with the other superbattleships," Tan!Stalla ordered. "We're to form a wall between the Kanzi and the rest of our fleet, just in case."

"Proton beams!" Nidei snapped. "Multiple Kanzi ships are firing on each other. So far, shields appear to be..."

A damaged battleship vanished in a ball of fire.

"...holding," Nidei finished their now-obsolete sentence. "Sir? What do we do?"

"We continue the landings and hold a barrier position against

Kanzi movements against our fleet," Tan!Stalla said gently. "The Kanzi will deal with their own problems. Or not, as the case may be."

Icons on Morgan's display marked the first ships to fire. There was no counterfire for several seconds, several ships attempting to interpose their shields to keep lighter siblings intact...and then the squadron of superbattleships around Cawl's flagship came under fire themselves.

Cawl's people *still* didn't fire...but they did move. Ten superbattleships were suddenly *shield-to-shield* with a single ship.

That ship stopped firing as shuttles swarmed over the gap. The unspoken message had been received.

The scene was repeated across the fleet. Battleships tried to maneuver and found themselves pinned between two superbattleships. Superbattleships fired on their sisters and found themselves boxed in by a dozen other ships.

It wasn't bloodless. One of the rogue superbattleships *did* try to keep firing after a dozen battleships boxed her in. Morgan's scans showed they badly damaged one of the battleships—before being *obliterated* by the return fire.

"Seven minutes to launch a prepared mutiny," Morgan finally noted. "Looks like about fifteen to end it."

Every ship that had tried to move against Cawl was stopped now, with shuttles swarming over them. The Fleet Master, it seemed, had been *far* more ready than his opposition.

"I guess that only leaves one question, doesn't it?" Ichri asked softly. "In the eyes of the Theocracy...which side is the traitors?"

CHAPTER SIXTY-TWO

"Grand Master," Harriet greeted her new guest with a formal salute. "Welcome aboard the A!Tol Imperial battleship *Ajax*."

The white-uniformed Kanzi drew himself up to his full height and glared up at her.

"Let us not pretend I am happy with how this ends, Fleet Lord," he said bitterly. "God's will was made known to us. You will see the truth in the end."

"All I see is that a bunch of exiled wannabe genocides stumbled onto a pile of Precursor tech that allowed them to get into a *lot* of trouble," she said sweetly. "The Imperium never forgot you. We just thought you were all dead. Fortunately for you, my Empress declined to order me to make that true."

Harriet was *not* a tall woman, but the diminutive Japanese Fleet Lord towered over the Grand Master—who *still* had not given them a name.

"You have what you desired," he told her. "I am your prisoner. So is the Conclave. Armored boots march the streets of my cities, and our divine mission has failed. Just know that our task *was* divine and while I bow to the reality today, *God* cannot be thwarted."

"If your oath was anything like the ones Fleet Master Cawl swore, I'd be hoping he could be thwarted," Harriet pointed out. "You did, after all, hand us the Conclave on a silver platter."

"I swore an oath before God to protect my people, to guard the Conclave, and to deliver upon our sacred mission of purifying the galaxy," the Grand Master told her. "I failed one. To keep another, I broke the last. I will face His Judgment. So will you."

"I'll worry about that when it comes to it," she told him. "Marines, see the Grand Master to his cell. I suspect he'll find the accommodations far more congenial than we would if the situation were reversed."

That got a small nod of acknowledgment from the Grand Master before he was led away. More prisoners were being led off the shuttles, but they didn't need her personal acknowledgment. Key military and political leaders were being moved off-world and imprisoned aboard Imperial vessels in orbit.

They were probably safer up there. Jaltal's populace was swinging between horror at the destruction of the cloner that seemed to have birthed ninety-plus percent of the population, fear of the power-armored soldiers now patrolling their streets, and anger at the surrender.

For now, most of that anger was directed at their government—but Harriet had already put out the call. She had an army on its way.

She was going to need it!

EVEN WITHOUT THE Imperial Marine divisions she'd been promised, Harriet still had access to a stunning number of soldiers. It wouldn't have been enough to *conquer* a planet, but it was enough to control a planet that had surrendered.

She hoped. Planetary occupation was outside her skillset, and she was going to be leaning on her Marine officers.

"Fleet Lord." Harriet wasn't surprised to see Koanest sticking her head into her office, though she was early.

"Koanest. I didn't think the Marines were due for another hundredth-cycle at least." She waved her display closed and gestured for the Yin to enter. "What's going on?"

"Someone else is here to see you," her operations officer told her. "I'm going to go give the Marines an excuse to buy you at least an extra hundredth-cycle. Should I ask them for more?"

Harriet was about to ask what the Yin Captain was going on about...and then Fleet Master Cawl stepped through the door.

Standing next to Koanest, the color difference between the pale blue feathery fur of the Yin officer and the dark blue, catlike fur of the Kanzi warlord was sharp. The Yin also towered over Cawl by at least fifty centimeters.

The Fleet Master leaned on his cane and smiled apologetically at Harriet. She was struck once again by just how *human* any Kanzi looked. They were covered in short blue fur and could *purr*, but otherwise, they could easily pass for a human pre-teen.

"Get me at least a twentieth-cycle, Captain Koanest," Harriet ordered. "I'll be engaging a full privacy seal."

"Understood, Fleet Lord." Koanest saluted and stepped outside. Even with the full privacy seal, the Yin officer was one of the three people on the ship who could override Harriet's privacy settings—the other two were *Ajax*'s Captain and head doctor.

Cawl silently took a seat across from her and produced a small bottle of a blue liquid from inside his uniform jacket.

"Do you have glasses, Fleet Lord?" he asked softly. "I believe you've had pila juice. Did the Duchess or I introduce you to pila liqueur as well?"

The bottle was *tiny*, maybe enough for three shots. Shaking her head, Harriet pulled out the set of porcelain cups she used for sake.

"Bond was very impressed with the juice, but I don't think even she encountered an alcoholic form of it," she admitted.

Cawl neatly filled two cups from the tiny bottle. They each took a cup and Harriet studied the dark blue liquid.

It smelled like a stronger form of pila, the strangely delicious juice that Annette Bond had brought back to Earth after forging the alliance with the Theocracy.

"*Kanpai*," she told the Kanzi. Both of them slugged back the drink and she blinked. That was...much stronger than she'd been anticipating.

"'Empty cup,' I see," Cawl echoed the translation of the Japanese back at her. "Fitting."

"My people's other toast is for more enthusiastic affairs," Harriet said with a chuckle. "*That* translates to 'to live ten thousand years.'"

"That would not be what either of us is expecting," the Kanzi replied. "Especially not if it works how the Taljzi's 'immortality' was working."

Harriet shivered. Apparently, each of the *seven thousand* copies of a person produced after they walked into the cloner had all of their memories...but was at the prime of young adult health, regardless of the age of the individual the cloner had just eaten.

The Grand Master had overreacted to the sight of a starkiller, but so had thousands—*millions*—of his officers. Because every single one of them knew what a starkiller was and had memories of seeing one fired.

"With modern medicine, I can expect to live four or five hundred long-cycles," Harriet replied. "A bit over two hundred years as humanity tracks time. I'm content with that, I think."

"I'm already over two hundred long-cycles old," Cawl pointed out. "Traditionally, I'd expect another hundred at least. We'll see how that goes."

"How so?" Harriet asked carefully.

He poured new drinks, emptying the bottle.

"It was never relevant to your interests that I had a force of Inquisitors, sworn to High Priestess Karal, amongst my fleet," Cawl said slowly. "They were why I knew what was coming and was ready for it when they finally decided to act.

"And they have now completed their interrogations."

"They confirmed what you were saying about the First Priest?" Harriet asked.

"And then a thousand times more," he admitted. "You should know that I have received orders to break the alliance and destroy your fleet."

She froze with the cup of liqueur at her lips.

"I presume you do not intend to follow those orders," she said.

"I do not," Cawl confirmed. "Which means I am now a traitor in active rebellion against my government...but then, my government has betrayed our High Priestess and sealed her under house arrest."

He shook his head and swallowed the liqueur.

"I have to leave," he told her. "And take the Gloried Armada with me. We've finished sweeping the Taljzi battleships. They're now disabled and orbiting B, a long way from any Taljzi with ideas.

"I can leave some ships, depending on what you need."

"I still have almost five hundred capital ships," Harriet said quietly. "If I can't restrain a defeated enemy with that, I need to turn in my uniform. We've lost too much, come too far, to fail now because the prisoners had funky ideas."

She set her empty cup back down on her desk while she considered the situation, humming quietly to herself.

"I'm guessing that *my* sending ships with *you* is a terrible idea," she finally said. "I suppose that means all I can do is wish you luck?"

"Keep the Taljzi dealt with," he told her. "That's all of the help I need."

"You have a plan?" she asked.

"The First Priest and his allies are currently pretending to be speaking for the High Priestess, so they haven't been able to do too much damage yet—or to even truly prepare for civil war." Cawl looked down at the cane in his lap.

"I'm hoping a strike directly at Arjzi will allow me to liberate Karal and end this fight before it begins."

"And what are you *expecting?*" Harriet asked.

"That I will liberate Arjzi and Karal, but the First Priest will have an escape plan and allies—Clans and star systems—that he can call to his banner. I believe I can safely retrieve my High Priestess, but I do not expect that to be the end."

He shrugged.

"If I fail, they will turn on you," he told Harriet bluntly. "But this is not the kind of war where you can help me."

"Then I send our hopes with you," she replied. "And a warning for the entire Theocracy: we will *only* honor the alliance with Karal... or you. If we do not know the leadership of the Kanzi, we cannot trust the Kanzi.

"Blood and history run far too deep for that."

"I will endeavor to save the Theocracy," Cawl said quietly. "God willing, Karal and I will both live. If we do not...then God willing, I will save a Theocracy that will rebuild that trust."

"May your God guide you to safety, Fleet Master Cawl," Harriet told him, offering her hand across the table.

"It has been an honor to fight by your side."

CHAPTER SIXTY-THREE

JEAN VILLENEUVE HAD FINALLY RETRIEVED HER SHUTTLES, AND Morgan stood in the shuttle bay, waiting to see which of the pilots she'd sent on a suicide run came home.

Somehow, she wasn't surprised to see that it was Donnelly missing. The Texan was the one who'd realized they *could* fire through the portal...but she suspected he'd done the math on the lost impact energy from the process and concluded it wasn't going to be enough.

"Lesser Speaker Istil!. Lesser Speaker Ando Kal," she greeted the A!Tol and Anbrai pilots as they stepped onto the metal of *Villeneuve*'s decks. "Welcome home. You did it."

"You mean Donnelly did it," Istil! corrected. "The idiot left me a recording. He wanted to be certain, he said."

"He made certain," Morgan confirmed. "Rammed his shuttle into the center of the cloner and overloaded his fusion core. Boom."

"I heard they surrendered," Kal rumbled. "That was enough, was it?"

"We also disabled all four superfortresses and wiped out three-quarters of their fleet," she replied. "We're going to be picking through Taljzi tech databases for a while."

And Mesharom. The scientists and engineers at DragonWorks were going to be *ecstatic* when the first ships made it home. That was part of why *Jean Villeneuve* was there at the hyperspace rendezvous with the logistics fleet.

While the pilots they'd sent out were coming back, other shuttles were transferring the molecular-circuitry crystals containing *Blade's* databases to one of the *Bellerophon*-class ships tasked to escort their cripples home.

"We're sending those databases home," she told them. "Everything's loaded aboard *Horatio*. Squadron Lord Sun is escorting our cripples back to Sol. He's supposed to pick up the third wave of Marines there and come back, but his people will get *some* leave."

"And us?" Kal asked, the barrel-torsoed and four legged alien looming over even Istil!'s bulk.

"We're backing up the occupation force for the foreseeable future," Morgan replied. "You're mostly going to be flying Marines around, I suspect, with the occasional ground attack run.

"Nothing like what you just pulled," she promised. "*That* stunt will be getting you two and Donnelly medals."

Posthumous highest award for valor–type medals for Kenneth Donnelly. Morgan doubted it would be any solace to his mother.

"That's tomorrow's waters, I suppose," Istil! replied. "For now, I'm looking forward to my own bed."

"Get to it," Morgan ordered. "You did well. All of you. I don't know if disabling the fortresses would have been enough if that Precursor monstrosity was still intact."

"Deeper waters than I swim," Kal rumbled. "We just do the job."

Morgan chuckled and gestured for the two pilots to get back to their quarters. There would be a lot for them to do back in PG-Six.

A lot for *Jean Villeneuve's* First Sword to do, too. Escorting the logistics fleet into the system was going to be the closest thing to quiet Morgan could see in the near future.

She was looking forward to a challenge that *didn't* involve anyone shooting at her with Precursor superweapons.

"SO, I GOT YOUR MESSAGE."

Arriving back in PG-Six, the mail call had contained a recording from Victoria Antonova. Morgan had hesitated, but she'd been going off shift...and she needed to know what Victoria had said.

One way or another, she needed to know.

The blonde woman in the recording was smiling, though, and that was probably a good sign. She didn't look like she'd been crying. Maybe a bit overworked, but she *was* the communications officer for an entire sixteen-ship squadron of superbattleships.

"I love you, Morgan Casimir," Victoria continued. "And you're an idiot."

Morgan winced.

"I'm not trapped by you. Never was. Never will be. I'm waiting for you because I *want* to." She raised a hand as Morgan released a level of tension she hadn't realized she'd been holding.

"I've been briefed on PG-Six," Victoria noted. "That was hell. I didn't get everything, I'm guessing, but I did get that *Villeneuve* is held up in occupation garrison duty for a while. Rumor has it there's a *plan* for limiting how long any ship holds that duty, but no one has really sorted it out yet.

"After all, it's not like we've got another seven hundred fully refitted capital ships floating around to replace Tenth Fleet."

Not yet, anyway, Morgan reflected. There were at least four hundred ships being refitted and another four hundred under construction across the Imperium. The Empress had been preparing for a long war against the Taljzi.

"I'm guessing you're looking at a long-cycle before you get leave, though," Victoria continued. "So, you and I keep trading messages for all that time." She grinned. "Once you're off top-secret-every-message-is-reviewed-before-delivery status, I may even start sending you *dirty* messages. You've been gone longer than I'd like.

"But I can wait six months, Morgan Casimir. And I will. And the only price I'm going to demand is that when you next get leave, you're spending it on Earth. With me. And you better not be expecting to get out of bed for at *least* the first week."

Victoria was now grinning.

"We'll loop back and forth, my love, and hyperfold coms let us do just that. We'll steal what time we can, and if there comes a point where one of us can't take it anymore, we'll deal with it then.

"But I *will not* give you up out of fear of a future that will not come. And you damn well better believe I won't let you do so, either."

Morgan couldn't help but return the grin of her lover's image. Right then, at that moment, she was certain they *could* make it work.

Like Victoria said, they might not...but that was for the future.

"I love you and I await your next message with bated breath," Victoria concluded. "*Do vstrechi, moya lyubov.*"

The recording ended and Morgan inhaled a long, surprisingly relaxed breath.

The war was won. She had an amazingly patient and understanding girlfriend. She had what was unquestionably the best possible position for an officer of her rank in the Imperial Navy.

She was also trapped in occupation-garrison duty, but nothing could be perfect.

Life was good.

She had no idea how long that would last, but she could hang on to that for today.

JOIN THE MAILING LIST

Love Glynn Stewart's books? Join the mailing list at

GLYNNSTEWART.COM / MAILING-LIST /

to know as soon as new books are released, special announcements, and a chance to win free paperbacks.

ABOUT THE AUTHOR

Glynn Stewart is the author of *Starship's Mage,* a bestselling science fiction and fantasy series where faster-than-light travel is possible–but only because of magic. His other works include science fiction series *Duchy of Terra, Castle Federation* and *Vigilante,* as well as the urban fantasy series *ONSET* and *Changeling Blood.*

Writing managed to liberate Glynn from a bleak future as an accountant. With his personality and hope for a high-tech future intact, he lives in Kitchener, Ontario with his partner, their cats, and an unstoppable writing habit.

VISIT GLYNNSTEWART.COM FOR NEW RELEASE UPDATES

 facebook.com/glynnstewartauthor

OTHER BOOKS
BY GLYNN STEWART

For release announcements join the
mailing list or visit **GlynnStewart.com**

STARSHIP'S MAGE

Starship's Mage
Hand of Mars
Voice of Mars
Alien Arcana
Judgment of Mars
UnArcana Stars
Sword of Mars
Mountain of Mars
The Service of Mars
A Darker Magic
Mage-Commander (upcoming)

Starship's Mage: Red Falcon
Interstellar Mage
Mage-Provocateur
Agents of Mars

Pulsar Race: A Starship's Mage Universe Novella

DUCHY OF TERRA

The Terran Privateer
Duchess of Terra
Terra and Imperium
Darkness Beyond
Shield of Terra
Imperium Defiant
Relics of Eternity
Shadows of the Fall
Eyes of Tomorrow

VIGILANTE
(WITH TERRY MIXON)
Heart of Vengeance
Oath of Vengeance

Bound By Stars: A Vigilante Series
(With Terry Mixon)
Bound By Law
Bound by Honor
Bound by Blood

TEER AND KARD
Wardtown
Blood Ward

CHANGELING BLOOD
Changeling's Fealty
Hunter's Oath
Noble's Honor
Fae, Flames & Fedoras: A Changeling Blood Novella

ONSET
ONSET: To Serve and Protect
ONSET: My Enemy's Enemy
ONSET: Blood of the Innocent
ONSET: Stay of Execution
Murder by Magic: An ONSET Novella

FANTASY STAND ALONE NOVELS
Children of Prophecy
City in the Sky

Made in the USA
Middletown, DE
14 December 2023

45588801R00279